DEDICATION

To the ones who swore they'd ruin us, only to end up on their knees, begging for our mercy instead.

LORENZO'S CLAIM

OATHS AND BETRAYAL

BOOK ONE

SAMANTHA JAYNE

COPYRIGHT

WARNING

Lorenzo's Claim is strictly a work of fiction.

Trigger Warnings include but are not limited to: Graphic violence, alcohol use, knife play, breath play, kidnapping/abduction, assault, death, torture, criminal activities, sexual explicit scenes.

<u>Anastacia</u>

I thought I was attending a wedding.
But what I didn't realise was that it was mine.
Lorenzo Ricci is cold, commanding and the last man I'd ever choose.
I'm told I'm his now, bound by a vow I never agreed to.
But he'll learn quickly enough that I don't break, and I certainly don't bow.
Not even for him.

<u>Lorenzo</u>

This marriage isn't about love.
It's about power, control, and revenge.
Anastacia Fedorov is the final piece in a plan I've spent years perfecting.
She's fire wrapped in silk, more defiant, and far more dangerous than I ever expected.
I told myself I'd use her and walk away.
But what I didn't plan on, was wanting more.

PLAYLIST

Blood Oath - Henri Werner
Addicted - Ross Loudon
Fuck Me Like You Hate Me - Jutes
Love Looks Pretty On You - Nessa Barrett
Dark Romance (Remixed Slow) - TfamilyRocky
Queen - Loren Gray
100 Ways - Austin Hull
The Death Of Peace Of Mind - Bad Omens
I Wanna Be Your Slave - Måneskin
Can't Help Falling in Love With You - Travis Atreo
My Songs Know What You Did In The Dark - Fall Out Boy
Let The World Burn (Remix) - Chris Grey, G-Eazy & Ari Abdul
The First Time - Damiano David
Good For You - Selena Gomez, A$AP, Rocky
Play with Fire - Sam Tinnesz, Yacht Money
It's ok, I'm ok - Tate McRae
Fetish - Selena Gomez, Gucci Mane
PILLOWTALK - Zayn

Shadow You - Henri Werner & Shivers
Scream My Name - Thomas LaRosa
Good Girl (Praise) - Nation Haven

You can find the complete playlist on Spotify

PROLOGUE

ANASTACIA

ANOTHER DAY, ANOTHER WEDDING.

Thankfully, this wasn't mine, though. I drew the line at that kind of crap, much to my father's disappointment.

Today was the unfortunate day that we'd have to attend Lorenzo Ricci's wedding, the newest Don of the Sicilian Mafia. He was a real coldhearted prick, apparently. I just couldn't help but feel sorry for the poor woman that had to marry him. Probably the apple of her daddy's eye, but for the right price, she was nothing but a pawn in their game.

I saw it one too many times. No matter how many times my father tried to persuade me into a marriage arrangement, it was never an option. Fair enough, he did have the final say, but he knew I wasn't quite there yet. I was only twenty-one. That was no age to play wifey to some psychopath.

My father wasn't just anybody. He was Victor Fedorov, *Pakhan* of the *Bratva*.

Hated by many.

But respected by many more.

He had groomed and readied my older brother, Miles, to take his position as Pakhan, despite me being better than him at pretty much everything. That wasn't how it worked. My father knew Miles had to be the one to take over, but fuck, did he make him work for it.

He made him earn it.

But then again, so did I.

While my father was focusing on Miles, my grandfather focused on me and made it known to my father just how lethal I would become. He tried to make him see that Miles was the wrong choice, and I was the right one. But his mind never swayed. No matter how invisible he made me feel, I still loved him, just as he expected me to. But that didn't mean I didn't resent his decisions.

"Anastacia, are you ready?" My mother's voice came from the other side of my bedroom door. "We really do need to leave." It was clear she was irritated by the tone of her voice and the tapping of her foot I could hear against the marble.

Of course I was ready, she'd made sure of that this morning. Whoever thought having a morning wedding was a good idea, really needed talking to.

"Yes, give me two minutes." I sighed, dusting the smallest amount of gloss over my lips.

I glanced at myself in the mirror. I'd chosen a black floor-length gown for the occasion. The expertly tailored dress hugged my body, tracing every contour from my neckline to the floor. The daring thigh-high split made me smile to myself, knowing that my mama would disapprove. Our relationship was anything but sunshine and roses, all she truly ever wished for was a daughter she could shop with but that wasn't me. I would rather have had my weapon of choice over Daddy's credit card any day of the week.

I scoffed at the idea of coming face-to-face with the countless sons of my father's many alliances. Although, he would have had more if it wasn't for Lorenzo Ricci's father. They were best friends once upon a time, but all that ended when Franco bled out in Lorenzo's arms after he crossed the Fedorov family, leading me to wonder why on earth we had to attend this shit show of a wedding.

"Anastacia!" Mama snapped as I yanked the door open with a forced smile. "Oh, that dress is, umm, well it's—" She was speechless and not in the way she had hoped to be.

"How about I stay home and stick burning hot needles in my eyes? I'm sure that'd be better than what I'm about to endure." I scoffed, breezing past her, ignoring her sighs of annoyance.

"Don't be ridiculous. It'll be a lovely wedding. You'll have a great time. Besides, you could meet—"

"Stop pushing it. Me falling head over heels with some jumped-up twat of an heir, isn't on the cards for me." I descended the stairs with her hot on my heels, her creamy blonde bob bouncing as she walked. Her cherry red lips were undoubtedly pursed as though she'd just sucked on a lemon.

"Not all of them are jumped-up, Anastacia. Some are actually rather lovely."

I ignored her comments as my father came into view, looking sharp in his tux. He turned to face me, a pearly white smile appearing on his face. He stood beside my brother, Miles, who barely offered me a smile.

"Ty vyglyadish' prekrasno." My father's lips turned up at the corners as if threatening to smile.

"Thank you."

"Russian, please," he demanded, his smile not faltering.

"*Spasibo.*" I smiled, nodding my head towards him.

"*Mozhet byt', eto plat'ye nemnogo otkrovenno, net?*" He pinched the bridge of his nose, clearly also hating my choice of dress for today.

"No, it's not too revealing. Besides, I don't see why it matters anyway." I rolled my eyes, which earned me a disapproving look from my mother.

"Anastacia, just for today, can you pretend to be somewhat

happy? I promise it won't be that bad." He sounded so sure, but it was a shame that I wasn't equally as certain.

"I guess I'll be the judge of how bad it is." I forced a smile, which completely went unnoticed by him and my mother.

"That's my girl. Now, shall we get going? We don't want to be late." He held out his arm to me as my mother accepted the one Miles held out to her.

He was and always would be her golden child.

I looked towards the door where Chad stood, waiting for us. He was one of my father's most trusted men, as well as my childhood friend.

"Does it matter? You can't stand the guy anyway." I rolled my eyes as I accepted his arm. "I don't understand why we're going. You both have unresolved issues with one another."

"Because, Anastacia, after today we'll have buried the hatchet, and hopefully after he and I sit down later this evening, we'll be able to rebuild our alliance once more." He was hopeful. I, on the other hand, couldn't have cared less. "Hence the invitation."

"All I can say to you is good luck."

"Thank you, but trust me, this will be good for us." He nodded at Chad, who mirrored his action. "You know what to do while we're gone, don't you?"

"I do, Boss." He nodded yet again, before offering me a friendly smile.

"See ya later, Chad." I waved before letting my father lead us out the door to our waiting car.

I settled into the back seat. As the car pulled away from the house, I noticed my father's knee start to bounce, just slightly at first. He shifted in his seat, cleared his throat, and tugged at his sleeve like it was too tight. His eyes flicked from me to the side window, though there wasn't much to see. He let a sigh slip out—sharp and quick, as he folded his arms, then unfolded them again.

I didn't say anything. I knew the signs. He got like this sometimes—for reasons he rarely shared. Reasons I didn't care to know either.

"*Ya lyublyu tebya.*" The corners of his mouth lifted, but tension still clung to his face.

It was rare, and strange to hear him say he loved me. Expressing affection had never been something he did easily, especially when it came to me.

"I love you too."

I

LORENZO

Securing the final cufflink on my shirt cuff, I couldn't stop my mind from disappearing to the darkest time of my life. Reliving every second of that night was something that replayed in my mind like a broken record. His final words haunted me until this day. I already knew he'd never betray his dearest friend and ally, so why didn't the cunt that took his life know it too?

"I didn't do what he thinks. I didn't betray them." His voice was strained, the pain coursing through him as he struggled to speak.

As I held him in my arms, all I could do was watch him bleed out, knowing there was nothing I could do to save his life. It was already too late. My father was shot for a mistake. He was shot for something he was fucking framed for, and I knew just how to make the man who cowardly pulled the trigger pay.

"If he doesn't believe me, then be the leader I raised you to be and make him pay in worse ways than death." And with that, my father, the man I idolised, was gone. My heart ached as I cradled his body close to mine.

I vowed to myself that I'd make him pay. Death was too good for him. I had to hit him where it hurt the most—his achilles heel.

After today, the betrayal would begin. A betrayal he would never expect. I may have already lied to get exactly what I wanted. I may have already promised to deliver the things he asked, but then again, some promises were made to be broken, no?

"Boss, you ready?" Red asked, closing the door behind him as he handed me a tumbler of whiskey.

"Am I ready to have a wife? No." I scoffed. "Am I ready to break her until there's nothing left? Too right, I am." I smirked, knocking back the two fingers worth of amber liquid.

"Do you think she really deserves that? She's an innocent party in all this." Red was as fucked up as the next person, but what many didn't know was that he had a heart of gold, and I could see he was conflicted.

"I was innocent too, remember?" I asked, not giving him time to answer. "She's just collateral damage, Red, that's all." I sighed. "I will destroy her. I'll leave her broken, so she has nothing left."

"Boss—"

"Her father took mine from me, so I plan on taking his daughter from him. And right before he dies, I'll tell him all the ways I wounded her, and how once he's gone, so will she be. He'll die not knowing the fate of his daughter. Maybe she'll end up beside him, her fate the same as his. How poetic is that?" I laughed as Red let out a deep sigh, obviously thinking about the poor princess I was about to marry.

"Mate, I get you're still cut up about your father, but she—"

"She's nothing, Red. The sooner you realise that, the better it is for all of us." I gritted my teeth, anger coursing through me.

"Okay, just answer me this, does she even know?" He rubbed the back of his neck, already privy to the answer.

"No, I made sure he knew to keep it that way." I chuckled. "I told that snake that if he allowed me to marry his daughter, our alliance would be as strong as it once was. His only request was for me to love and protect her, and of course, I agreed. But that cunt doesn't need to know I didn't mean it." I chuckled. "She'll hate him for arranging this marriage without her knowing. She won't be able to turn to him when I begin to break her down piece by piece. And just when she might let him in again, I'll end him."

"How could he bring her here without her having a clue. How could he do that to his daughter?" I saw a look of disappointment flash across his face.

"I don't give a shit how he deals with his family. They're his issue, not mine, so let's just leave it at that now that I know what I'm doing."

"Alright, you know best." Red nodded as Gino and Emmet entered the side room.

"Does he, though?" Gino chuckled.

These three weren't just my most trusted men, they were my friends. And believe me, I didn't have many of those.

Didn't need them.

"I do, Gino, yeah," I teased.

"They've arrived." Emmet confirmed, glancing at his watch. "Right on time, too." He put his hand firmly on my shoulder. "Have you actually seen the woman, mate? She's a knockout."

To be honest, I hadn't seen her. Never desired to. A plan was a plan.

"I think even you might struggle to break her. She doesn't seem the type." Gino sucked in a *"you're fucked"* breath, barely hiding his amusement.

"We'll see just what type she is, won't we?" I scoffed, knowing deep down just how easy it would be.

"I will say one thing, though. She didn't look happy about this whole situation." Emmet shrugged. "I saw Lee dragging her back here."

"Good, I'm glad." Smiling, I finished off the last of the cigarette I'd lit previously. "I'd have paid to see that."

I strolled towards the foot of the aisle, still not having seen my bride-to-be. I would soon, though, and I couldn't wait.

"You know every man in this room is jealous of you right now, don't you?" Gino eyed the many men that sat in the guest seats and I couldn't care less. "Many have asked for her hand in marriage for their sons or themselves, but that fucker shot each and every one of them down. He must really like you," he tormented.

"You know he can't stand me, but then again, the feeling is mutual. He's just doing this to rebuild the alliance he once had. And I'll make him think he's got it." I smirked. "For now."

"And you're sure you ain't going to fall in love with little miss perfect?" Emmet asked, and I knew he was taking the piss.

"Emmet, say the word love again and I'll rearrange you until you're unrecognisable." I smiled, and to be honest, it was the first genuine smile I'd had of the day.

"You can leave. You don't need to do this," my mother said as she stopped in front of me.

"I know you don't agree with my plan, Mama, but I have to do this." I kissed her cheek as she let out a sigh of disappointment.

"As you've said, but Lorenzo—"

I led her to her seat, not wanting to continue this conversation anymore. "Mama, just sit back and enjoy the wedding."

The faint sound of music echoed through the venue as I knew it was time to come face-to-face with Anastacia Fedorov—Victor's little princess, the apple of his eye, and the final one who'd see him before I made him suffer worse than my father did.

I glanced at the double doors that swung open with force, and that's when I saw her. All five-foot-four of her. I watched with interest as she reluctantly walked down the aisle beside Victor. She didn't hold his arm like you'd expect a good mafia daughter to. Instead, she kept her distance, her beautiful yet delicate face marred with an anger so visible she could've blown her top any second. I would have had to be an idiot to not notice just how stunning she was, but none of that mattered. Her beauty meant nothing to me. She walked towards me as if she was walking the plank to her own death, only there was no fear hidden in those icy blue eyes. There was something slightly unnerving about her expression, and I was never unnerved.

She walked towards me in a black gown. Surely she wasn't going to marry me in that?

Wait a damn minute... Why wasn't she in the dress I'd arranged for her?!

Well, I guess we all knew how she felt about marrying me.

The dress she'd chosen was obviously made for her. It fit perfectly around her petite frame, clinging to her breasts and left very little to the imagination. Her ash blonde hair fell in waves, tumbling to her waist. *Fuck me. Was she sent to test my willpower?*

I could tell just by looking at her that she was just as powerful as her father, if not more. She held everyone's attention, including my own as I figured out that I'd have to come up with new ways for my plan to succeed. If I thought making her fall in love with me would be easy, I couldn't have been more wrong. But then again, I did love myself a challenge.

Most of the men in this room looked at me with envy, and if given the chance, they'd have ended me and taken her for themselves. Now I understood why men said she would bring them to their knees with her presence alone.

The second they reached me, Victor smiled but Anastacia looked as though she was planning my death in a thousand different ways. I doubt she'd manage it, though it was funny to see the thought cross the blue of her eyes.

This plan might have actually ended up being somewhat fun.

"Hello, wife." I smiled.

"Get fucked, you psychotic asshole." She scoffed as Red sucked in a sharp breath from behind me.

My smile fell, as I never tolerated being spoken to in that way, especially not by someone like *her.* "I can tell we're going to be very happy together."

I gripped her wrist, tighter than she expected, but she never faltered as I pulled her in front of me. Victor was about to speak when Florence forced him into the chair beside her. She knew Anastacia was mine now, and there was nothing anyone could do about it.

"I'd rather die a thousand deaths than be with someone like you," Anastacia snarled, ripping her arm away.

I leaned into her as I noticed her body tense ever so slightly. Not much, but just enough to know I had the upper hand. "It looks like your Daddy didn't give you a choice, though, did he?" I whispered, so only she could hear. "He practically sold you to me for an alliance."

"Fuck you," she sneered.

"You're mine. You belong to me now, Anastacia."

2

ANASTACIA

The second the car stopped, my father turned to face me, taking my hands in his as if he was about to ruin my whole life.

"Anastacia," he started, his eyes unable to meet mine. "I'm sorry I had to do it this way, you would never have agreed otherwise." He sighed.

"Sorry? Agreed to what?" I asked, already dreading the answer.

"I made a deal with Lorenzo Ricci." He let out a ragged breath. "We can rebuild our alliance, but he wanted one thing."

"Don't say it. Don't you dare say it!" I snapped, but I knew exactly what the man I called my father had done.

"He wanted to marry you..." His eyes met mine, and it was as though he was drained of any emotion. "Today you'll marry Lorenzo, and our alliance will be as strong as it once was."

"I can't believe you." I shoved the door open to make my getaway.

I made it a few feet before Miles stopped me, and then it dawned on me.

My brother knew, too. He lied to me, too.

"Let go of me, Miles!" My hands collided with his chest in an almighty thwack as he winced at the hit. "I'm not getting married!"

"Anastacia, you need to do this," Miles demanded, gripping the tops of my arms tighter.

"For who?!"

"For Pa!" Miles shouted as I felt my parents' eyes on us.

"Why should I?! Did he care about me when he made that stupid deal?!" I was livid. I couldn't fathom what was going on or why my own father did this to me. "I'm not marrying him, Miles!"

"Ana—"

"You knew and you didn't tell me. How could you do that to me?" I whispered, the pain stung at how my family hid it from me. At their betrayal.

"Because we knew if we told you that you wouldn't go along with it." He sighed, clearly torn between his loyalty to our father and to me.

"How do you know? If my so-called father would have sat down and explained everything to me, I might have listened. I know your loyalty to Victor is stronger than to me but to be kept in the dark is messed up! Why should I be the one to give up my life? Why should I suffer while you three sit in your ivory tower?!" I shouted.

I could feel my chest heaving, feel the heat rising under my skin like I was about to explode. "I didn't ask for this! I didn't ask to be lied to, manipulated, thrown into something I didn't even know existed!" My voice rose, sharp and raw, cutting through the air. "You should've told me. You *all* should've told me. But I was just easier to sacrifice, wasn't I?"

"Sis—" Miles started again, not knowing what to say, or if he did, it was too late.

"No, you lost the right to call me that the moment you went against me." I narrowed my eyes, shooting daggers at him and causing him to back off if only just a little. "I don't have a family anymore." I stormed past him, marching to the beat of my own drum when a burly figure stepped in the way.

"Your husband-to-be is that way, princess." A man dressed in a three-piece suit smiled, a gold tooth catching my eye, as did the scar that ran down the middle of his face.

"You can tell that prick to get fucked. I'm leaving," I said on an eye roll.

He cocked his head to the side, the bones in his neck cracking as he grasped my wrist tightly and dragged me back towards the venue.

"Get off of me!" I screamed, but it was no use. He had one job and one job only, and that was to get me to that altar.

"Anastacia, stop fighting. You're making this harder." My father sighed, running his hand through his hair with irritation.

"Don't say another word!" I snapped at my father. "You three are dead to me, do you hear me?" I couldn't control the words that left my mouth. My hands were balled into fists at my sides, nails digging into my palms until I felt the sting of skin breaking. "I'm going to marry that psychotic bastard inside for your alliance, but I don't want to hear a word from you again." I snatched my arm away from the guy who had loosened his grip on me. Did he feel sorry for me? Was that it?

I didn't need anyone's pity.

I didn't need anyone anymore, period.

"Anastacia, sweetheart, there is a white dress for you inside. Lorenzo's choice, apparently." My mother smiled, and call me mistaken, but she actually looked happy that I was marrying someone.

"No thanks. I'll walk to my death sentence in this. Seems quite fitting, doesn't it?" I shot her a glance, as she gasped.

My father joined me at my side, his eyes darting between my mother and I. "Anastacia, would you believe me if I said I was sorry?"

"No, I wouldn't. If you were sorry, you wouldn't have done it. You sold me to what I guessed was the highest bidder. Sold me for an alliance that clearly means more to you than I do." I started my walk up the few steps to the entrance.

"That's not true," he shouted after me.

I didn't give him the respect of turning around. He didn't deserve it.

"If that's what you need to tell yourself to sleep at night, carry on." I breathed, taking a moment to truly internalise what I was about to do.

My father appeared at my side, holding out his arm to walk me down the aisle like you saw in movies. I paused, not taking it now or even a minute later. He could get fucked.

"Anastacia, we need to be seen as united. What will it look like if you can barely look at me?" He touched my elbow, trying to find some sort of common ground.

"We were united until about ten minutes ago, but now you three are on your own, just as I am. I don't want to hold your arm, *Victor*. I don't want to look you in the eye, and I most certainly don't care what anyone inside thinks." I blinked back the tears, not wanting to come across as weak or bothered. "I can't even imagine what *dedushka* would think of you now. He'd be turning over in his grave at what you're doing."

"Don't," he admonished.

"Why? Does hearing little home truths hurt?" I scoffed. "Is *babushka* inside?"

"No, she doesn't know." He hung his head. He had to know just how fucked up all this sounded.

"Of course she doesn't, because she feels the same way *dedushka* would have, and as I do."

The faint sound of music came from the other side of the door, and I knew it was time.

Time to walk away from my family and into something unknown.

I kept my distance from my father as I walked towards a man I had only ever heard of. One I didn't know and didn't wish to know. I kept my eyes fixed on the registrar waiting for me at the front. I didn't look at Lorenzo, not even to see what he looked like. What was the point? The deal was done. Appearances meant nothing.

"*Ulybka, Anastacia,*" my father coaxed from beside me.

"I will when I have something to smile about." I swallowed the acid that rose in my throat as I took my final steps toward Lorenzo Ricci.

I wouldn't run. I wouldn't show any signs of weakness to that prick. I would be the woman my grandfather taught me to be. A woman who would never be ruled and dominated by a man, especially not one like Lorenzo.

"Hello, wife." The smug bastard smiled.

"Get fucked, you psychotic asshole." I scoffed, my head snapping towards a man with hair brighter than the sun. It was redder than red. He sucked in a sharp breath, clearly not used to people disrespecting their boss.

"I can tell we're going to be very happy together." His smile fell, and I knew the prince wasn't happy.

He gripped my wrist, tighter than I'd have liked—actually, scratch that—I didn't want him to touch me at all. My face remained stoic and unreadable. I never once let my mask slip. He yanked me into him, our bodies almost colliding. I couldn't hide my scowl as my father stepped away to join my mother.

That woman seemed more into this marriage than anyone else. Hell, maybe she was the one who pushed for it, but she'd never admit that to my face. I doubted my father would either. Lorenzo might have thought I belonged to him now, but the sooner he realised I belonged to nobody, the better it would be.

"I'd rather die a thousand deaths than be with someone like you," I snarled, snatching my arm away, wanting to keep my distance but it was short-lived.

He leaned into me. I couldn't disguise the fact my body had tensed ever so slightly. It was clear he thought he had the upper hand, but in reality, that'd never happen. "It looks like your Daddy didn't give you a choice, though, did he?" he whispered so only I was able to hear. "He practically sold you to me for an alliance."

My words sliced through the tense air, "Fuck you," I seethed, my voice trembling with fury. My heart pounded like a drum in my chest as I glared at the man standing before me. His face remained unreadable, I couldn't work out if he was pissed off or shocked. The room felt small and suffocating, filled with the weight of my resentment and my unwillingness to accept a future I didn't want.

"You're mine. You belong to me now, Anastacia."

"Over my dead body." I leaned in closer than he did, resting my hands on his chest and gaining the upper hand. I gently grazed his earlobe with my lips, sensing the quickening of his heartbeat under my touch. "If you plan on using the outdated line of *'that can be arranged'* just know it doesn't work on me, Ricci." I smirked as I distanced myself, knowing I'd gotten under his skin.

I'd unnerved him. It was written all over his face. He looked more like one of those cartoon characters where steam was coming out of his ears. Like he was about to combust at any second.

It looked like Ricci had met his match, and all I had to say to him was good luck.

I tuned everything out as the registrar recited what he was supposed to up until it was time for us to say 'I *do.'* I was dreading it. I never wanted to say 'I do' to anyone, let alone to this jumped-up prick. It was obvious that he basically thought the sun shone out of his ass.

"Anastacia Katerina Fedorov, do you solemnly promise to love, honour, and respect Lorenzo Franco Ricci for as long as you both shall live?" The registrar asked as Lorenzo trained his gaze on me, as if he expected me to refuse, but no matter how much I wanted to say it, I wouldn't.

My family might have thrown me into the lion's den, but I knew what was expected of me, and I wouldn't fail. I had never failed at anything, and I didn't plan on starting now. I glanced at my future husband for a second, taking in all his features. He was annoyingly handsome, I'd give him that. Fire danced within his caramel eyes as they narrowed the longer I looked at him, trying to work out what I was doing. A couple of jet-black strands fell down onto his forehead as the rest was tousled and pushed back in a minimal way. My eyes snagged on the deep scar that ran in a perfect line across his sculpted cheekbone.

"Miss Fedorov?" The registrar prompted, interrupting my thoughts.

"It's a simple yes, Ana." Lorenzo scoffed, my nickname rolling off his tongue like acid. "Or if you want to be traditional, it's three letters, two words. You choose." He smiled, cocking his head to the side.

"If I have to." I smirked.

"Lorenzo Franco Ricci, do you solemnly promise to love, honour, and respect Anastacia Katerina Fedorov for as long as you both shall live?"

"Yes." Short and to the point. What more could I expect, really?

"As a symbol of your promise, please place your ring on Anastacia's finger." The registrar smiled, thinking he was joining two people in marriage who loved each other.

Lorenzo took the ring from the red-headed man before bringing it to my finger.

"I don't wear jewellery, so you can keep that." I practically heard my father sigh with disappointment.

"Either you let me put this ring on your finger voluntarily, or I'll glue it on. It's your choice." Lorenzo grabbed my hand, bringing it to where he needed it before forcefully thrusting the thin diamond band over my knuckle.

It felt like he had just placed a noose around my neck as my skin burned slightly. *Asshole.*

"As a symbol of your promise, please place your ring on Lorenzo's finger." *My turn.*

I took the ring from Lorenzo as he produced a solid black band, no doubt to match his heart. I placed it on his finger, sliding it down past his knuckle until it couldn't go any farther. He didn't flinch, nor did he look at what I was doing. He just continued to watch me.

"I now pronounce you husband and wife, you may kiss!" The registrar cheered from in front of us, stepping back to allow us our space.

Lorenzo gripped the back of my neck tightly, pulling me into him as he towered over me. He pressed his lips against my own, catching me off guard. This bastard tried to put on a show for whoever was watching, and I wasn't having it.

I had never kissed anyone before, and I didn't plan on this man being the one that made me weak in the knees. His fingers tangled in my hair, and by that point I was done. I nipped his lower lip with my teeth, tasting blood instantly. He pulled back just enough to silently let me know what a massive mistake I'd made, but I didn't care. It was worth it just to get this asshole off of me.

"It seems I've got myself a livewire." He chuckled, his tongue clearing the blood from his lip. "I think we're going to have some fun, wife."

"Fuck off with that wife shit. I'd rather not be reminded."

"Alright, Ana," he said with a lopsided smile.

"I allow very few people to call me Ana, only people who are dear and close to me. You, Ricci, will never be close enough."

"You can't get much closer than a husband," he whispered against my ear.

"Husband on paper, that's all. Don't expect anything other than that." I turned to the guests who were still clapping and smiling as I readied myself to walk towards wherever I was needed next.

Lorenzo took my hand in his, almost crushing it in his vice grip. "Not so fast, princess."

"Unless you want to bleed to death in your sleep, I suggest you stop with the nicknames," I threatened through a fake smile.

"I look forward to the challenge."

He took the first step. I had no choice but to follow, my parents beaming with pride, which sickened me to my core. How could they sit there clapping and smiling when they did this?

"From here on out, you're mine," Lorenzo added.

"I'm nobody's, especially not yours."

And I never would be.

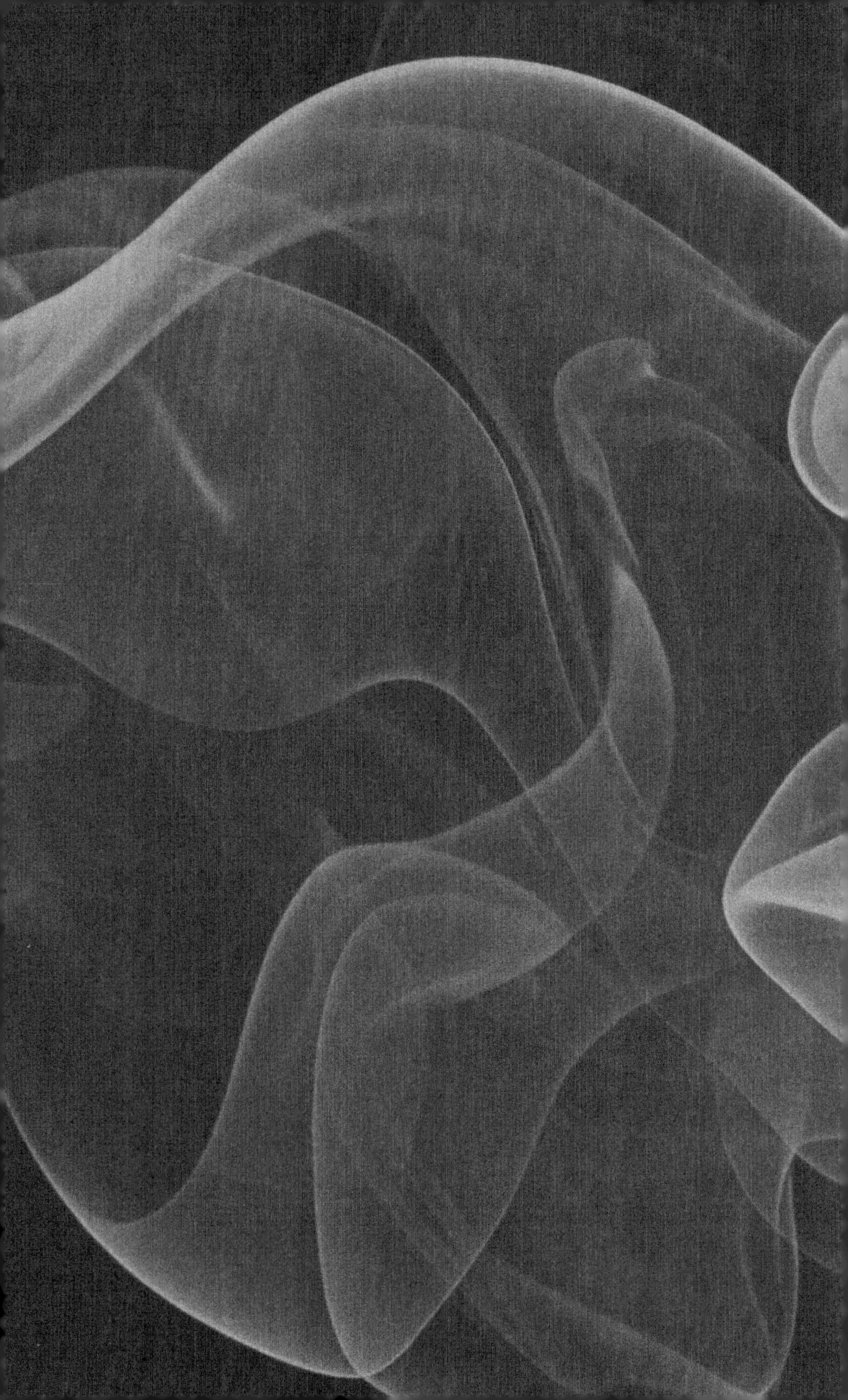

3

LORENZO

I WAS RECALCULATING THE PLAN IN MY HEAD AS I LED THE LITTLE LIVE WIRE back up the aisle. Her hand was drowned by my own as it fit perfectly within my calloused palms. The warmth of her skin against mine wasn't something I was used to.

I couldn't say I completely hated it, but then again, I didn't like it either. It was an unusual feeling, and one I didn't plan on working out. She was a pawn in my game, that was all. Nothing more, nothing less.

"I'm nobody's, especially not yours." Anastacia scoffed with disgust as we stepped outside, away from family and guests.

"Oh, really?" I smirked as we rounded the corner out of sight. I pressed her delicate body up against the stone wall. She didn't falter or seem to fear me. Her eyes never left mine. I couldn't quite work out if she was challenging me or staring into my soul. "Every inch of you is mine, wife. You belong to me, and there is nothing you can do to change that." Her lips parted slightly as the gentle breeze blew her hair, the scent of her floral perfume filling the air around us.

"There is plenty I can do to change that. And most include you being six feet under," she threatened, her anger rearing its ugly head.

"Now, can we get whatever shit you've planned over with so I can get this dress off?" She sneered, a smile threatening the corners of my lips as she continued. "And no, you aren't taking my dress off. If you ever try it, you'll lose all ten fingers along with something else."

Shit, this was going to be harder than I thought. She didn't seem like the type that was easy to break and dispose of.

"Anastacia, I think you seem to forget who you're speaking to." There was no hint of humour in my voice, and she knew she was crossing the invisible line, but she didn't seem to care. She was already getting on my last damn nerve. "Do you know what I do to people who speak to me the way you have over the last hour?"

"No, and quite frankly, I don't give a shit what you do to people with an attitude like mine, and do you know why?" She smirked.

"Enlighten me," I said, her eyes twinkling with happiness at getting to explain herself.

"Because you should see what I do to people with an attitude like *yours*." She leaned into me, her tits now pressed against my chest. She craned her neck to look up at me, her once icy blue eyes darkened with mischief. "I was trained by Aleksander Fedorov. He taught me every single thing he knew. Things that would make your insides churn and your toes curl." Her mouth hardened as she finished her sentence.

I had heard of Aleksander Fedorov. There wasn't a person in our world that hadn't. He was as psychotic as they came. A brutal bastard who trained his son to be a carbon copy of himself, and by the sounds of it, he chose Ana over Miles to focus on. A choice some may have frowned upon, but seeing her here now... He made the right choice. She wasn't some delicate Mafia princess who wanted her husband's credit card for fancy shit. No, she was something else entirely. The plan would never change on my part, no matter how turned on I was by her attitude. It would be harder to execute, but I could do it. I had no doubt in myself.

"I may have married you, Ricci, but believe me, don't think for one minute I'll be sharing a room with you, sharing a bed, or even breathing the same air as you," she snapped, trying her best to remove herself from my hold that only got tighter every time she wriggled.

"You sound so sure of yourself, wife." I chuckled, narrowing my eyes as she rolled hers. "But you should know, I don't like playing games as much as you seem to enjoy them," I whispered in her ear, my lips brushing her earlobe.

"I don't see myself enjoying anything when I'm in your presence." She grimaced, her words spilling from her mouth like venom.

"How about when I fuck you until you're begging for more, would you enjoy it then?" I tightened my hand around her waist, securing her to me.

"Nothing, and I repeat *nothing*, will ever happen between us, so you and lefty may as well get used to one another." She smugly smiled, not batting an eyelid at my comments. She had a reply for each and every one.

"Or how about I fuck that pretty little mouth of yours instead?" I trailed the pad of my thumb across her lower lip before she turned her head away from me. "I can't wait to hear you beg for it."

"I have never been one to beg, and I don't plan on starting when it comes to you." She tried to sound convincing, but I could have sworn I heard her voice jump an octave.

"I wouldn't be so sure."

We were locked on one another for a second, her eyes not leaving mine. She was strong-willed, not wanting to look weak and gullible to someone like me. I had to admit, I admired that, even if it was just a little.

I felt Red silently join us, waiting for a moment before clearing his throat to speak. "The car is ready." She snapped her head towards Red, who looked pretty sheepish, not knowing whether he should have interrupted whatever this was or not.

"Good. We'll be right there." I let my guard down for a second as she managed to free herself from my grip, a triumphant expression now gracing her breathtaking face.

"No, we're coming now." She smiled sweetly at Red, whose cheeks flushed the same colour as his hair. *Brilliant*. This woman was going to screw up everything. She stomped off to the waiting car, ready to head to the reception and not once looking back at the pair of us.

"This just got harder didn't it?" Red asked, finishing his cigarette. "And no, mate, I'm not talking about your dick."

"Fuck off, Red." I snapped. "I was expecting her to be timid—a 'yes sir, no sir' kind of woman but she's anything but, She's a nightmare!" I ran my hand through my hair in frustration. "That family will pay, and trust me, no matter how strong she thinks she is, I'll always be stronger."

"If you say so." He laughed, and I swore if he wasn't one of my best friends he would have had a bullet in his head already. "You can always rethink the whole plan. She might be good for you."

"How about you rewind and think about what you say before you say it. She won't be good for me. The only person she'd be good for is the devil."

"So, you, then." He nudged me with his elbow before heading towards the driver's seat of the car.

I slid into the seat beside Anastacia, who didn't even have enough respect to look at me. She kept her gaze trained on the window.

"Didn't your father teach you any manners?" I asked, unbuttoning my suit jacket.

"Not that it's any of your business, but he taught me very little actually. Besides, my father sold me to you. As far as I'm concerned, he's dead to me."

Brilliant. At this rate she wouldn't even bloody care if I killed her father.

I caught Red glancing in the rearview mirror at me with an amused twinkle in his eye.

"What? No words?" She shifted in her seat, finally looking at me. "Did you really think I'd be over the moon with this shit show? That I'd thank him for selling me to you to save his alliance, the one that went to shit when he pulled the trigger on your backstabbing father?!" Her venomous tone was enough to send me over the edge.

Red swiftly exited the car, leaving the engine running. I yanked her onto my lap as a gasp of shock left her lips. My fingers dug into her flawless skin. She didn't have a chance to try and slip her mask into place.

"Say one more fucking word about my father, and I'll pay your dear *babushka* a visit." I fisted her hair at the nape of her neck, bringing her ear to my lips. "I noticed she wasn't watching us get married today, meaning she doesn't support what your father agreed to. Therefore, she's currently the only one you truly care about. It would be awful for something to happen to her, wouldn't it?"

"How do you know about her?" she asked, a slight quiver apparent in her voice. Gone was the Anastacia who didn't falter.

"I know more than you think I do. Didn't you think I'd do my research before asking to marry you?" The ball was back in my court, and I loved it. "So, tell me, are you going to repeat what you said or be a good girl and refrain from mentioning him again?"

"Noted." One simple word and she was back on top. With the fear gone, her mask slipped into place, and her body offered no signs of panic.

I placed her back in her seat as she folded her arms across her chest, pushing her breasts up, which was hard not to notice. I tapped on the window, signalling Red to get back in the car.

"We're going to put on a front at the reception. You'll play the perfect wife, you'll dance with your father if that's what he wants, and then I will take you home."

"Your home will never be my home," she scoffed, unable to hide the disgust in her voice. "Stop speaking to me like you'll own me because that'll never happen."

"But I already own you, Anastacia Katerina Ricci."

That didn't even get a damn reply. She had decided to give me the cold shoulder and the silent treatment. *Lucky me.* She was stubborn, I'd give her that.

Red cleared his throat from the driver's seat. "I'm Red, by the way." He smiled, blatantly ignoring what I said prior to the wedding. I knew he wouldn't be able to treat her like shit. It was inevitable, to be honest.

"Hey, Red," she replied angelically, and it was the first time I'd seen a genuine smile from her.

I loved how she was nice to someone who could hack up someone with his eyes shut, but then again, she hadn't seen that side of him yet. I shot him a look in the mirror that I hoped reminded him of our previous conversation, before he quickly focused his attention back on the road ahead.

"You don't need to speak to him." I twirled the ring on my finger, a strange feeling.

"Oh, so I'll just be a wife who stays silent then and does everything her husband wants, is that it? You say jump, and I say how high?" *Wow.* She was on fire.

"Yes, that's what I expect from my wife."

"What you want and what you get are two completely different things, Ricci. I'm afraid you're going to be severely disappointed with the wife you've gotten," she said with no emotion. There was no life behind her eyes. It was as though the second her father revealed the news, she'd died inside.

"It's an easy fix." I heard Red clearing his throat as I spoke as if to tell me to just shut up. He might have been right, but it was incredibly hard not to keep going, to keep pushing her to her breaking point that early on.

I relaxed back in my seat, unable to look at anything else other than her. Even her side profile was breathtaking. I had never seen a woman as painfully beautiful as her. I tried my best to work her out, trying to see how many layers she had. How hard I'd have to work. I even tried to think of ways to get her close to her father again, so that way when I ripped him from her, she'd be devastated.

"You can quit looking at me," she snapped.

"Don't flatter yourself. I was merely planning ways to kill you, that's all," I teased, seeing if she would let her guard down just a little.

"Do it. Kill me right here, because death would be a whole lot better than being married to you." She whipped the gun from my waistband, unlocking it without thinking. She held it to her temple with a smile. "Or better yet, I could do it myself. What do you think?" She was a menace. All it took was one slip of her finger, and she'd have been a goner.

"Anastacia, give me the gun. Now," I demanded, holding out my hand to give her the chance. I couldn't snatch it from her. I couldn't risk the aftermath.

"Why? Scared I'll ruin your pretty leather interior?" She laughed, and I could have sworn I physically felt sick as my stomach dropped.

Red slowly pulled over, wanting to minimise the risk.

"Anastacia. Now," I demanded once more, pissed that she didn't listen.

She huffed with an eye roll before locking the gun with ease and placing it in my palm. "You're no fun, are you?" She scoffed.

"Fun? Fucking, fun?! You just held a gun to your head. I'd hardly call that the best time of my life." I threw the locked gun on the passenger seat as Red finally let out the breath he'd been holding. "Do that again and I swear I'll—"

"You swear, you'll what? You're all talk and no action." She turned her back to me as if she hadn't just acted like a psychopath.

I hadn't quite worked out if this was going to be enjoyable or a nightmare, but I'd find out soon enough. The car came to a halt as Red quickly jumped out to open Anastacia's door.

"It looks like your father is waiting for you, Mrs. Ricci." He smiled the biggest damn smile I'd ever seen as he spoke.

"Don't call me that. It makes me feel like his asset, and I'm not. You can call me Ana, though."

Wait a damn minute. She said only a selected few called her Ana, and how the hell was Red one of them?! She met him two damn minutes ago. Alright, it was longer than that, but what difference did it make?

"Okay, Ana, your father is waiting for you."

"I think I'd rather walk in with the asshole in the backseat than speak to my father." She graced us with a genuine laugh.

"I can make it happen," he assured her, clocking my gaze over her shoulder. "Out you get, Boss," he teased, and I swear I could have killed the bastard.

"I feel honoured," I joked without breaking a smile.

"Good for you," she replied in jest.

She didn't take my hand nor my arm, but she walked beside me, making sure she didn't touch me as we reached the entrance.

"Anastacia." Victor called as she walked past him, giving him no respect whatsoever.

"Not now, Victor," I interjected as he remained rooted to the spot.

He clearly wanted to keep the peace, but as far as I was concerned, there wasn't any, and there never would be.

We entered the reception as we were greeted with claps and cheers. I took her hand in mine as I led her to her seat. She didn't try to snatch it away nor did she make a snide comment. She just went along with it. Was it some sort of game, or was she genuinely good at putting on a front for everyone?

She lowered herself gracefully onto her chair as I settled into mine beside her. We had a secluded table, just the two of us. Of course, that was my mama's doing. She was determined to make me change my mind and fall in love with this angelic psychopath.

"You two look exquisite together." My mother appeared with a beaming smile, one that Anastacia mirrored. "Anastacia, you look beautiful. My son finally did something right for a change." She shot me a glance, and I knew once again that she didn't approve.

"Thank you, Mrs. Ricci. It's lovely to meet you." That sweet smile had everyone in this room fooled—everyone except me.

"Likewise, and please, call me Carmella." My mother kissed both of Anastacia's cheeks before heading off to take her seat.

"I see you smile for everyone except me. That hurts, you know," I teased.

"I sincerely doubt it does, but even if it did, you'll get over it." She winked as she seductively wrapped her lips around the straw of the signature cocktail. Another one of my mother's ideas. I doubted Anastacia even realised how sexy she looked at that moment. All I could think about was how perfect she'd look on her knees with her lips wrapped around my cock.

Time passed quickly until it was time for the father-daughter dance. Something I wasn't sure she'd actually agree to, but when Victor stood before her with his hand outstretched, she had a change of heart to her earlier words and placed her dainty hand in his tattooed one.

I guessed she didn't want the alliances in the room to look down on him. I relaxed back in my chair, watching him twirl her around the floor, but not once did she smile. She was closed off, unable to scream and shout at him like she probably wanted to.

As my eyes drifted over them, she distanced herself. Her expression changed, her brows furrowed, knitting in the middle as she gritted her teeth whenever she spoke, and it didn't take me long to realise how heated things were getting between them.

Fuck it.

She may not like me, and I didn't like her either, but there was no way I could sit there and let Victor talk to Anastacia in whatever way he was. I couldn't hear what was being said, but judging by their faces, it wasn't good.

I rose from my seat, not wasting another second as I strode over to where they were on the dance floor.

"Anastacia, we're leaving. Say goodbye." I spoke firmly, not wanting to look as though I was trying to comfort her in any way.

"There's no need. I was done here anyway. No need for goodbyes as I've said all I needed to earlier." She breathed out, composing herself. "I'll be in the car."

"Red will walk you out."

"I don't need a babysitter." She scowled at the thought.

"There are many people here that I still don't trust." I glanced at Victor who had no idea I was talking about him. "Red will take you to the car and wait with you."

She gave up the fight as Red lifted a hand from where he stood by the exit.

"Lorenzo, I was speaking with my daughter, you had no right to interrupt that way," he snapped the second she was out of earshot.

"Victor, I can interrupt anyway I want since she's now my wife. You didn't give a shit about her when you practically sold her to me, or when you brought her to our wedding under false pretences, so I suggest you give her time."

"Lorenzo, we still have things we need to discuss." He didn't even acknowledge anything that was said about his own daughter. He went straight back to business. Did he even care about her at all? Was he bothered?

"Our alliance is valid. There is nothing we need to discuss." I turned my back to him, not wanting to keep this shit going any longer than needed.

"How dare you turn your back to me, boy," he seethed, gaining some extra attention. *Boy, fucking boy?!* The anger that pumped through my veins was more than I usually felt, but I knew I couldn't kill the bastard in the middle of the wedding reception, so I kept my cool as well as I could. "Where's the damn respect?!"

"Respect is earned, not given." I turned back to face him, my voice unnervingly calm and collected. "You are my wife's father, that is all. You're lucky I don't put a bullet in that skull of yours after that disrespectful comment." I breathed, still trying to keep my gun tucked away. "Enjoy the rest of the evening." I extended my hand to him which he happily shook. It's not something I wanted to do nor was it something he deserved, but I needed this man to let his guard down with me. I needed him to not expect anything when I led him to his death.

"Good luck with her, Lorenzo." Her mother smiled from beside Victor. I'd almost forgotten she was there, to be honest. There was something about her wishing me luck that didn't sit right with me. Clearly, Ana's own parents didn't give a shit about her.

I nodded curtly before heading off to check if my wife actually did as she was told and waited in the car with Red.

Much to my surprise, she did.

Wow, I guess she could follow orders.

Good to know.

And now that all the legal and important shit was out of the way, I could focus on putting my plan into action.

Let the games begin, wife.

4

ANASTACIA

I GLANCED DOWN AT THE BAND ON MY FINGER, FEELING SICK AT THE EVENTS of today. How could my father do that to me? He was a man I once looked up to, alongside Artem, his original right hand, however, he left out of the blue. He was more like a father to me than Victor ever was, and what's worse, my father didn't seem to care. His focus was Miles, Miles, and Miles. I knew deep down he felt no remorse about packing me up and handing me to Lorenzo Ricci. I supposed having me gone would be one less thing for him to worry about.

"Anastacia, are you okay?" Red asked from the driver's seat.

"It's Ana, Red, and I'm fine," I lied. I wasn't okay. I would never be fine, but I had to grin and bear it just as I had many things in my life.

"You don't need to lie. He might be my boss as well as my friend but—"

"But what, Red?" Lorenzo snapped as he slammed the door behind him. I hadn't even noticed him open the damn thing.

"Nothing, just nothing." He sighed, perhaps feeling sorry for me, but he didn't need to. Give me a day or two and I would genuinely be fine.

Fine... A word I hated. I always knew my mother wasn't okay when she used the word fine, and now I couldn't stop saying it. It flowed out of me like bloody water.

"Let's go. We have that meeting to get to tonight, and we can't be late." Lorenzo tapped on his phone, not paying attention to anything else.

"At least I won't have to deal with you tonight then. I guess my prayers have been answered," I teased, turning my attention to the passing nature. "You'll probably end the night with a quick fuck to get your rocks off."

"Jealous, wife?" he asked, cracking his neck.

"Of the poor woman who has to fuck you?" I scoffed. "Not in the slightest."

He chuckled before the car fell completely silent. I was in the process of working out if that was a good thing or something incredibly bad. Then suddenly I had my answer, Lorenzo gripped my chin between his thumb and forefinger, forcing me to look at him. He leaned into me, the warmth of his breath brushing my ear.

"That mouth is going to get you into trouble, Anastacia," he hissed.

"I doubt that, but then again, you won't be paying much attention to me after today anyway. As you said, you want a quiet wife. I'm guessing one that's seen and not heard." I bit back, not faltering or letting myself seem rattled by him or the words he spoke.

"And is that what my wife craves? My attention?" He brushed his thumb over my lower lip, making my skin prickle unexpectedly. *Dammit.*

"I don't need, nor do I want, your attention. I'm content being alone." I let out a steady breath, my confidence coming back in full force.

"Lying isn't a good look on you." In one swift move, he fisted my hair, causing my head to jerk back just enough so he had access to my bare neck. His stubble scratched my sensitive skin before he roughly sucked on my neck. *Did that bastard just give me a mother-fucking hickey?!*

I saw red. Rearing my hand back, I wasted no time in letting it collide with his face. The sting radiated through my palm and his cheek reddened.

"Touch me again and it'll be more than just a slap," I threatened, shoving his body away from mine as I saw the rage written all over his face. "Why would you do that anyway?!"

"I can do whatever I want with my wife. At least now any man who sees you without me by your side will know you're taken."

"And the ring on my finger isn't indication enough?" I threw my hands up in despair, wanting to smash his damn face in.

"No, not nearly enough." He scowled, his eyes darkening as he spoke.

I turned my back to him, not wanting to feed his ego with more attention. No matter if it was good or bad, he didn't deserve it.

It wasn't long before we turned onto a long gravel driveway that led to what could only be his house. It was magnificent, I had to admit. It was grander than the one I shared with my family. The driveway must have been over a mile long and was shaded by bushes and trees, hiding security cameras no doubt. As we reached the entrance, we circled around a fountain that replicated a work of art. Red parked at the bottom of the steps leading to the front door.

"Welcome to your new home, Ana."

Lorenzo huffed like a child as he exited the car, slamming the door behind him.

"Well, this is going to be fun." I laughed as Red tried his best not to join in.

"I promise, he isn't bad. I've known him since we were kids." His promises meant nothing to me. I hadn't known him long enough to trust him yet.

I was about to respond when Lorenzo yanked the door open, almost taking it off its hinges.

"Out," he demanded, his hand hooked over the top of the door in a tight grasp as he waited.

"You know, a please would be nice," I teased. It was worth it. He looked just about ready to combust.

I exited the car, not waiting for Lorenzo as I made my way up the stairs. I didn't need to look to know he was striding after me, I felt his presence close behind.

"Why don't you slow down since you have no idea where you're going?"

"Oh, silly me. I thought that big thing in front of me with a handle was the door. Have I been wrong all these years?" I gasped sarcastically.

I heard two men chuckle from the car. Red had been joined by another guy, who I saw beside Lorenzo at the wedding. My assumption was that he was a friend as well since he wouldn't have gotten away with that laugh otherwise.

"You two can shut up," he snapped, directing his anger at them both.

"If you're going to get so worked up about it, lead the way, your highness." I curtsied as he stormed past me.

"No, I'm done. I'm fucking done." Red cackled, not able to control his laughter anymore.

"Red, I swear to God if you don't shut up, I'll gut you from navel to mouth, friend or not." Lorenzo shoved the door open as Red stifled his next bout of laughter.

I followed him into the foyer of his home and was immediately slack-jawed. I couldn't believe how immaculate and stunning it was. There were bay windows overlooking a lake on either side of the staircase opposite me, the body of water picturesque. It seemed serene and peaceful, everything this marriage wouldn't be.

The staircase parted at the top, leading to different sides of the house. Hopefully I'd be far enough from him to keep my distance. Although the house was so breathtakingly beautiful, it was incredibly sparse. There were no flowers or pictures. It just felt empty and lifeless.

"Welcome home," Lorenzo said from behind me, closing the door to everyone else outside.

"I've already told you that this won't be my home."

His hand snaked around my waist, the back of my head colliding with his shoulder. He brushed my hair over my shoulder as he brought his lips to my ear.

"It already is," he whispered, sending a shiver down my spine and not in a way I liked.

"Can you show me to my room, please?" I asked as politely as possible, wanting to get this shit day over with.

"Your room? Correct me if I'm wrong but we're married now. Husbands and wives share a room, bed, and many other things." He ran his tongue over the hickey he left not that long ago.

"We will share nothing, believe me. Now, do I have my own room or do I need to find one myself?" I twisted in his arms, challenging his authority. "I'd hate to stumble into someone else's room and maybe even fall into bed with—"

"Don't you dare finish that sentence!" he ordered. "You have your own room. Your bags are already waiting inside." He cleared his throat as I stepped away from him. "I have a meeting to get to. Take a left at the top of the stairs, follow the corridor until the end, and your door is on the right next to mine."

"Don't trust me to be at the opposite end of the house, no?"

"You've got your own room, Anastacia. Don't push the rest," he snapped, turning his back to me as he slipped out the door without another word.

I had a feeling he didn't trust that I wouldn't pull a moonlight flit, hence why he wanted me in the room beside his. But at least there was a wall between us. I guessed that was something.

I glanced around, hearing the television blaring from what I assumed was the living room or a hang out area for his men.

Ignoring that, I climbed the stairs, following Lorenzo's instructions.

I didn't know what to expect upon opening the door to my room but it wasn't what I saw. My bags were at the foot of the four-poster bed that sat in the middle of the room, the walls a soft cotton white with petal pink accents dotted around the room. As beautiful as all this was, the one thing that captured my attention was the view. It was the same as the one I saw earlier with the lake in the back garden. The remainder of the afternoon sun reflected on the water as the trees that surrounded it blew gently in the breeze. The only good thing about living in Lorenzo's house would be the scenery, nothing else.

I quickly rummaged through one of my bags to find a comfier alternative to the dress I was wearing. I came across a note instead.

Ana, I'm so sorry. I only found out about what was happening this morning. Your father was incredibly tight-lipped about the marriage arrangement, and by the time I found out, I couldn't get near you to let you know. I packed your bags for you. Everything I could manage is in them. If you need anything, you know where I am. The house won't be the same without you. Please forgive me. - Chad

I dropped the note back into my bag in desperate need of some shorts and tank top, anything to replace this damn dress, but then something else caught my eye and I had an idea... Probably one that would get me into trouble, but fuck it. You only lived once, right?

I dialled my best friend's number, and within two rings, she answered.

"Where the hell have you been? I've called you multiple times today!" Robin asked, worry coating her voice.

"Getting married." I sighed as the line went silent for a second.

"I'm sorry. I must have misheard you. You got married?" She stumbled over her words, and I knew how real the shock was.

"My father made a damn deal with the devil in disguise."

"Of course it was your father's doing... Are you okay?" she questioned, her voice softer than before.

"I don't know. I hate him." I groaned, just thinking about the cocky bastard made my blood boil.

"Who? Your father or husband?" She chuckled, trying her best to lighten the mood.

"Well, both, but mainly Lorenzo Ricci, the asshole that is now my husband." I couldn't help but roll my eyes, which she instantly knew because we had that kind of friendship.

"He sounds hot, though," she teased.

"Alright, he's hot, yeah, but that doesn't mean I want to be married to him." I sighed. "Anyway, that's not why I called."

She gasped. "You're sneaking out, aren't you?"

"Indeed, I am. Meet you at that newer place in town?" I asked, already knowing her answer.

"I'll call Tay and meet you there in a couple of hours. Think of tonight as your bachelorette party since we didn't get to throw you one. Get drunk and get fucked. Tonight is your night, baby!" She knew I wouldn't fuck anyone, but that never stopped her from saying it every single time we snuck out to bars and clubs. When I lived at home, my father never approved of me going out. Then again, he barely approved of me doing anything.

AFTER SHOWERING AND GETTING READY, I felt the adrenaline coursing through my veins as I prepared to execute my plan. Sneaking out of a house unfamiliar to me promised to be more challenging than I had anticipated. Nevertheless, I was determined to give it a shot. I moved stealthily through the dimly lit corridors, slipping past the rooms where the men I had yet to meet were residing, my heart pounding in my chest. So far, so good.

The real challenge awaited outside, where the men patrolling the grounds and the gate were more vigilant, their eyes scanning the surroundings with practiced precision. Yet, by some stroke of luck—or perhaps a small miracle—I managed to evade their notice. I slipped through the narrow pedestrian gate nestled beside the imposing electric one, which loomed silently, locked and unyielding.

Wow, that wasn't too bad.

I bet I was caught on the cameras, but by the time they noticed anything, I'd be long gone.

See you in the morning, Ricci.

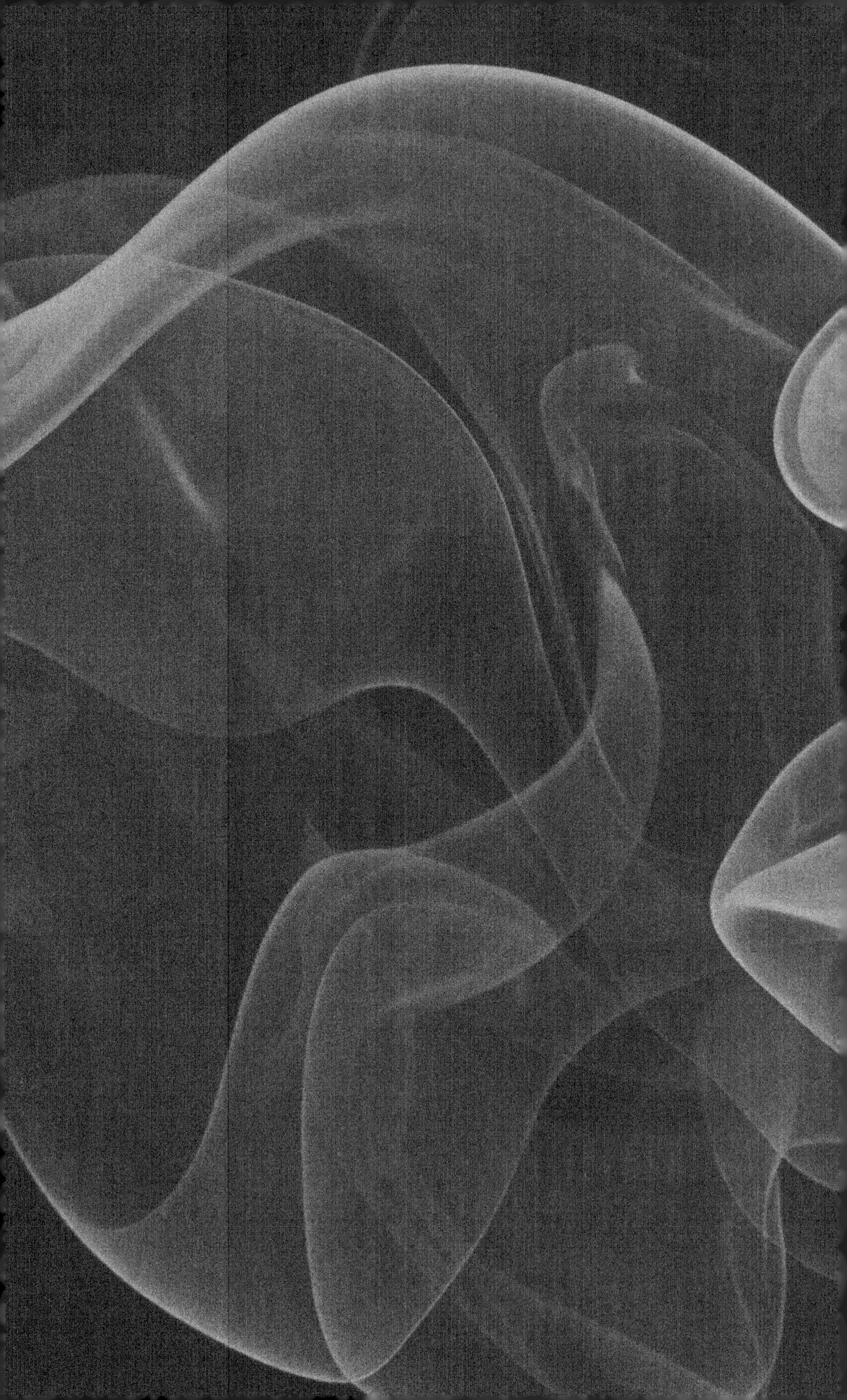

5

LORENZO

Relaxing back against the plush booth, I enjoyed the two fingers worth of whiskey I poured myself. I glanced down at one of my many empires. It was one of the newer establishments. One that was doing pretty well. It was crowded tonight, which meant my pockets would be well and truly lined by the end of it.

"Boss, Rox has arrived," Finn called from the door, glancing at his watch to check he was on time.

He wasn't.

"Only fifteen minutes late." I scoffed, downing the amber liquid.

Within seconds, Rox Marshall swanned into the private lounge. He was a complete and utter cock, but we needed a new arms supplier after our most recent one was hacked apart and buried all over due to a monumental fuck up.

"Mr. Ricci, it's a pleasure." A wide smile stretched across his face, revealing a glinting gold canine tooth that immediately captured my attention. He was a middle-aged man, his hair slicked back with an excessive amount of gel, giving it a shiny, almost wet look. It was as if he believed more was always better, not realising it left him with a helmet-like appearance. I found myself instinctively wary, certain that he should steer clear of any open flames unless he wanted to become a human torch.

"You're fifteen minutes late," I told him, letting him know we weren't off to a good start.

"I know and I apologise for that, but I met this woman outside, and I couldn't say no to getting my dick wet, could I?" He laughed, but it wasn't reciprocated by anyone in the room.

"Business comes first, Mr. Marshall, so if you can manage to keep your cock in your pants for another hour, that would be appreciated." As I slid into the booth, he shifted uncomfortably across the table, his eyes darting away from mine. His throat bobbed with a tense swallow, and a faint flush crept up his neck, betraying the embarrassment that lingered from his recent behaviour.

"Of course, it won't happen again," he assured me.

"Too right, it won't." I tensed my jaw as I cracked my neck. "I don't take kindly to being fucked around, so can I count on you to not fuck it up?"

"You can, you have my word." He held out his hand, securing his word with a handshake, but only time would tell how genuine he truly was.

"Okay, let's begin." I smiled, sliding him a glass of whiskey.

We spent the next hour meticulously dissecting every last detail of our partnership, leaving no stone unturned, as we discussed the intricacies of what it would entail. We delved into the nuances of each party's share, ensuring clarity and fairness in the distribution of profits. The moment he grasped the full extent of the money he stood to gain from each transaction, his eyes lit up like a damn Christmas tree.

"So, by the look on your face, I take it we have ourselves a deal?" I asked, crossing my ankle across my thigh, awaiting his response.

"Indeed, we do, Lorenzo." He clapped his hands together with delight before downing his shot of premium whiskey.

"Perfect, just as expected. Now, you'll be dealing with Red

regarding the contract." I gave Red a quick curt nod as he set the contract down in front of Rox with a pen.

"I'm sorry, a contract?" Rox cleared his throat, taken aback at the fact I was asking him to sign on the dotted line. He could barely hide the astonishment in his voice.

"Unfortunately, some can't be trusted with cuts and such." I said as he arched his brow as if to question me. "I'm sure you understand, don't you?" I narrowed my eyes as he nodded rapidly. "Red, I'm leaving you to get this sorted and squared away."

"Of course, Boss." He explained the contract to Rox, who listened carefully to every detail before enthusiastically signing his name in permanent ink.

But we all knew that all it took was one slip up for Rox to end up like the others.

"Now that that's done, how about we enjoy a drink to toast what will hopefully be a long and respected partnership?" I asked once all the t's were crossed and i's were dotted.

His eyes sparkled with enthusiasm as he leaned back in his chair, a wide grin spreading across his face. "I think a drink sounds like the perfect way to solidify our partnership," he declared, his voice filled with a warmth that matched the atmosphere of the dimly lit area around us.

As we enjoyed the first round of drinks, Red caught the eye of a violet-haired girl practically wearing next to nothing. He wriggled his brows at me. I chuckled before giving him the go ahead to do whatever it was he planned on doing tonight.

"I must say, your men have exquisite taste." Rox smacked his lips as he poured himself another whiskey.

"That's questionable at times." I laughed as I checked my phone, seeing if there was an update on my wife, who I expected had either trashed her room in anger at being married to me or had already fallen asleep whilst cursing my name.

"I'll tell you what isn't questionable," Rox responded, his focus clearly drawn elsewhere.

"Enlighten me." I glanced up at him briefly, waiting to see what had captivated him.

"That gorgeous blonde over there. The one with the incredible legs. I wouldn't mind having them thrown over my shoulders, if you know what I mean?" His tongue darted out, wetting his lower lip.

I followed his gaze and realised the woman he was salivating over was none other than my woman! *My wife!*

He continued to run his mouth, making his interest in Anastacia known as she gracefully swayed her petite hips in time with the pulsating music. She was an electrifying presence, a fiery force of nature that was almost impossible to contain. I studied every inch of her. Starting from those fuck-me heels to the hem of her figure-hugging dress, the one that just barely covered her perfect ass.

Her hair was slicked back in a ponytail that highlighted her flawless features. Then, there were her lips. Painted a deep cherry red, they made my cock twitch as the thought of having them wrapped around me became all too much.

I continued to watch her as I blocked Rox out. She dismissed any man that came near her, too focused on dancing with her two female friends. *Good girl.* I could tell just by looking at them that they'd been friends since diapers or close enough.

Rox stood, ready to excuse himself so he could make a move on my wife.

"Am I keeping you, Rox?" I asked, narrowing my eyes at him.

"Actually, I'm going to see if she'd be up for a good time." *She would be but not with you, you deluded prick.*

"I suggest you sit your ass back down and keep those filthy hands to yourself unless you want to lose them," I snapped, slamming my glass on the table.

I watched as his face fell, completely unaware of what he did wrong as he lowered himself back onto his seat.

“I’m sorry. I shouldn’t be trying to score with someone else after I was already late. I’ll head down once we’re done here.” He leaned back, wiping his sweaty palms on his slacks.

“I don’t give a shit if you want to score, get lucky, or get your dick wet. What you do with that nasty thing is none of my business, but when you mention her, it becomes mine.” He side-eyed me, still trying to look at her as I spoke. “Look at me when I’m speaking to you.”

His head snapped towards me, and I noticed an expression I knew all too well... *Fear.*

I leaned forward, my voice low and firm as I locked eyes with him. "My wife is off-limits to anyone but me, do you understand?" The tension in the room was palpable, and I could feel the intensity of my own words vibrating in the air. There was an unmistakable edge of possessiveness that laced my tone.

“Your wife, huh?” He chuckled.

“I said, do you understand me?!” I demanded, slamming my fist on the table as it rattled beneath me. My men stepped forward, ready to intervene, but the second I shook my head, they returned to their positions.

“Oh, I do, but answer me this—if she is your wife then where’s her wedding ring?” He tapped his finger against his non-existent lips, questioning me.

My eyes locked on her ring finger and there it was... Bare. No wedding band in sight.

“So, no ring means fair game, right?”

Bastard.

That was my breaking point. A surge of adrenaline coursed through me, and before I knew it, my hands gripped the edge of the table, flipping it violently across the room with a crash that echoed like a thunderclap. The path to Rox was clear, and I moved swiftly, each step fuelled by an uncontainable fury. In an instant, my fingers clamped around his neck, the skin beneath my grip hot and pulsing. His eyes widened, round and glassy, as my hold constricted, cutting off his breath and reflecting the intensity of the moment.

"My wife will never be fair game!" I hissed through clenched teeth. "She belongs to me and me alone." I declared, my voice steady and cold, my words slicing through the tension like a blade. He wheezed and sputtered, struggling to draw a breath. I leaned in closer, my gaze unyielding. "Now, I'm going to ask you one more time, do you understand me?!"

"Y-yes, I u-understand," he choked out, his ringed fingers clawing at my wrist.

Once I was satisfied, I released him. My eyes never left his beady gaze.

"Please accept my apology, Lorenzo. I truly had no idea," he spluttered as he rubbed his neck.

"Yeah, well, now you do." I smoothed down my dishevelled shirt. "Make it known that Anastacia Fedorov is now Anastacia Ricci, and if anyone lays a finger on her, I'll torture them in ways they'd never be able to think up themselves."

"You married Victor Fedorov's daughter?" he asked, again, not realising who she truly was.

"I did, but as I said, she's a Ricci as of today."

"Let me get this straight—it's your wedding night, and you're here? Doing business with me?" He tsked, taken aback. After hearing it, I realised how shitty it sounded.

"Yeah, but I'm done now, and so is she." I said, knocking back the whiskey Gino handed me.

"Lorenzo, I apologise again, and I hope this doesn't affect our working relationship." He sheepishly smiled.

"Our working relationship will be just fine as long as you keep your eyes and hands off what's mine." I handed him my empty glass as he nodded. "Now, if you'll excuse me, I need to pay my wife a little visit. Gino will see you out." I didn't wait for him to respond. There was no point. I strode out of the private room, down the spiral staircase, and onto the crowded dance floor.

It didn't take me long to find her. I would have spotted her anywhere. I watched her sensually move her body to the music with each step I took. The thought of wrapping her ponytail around my fist while slamming into her tight pussy taunted me as my cock strained against the constraints of my suit pants. Her hands slid seductively over every inch of her body, sending me into some sort of trance. I shook myself out of it quickly enough, remembering that she was just a pawn in my game.

Her intoxicating scent filled my senses as I slowly invaded her personal space. She was completely oblivious to me being there, which made my next move all the more sweeter. I slid my arm around her waist from behind, securing her body to mine and bringing my lips to her ear so I'd be heard over the music.

"Enjoying yourself, wife?" I whispered as I felt a gasp leave her lips, her heart racing faster than what her dancing had caused.

I stole a glance at her friends who were somewhere between shock and drunken happiness.

"Don't worry, I'm her husband," I assured them, playing the part all too well.

"We'll grab another drink and leave you both to it." They giggled.

"Your drinks are on the house. Just tell them Lorenzo sent you, and there should be no issues." And with that, they departed, leaving us alone.

"Where is your ring, Ana?" I asked, my voice a tense whisper as I struggled to keep my composure. I teased her bare finger with my own. Each second that passed without an answer only fuelled the heat rising in my chest.

"First of all, it's Anastacia. And secondly, it's at home in the drawer beside my bed. Next question." She sarcastically smiled, riling me up even more.

"It's supposed to be on your finger," I growled.

"Well, it's not, is it?" She held up her hand to show me her bare finger, a smug look written all over her face.

"Don't worry, I'll ensure it will be," I assured her. "Now, care to tell me why you snuck out and why you're in my club? Did you crave my attention that much, or did you want to get a rise out of me?" I spun her to face me. Her lips parted, ready to give me a mouthful. "Before you open that pretty little mouth of yours to surprise me with yet another smart ass remark, remember who you're speaking to," I warned as my fingers brushed the hickey on her neck. The one she tried to cover up with layers of make-up.

"Oh, don't worry. I know who I'm talking to." She chuckled with an eye roll.

Was she drunk?

"And who's that?"

"A damn stalker, that's who." She sneered, trying to turn away from me, which of course, I didn't allow. "Get your hands off me!" She fisted my shirt, as anger radiated from her.

"I don't think I will." I tightened my hold as she let out a pissed off sigh. "Come with me," I demanded, but there were no signs of movement.

"I'm going nowhere with you," she declared, her voice tinged with defiance. Her piercing blue eyes narrowed to icy slits, reflecting the storm of emotions swirling within her as she clenched her fists harder.

"It's admirable that you think you have a choice," I said, my voice laced with a mix of sarcasm and amusement. I gently released my grip, letting my hands fall away from her, and in one fluid, decisive motion, hoisted her over my shoulder. Her weight settled comfortably as I adjusted my stance, feeling the soft fabric of her dress brush against my cheek, while her startled gasp echoed in the air.

I weaved my way across the pulsating dance floor, feeling her tiny fists hammering against my back in an attempt to inflict pain. We navigated through the throng of gyrating bodies, the crowd too engrossed in their own rhythm and music to pay any attention to us. I sprinted up the winding staircase, until I reached the secluded haven of the private room. Only then did I stop, quickly pulling the door shut to block out everything else.

"Put me down right now or I'll—" She strained. Being upside down had its perks.

"You'll what? Call Daddy Dearest or someone else to tattle on me?" I chuckled as I set her down, and for some inexplicable reason, I steadied her so she didn't break her neck in those damn heels. "Why are you here, Ana?" I dipped my head just enough for the warmth of her vodka-infused breath to mingle with my own.

"I don't see how it's your business, to be honest." She had an answer for absolutely everything.

"Since I'm your husband, it has everything to do with me." I was so tempted to taste her, just once, to get it out of my system.

"You wish it did, you mean." She giggled.

"You're drunk, aren't you?" I rubbed my temples as she shrugged her shoulders. "How much have you had to drink?" I asked.

"I might be drunk, but then again, I might not be," she joked sarcastically as she rolled her eyes in annoyance.

"Fuck sake," I snapped. It was clear she was barely paying attention to me. She was probably planning her next pain in the ass remark. "All you had to do tonight was behave, was it really that hard?"

"Yeah, I didn't feel like doing that." She stepped closer to me, capturing my attention. "And I actually don't plan on ever behaving with you."

"Right, I'm taking you home. We'll discuss this when you aren't intoxicated."

"I was celebrating getting married." Her lips twisted up at the corners. "Eh, who am I kidding? I can't lie that well." She laughed, swaying side to side. "But on a serious note, I'm not going anywhere with you."

"I'm not playing games. Do as you're told!" But of course, she didn't. She turned on those death trap heels of hers and stalked off towards where I had sat with Rox not that long ago.

"Anastacia." I sighed, catching up to her in two strides. I tossed her effortlessly over my shoulder once again as if she was nothing but a rag doll.

"If you don't put me down, I swear I'll feed you your own dick!" she screamed as her head dangled down my back.

"I look forward to the challenge, Mrs. Ricci," I teased, laughing until I met Gino who was already waiting with the car.

"Lorenzo?" He arched his brow, questioning what was going on. "I'm not entirely sure what's going on here."

"What's going on is this dickhead thinks he owns me. All because we're married," she piped up from behind me.

"My wife decided to sneak out tonight. She's intoxicated and quite irritating."

Gino let out a throaty laugh as Anastacia continued to pound my back. Someone so dainty sure could pack a punch. "Let's just get her home."

I carefully placed her on the backseat. Although, I should have bloody thrown her in there instead. Maybe I wasn't feeling as heartless as I should have been.

"Are you joining me in the front, or are you keeping Anastacia company?" he asked, already rounding to the driver's side.

"I better watch her in the back. She seems to be good when it comes to escaping." I scoffed as he smiled.

I slid in beside her, noticing she hadn't yet secured herself.

"Put your belt on," I ordered as I clicked mine into place. There was no movement as it was pretty damn clear she was doing her best to make my life hell.

"Anastacia, I said put your—"

"I heard you! I'm not a damn child!" She reached over and clicked her belt into place before turning around to face me. "Thanks for ruining my night, by the way."

"My pleasure."

Gino began the drive home, nobody saying a word for a while. Jazz music filled the car, and I suddenly felt something drop onto my shoulder. Moving my head carefully, I noticed Anastacia had fallen asleep and unintentionally rested her head on me. I studied her for a moment. Her face serene as if she didn't have a care in the world. Her lips curled upwards into a gentle smile, and it made me wonder what she was dreaming about. There was no way it was me, otherwise she'd be scowling.

"If I didn't know you, I'd say you look like a man admiring his wife," Gino piped up from the driver's seat.

"Good job. You know the truth then," I whispered.

"I know I do, but it's not too late to—"

"Drop it, Gino. You know my reasons, as well as my feelings, behind everything. Never question me or my plans again." I shut him down, or so I thought, but he felt the need to continue.

"I know that but I saw how you reacted with Rox, and yes, I've seen that side of you, but never because of a woman." He caught my eye in the rearview mirror, and I could tell he was trying his best to see if he could change my mind or get me to admit some nonexistent feelings.

"That woman is my wife, and there is no way in hell I'd let Rox anywhere near her. I don't like sharing what's mine. It meant nothing." I narrowed my eyes at him as he quickly dropped the subject. "Let's just get her home, and then, I'll deal with the fuckers that let her slip past them."

We pulled up to the house, and she showed no signs of waking up whatsoever. I had no idea what to do since I had never been in this situation before. I was removing her seatbelt when the door flung open, revealing one of my men who clearly had too much to drink.

"Boss, who's the woman?" He questioned, already pissing me off. I ignored his stupid remark as I scooped her into my arms with ease before carrying her up the steps to the front door. I could feel him following behind. "You don't fancy sharing her then?" *Cunt.*

My guys had been briefed relentlessly for today. They knew I was getting married, and that she'd be here. Was he so drunk that he forgot something that important?

I tightened my grip on her, refusing to let her slip from my embrace as I reached behind to draw my gun from the back of my waistband. "I don't share my wife," I declared, my voice a low growl filled with unwavering determination. I levelled the weapon at his head, watching as his jaw went slack and his eyes widened in sheer disbelief.

"Shit, Boss, I forgot. I had one too many. I—"

I interrupted him abruptly with a single bullet piercing the space between his eyes, and he crumpled to the floor in a lifeless heap. Everything around us was suddenly silent, except for the echoing ring of the gunshot. I glanced down at Anastacia, who lay undisturbed, her breathing steady and unbroken. The fact that she didn't stir, even as the sharp crack of the gunfire shattered the silence, left me baffled.

"Clean this shit up," I ordered, as Gino had already pulled out his phone to call Red.

The second I entered the lobby, the men I trusted tonight were lined up looking sheepish. *As they should.*

"Boss," Wes started.

"I don't want to hear it. You all fucked up tonight, and once I put my wife to bed, I'll be back to deal with each and every one of you," I snapped, not wanting to waste my time on them any longer.

I ascended the stairs, making a beeline for Anastacia's bedroom. I was in for a treat the second I reached the door, realising it was bloody locked. *Why the hell did I install a lock on her door?!* I could have kicked it in, but I didn't fancy ruining my house just so she could sleep in her own bed.

I looked down at her body, knowing her dress had nowhere to hide a key, and we'd obviously left her bag in the car.

Could I have asked someone to grab it for me? Yes, I could have.

Was I going to? No, I wasn't.

Knowing she'd wake up tomorrow with a shitty attitude was enough for me. Plus, I was actually looking forward to seeing what smart remarks she had in store for me.

6

ANASTACIA

I STRAINED MY EYES OPEN, THE EARLY MORNING SUNLIGHT STREAMING through the heavy curtains. My head was pounding, but I guessed that was from the effects of a good night out. Well, until that prick ruined it. I stretched my arms out, the black sheets enveloping my body.

Wait a minute... These weren't my sheets... Were these...

Bastard!

"Lorenzo fucking Ricci!" I snapped, sitting bolt upright, the thumping in my head now gone. "I'm going to kill you, you son of a bitch!" Of course, he was nowhere to be seen.

I climbed out of bed and exited his room, finding my bag outside of mine with a small note attached to it.

Next time you want to drink that much, don't forget your damn purse. Oh, and by the way, the lock has now been removed. - Lorenzo

I snatched my purse off the floor and debated finding him and gutting the bastard, but I prioritised taking a shower first and washing all the shit from yesterday away.

After changing into a pair of ripped jeans and an oversized knit, I felt fresh and ready to face my so-called husband. I debated putting my wedding ring on, but honestly, why the hell should I? It wasn't like this was a real marriage filled with love and loyalty, so why bother?

I followed the voices I heard as I neared a room with a closed door. Not bothering to knock, I barged into what I guessed was his office. Seven or eight pairs of eyes landed on me the second I almost took the door off its hinges.

"You bastard!" I yelled, not caring who was watching.

"Team, say good morning to my wife," he teased, looking incredibly pleased with himself.

They all smiled in unison and muttered out, "Good morning."

"Now, get out," he ordered.

"I'm not done, so no, I won't get out." I folded my arms across my chest, standing my ground.

"I didn't mean you, *la mia bella ragazza*." He settled back in his chair, calling me something in Italian that I'd need to search the meaning of later. "Don't keep jumping to conclusions." He chuckled, sending the team out with a flick of his wrist.

"What the fuck did you do?!"

He grinned, his eyes twinkling with self-satisfaction, as he recounted the evening. "I put my intoxicated wife to bed." He said, his voice dripping with smugness.

"I know that, but you put me in the wrong one!" I threw my hands up in the air, clearly getting nowhere with his sarcastic ass.

"Well, if you hadn't locked your door, got drunk, and fell asleep in the car then I would have been able to put you in the right one."

"You could have woken me up!" I sighed, my blood boiling.

"Oh, trust me, I tried but you even slept through a damn

gunshot. There was no waking you up." Lorenzo rose from his chair as he spoke, his eyes never leaving mine.

"You stay over there. You've already done enough." I reached behind my back, putting my hand on the handle of the door, readying my escape.

"What you did last night was incredibly stupid and reckless." He stopped before me, gripping my wrist as I held on to the metal. "You're married to *me*. You're the daughter of a *Fedorov*. You have countless targets on your back, and you swan around without a care in the world." His jaw clenched and his eyes narrowed, the lines on his forehead deepening as the smug grin he had worn moments before vanished. His lips pressed into a tight line, and he let out a sharp breath through his nose, exuding a palpable wave of frustration.

"I can protect myself. I don't need you or anyone else watching my every move." I scoffed as he pressed my body against the door, slowly suffocating me.

"That's where you're wrong. You're my wife, and you will do as you're told, when you're told." He grabbed my face with one hand, holding me to his body with the other. "Where is your ring, Anastacia?" he demanded, his gaze dropping to my bare finger, just as they did the night before.

"Where it belongs."

"Well, it clearly isn't. I already told you if you didn't wear it, I'd glue it to your finger." He craned his neck, bringing his lips an inch from mine, the warmth of his breath teasing my skin. "Would you rather I tattooed my name on you instead?"

"I'd rather not be married to you in general." I thrashed my head, wanting to get the hell away from him but it only made him tighten his hold on me.

"Well, we can't always get what we want." His eyes darkened with each word he said. "Now, be a good girl and do as you're told."

I slapped his face with such force that my hand went numb, a tingling sensation spreading up my arm. "Don't tell me what to do!" I demanded, my voice shaking as anger spilled out of me like a torrent of water bursting through a dam.

I expected him to retaliate, but he just stood there with a smile. One that unsettled me.

His eyes searched mine for a split second. I had no idea what he was looking for but then I realised. He was hoping for the smallest hint of approval. I didn't get the chance to answer because his lips collided with mine in a ferocious crash, a violent clash of heat and fury. There was nothing loving about it. It was as though we were fighting a war with mouths instead of fists, the pair of us so desperate to come out on top.

His anger and frustration poured into me like lava, dangerous and destructive. My body began to betray my mind as I kissed him back with the exact same venom. I couldn't see or feel anything other than us. Not that there would ever be an us. I vowed to myself that I'd never lose my power to him, never give him what he wanted. Yet here I was, doing the opposite.

He fisted my hair tighter, wrapping one braid around his hand and possessing me with every stroke of his tongue. And although I felt nothing but hate for this man, desire crept through the cracks in my invisible amour. I tried to drown out any unwanted thoughts that played on my mind but the way he controlled me was making it so hard.

He teased my lower lip between his teeth, breaking the skin. All I could taste was my own blood, metallic and warm. He was draining the power from me second by second, and I couldn't let that happen.

"You keep surprising me, Ana," he growled, my blood painting his lips too.

"What were you expecting? A timid princess who was trained by her family to be the perfect housewife?" I whispered. "I'm not my mother, Lorenzo. You don't get perfect."

"Perfect is overrated." He sucked my lip into his mouth before devouring me again. His lips moved to my neck, roughly sucking on my skin as I let out an unexpected moan. "You'll never escape me, wife. You are mine until I say otherwise."

"Your say is irrelevant to me." I scoffed.

"My say is everything. I chose you, and you're going to obey me. No matter how long it takes, you'll obey your husband."

"You're deluded if you think that will ever happen," I snapped back, my breathing rugged. My words were thick with hate and cut through the air like a whip.

He yanked my face back to his, his lips colliding with mine before I had a chance to say anything else. As he overpowered me, I kissed him back with every ounce of resentment I was holding onto and the bastard knew it. He kissed me with more aggression and force than before as I felt the heat of his body seep into mine. My body pulsed with anger, there was no grace, no gentleness, just us fighting for dominance.

I dug my nails into his back with as much force as I could. The sound of the hiss leaving his lips filled me with satisfaction.

"Stay away from me." My chest heaved as his eyes dropped to my breasts. "Whatever that was will never happen again."I whispered, as I found the strength to shove him away. I couldn't give in to him. I couldn't let him think kissing me would be as easy as this or that it would change anything. It changed nothing.

"Put your ring on," he said, making it clear he was still wearing his own by lifting his hand and twisting it around his finger with his thumb.

"*Idi poigray v probke, chertov zasranets.*" I smiled, knowing he had no clue what I just said. "*Ya zastavlyu tebya podavit'sya etim kol'tsom.*"

I yanked the door open, coming face to face with the men who Lorenzo sent out not that long ago.

"He's all yours." I smiled sweetly as I left the team in my wake.

That man had another thing coming if he thought I'd obey him.

I didn't even know the meaning of the word.

7

LORENZO

"Red, get the fuck in here," I ordered as he hurried back into the office, trying to hide his smile the best he could. "Translate what my wife just said to me."

"Well, for starters, she told you to go play in traffic, you fucking asshole." I narrowed my eyes at him as he held his hands up in surrender. "Hey, her words, not mine."

"Next thing."

"I'll make you choke on that ring," he translated.

"I'm going to need you to teach me some Russian, Red." I smiled, always ready to get one up on my new, pain-in-the-ass wife.

"Gladly." He patted my shoulder with a look I wasn't quite sure of. "She's keeping you on your toes, isn't she?"

"She's something, that's for sure."

"I'm sure you don't give two shits about my opinion, but I'm going to give it to you anyway." He lit a cigarette before continuing. "I think she's good for you, and honestly, I think she's exactly what you need."

"You're right. I don't give two shits." I scoffed. "But I think I'll keep her after I kill her father. It'll be fun."

"You think you'll break her by taking him out, but I think it'll be the opposite. She'll set out her own plan. One that involves making you pay. She won't be a sobbing, broken mess. You and I both know it."

"You know how much I love a challenge, Red."

I was about to call the team back into the office when Finn barged in, looking a little dishevelled.

"Boss, I just thought you should know..." He paused, taking in my appearance. "You know you're bleeding, right?" I looked over my shoulder, noticing the blood that seeped through my shirt, the blood Anastacia had drawn during our heated moment.

"Spit it out, Finn," I ordered, not caring about how my shirt looked.

"There's some guy parked at the front gate. He said he's here for Anastacia," he responded, pissing me off.

"What guy?!"

Finn clenched his jaw, his eyes narrowing with irritation. "He said his name's Chad," he muttered, his voice tinged with frustration as he matched my own simmering anger.

Chad.

The same fucking Chad that said the house wouldn't be the same without Anastacia.

Oh, yeah, I found the note he'd written to Ana, in what I bet was his best damn handwriting. Not that I was snooping or anything when I came across that piece of paper. It was just sitting there on top of one of her unpacked bags when I had the lock removed earlier. And now that bastard was here to see her? Who the hell did he think he was to turn up uninvited and unannounced at my house?!

"The lot of you stay here. We still have shit to deal with." That wasn't a request. It was an order.

As I rounded the corner to the foyer area, I saw her heading towards the front door.

"Where do you think you're going?!" I bellowed as her body stilled at the sound of my voice.

"Out. What's it to you?" She didn't turn to look at me. She didn't hold that much respect for me.

Yet, anyway.

"I'm going to ask you again. Where do you think you're going?!" I was beyond irritated. She was truly testing my patience.

"I told you—out." She breathed, remaining calmer than expected.

"Red will take you where you need to go. You don't go out alone or without one of my men anymore," I ordered, gaining her attention as she turned around to face me.

"I don't need a damn chaperone, Lorenzo. I'm a grown ass woman!" she bit back. And there she was. She couldn't keep that anger hidden for long.

"That wasn't a request, Anastacia." I closed the distance between us, pushing her dainty body against the door behind her, the metal biting into her back. She peeked up through her lashes, challenging me yet again. "You can send Chad on his merry fucking way and take Red where you need to go." The way her lips parted and eyes darkened made my cock ache with need. How was it possible to want to murder her, yet devour her in the space of a couple of seconds?

A soft giggle left her bare lips as I cocked my head to the side, trying to work out what the hell she was laughing at.

"It seems my wife finds something funny. Care to enlighten me?" I whispered, forcing her face closer to my own and causing her to rise up onto her tiptoes.

"Sure, I just think it's laughable that you think you hold any authority over who my friends are." She smirked.

"I don't give a shit, Anastacia. Let him find his own wife to have fun with because it won't be mine."

"Is someone jealous?" She questioned, her face one of pure delight and amusement.

"Don't test me. I'm not in the mood for your games today." I pressed my hand against the door beside her head. "Take Red where you need to go and tell Chad to fuck off back home."

"Ask me nicely."

"I'm not about to stand here and say please so you do as you're told." I declared, my voice still tinged with frustration. Although I had managed to steady my breathing a little, the tension in my shoulders revealed I was far from fully composed.

"Then, no, I won't be asking Red to take me." *Why was she being so damn difficult?!*

"You are not going with Charlie," I snapped, pulling her body into mine as she fit perfectly.

"You mean Chad?" She asked, arching her brow.

"I don't care if his name's Tom, Dick, or Harry. You're not going with him."

"I am. So either you remove your hands yourself or I'll remove them in a way I see fit, and it won't be friendly," she threatened.

"Ana—"

"No, Lorenzo. I will do as I like. You cannot lock me up in here until I choose to obey. It'll never work." Her voice softened as she spoke calmly, trying to get through to me.

I could hear the sound of the engine running outside before the dick who was driving sounded his horn to signal her to hurry up.

"Don't even think about it," I warned, my voice nowhere near as calm as hers. "I've already told you not to test me."

"Or, what? What are you going to do about it?" She turned her back to me, her ass pressing against me. She knew exactly what she was doing whether she meant to or not.

"Fuck you right here. And let everyone hear you scream the name of the man you belong to." I watched her face closely as she glanced up at me over her shoulder. Her pupils dilated a minuscule amount as her lips parted and she swallowed hard. "Is that what you want,

Ana?" I growled against her ear as her breath hitched in her throat, something she tried to hide.

"I have somewhere I need to be." She sighed.

"Then let someone I trust take you." I whispered, trying my best to relax.

"I'm not going to keep repeating the same part of this argument." She groaned with irritation as she pushed my body away from her with her ass. "Goodbye, Lorenzo," she whispered, ignoring everything I just said as she yanked the door open with force.

"Anastacia, I don't trust that man," I roared as she descended the outside steps.

"I don't need you to trust him," she shouted back, not caring what I said or thought.

She opened the car door as I screamed her name, only to be ignored. She exchanged a few words with that smug cunt in the front seat before he revved the engine.

"Red!" I shouted, my voice echoing through the hallway

"Want me to follow them?" he asked.

"Yes, do it now. Don't lose them, and let me know exactly where my troublesome wife needed to go."

"Already on it." He nodded before heading to the garage to his car.

After calling the front gate to stall them for just long enough so Red could catch up without being seen, I called her phone a ridiculous number of times.

Voicemail, brilliant.

She really was intending to test my patience, wasn't she?

"Gino, cancel the meetings outside the house for the day or move them here. I want to be here when she decides to return," I snapped, sparking up a cigarette.

"Mate, I think you should maybe give her some space when she returns. I'd rather not clean up a bloodbath between you both tonight."

"With all due respect, Gino, she went against me today. She ignored my word, and you know my word is final," I seethed. "The only blood you'll be cleaning up tonight will be hers if she doesn't start to fucking listen."

"Lorenzo, you wouldn't hurt her." He sounded so sure of himself.

"You have no idea of the things that woman would drive me to." I sighed.

Of course, I wouldn't hurt her, but that woman had been here one damn day. She was already driving me to the edge.

"Drink?" He rapidly changed the subject. Good man.

"Drink." I confirmed as we headed back to the office.

"Things are new and unusual for the both of you right now. You need to try and refrain from losing your shit when she doesn't do what you want. I know that'll be hard for you, though," he teased.

"No, I know that, but she makes it so hard. Why is she so difficult?!"

"Why are you?" He laughed, pouring me a triple whiskey.

He got me there. I was a difficult bastard. I never claimed I wasn't, but Ana was a whole new kind of difficult. I genuinely thought I had nothing on her.

"Finn, continue calling my wife's number, would you? She's clearly ignoring me."

"About that... She actually left her phone on the side table by the door." He handed it to me. "My guess is that she wanted to piss you off even more than she already did."

"Thanks for pointing that out, I wouldn't have realised that otherwise." I slammed her phone against my desk, the screen shattering beneath my palm.

"My bad. Sorry, Boss." Finn smiled sheepishly. He was the youngest of the team, and honestly, he was a good kid. He just needed to think before he spoke.

"It's alright. Just keep me updated on when she returns."

I would be waiting for her, ready to show her exactly what happened when she didn't listen.

8

ANASTACIA

"Everything alright?" Chad questioned the second I slid into the front seat.

"Yeah, everything's fine. Why do you ask?" I couldn't truly bring myself to open up and tell him just how much of a bastard Lorenzo was. I clocked my husband in the side view mirror as he ran his hands through his hair in anger.

"You know, I don't think I've ever seen you run that fast before," Chad joked, keeping his eyes trained on the driveway ahead.

"Fuck off! You know I have. I used to run circles around Miles!"

He threw his head back, letting out a throaty laugh as we pulled up to the gate. A man I had never seen before strolled up to Chad's open window, not saying a word. I expected him to give some kind of warning from Lorenzo but that never came and I quickly realised. He was stalling us, wasting time for one of his men to catch up.

"Can you please just open the gate? I have somewhere I need to be." I smiled, awaiting his response. He nodded at the other guard who politely opened the gate for us. "Thank you."

"What was all that about?" Chad asked, completely oblivious to what just happened.

"Nothing, just drive."

"Where to, Miss Fedorov?" He smiled, strumming his fingers on the wheel.

"You know that's no longer my name. Well, legally, anyway." I sighed, wishing that wasn't the case.

"You'll always be a Fedorov to me." He sped off down the road as I turned the music up, enjoying the freedom. Freedom that would be ripped away from me the second I walked back through those doors later. "So, where am I taking you?"

"To see my *babushka*, please." The thought of seeing her filled me with happiness. Besides my *dedushka*, she was always my favourite.

"Stopping at the usual place first?"

"Of course." There was no need to specify the plan. He knew it like the back of his hand. It was one we did every week. "Do you mind if I sit in silence for a bit?"

"Not at all. I was expecting it, to be honest. You've had an eventful twenty-four hours."

I tutted, agreeing with him. Although, eventful wasn't quite the word I'd use.

After about twenty minutes, we reached our first destination. One I used to lose myself in as a child.

"I won't be long," I assured Chad as I quickly exited the car before he could ask me if he could tag along.

I entered the old-school flower shop situated on the main strip of town, an array of flowers decorated the inside and out. It was so familiar to me. Nothing had changed in all the years it had been open. I used to visit weekly with my grandmother to collect her favourite pink lilies. I was obsessed with flowers, and to be honest, they were still one of my favourite things. My grandfather and I used to spend hours tending to the garden, and when he passed away, my grandmother took his place by my side.

"Anastacia, my darling, how are you?" Marilyn, my father's aunt cooed as she pulled me into a hug. "Your order is ready."

"Well, I'm married. Surprise!" I groaned as she gasped at the news.

"I cannot believe your father would do such a damn thing! I could wring his neck!"

"I can't believe it either, and get this, he sprung it on me outside the venue! I thought I was attending a typical mafia wedding. But no, it was *mine*." I breathed, trying not to let my emotions get the better of me.

"Tell me, is your husband a good one, at least?" *I wished.*

"My husband is Lorenzo Ricci. I don't think there is any good in him."

"Is your father fucking mad?! Excuse my language, but I swear he doesn't think most of the time." She threw her arms up in frustration.

"Clearly." I laughed, but it was all fake. No feelings attached.

"You know where I am if you need anything, even if it's just a call." She patted my cheek gently, the familiar smell of peppermint and floral hues taking me back to simpler times.

"I know, thank you. It means a lot." She handed me the usual bunch of lilies, beautifully wrapped. "How much do I owe you?"

"You ask me every week, darling, and the answer is always the same. Nothing."

"Fine, but here's a tip for the beautiful flowers." I grinned, leaving a fifty on the counter.

"You're as stubborn as my brother. The same brother who'd be turning in his grave if he knew the deal your father made." She scoffed, her irritation levels rising yet again. "Look after yourself. Show that husband of yours just who you are, who your grandfather taught you to be." She winked, her support well and truly needed.

"Don't worry, I will." I blew her a kiss from the door before heading back to the car.

I knew I was being followed the second I stepped foot outside

Marilyn's shop. Lorenzo had sent someone after me, wanting to know my every damn move.

Psychopath.

"All sorted?" Chad asked as I climbed inside the car.

"Yeah, let's go." I fastened my seatbelt as he set off down the road to our final destination.

We drove across town to where my grandmother resided in a secluded care home. She barely had any time left, and each week I visited, it got harder. I'd grown up with her, spending the majority of my time at my grandparents' house. Visiting her was my favourite part of the week. Knowing that she was getting worse day by day, and that one day I'd be without her, killed me inside.

"Ana, you can stop coming here if it's too hard," Chad said softly, his voice gentle and understanding.

"I could never stop visiting her. She needs me just like I need her." I retrieved the flowers as he pulled up to the large building. "You don't need to wait. I'll make my own way home."

"Without a phone? Don't be silly. I'll park up and wait." He smiled as I exited the car.

I climbed the worn stone steps, feeling the coolness of the railing beneath my hand, and entered the old yet elegant building. The nurses greeted me with warm smiles and cheerful hellos, their faces as friendly and welcoming as they were every week. Inside, the high-beamed ceilings stretched above me like the nave of a cathedral, while vibrant paintings and black-and-white photographs lined the walls, capturing moments of history and beauty. Through the tall double doors at the back, the view unfurled like a masterpiece, offering a sprawling landscape that seemed to breathe life into the very structure of the building.

My grandmother caught my eye through the window as she sat on a bench under the shade of her favourite oak tree with a book in hand and a red cardigan draped over her shoulders. The very same one my grandfather bought her the year he died.

"Go on out, Anastacia. She's waiting for you." One of the nurses smiled, capturing my attention.

"Thank you. How is she today?" I asked, turning my attention to the nurse.

"She's okay. Today has been one of her better days." She squeezed my hand before she wandered back to tend to another patient.

I hurried out to the garden, my grandmother's face lighting up the second she looked up from her book. A smile spread across her lips, one that could brighten my day in seconds.

"*Vot moya devushka.*" She held her arms open as I wrapped mine around her. "Come and sit beside me. I was just reading to your grandfather." She glanced up at the clouds, just as she always did when she read out loud.

"His favourite story again?"

"Of course, and I have to admit, over the years it's become mine, too." She patted the empty seat beside her. I lowered myself onto it.

"These are for you, *babushka*." I handed her the flowers, watching her inhale the fresh scent.

"I love them, thank you." She turned to me, giving me her full attention. "I'm sorry I wasn't at your wedding, darling, but I couldn't witness something I didn't agree with." She sighed, placing her hand on mine. "I wanted to see you get married for love, not for an alliance."

"You know Papa always gets his own way. As does Lorenzo, or so he likes to think." I scoffed.

"Exactly. You have to let him *think* he gets his own way. Let him believe he is the one on top when really you're the one determining everything." She spoke from experience, and I admired that. "Your grandfather was my arranged marriage. Luckily, he was different, but I made it clear to your father that I never wanted you to go through that."

"I don't think he listened. Neither did Mama."

"Your mother doesn't know how to say no to your father. She's always been the same, darling. If he wanted you to marry Lorenzo, she was never going to get in his way. You and I both know that." She was right, I did. "Your *dedushka* taught you well, my darling, and if that man puts a foot out of line or harms one hair on your head, you do what your *dedushka* taught you. No second guessing, just gut the bastard."

"*Babushka*!" My mouth fell open. I had never heard her speak this way. She was always the softer one out of my grandparents.

"You are my angel, and if you don't do what's needed, then I will." Lorenzo hadn't done anything that warranted being gutted alive, but it was good to know she had my back no matter what. "I've heard stories about that man. I know he still holds a grudge for your father too. Just be careful. I don't trust him. Not yet, anyway. Not until he shows me he's different."

"You'll be waiting a really long time then," I teased.

"You know I don't have that long left, my darling. But I hope that maybe, just maybe, he can show me why he deserves you." She squeezed my hand tightly, her words causing my heart to physically ache as I fought back the tears. "Oh, my angel, please don't get upset."

"I'm sorry, *babushka*. It's just hard to think of my life without you." I sighed, knowing that when she's gone, I'd be alone.

"Your life will move on. You'll have children of your own to love and cherish. You'll see how they brighten your life, just like you did mine. I know I am only your *babushka,* but you lit up mine and your grandfather's life the second you came into it."

"I love you." I rested my head on her shoulder as she wrapped her arm around me.

"And I love you." We sat in silence for a moment, enjoying the scenery and each other's company.

"You do know I'll never have children with that man, don't you?" I scrunched my nose up in disgust.

"If you don't want to have children with him, that's your choice. Don't let your family or anyone else bully you into giving him an heir. Only you know what's right and what's not."

"I won't. Marrying him wasn't my choice, but what happens from here on out is." I smiled, thinking of the many ways I could kill Lorenzo and make it seem like an accident.

That would be fun.

"That's my girl," she whispered. "Never forget who you are. Never let that man dull the sparkle I adore."

"I won't, I promise," I assured her. I always kept my promises to her. She knew that.

As the sun set beyond the trees, I realised I had been out all day. Lorenzo was well and truly going to lose his shit when I got home, but I didn't care. He could throw as many tantrums as he wanted. It wouldn't change anything.

"Ana, sorry to bother you both. I just wanted to check if you were okay," Chad piped up from beside us.

"Chad, sweetheart, thank you for bringing my girl to see me again. Sorry, I didn't realise you were waiting for her outside." My grandmother stood gingerly as she wrapped her arms around him in a warm embrace.

"Don't apologise, Evelina. It's my pleasure." He caught my eye over her shoulder, smiling softly.

"Maybe you can teach her husband how to be a gentleman." She giggled, releasing him.

"Okay, that's enough. Let's get you inside for dinner." I sighed, changing the subject swiftly.

After we said our goodbyes, Chad drove me home, the dread creeping in as we neared the house.

"You're quiet, you alright?" he asked, breaking the silence.

"I'm fine, just thinking." He didn't push or pry. He always knew not to if I didn't go into detail.

HE PULLED up outside the front steps and my heart sank at the thought of coming face-to-face with Lorenzo's asshole attitude. All I genuinely wanted was to lose myself between the sheets and have a good night's sleep.

"I'll see you soon." I smiled, putting on a front for Chad, not wanting him to worry.

His smile mirrored my own, but there was more concern behind his than mine.

As I made my way up the steps, Gino appeared at the front door. It didn't take long for me to realise he was trying to warn me about the mood Lorenzo was in.

"No Red?" I asked, Gino's eyes widening at the question. "Oh, come on, Gino. I know he was tailing me all damn day. Maybe next time Lorenzo should send someone whose hair doesn't need its own warning."

"He's not happy, you know." He pinched the bridge of his nose.

"He never seems to be." I walked around him, but then he gently stopped me.

"Anastacia, he's... How do I put this?"

"Ignorant, difficult, *an asshole*? I can continue if you'd like?" I asked as he let out a long, steady breath.

"Just maybe give him a chance. I know he's difficult, and he needs to work on his temper, but believe me. He's not as bad as you think." He sighed.

"Are you trying to convince me or yourself?" I didn't give him a chance to respond. I wanted to dart to my room in an effort to go unnoticed.

But that was wishful thinking.

"Ana-*fucking*-stacia!"

Here we go... Round one.

9

LORENZO

"She's just pulling in, Boss," Finn notified me as the news fed through his earpiece.

"Wonderful. Gino, go get the door for her but don't speak to her," I ordered. "The rest of you, make yourself scarce. I don't want to see a single one of you loitering around, understand?" I snapped, stubbing my cigarette out in the ashtray.

"Understood, Boss," they said in unison before scurrying off like ants.

I was ready to lose my shit the second I saw her. She'd gone against my word and disappeared all day without her phone. The one that was still smashed to bits on my desk.

I had smoked more cigarettes today than any other day. The stress that woman caused me was going to send me into an early grave.

I could be patient and lenient but not with her. It was too damn hard. Red had kept me up to date on her whereabouts. Every single move she made, I knew about. She knew he was there. He didn't try to hide it, and I wanted it that way. I wanted her to know she'd never escape me.

As I rounded the corner to the foyer, I saw her ascending the stairs. As instructed, my men made themselves unnoticeable.

"Ana-*fucking*-stacia!" I shouted as her body stilled in place on the third step. "What time do you call this?!"

She glanced at her watch before turning to face me. "It's actually—"

"Don't be smart," I sighed in frustration, she could barely hide her amusement. "Is something funny?"

"Just how worked up you are. I went out and came back to this hellhole. Does it matter what the time is?!" She turned on her heel, climbing each step faster than the last.

"Don't walk away from me!" I called after her, but did she stop? Of course not.

"Goodnight, Lorenzo." She waved from over her shoulder, disappearing from view as she turned down the corridor.

She was dreaming if she thought that was the end of this argument. She had some explaining to do. This wasn't over. I stalked after her, not getting to her fast enough before her door closed. I twisted the knob and pushed inside, a string of curses coming from her as she remembered she no longer had a lock.

Poor princess.

I shoved the door open with a forceful push as it banged against the wall, drawing her attention towards me immediately. Her head snapped in my direction, eyes narrowed, and her jaw set in a hard line, clearly bracing herself for the confrontation she knew was coming. She stood up straight, shoulders pulled back, and faced me directly, her stance a challenge, daring me to speak first. My heart pounded in my chest, fuelled by the anger coursing through my veins, and I could feel the heat rising to my face. I was beyond furious, ready to unleash the torrent of words that had been building inside me.

"You won't do what you did today again, do you understand?" I snapped, kicking the door closed behind me.

"I understand you but that doesn't mean I'll agree and listen." She barely looked at me as she undid one of her braids. "Treat me with a little respect and I might do what you say."

"Respect works both ways, Ana." I edged nearer to her as she deftly worked her fingers through the intricate loops of her other braid, the strands unraveling like a cascade of silk. Anticipating her to retreat, I was surprised when she remained still, rooted to the spot. The only motion was the gentle rise and fall of her chest, synchronised with her calm, steady breaths.

"Respect is earned, Lorenzo, and so far, you've done nothing to earn it.." She ran her fingers through her crinkled hair as her eyes met mine. "You are nothing but a jumped-up prick playing leader."

"Drop the smartass remarks and attitude," I insisted, taking yet another step closer.

"Or, what? What can you seriously do to me?" she challenged.

"I'll make that fucking attitude drip out of you."

My eyes never left hers and her hands travelled to her waistband. Her movements were fluid, almost like a dance, each gesture confident and assured. I was mesmerised. She had caught my attention, but that was for an entirely different reason than I anticipated. I never thought she'd have the balls to do half of what she did.

She stepped forward, bringing her body close enough to mine in order to drive the blade of her knife just beneath my shoulder, her expression changing from somewhat emotional to something much more sinister. There was no hesitation in her movements, just a cold-hearted woman who had been trained by the best. Pain radiated through me as blood seeped through my shirt.

I stood, unnerved by what she'd done to me as a moan escaped my lips. I fed off of the pain. My body tightened beneath her grip as she kept the blade lodged into place. I had let my guard down for a split second. Something I'd never done, and never planned to do again.

"Is this what you like, Lorenzo?" She purred against my ear, her voice low and seductive. She twisted the knife into my flesh, knowing exactly how far she could take it before it got too dangerous. "Does this turn you on?" She stroked my cock through my pants, feeling just how much I loved it. Maybe it was fucked up to like this kind of shit, but I couldn't help but thrive off her authority and dominance.

She admired the scarlet stains that soaked through what was once my white shirt as she slowly removed her blade, her hand steady and somewhat gentle. I let out a low grunt that rumbled through my chest as the tip grazed more skin on the way out.

She brought the knife to her lips before running her tongue along the blood-coated steel. *Fuck, that must have been the hottest shit I'd ever seen.* "You can leave. You've served your purpose." She threw the weapon onto the carpet, letting whatever blood was left decorate it.

I had no fucking idea what came over me, but I couldn't stop myself nor did I want to. Not when her cold, judgemental eyes were locked on mine. The air between us was thick and heavy as I gripped her neck, her lips twisting up into a smile.

"Is that all you've got, husband?" she teased, but that wasn't all I had. I tightened my hold on her, feeling her pulse beneath my fingers as her breathing slowed slightly.

I was expecting her to beg me to release her but nothing seemed to faze her. Maybe her training was more intense than I thought. Maybe she could handle torture and pain better than the majority of my men.

"Do you think this hurts me, Lorenzo? Do you think I can't handle whatever it is you're doing?" She choked out as her finger found my wound. She applied pressure as she pressed on it. I exhaled sharply as I welcomed the pain.

I lifted her body from the floor by her neck and tossed her on the bed. Her eyes widened as mine darkened. "Spread your legs, wife."

"No," she whispered, her lips enunciating the word.

"Still so defiant?" I asked, not giving her time to answer. "Open your legs and show your husband what a good girl you are."

"And if I don't?" she questioned with confidence, perhaps wanting me to eat her pussy just as much as I did.

"Then I'll do it myself. Your choice."

A playful, mischievous smile danced across her lips, and for a fleeting second, I anticipated resistance from her. Instead, she surprised me. With deliberate movements, she unbuttoned her jeans, shimmying her body gracefully out of the snug fabric. Her lace thong slipped off along with the denim, sliding down her legs in one smooth motion. She let her legs fall open, revealing just how wet she was. Her fingers traced patterns across her delicate skin, leaving a trail of anticipation in their wake.

"Don't touch yourself, Anastacia." I shrugged off my shirt as she admired her handiwork. "The only person allowed to touch you is me. The only person to make you come is me, and if you wish to do so, you'll ask for your husband's permission first." I dropped to my knees, grabbing her legs so I could pull her to the edge of the bed. "I own every inch of you, Ana."

I slid two fingers inside her as a sweet moan left her lips. She was so deliciously tight as she clenched around my fingers. Circling my thumb on her clit, I watched as she let her head fall back before another moan escaped her.

"I never thought I'd see Lorenzo Ricci on his knees," she breathed, a soft whimper escaped her lips, charged with anticipation, as I intensified my movements, curling my fingers inside of her, hitting exactly where I wanted to hear those delicious moans.

"You'll only ever see me on my knees when I'm eating your pussy, wife." I ran my tongue along her inner thigh, leaving a trail of fire in my wake before nipping her skin and decorating her with another hickey.

She exhaled a sharp breath as I continued to work her pussy, adding another finger inside of her. I couldn't stop. I wanted to punish her for what she did to me. Wanted her to feel the fire and desire before I ripped it from her. I may have wanted to despise her but all I did was crave her.

I flicked my tongue over her clit as the sounds of her sweet moans made my cock twitch. Her body reacted to my touch instantly, no matter how much she'd deny it, I knew. I sucked on her clit as my fingers fucked her harder and deeper. "Is this what you want, wife?"

"Y-yes..." she managed to say, trying to chase her next breath. "But not with you."

"Try that again." I pushed another finger inside her as a whimper played on her lips. "Because your body gives you away."

"Y-yes. I want it." She whimpered, unable to hide it any longer.

I sucked on her clit, revelling in the taste of her, and fuck, did she taste like forbidden fruit. *Only she wasn't forbidden, she was mine.*

Her pussy tightened with need as she tried to maintain her control. I flattened my tongue, slipping it up and down her clit. Every time I felt how close she was getting, I slowed my pace, dangling her over the edge.

"F-fuck." She moaned as her hand fisted my hair.

"You're mine, Ana." I breathed against her pussy, the warmth of my breath sending goosebumps over her skin.

"I'll never be yours."

"You..." I lightly spanked her sensitive clit as she moaned in ecstasy.

"Are."

Spank.

"Mine."

Spank.

"Fuck, Lorenzo." She was almost there, she was so damn close.

"If you want to come, then beg," I growled, grazing her clit with my teeth.

"I'll never beg you." Her head snapped up, her eyes meeting mine as she watched me flick my tongue across her sensitive flesh. I'd never tasted something as intoxicating as her.

A sly smile spread across my lips as I slowly removed my fingers from her, her eyes widened in surprise. She knew exactly what I was doing. She didn't want to beg, that was fine, but I wouldn't let her finish. I wouldn't let her come.

"What are you doing?" she snapped. The look of anger and disbelief on her face was priceless.

"You should have begged." I smirked.

"I hate you," she sneered, sitting bolt upright in bed.

Did I want to claim her orgasm? Of course I did, but I wouldn't until she begged me.

"Good." I winked and left her close to the edge and alone.

THE FOLLOWING MORNING, I relaxed in my office, sipping an espresso as I waited for the wrath of my wife after denying her.

"You look incredibly smug today." Red arched his brow as I chuckled from behind my cup.

"No, not smug, just waiting and preparing myself for Ana's arrival. She'll have plenty to say this morning." I placed the cup on the desk as Red sank into the chair opposite me.

"She sure had a lot to say last night when she stabbed you." Red laughed. "Gino said he'd never seen an entry so clean."

"She knows what she's doing, that's why. I underestimated her." I tsked.

"Enzo, you honestly did. Do you really think she would want anything to do with you after you kill her father?" Red asked.

"She's turned her back on her family, she has nobody other than me and her dear grandmother, and as you know she doesn't have much time left."

"And you don't think she'll just up and leave? Disappear without a trace?" he questioned.

"That woman is my wife, she will remain with me, whether she hates me or not. I will not let her leave my side." I grinned, thinking just how much fun it would be.

"So, you don't want her to end up like her father then? Was all that at the wedding just talk?"

"Red, you know I'd never kill my wife, even if she begged me, I wouldn't," I smiled, knowing she'd never beg for anything, she showed me that last night.

I glanced at my watch, strumming my fingers on the desk. *Seven-thirty.* It might have still been early for her. I wasn't sure what her routine looked like yet but I would soon enough.

"Do you think Ana would feel anything if you kill her father? You know the mentality they have. The mentality she was probably brought up with." Red was as clued in as I was.

"I guess time will tell, won't it?" I said, sipping my coffee. "But she'll have to live with the memories of her father's death, just like I did mine, and whether she loves him or not, it still won't be an easy memory to live with."

"Do you care about her? Even just a little bit?" he asked.

"You already know the answer to that, Red."

"Alright." He nodded. "But let me ask you something, why did you kill Joey then? If you don't care about her?"

"Because that bastard made a comment about sharing her, and even if I don't care about her, she's still my wife and nobody will ever speak about her that way." I placed my cup back on the desk, keeping my eyes firmly on my friend who wanted me to falter, and wanted me to let my guard down. But I wouldn't.

"So, Joey ended the night with a bullet in his head, and Rox almost choked to death. Yeah, it sounds like you really can't stand her," he laughed.

"I swear to God, Red, if you—" I was interrupted by a knock on the door. "There she is."

"And that's my cue to leave." He beamed, slapping his palms on his thighs as he stood to open the door. "Morning, Ana."

It took me a minute to register that she may as well have been wearing nothing at all. Her pale pink satin pyjama shorts barely covered her ass as the matching top stopped just below her breasts. I cracked my neck to the side, my fists tightening where they rested on the desk as I allowed my eyes to roam over every inch of her.

What was she playing at?!

"Morning, Red." She flashed him the sweetest smile, but all I got was a venomous one. "Lorenzo." She winced as if it killed her inside to say my name.

"Morning, wife," I managed through clenched teeth.

Red left us alone, closing the door behind him. She lowered herself into the same seat he was previously in, and despite how I left her last night, she looked very satisfied.

"Got something you want to say?" She relaxed her forearms on the arms of the chair as she seductively crossed her legs. I fought the urge to look.

"A couple of things, yes." I leant forward, my eyes meeting hers.

"Well, go for it, I'm waiting."

"You're looking incredibly satisfied for someone who wasn't allowed to come last night." I strummed my finger on my lip, waiting to hear exactly what she had to say.

"Who said I wasn't allowed to come? You?" She rolled her eyes with a cheeky giggle. "I don't need you to make me come, Lorenzo. I can do it pretty damn good on my own."

Excuse me?

"I should thank you, actually. That shower head had the perfect spray to get me off." She looked so smug as she spoke, and I should have hated it, but all I wanted to do was bend her over my desk. "So, just know I don't need you to make me come nor do I need to beg for release." She rose from the chair, her shorts riding up even more than before. "Enjoy the rest of your morning."

"And do you think I have nothing more to say? Trust me, Ana, I'm not done," I informed her, pushing the chair back as it toppled to the floor.

"I didn't think you were." She paused near the door, knowing I'd be behind her in a split second.

I pushed her body against the hard wood as her palms flattened against it. A sharp breath escaped her, and she side-eyed me. She was trapped, and I loved it.

"Want to finish what you started?" she challenged.

I teased the waistband of her shorts before sliding them down her legs. She was naked underneath. It angered me knowing she was waltzing around the house with next to nothing on in front of whoever was around.

"Never wear these around the house again," I whispered as I kneed her legs open. I slowly ran my finger along her slit as she let out a shaky breath, giving into me already.

"I won't beg, Lorenzo," she murmured.

"We'll see." I ran my tongue along her neck, tracing the hickey I gave her, the anticipation building rapidly. "You can't defy me, Ana."

I spun her around to face me as her chest began to heave with need and desire. I forced her leg to wrap around my hip while my thigh pressed between hers, keeping her where I wanted her. I sank my fingers deep inside her. Watching her bite back a moan was everything I never knew I needed. Her body was betraying her and I loved it, knowing there was nothing she could do about it but give me all of her.

"You're so wet for your husband. Good girl," I growled against her ear. "Even though you hate me."

I thrusted my fingers into her, hard and relentless, as her body arched into mine. I continued to pin her to the door. My free hand tangled in her hair, pulling her head back to expose the delicate curve of her neck.

Her eyes squeezed shut, her body trembling as my fingers moved faster, pushing her to the edge. She may hate me. She may hate the way I was making her feel. She may even hate the struggle she was having between giving in and letting go or walking away.

"You belong to me, wife." I hit the spot she needed, and she let out a moan of desire.

"Never." She gasped, her voice barely audible as she struggled to catch her breath.

I tightened my grip on her hair, digging my fingers into her scalp as I leaned into her, my lips brushing her ear. "Liar," I whispered.

I curled my fingers inside her, pressing my thumb against her clit. That's when the control she wanted shattered. A broken, delicious moan escaped her lips as her nails dug into my shoulder. I wasn't going to let her come yet. I'd lead her to the edge and dangle her there for as long as I wanted.

"Say it," I demanded, her gasps and moans mingling in the air. "Say who you belong to."

She bit her lip, forcing herself not to speak, knowing if she did, I'd win. I circled my thumb over her sensitive clit as I continued to fuck her with my fingers.

"I can't." It almost sounded like a plea as her eyes flickered open to meet mine.

"Say it, Ana." With one forceful thrust, her lips parted and I knew she was about to say those words. "You know you want to."

"I'm yours, you bastard," she snapped, anger and pleasure mixing within her.

"Too right, you are." I smirked, sounding all too smug and satisfied as her body shook against mine. "You're mine whether you like it or not."

"Lorenzo." She breathed, but my name was lost in her moans.

"Come for me," I ordered as she finally let go. Her legs trembled, and she chased the orgasm that surged through her. All the willpower she held when she walked in had vanished from within her.

I released her hair, sliding my hand down her body to grip her hip. Bringing her body against mine, my erection was hard and insistent against her thigh.

"Do you really think this changes anything?" she just about managed to say, her voice weak and unconvincing.

I let out a low chuckle. "It changes everything." I smiled, brushing my lips against hers before pulling away. "You're mine now, Ana, and trust me, I'll make sure you never forget it."

I let go of her and took a step back, smoothing the wrinkles from my shirt with deliberate movements, trying to act as if our moment hadn't just unravelled me slightly. She leaned against the door, her hair cascading over her shoulders, eyes bright and alive, and I couldn't help but acknowledge how beautiful she looked.

"The only person to make you come will be me. Nobody or nothing else."

She clenched her fists. Her nails dug into her palms as she fought the urge to scream at me. She may have hated me more than she hated anyone, yet she just came all over my fingers like a good fucking girl.

10

ANASTACIA

I'D BEEN ALONE ALL EVENING EXCEPT FOR THE GUARDS WHO PATROLLED THE area outside. I had no idea where Lorenzo and his men had gone, but to be honest, I didn't really care.

I had just put a tray of muffins in the oven when I heard the front door open and close. His men entered the kitchen first, startled by me standing there. I didn't bat an eyelid to them strolling in so late. I was used to it.

"Shit, sorry, Ana. We just needed a drink." Red held up his bloody hand, but it wasn't his own blood, that much was obvious.

"No worries." I grabbed the whiskey from the cabinet and slid it across the counter followed by tumblers.

"Cheers, A." Emmet tipped his head with thanks.

Another new nickname. Not that I minded when it came from any of these guys. They were pretty decent compared to some others I grew up around.

I glanced up as Lorenzo came into view. His clothes were drenched in blood, the dark crimson staining his shirt, pants, and even his face. His left hand was sliced open as dried blood decorated his wedding band while fresh blood dripped down his fingers onto the marble floor. The wound I inflicted on him last night was split open as blood continued to seep out. He looked like a man who had just emerged from hell.

"What the hell happened to you?!" I asked, trying to not sound worried.

Lorenzo's head snapped up, his gaze locking onto mine like a predator. His face relaxed for a split second, before his jaw tensed once more.

"You don't need to worry, it's nothing," he growled, his voice rough and low.

He tried to step past me to grab a drink, but I stopped him.

"Get out of the way, Ana," he sighed, and for a second it almost sounded like he was trying to be somewhat nice.

Who was I kidding, he wasn't nice.

"No, let me see your wound first," I prompted, crossing my arms over my chest as I continued to block his path.

He let out a bitter, hollow laugh, the sound grating against the silence. "You mean, the one you inflicted on me yesterday?" He breathed. "Save your compassion. I don't need it." His words were meant to hurt, but they didn't even break the surface with me. He tried to brush past me again, but I stood my ground, my gaze unwavering.

"It's not compassion," I muttered, reaching out to grab his arm before he had time to snatch it away. He flinched, his body tensing beneath my hold. "Sit your stubborn ass down," I demanded, which was something he clearly wasn't used to.

He ripped his arm away as his voice dropped into a dangerous whisper. "Don't pretend you actually give a shit, Ana. We both know you would rather I bleed to death." His words were as harsh as a slap, cold and cruel, but there was a flicker of truth in them that I couldn't deny.

My jaw tightened, my lips pressing into a thin line, and for a moment, I wanted to walk away. Instead, I grabbed the first aid kit from the cupboard beside me. "It won't take long and then we can carry on as we were."

He reluctantly surrendered to the situation, peeling off his shirt with a resigned shrug, his eyes fixing on me with a complex blend of amusement and simmering resentment. The atmosphere between us felt heavy and charged, a palpable tension that was unmistakable to anyone nearby, like an electrified wire humming with our shared animosity.

I set to work cleaning the wound with an antibacterial wipe, the sharp scent of antiseptic mingling with the air, while his expression remained impassive and indifferent, a mask of stoicism. The silence was a welcome balm, a brief respite from our unspoken conflict, until he broke it, his voice cutting through the stillness.

"You think you're so much better than me, don't you?" he asked, downing the drink Red handed him. It was clear he already had a few wherever he'd been and didn't need anymore.

"You prove just how much better I am than you with each passing day. I don't need to think about it." I scoffed, not giving him the satisfaction of arguing. He wasn't worth it.

He let out a harsh, bitter laugh. "You'll only ever be good enough to warm my bed for me." He smirked. "Because remember, you're mine."

For a moment, I froze, but the anger quickly dominated my body as I slammed my fist into his face, the sound of the punch echoing the kitchen. "How about you fuck off, Lorenzo?" I shoved him off of me with such force even he was taken aback. "I hope you rot in hell."

His hand flew to his mouth, fresh blood from his split lip smearing on his thumb. A twisted smirk played on his face as he wiped the blood away. "Fuck this. I'm going to bed."

He stormed out of the kitchen and thudded up the stairs, blood still trailing behind him. My hand was throbbing as I watched him go, but the pain was nothing compared to the rage that continued to course through my veins. I hated everything about him. The way he spoke. The way he made me feel and just him in general.

"Are you okay, Ana?" Red asked, retrieving ice from the freezer. "Give me your hand." I did as he asked, letting him place the ice on my knuckles.

"Why is his face so fucking hard?" I laughed, trying to make light of the situation.

"He didn't mean what he said. He had a shitty night, and he shouldn't have taken it out on you." Emmet softly smiled from the chair.

"Let me guess, it was a torture that ended in no answers?"

"How did you know that?" Red asked, genuine confusion written all over his face.

"When you've lived with a father like mine, it's clear enough." I took the ice from him. "Can you grab those muffins from the oven? They should be done in about ten minutes. I need to go to bed."

"Only if we can have some?" Red asked with a beaming smile.

"Of course, just don't give any to that bastard."

I meant every word, he deserved nothing.

WITH THE REST of the house asleep, I ended up in the gym close to Lorenzo's home office. While growing up the gym had always been my sanctuary, it was a place I could let everything go, including this arranged marriage.

The far wall had many marks in it, from what looked to be from knife practice. I pulled out my two favourite knives from my waistband and let out a steady breath before imagining Lorenzo's face in the middle of the wall. Letting the first one go, I felt more alive than I had the last couple of days. It was how it used to be. How it always was. Just me, alone with my thoughts.

Or so I thought...

I didn't need to see him to know he was hidden in the shadows, watching my every move. I launched my second knife towards the wall, the blade swishing through the air beneath the dim lighting. My grandfather taught me how to use a blade, and by the time he was finished, I could hit a bullseye with my eyes shut. Tonight was originally about me, but now it was about giving a middle finger to the man who belittled me earlier.

I retrieved my knives from the wall, and as expected, they both hit the bullseye mark. There were many attempts on that wall that hadn't.

"You can stop hiding." Venom laced my voice as he suddenly came into view. "I don't know how you have the balls to come in here after how you spoke to me in front of everyone." I scowled. "You're proving to be a shit husband, Lorenzo. An arranged *mistake*."

Lorenzo's smirk didn't falter, but his eyes narrowed, a spark of something dangerous and alluring flickering in their depths. "Yet, here you are putting on a show for that same shit husband." He whispered. "Tell me, wife, what else did your grandfather teach you? Are you all knives and no skill?"

His words struck a nerve. My grip tightened on the hilt on the knife until my knuckles turned white. I felt the rage simmering beneath the surface, threatening to boil over. I couldn't hold it in any longer. With a quick motion, I threw the knife towards him, embedding it into the wooden beam above his head. The sound of the blade sinking into the wood was sharp and music to my ears. I just wished I'd aimed lower.

His smirk faltered for a fraction of a second before he recovered, his expression smoothing into something cool and detached. "Impressive." He chuckled, stepping even closer. "But a real fight isn't about tricks, Ana. It's all about control, and if what happened in my office this morning is anything to go by, you have very little."

I took a second to study him. He wore sweats and a tank, showing off the tattoo that decorated his chest and both arms, something I hadn't truly paid attention to before. I wondered if there was a story behind them, but then had to give my head a mental shake because I didn't actually care what story they held.

"Spar with me. Show me what you've got."

"Why? What's in it for you?" I questioned.

"I need to know my wife can protect herself if ever she needs to, so spar with me." He closed the distance between us. "That wasn't a request." He grabbed my wrist, pulling my body flush to his. "It was an order."

"It always is with you, isn't it?" I asked rhetorically, already knowing his answer. "Are you sure you can handle it, Lorenzo?"

"Don't worry about me. I can handle you just fine." He chuckled as he leaned into me, the woodsy scent of his cologne invading my senses more than I would have liked. My eyes fell to the bandaged wound I caused, and I couldn't hide the proud smile on my face.

The air crackled with tension, charged with unspoken hostility that had defined our marriage since the start—which was a mere few days ago. His gaze met mine as he challenged me.

"Alright, let's spar, but don't come crying to me when I put you on your ass." I laughed, throwing my other knife to the floor.

"I'll take that risk." His smile faded, replaced with something darker and more primal.

He removed his tank, throwing it off to the side. My gaze dropped for a second, admiring his chiseled torso.

"My eyes are up here." He teased, his breath warm against my skin.

"I wasn't looking. Don't flatter yourself." I scoffed.

We circled one another like predators, the gym morphing into a fierce battleground where every step, every breath, reverberated as a calculated move in our tense game of cat and mouse. The air was thick with anticipation, and my heart pounded like a drum in my chest, a relentless rhythm that fuelled my heightened senses. I could feel every muscle tense, every nerve on edge, as I meticulously tracked his every move, noting the subtle shifts in his stance, and the glint of determination in his eyes.

Lorenzo struck first, his movement swift and deliberate, his hand darting out like a striking serpent to seize my waist. But I was prepared, my muscles coiled and ready to spring. With a fluid twist, I slipped from his grasp, my body weaving around him like a dancer evading an unwanted partner. My own hand lashed out in a swift arc, targeting the vulnerable spot beneath his ear where the skin was tender and exposed. Yet, with infuriating agility, the bastard deflected my strike, his reflexes as sharp as his intentions.

"Not bad." He nodded. "But you're holding back."

"And you're overconfident," I retorted, my voice steady despite my racing pulse. I kneed him in the thigh, one sharp strike, hoping to weaken him, but as he absorbed the blow, his hand gripped my wrist, spinning me into him. His chest collided with my back as I let him have that one.

"You can't win," he murmured as I tried to break free. I knew I could but I'd underestimated his strength. He was relentless, and I could feel my skin bruising beneath his hold.

Maybe it wasn't the original move I'd have chosen, but without thinking, I reared my head back, head butting him in the face. It might have been a desperate move, but it worked, catching him off guard as he released me. "Fuck," he cursed, his chest heaving as he tried to regain his composure.

I watched as he straightened his body, his hand rubbing at the sore spot on his forehead where I'd struck him. His gaze was dark, his expression unreadable as he yanked me back into him. "You're full of surprises, wife, but this isn't over."

"It'll never be over with us, will it?" I scoffed, challenging him, and not giving in.

"Not until I put you on the floor in triumph." His lips twisted up into a dangerous smile.

"Okay, no holding back," I promised.

We circled each other once more, tension crackling in the air as adrenaline coursed through my veins like an electric current. My mind raced, calculating my next move with precision. He was undeniably strong and skilled, a formidable opponent in his own right, but I had my own set of strengths honed over years of training. My grandfather's lessons echoed in my mind, a testament to the discipline and skill he had instilled in me. I wasn't about to let Lorenzo underestimate me once again. The determination in my eyes was a silent promise that this time, I would not be taken lightly.

He lunged at me with a sudden burst of energy, his movements swift and meticulously calculated. But I was prepared, my senses heightened and my stance steady. I sidestepped gracefully, targeting his arm with precision. As anticipated, he dodged my strike with a fluid motion, his reflexes as impressive as ever. We continued our intricate dance, moving around the mat that lay at the centre of the gym, our feet barely making a whisper against its surface. The room was silent except for the rhythmic sound of our breathing and the occasional thud of our bodies colliding with intent and force.

There was something about Lorenzo tonight that I couldn't put my finger on. His eyes darkened when he looked at me, his grip lingering a moment longer than I expected. It was hard not to feel the heat building low in my stomach. What should have felt like pure anger was something far more dangerous.

What the fuck was going on with me?! He was an absolute bastard, but the things he could do with his fingers and mouth were out of this world. Unwanted, but incredible.

We paused for a second, our chests heaving and eyes locked, both wondering who would emerge victorious.

"I have to admit, tonight has been entertaining." He whispered, his breathing more ragged than before.

"What part? When you spoke to me like shit in the kitchen or now?" I asked as his arm snaked around my waist firmly.

He inched his face closer to mine, his breath mingling with my own. I could feel the rapid beat of his heart, matching my own.

"Here. Now." He breathed. "You distracted me, though."

"How did I manage to do that?" I asked as his fingers traced the line of my jaw, sending unusual sparks through my body.

"By this," he said, his voice rougher than before. "By the way you move, and the way you fight me. No matter what I throw at you, you give what you get."

"Careful, Lorenzo, you sound like you're softening towards me." I laughed, his jaw ticking at my words.

"That'll never happen, just remember that," he murmured as I tried to pull away. He stopped me. "God, Anastacia, I can't stand you, but all I want to do is kiss you," he growled.

"Do you think you can walk in here and just—" I began, my voice getting cut off as he leaned into me, his lips brushing my ear.

"Just, what?" He smirked. "Use you? Fuck you, perhaps?"

"You're a prick," I hissed.

"And you're a liar," he countered. "You want this as much as I do."

I opened my mouth to deny it, of course I did, but the words caught in my throat when he slammed his lips to mine. The kiss was fierce, demanding, and so fucking hot. I knew I should've ended this game, but his words, his touch, his proximity was all too much.

"You know I'll regret whatever this is after, don't you?" I murmured against his lips.

"So will I," he retorted back, his feelings matching mine as his voice was hoarse with desire.

The kiss grew more urgent and intense as my clothes became an obstacle to him. With a swift, tearing motion, he ripped open my tank top, letting the shredded fabric fall carelessly to the floor. His eyes descended to my exposed breasts, his gaze was filled with hunger and urgency. He pressed me firmly against the sturdy beam, where my knife still hung, while his lips traveled a rough, passionate path down my neck, leaving a tingling trail in their wake. His hands cupped my breasts, his touch igniting a cascade of pleasure that rippled through my entire being. I arched towards him involuntarily, momentarily forgetting the animosity that had once consumed me, as my fingers wove themselves through his thick hair, pulling him closer.

"Fuck." I moaned as his dominance took over.

Lorenzo's hands moved lower, his touch deliberate and skilled. "Tell me to stop." His words were firm, but I couldn't tell him despite wanting to. My body betrayed me, but I didn't care. "You can't, can you?"

"I can, but I won't tonight." I managed.

His grin was smug and triumphant, but he hadn't won yet. He wouldn't touch me tonight. I'd be the one to make him come this time.

"You're not in control here, Lorenzo."

"Neither are you, but we can pretend, can't we?" He dipped his head lower, his mouth hovering over the swell of my breast.

I pushed down his sweats. His cock sprung from its restraints, a series of metal bars on the sensitive underside of it. He had a Jacob's ladder piercing. I could only imagine what it would feel like as he fucked me, a mixture of pain and pleasure intertwined. His cock throbbed with need as I wrapped my hand around him, my touch firm but gentle. "Fuck, Ana." He moaned, his head falling against mine as I stroked him with slow, deliberate movements. "Are you trying to kill me?"

"Maybe," I responded, our eyes meeting for a second. My confidence soared as my touch weakened him slowly.

"Then get on your knees and suck my cock, wife," he ordered.

For once, I didn't fight against him. I didn't even hesitate, I was fully aware that I could turn the tables on him just as he had done to me earlier that day. I slowly sank to my knees, flicking out my tongue, the tip grazing the first bar and sending a jolt of pleasure coursing through his body. A secretive smile played on my lips, knowing I would make him savour every electrifying second. My warm breath ghosted over each bar as I took him into my mouth, moving slowly at first, wanting him to become as lost in the moment as I had been that morning.

Teasing his sensitive skin beneath the cool metal, he let out a deep groan. His fingers tangled tightly in my hair, pulling me closer. My mouth travelled rhythmically up and down the length of his cock, while my hand firmly gripped the base, both working in perfect harmony. Each calculated movement was deliberate, and designed to push him closer to an explosive climax, sending him rocketing over the edge with pleasure.

Slowly, inch by inch, I took him deeper as he thrusted into my mouth. His hips moved, trying to take control but I wouldn't let him have it. I quickly regained dominance whilst tracing the length of his cock with my tongue in a way that had him cursing my name repeatedly. I sucked gently as my cheeks hollowed. His fist tightened and I knew I had him where I wanted him. I gripped the backs of his thighs as tears sprung to my eyes.

"Good girl." His voice was hoarse as his eyes burned into me. He was enjoying watching me on my knees for him. "I never knew my wife would be able to take me so well." I moaned around his length, enjoying knowing I could get him off any way I wanted.

He pulled my mouth from him by my hair, my lips swollen and ready for more. "You're going to take everything I give you. Don't waste a drop." I slid my mouth down his cock once more, listening to the sound of his moans filling the air around us.

"Fuck!" he hissed as I dug my nails into his skin.

His cock twitched against my tongue. He was close. Taking him deeper than before, I pushed him over the edge. His body tensed as his come hit the back of my throat.

"Ana." He roared his release, my scalp burning beneath his hold as he tightened his fist.

His breaths came out ragged as I pulled my mouth from his cock, swallowing every last drop just like he wanted.

"I think," he said, his voice steady despite his heaving breaths, "that I've underestimated you for the last time."

I rose to my feet, my body flush with satisfaction as I felt as though I was back on top—right where I needed to be. But as our eyes met, I saw something beyond this game we played, beyond the power dynamics and the unspoken challenges. There was something hidden deep within his. Maybe it was a spark or a glimpse of a connection that threatened to unravel every single thing.

"Take my top. I don't know who you'll bump into at this time of night." He gave me no time to respond as he slipped it over my head. "Don't take that as me caring. I just don't feel like murdering any of my men tonight because they saw you half naked."

"Such a gentleman." I scoffed, feeling as though we were back to how we were earlier.

"I'm anything but one of those." He pulled up his sweats without taking his eyes off of me.

"Trust me, I know." I grabbed my knives and water bottle before making my way to the door.

"Ana," he called after me.

"Yeah?"

"This weekend, we have a dinner to attend. Your father will be in attendance." He breathed. "You will play the part of my loving wife. We cannot look like anything other than what people expect."

"And what might that be?" I didn't turn around. I kept my back to him as he spoke.

"My alliances expect perfection, especially since we're a newly married couple." There was a warning in his voice. I had to hide my laughter at the seriousness.

"We're anything but perfect." I scoffed. "My behaviour all depends on my mood, and I have no idea what mood I'll be in come the weekend."

"Anastacia," he warned.

"Goodnight, Lorenzo." I waved my hand over my shoulder and left him standing alone, just as he preferred to be.

What was that tonight?

I must have been out of my damn mind.

11

LORENZO

I STOOD BESIDE RED, WAITING FOR ANASTACIA AT THE FOOT OF THE STAIRS, hoping that tonight she behaved and acted as a wife should. Tonight wasn't just a ball nor was it only a dinner. It was us showing that we were united. I knew Anastacia had a hard time putting on that front, especially since I was the one requesting it.

"How do you think tonight will go?" he asked, smoothing down his jacket.

"Honestly, I have no idea. I told Anastacia exactly what I wanted from her, so I guess I have to hope she listened."

"Maybe you should ask her rather than demand, you know?" he responded with a soft smile.

"I don't think that woman would bloody listen, no matter if I asked or demanded it." I scoffed, shoving my hand in my pocket.

The air shifted around me, turning that same level of tense it always did when she was near.

"I'll meet you in the car." Red beamed as he left the pair of us alone.

I turned my head to see what daring number Anastacia wore but my breath hitched in my throat. She was a vision, her gown a deep sapphire that hugged her frame. But it wasn't her dress that caught my attention. It was her eyes. That piercing blue that seemed to hold my gaze. Her lips curved up ever so slightly, as if mocking me for admiring her, as if she knew her appearance captured my attention.

She descended the stairs with the grace of a woman who knew just how much she was worth, each step calculated and deliberate. My jaw tightened as she came to a standstill at the bottom of the last step.

"You're late," I growled, my voice low and authoritative. My words cemented that I would always be in control. That I held the power between us.

"And you're still an asshole." She scoffed as she swanned past me without a care in the world. "Are you coming or are you just going to stand there?"

Her attitude was already in full force. Fuck, I had my work cut out for me tonight.

LUCKILY, the drive to the ball would be a short one. I took a moment to study her. The streetlights cast shadows on her cheekbones. Her lips parted ever so slightly. And her chest rose and fell softly as she breathed. She was a damn puzzle I had yet to solve. The woman wore her hatred towards me like a second skin but still managed to carry herself with the poise of a fucking queen.

Hell, I even respected her for it. Even though I despised her for the way she made me feel. Deep down, I was a little more alive than I'd felt in a long time. The hatred and banter between us was becoming part of my daily life and I had to admit, I enjoyed it.

"What do you want, Lorenzo?" she asked, her gaze focused on the passing buildings as she spoke.

"Nothing, just trying to predict if you're going to behave

tonight." I rested my hand on her thigh, squeezing it gently as if to warn her.

"I don't know yet. I haven't decided." She grabbed my hand, throwing it off her.

"Anastacia," I warned, but she wasn't in the listening mood.

"Oh, look, we're here."

I let out a sigh at just how insufferable she was as I exited the car, making my way to her door.

I held out my hand to her, which she took with very little hesitation, her fingers cool against my skin but her grip firm. "So, it looks like my wife *can* behave," I whispered, my lips bushing her ear as I leaned into her.

"And it looks like my husband can play the part of a gentleman all too well," she breathed with an eye roll.

"Touché." I chuckled. "Are you ready?"

"To put on an act? Sure." She glanced up at me. "Because that's what it'll be, us pretending. And Lorenzo, I'm a pretty good actress." She winked.

"Looks like your family is already here." I nodded towards Victor, Florence, and Miles, who were laughing and joking at the entrance. "Do you want to join in on whatever it looks like is splitting your papa's sides?"

"No, I don't. Let's just go inside. I'll speak to them when I feel like it."

I led her up the stairs as she neared her family. I truly expected her to at least smile at them, but she looked straight ahead, not giving any of them the time of day.

"*Anastacia,*" Victor called after her. "*Sobirayesh'sya li ty neuvazhitel'no otnosit'sya k svoyemu ottsu i ignorirovat' yego?*" He continued to speak to her in Russian. I was pissed that I couldn't understand it.

"*Da, Victor,*" she replied, her voice calm. All I knew was that she didn't call him Papa like she would have before he forced her to marry me. She only referred to him as Victor.

"Ana, don't be like that." Miles gripped the top of her arm, causing her to stop as my blood boiled at the way he thought it was okay to put his hand on her like that.

"Take your hands off my wife, Miles," I ordered. I didn't care if that was her brother. Nobody treated her that way.

"You've been her husband for two damn minutes, you have no right to speak to me that way. She's my sister." He scowled back. Ana let out a sigh, and I knew she'd had enough of this whole situation.

"It makes no difference if it's two minutes to two years, you will never lay a hand on my wife." I cracked my neck to the side. "Besides, it's a shame you didn't think much of your sister when you were backing Daddy Dearest over there." He was about to speak when I cut him off, returning my attention to Ana. "Shall we head inside?"

"Please."

As we stepped through the grand double doors of the ballroom, the glittering chandeliers casting a warm glow over the crowd, I noticed the way her eyes darted around the room, her lips parting slightly as if words were ready to spill out. Her smile, which had been gradually brightening her face like a sunrise, wavered for a moment, as though she was caught between speaking and holding back.

"I find it funny how you got on his case for acting a certain way when you're no better,"she said with no expression. "Practice what you preach, Lorenzo."

She slipped her hand from mine and gracefully navigated through the dense crowd, her movements fluid and purposeful, until she reached a small group of women gathered on the far side of the room. I recognised them immediately from the wedding; they were esteemed members of Victor's team, their presence commanding respect. My gaze remained fixed on her, tracing her path, when Red suddenly emerged at my side, his presence both familiar and unexpected.

"For a man who can't stand his wife, you sure can't take your eyes off her." He laughed, nudging my elbow.

"You're seeing things, mate. Delusional is what you are." I scoffed, my eyes remaining on Ana.

"Mhm, if you say so." He continued to try his best to wind me up. "Maybe I'll go and keep her company. She seems to like me," he bantered.

"Don't even think about it," I chuckled, relaxing slightly. "I'll see you later."

"I just got here, where are you going?" he asked, but I was sure he already knew the answer.

"To join my wife, she looks as though she could use some company."

"But she already has some," he directed his hand towards where she stood, smiling wider and brighter than I'd seen before.

"Not mine."

I strode confidently over to where Anastacia stood, her poised figure framed by the dim lighting overhead. As I approached, she turned her attention towards me, her smile as radiant as it was a moment ago, not once wavering. Yet, beneath that polished exterior, I knew it was a performance, a carefully crafted façade, and I hadn't yet decided if I wanted it to remain a mere act or transform into something genuine.

Who was I kidding, of course I didn't want it to be real.

"Lorenzo, you know I only just left you, right?" she said, her lips curving gently.

"Yes, but you're going to dance with me." I took her hand, not giving her a choice.

"Lorenzo," she gasped as I spun her into my arms.

"Ana," I responded, matching her tone.

"What have I told you about calling me that nickname?" she sighed, relaxing into my hold ever so slightly.

"I don't recall you saying anything about it," that was a lie, I knew she hated it, but that gave me all the more reason to use it. "Now, stop with the questions and dance with me."

"Why do you feel the need to put on a show? Why are you so bothered about what people think?" she asked, and the truth was, I didn't really care about what the other people in this room thought. I knew the majority envied my marriage to her.

"I don't give a shit what the people in this room think of me. I just wanted to show that we're united. That you chose me."

"I didn't choose you, though." she responded, as quick as ever.

I rested my hand on the small of her back as her body remained flush against mine. I knew her parents' eyes were on us, as well as many other alliances, so I played the part just as much as she did. But it was hard when her body fit perfectly against mine. It was as though she was put on this earth to be mine. All I could wonder was whose great idea that was.

Ah, yeah, mine.

"What did your father say to you?" I asked.

"If you want to know, you should take some lessons in Russian." Her lips turned up into a smile, and I could have sworn there was a genuineness hidden within it.

"Do you always have an answer for everything?"

"Of course." She nodded, placing her hand on my shoulder.

"You know, there are many men in this room that cannot seem to take their eyes off you." I scanned the room, instantly spotting gazes dropping the second I clocked them.

"Jealous?" she asked, her voice all sweet and innocent. Despite being anything but.

"Ana?" A male voice came from beside us.

"Hi, Chad." She gave him a full smile. Actually, scratch that, she beamed at the bastard.

"You look stunning tonight." Was this prick for real? "Do you want to dance?" he asked, clearly not realising I was standing right there.

My grip on her tightened. Her body stilled. Chad held out his hand as Anastacia remained torn at what to do.

"I'm here with my husband, Chad," she informed him as he shifted his gaze to me for a split second before he turned his attention back to my wife.

"Ana, come on. It's just one dance," he insisted, leaning in with a self-assured grin that made my skin prickle. "Lorenzo doesn't mind, do you?" he added, his voice dripping with arrogance, making my temper flare.

"I suggest you fuck off before I give everyone in this ballroom a show." I stepped closer to him, eyes including Victor's fell on us. "Meaning I'll carve you open from navel to mouth before turning your intestines into a noose." My threat hung heavy as his body stilled. His smile vanished, and I clocked a flicker of fear.

"Ana—"

"Don't speak to her. In fact, stay away from her. She is nothing to you," I warned.

"And what, she's everything to you?" he questioned, catching me off guard.

"That's none of your business, but by all means, keep talking and I'll slice that tongue right out of your vile mouth," I growled as Victor appeared beside us.

"What is going on here?" he asked, trying to judge the situation.

"I think you need to teach your team some manners, Fedorov." I clenched my teeth together, my jaw ticking with anger.

I felt the weight of Anastacia's gaze, practically pleading with me to stop, but I didn't. All that mattered was that Chad and everybody in this room knew she belonged to me. No matter how we felt towards one another, I would never let anyone take what was mine.

"He's sorry. He didn't mean to disrespect you." Victor held up his hands, his half bothered attempt at apologising.

"I don't need nor do I want an apology. Just keep your team away from my wife and me," I ordered.

"But he's more than just a member of my team, he's practically family." Victor smiled, trying to make light of everything.

"Well, he's not mine, is he?" I snapped, still feeling Anastacia's hand on my arm, which shocked me. She took putting on a show to a whole new level.

I pulled her away from them, leading her outside as she finally let go of me.

"You didn't need to do that!" she exclaimed, her voice rising in pitch. Her eyes, usually bright and warm, clouded over, narrowing into intense slits. Her hands tightened into fists at her sides, and her brows furrowed deeply, casting shadows over her face as she glared at me.

"If you talk to him again, I'll kill him," I whispered. "You are mine. Not his."

She jabbed her finger into my chest. "If you think you can control me, you're wrong." She pointed out, challenging my authority. "Was everything that just happened for show, letting everyone believe you'd kill for your wife?"

"I have already killed for you." I breathed.

"No, Lorenzo, you killed that man because you wanted to." She sighed.

"Yeah, you're right, I did." I said, taking that lie a little too far. I expected her face to fall, to show any other emotion than the one she was giving me, but it didn't.

"At least you were honest." She snatched her wrist from my hold. "I'm going to see if Red will drive me home. I'm done for the night."

"Ana—"

"Goodnight, Lorenzo."

And just like that, she was gone. I could have chased her, but my feet didn't move.

I pulled out my phone, dialling Red's number.

He answered within one ring. "Boss?"

"Ana wants you to take her home," I informed him.

"What did you do this time?"

"Just drive her home, Red. Leave her there and come back here," I ordered.

"You sure you want me to leave her there alone?" he asked. There was that damn concern again.

"Just do as I ask." I hung up the phone, not waiting for his reply.

Tonight was a complete shit show.

And I'd make her pay for walking out on me.

"ANA!" I called out, knowing if I called her name loud enough she'd wake up. "Ana!" Oh shit, she might just murder me. I clearly had too much to drink after she left me earlier.

"Lorenzo, shut up," Red hissed. "What's the point in waking her up? Are you dying for an argument, or what?"

"Those arguments are the best part of my day. I love to see how much she hates me." I laughed as all Red and Emmet could do was tut and sigh in annoyance. "Besides, she *should* wake up! She left her husband at that damn ball. What wife leaves their husband alone?"

"A smart one." Emmet scoffed. *Fuck sake, not him too.* "Don't wake her up, Lorenzo. Just talk about it in the morning."

"It might be too late for that." Gino cocked his head towards the stairs as we all glanced up to see my wife standing there in those delicious next to nothing pyjamas.

She was clearly pissed off, her expression the perfect mixture of annoyance and disgust. Lucky me.

"There she is, my ice queen wife." I cheered at her arrival, her lips pressed into a thin line as I could barely hide my amusement.

Everyone beside me froze, knowing the storm that was about to unleash. Her gaze locked onto mine with a certain ferocity that made each one of them flinch. As she made her way towards me, I drank in every inch of her.

"You embarrassed me tonight, Ana. Does it feel good knowing I had to spend the night alone covering for you?"

Her voice remained calm. "I embarrassed you? Wow, that's rich coming from a man who stumbled in here, calling my name at the top of his lungs to get my attention. We all know why I left, Lorenzo, and that's down to you and your bullshit."

"My wife should be seen, not heard." I scoffed, chuckling straight after. *God, how drunk was I? Why couldn't I stop talking?*

Everyone seemed to hold their breath as her hand shot out, her palm connecting with my cheek. A sharp crack echoed through the house as the force alone sent me stumbling backwards. Everyone remained silent, waiting for my next move.

I was beginning to think she enjoyed slapping me.

"I'll never be that wife, Lorenzo. If you long for one like that, I suggest you look elsewhere."

"You'd love that, wouldn't you?" I asked, suddenly becoming sober with each word she threw at me.

"Too right, I would. Good luck to her." She turned on her heel, retreating towards her bedroom.

"I'm not done, Ana," I called after her, but as usual, it gained no attention.

"Well, I am."

12

ANASTACIA

I SHUT THE DRUNK BASTARD OUT, AS I CLOSED THE DOOR BEHIND ME. HE didn't deserve the time I just gave him, but boy, did he deserve that slap. I pushed the chair from the corner to in front of the door. Well and truly keeping him out since he seemed to like pissing me off constantly.

One minute that man seemed to show something other than being a total bastard, but then he went and ruined it all by opening his big mouth.

There was a knock on the door, softer than I expected. "Ana, what have you got in front of the door?" he asked from the other side.

"None of your business! Now leave me alone." I climbed in bed and pulled the covers and pillow over my head, shutting out the drunk man who continued to knock on the door.

I could only hear muffled voices before retreating footsteps. Thank God he was gone, I wasn't in the mood to deal with anymore drunken behaviour and attitude tonight.

The phone Lorenzo had given me as a replacement for smashing my old one vibrated on the side.

Poking my hand out from the covers, I grabbed it and saw Chad's name gracing the screen. I opened the message he sent and read it.

Sorry about tonight. Are you okay? I worry about your safety with him.

I think you should worry about your own safety rather than mine. I'll be fine. Remember, I'm tougher than you.

How could I forget? You've beat my ass to the mat countless times.

Exactly, so you don't need to worry about me. He's a real pussycat.

I highly doubt that, but fine. You can call me anytime, though. You know that.

Thanks. Night.

Night.

Chad didn't need to worry about my safety with Lorenzo. Sure, he was a brute, an asshole, a real class A cunt—the list was endless—but I knew he'd never hurt me physically. Not in the way he threatened Chad with, anyway.

And even if he wanted to, I'd never let that happen.

THE FOLLOWING MORNING, the house was incredibly quiet. There was no sound of Lorenzo or his men. The silence was golden.

The sun shone brightly as I headed outside to the lake, the early morning grass cool beneath my bare feet. It was so serene out here. It was easy to forget the hellhole Lorenzo called his house was behind me, especially when this garden was a haven I definitely needed.

The warmth of the sun kissed my face as I let my head fall back, relishing in the feeling.

"Anastacia?" A female voice came from behind me.

I turned, coming face-to-face with Lorenzo's mother, a beautiful woman who was a similar age to my mother. Her hair was styled into a sleek chignon, and the minimal makeup she wore accentuated her features.

"Mrs. Ricci, hi." I smiled as she closed the rest of the gap between us.

"Oh, stop that, you can call me Carmella." She said with a gentle smile she sat down on the stool. "I'm guessing my son is either nursing a hangover or he had business to attend to."

"Well, I hope it's the first option." I sighed. "Oh, God, sorry, that's your son I'm wishing a hangover on."

"We all know he can be a complete prick at times. I can bet that last night was no different," she tutted. Her words made me feel as though she actually understood where I was coming from. "He was fine at the ball, but Red informed me that he didn't stop there. He continued to drink at the club."

"I don't know where he went or how much he drank, Carmella. All I know is that every single time he opens his mouth, he continues to put his foot in it. It's like he doesn't even try. He just wants to push my buttons. I don't know what his deal is, but it won't end well for one of us."

"I know. You'll need the patience of a saint to deal with my son. That's a given, and I admire you for not actually killing him yet. Although, I heard you tried." She laughed.

"I didn't try to *kill* him. I just let him know I wasn't the kind of wife he thought he was getting. He wants me to obey his every word and be a perfect housewife, but that's not me." I pinched the bridge of my nose, trying to shake him and his words out of my head.

"His father had the same attitude towards me. I guess that's why Lorenzo thinks you should be that way. I don't think he ever imagined he'd meet his match with his wife." She chuckled, taking my hand in hers. "His father wasn't the man he let everyone believe he was. Maybe in the beginning, but near the end, he was a horrible man. That rubbed off on Lorenzo. His father drummed his beliefs into him so damn hard, and with each day, my caring, loving boy became just like his father. It broke my heart."

"Carmella, I—"

"I'm not asking you to love him and obey him. I know that's a tall order, but don't write him off just yet. He might surprise you,"she said, a plea hidden beneath her words.

"I don't see how he'd ever surprise me, but I promise not to stab him anymore." We laughed in unison as I caught the unapproving stare of Lorenzo.

He stood at the door, arms folded in annoyance, and showed no signs of a hangover. Or if he did, he hid them well. Carmella clocked him next as she sighed at the attitude he was already carrying.

He crossed the garden in long, fast strides. "Mama, what are you doing here?" Oh, of course, the attitude was aimed solely at me. How wonderful.

"I came to see you but ran into your beautiful wife instead." She nudged her shoulder softly into mine with a smile before accepting Lorenzo's kisses on her cheeks.

"I can see that." He sent a side eyed glance my way.

"Lorenzo, that's enough. I found Anastacia, not the other way around."

"Carmella, it's fine. I'll see you again soon." As I was about to walk away, she stopped me before throwing her arms around me in a warm embrace. Something I hadn't even gotten from my own mother since the wedding.

"Mama, let her go. She seems to love storming off and leaving," he snapped, his gaze burning into me.

"I wonder why that is, Lorenzo." I scoffed. "Last night, you were a complete jerk. Exactly as you are now, and I don't need nor do I want to stand here and listen to it." He grabbed my arm as I walked past him.

I pulled the knife I had hidden from the pocket in my dress and pressed it against his neck with a smile so fucking big it could have been seen from space.

"I promised your mother I wouldn't stab you, but I didn't promise not to slit your throat," I threatened. "Take your fucking hand off of me before I open your neck so wide it'll make a torn pocket look like a pinhole."

"Just remember, Ana, you went from one cage to another. It's not your father holding the key this time, it's me." He replied as I softly pressed the blade into his skin, drawing blood.

"Lorenzo Ricci, that's enough." Carmella scolded him, but he didn't seem to care. I knew he never would.

I hated him with every fibre of my being.

"Carmella, it's fine. He's nothing but a thug with a bad temper." I muttered, lowering my blade, admiring the blood trickling down his neck. "It was lovely to see you." I tucked my blade away and shoved past Lorenzo, making my way towards the house.

I heard their raised voices as I slipped inside, coming face-to-face with Emmet in the kitchen.

"Alright, A." He smiled. "Nice lil' number you pulled out there."

"I doubt it made any kind of impact on him." I sighed, grabbing some fruit from the fridge. "Do you want a smoothie?"

"You makin' it?" He asked, a little taken aback.

"Don't look so surprised. I make a really good smoothie."

"Can I have one?" Red piped up from the doorway.

"Of course, I'll make enough for Gino, too."

"I wouldn't bother. He got lucky last night. He ain't here." Emmet wriggled his brows as the three of us burst out laughing for no real reason.

Just as we were enjoying the moment, Lorenzo entered the kitchen with Carmella at his side.

"What's going on in here?" Lorenzo questioned the second he stepped inside.

"Carmella, would you like a smoothie?" I asked, ignoring Lorenzo.

"Anastacia, did you hear me?!" He demanded.

"So, Red, what kind of smoothie do you want?" I blanked him yet again

"Everyone, out," Lorenzo ordered.

"Boss—" Emmet started but never got to finish whatever it was he wanted to say.

"I said out! Right now!" He turned to his mother. "You too, Mama. I need to talk to my wife."

"Lorenzo, stop this," she pleaded.

"Mama, please." It was the first time I ever heard him say please. "I'll speak to the two of you later." He directed his comment to Red and Emmet who nodded once before leaving.

Carmella looked at her son with disappointment and irritation before she exited the kitchen. Within a few seconds, the front door closed behind her.

"What are you playing at? You disrespect me in front of my mother, my men..." He growled, his voice slicing through the air as he confronted me with a fury that vibrated off the walls.

"Be careful. You'll pop a vein if you carry on," I taunted. I knew he hated my sarcasm, so I gave it by the bucketload.

He gripped my face, bringing it closer to him, and all I did was smile, something that only angered him more. His fingers dug into my skin, firm but not painful, as he pressed me into the counter.

"You're playing a dangerous game," he muttered, his breath hot against my lips. But I didn't flinch. I wouldn't.

I tilted my head back, taunting him as if daring him to make good on his unspoken threat. My smirk never wavered despite his anger boiling over.

"You're driving me insane," he snarled before his lips crashed against mine in a kiss that was anything but tender. It was rough, punishing, and fuelled by hate.

His mouth moved fiercely over mine, demanding and unrelenting, as if he wanted to punish me with the kiss alone. I resisted as I pushed at his chest, digging my nails into the skin beneath his black shirt. But Lorenzo wasn't one to yield. He pressed his body against mine, allowing no room between us as his grip descended to my neck.

His free hand dug into my hip possessively as he deepened the kiss, his tongue invading my mouth with a ferocity that mirrored his anger. I fought against him, my teeth grazing his lip as I tried to pull away. His strength was overwhelming, and his movements became sharp and urgent.

He abruptly broke the kiss, his forehead resting on mine as we struggled to catch our breath. His chest heaved as he glared down at me. "You think you can get away with whatever you like, don't you?"

"You don't scare me, Lorenzo." I grinned, challenging him.

I knew I was playing with fire. The anger radiated off him in waves, but the thrill was too irresistible to ignore.

Without warning, he pressed my body against the pantry door, the force almost knocking the breath out of me. He pinned my wrists above my head and loomed over me. "Are you sure?" he growled against my neck. "Do you want to play, wife? Is that why you defied me?"

"Do your worst, Ricci," I breathed as he trailed rough and needy kisses down my neck. His teeth occasionally grazed my skin, leaving marks to serve as a reminder of the moment we shared. I was no submissive, but there was something about Lorenzo that made me want to give him some control.

His hand slid up my thigh, his touch rough and desperate as he pushed my dress up around my waist. The anticipation built as he slid my lace panties to the side. "When will you learn to obey your husband and show him some respect?" he murmured against my lips.

I opened my mouth to respond, but he silenced me with another kiss, this one slower but just as intense. His tongue traced the seam on my lips, demanding entrance as his fingers teased my pussy. "Already so fucking wet," he growled as I gasped into his mouth, my body betraying my defiance as I arched into his touch. "You can't hide it from me, Anastacia." His voice was thick with satisfaction.

He slid his fingers inside me as I bit my lip to stifle a moan, my body trembling as he began to move, his touch rough, which was exactly what I needed and wanted. He worked my pussy with a rhythm that was both punishing and intoxicating.

"Say it," he demanded. "Say you'll obey me from now on."

"No," I whispered, my voice barely audible, despite my walls clenching around his fingers.

"Say it, Ana."

"Never." I moaned as he fucked me with his fingers, his thumb circling my clit.

"We'll see." He whispered.

His fingers sped up, pushing me closer to the edge. I dug my fingers into his shoulders, slowly letting him claim the orgasm that was surging through me.

"Come."

One word was all it took as my body shook with the force of my orgasm, my cries of pleasure echoing off the walls. "L-Lorenzo... Fuck!"

"*Ecco fatto, dammi tutto.*" I had no idea what he said but I let go, giving him everything my body had to offer. He took it willingly. "For someone who hates me, you seem to love it when I make you come."

"Does it make you feel good, Lorenzo?" I managed, my breaths ragged and shallow.

He removed his fingers from me, bringing them to his lips. He swirled his tongue around them, sucking off my come. "So fucking good."

"You're such a bastard." I scoffed as his mouth twisted up into half a smile.

"You weren't saying that a minute ago." He winked as I shoved him away from me.

"Listen, I may have had a few moments of weakness when it comes to you, but that stops now. This will never happen again." I rearranged my dress, squaring up to his much larger frame. "You are a mistake in every sense, Lorenzo."

"Who are you trying to convince? Me or yourself?"

I shoved past him, not giving him another moment of my time. He didn't deserve that, nor did he deserve me.

AFTER SLIPPING into a form fitting black dress, I made my way towards the garage where my car was parked.

"Where you goin'?" Emmet asked, catching me off guard.

"Out. I have somewhere I need to be." I smiled, hoping he wouldn't run to Lorenzo.

"A, you know I can't let you leave. We have orders."

"Emmet, with all due respect, you can tell my husband I said he can stick those orders up his ass. I have somewhere I need to be. It's an annual thing." I exited the house. Emmet was clearly torn, unsure over stopping me or finding Lorenzo.

"A," he sighed.

"See you later, Emmet." I smiled, heading out to the garage before he had a chance to say another word.

It felt good to be back behind the wheel again, I hadn't driven since moving in here and I missed it. It allowed me to feel free.

Speeding off down the driveway, I noticed Lorenzo driving the opposite way, our eyes meeting as we passed one another.

The gates were already open to let him in which gave me a quick getaway. I had a feeling he'd follow me, and I was right. The second I glanced in the mirror, I clocked him, driving like a maniac behind me.

Of course he'd turned around, how else would he survive the day if he didn't piss me off?

This man had no clue about this evening, but I'd enjoy watching it all unfold.

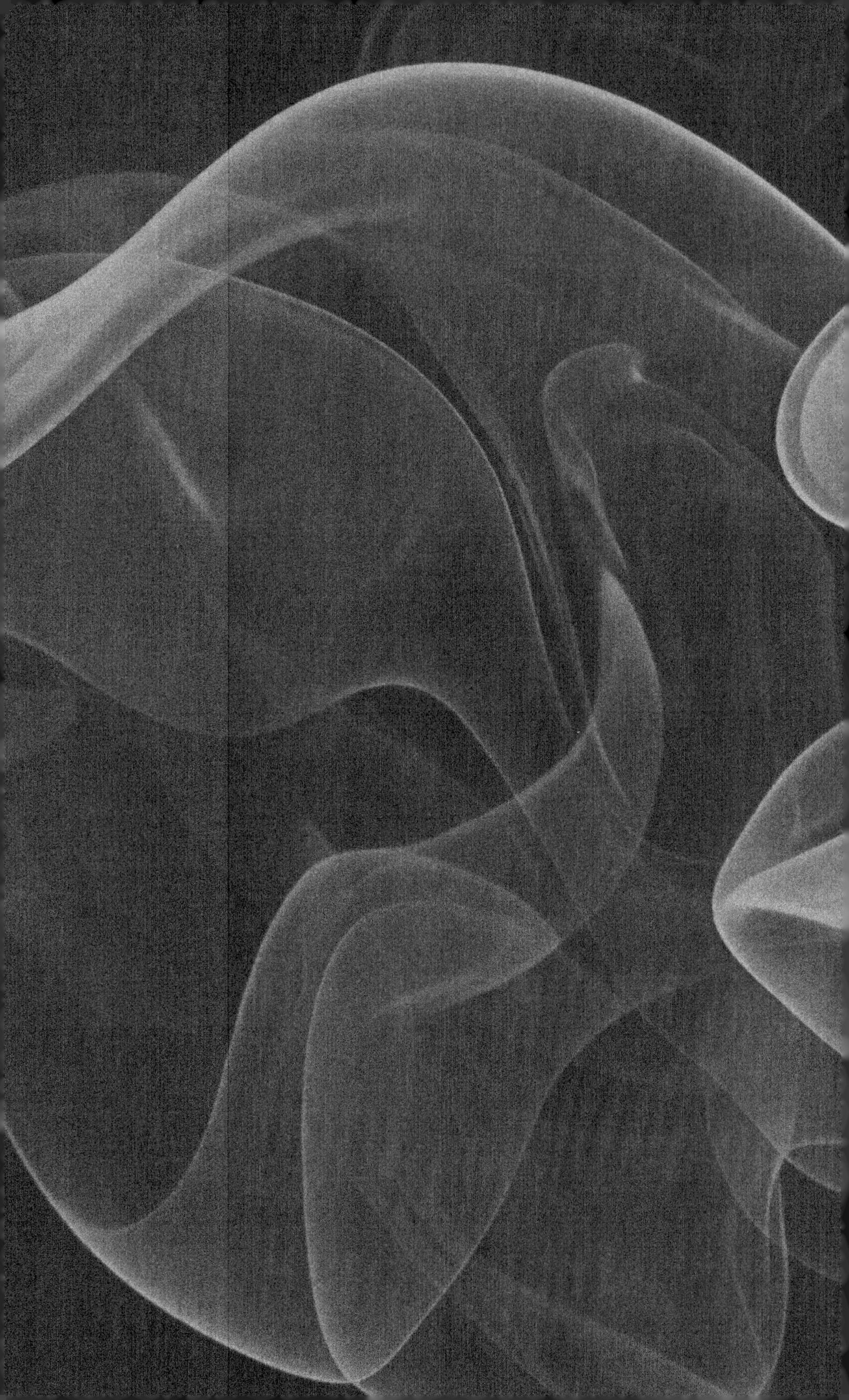

13

LORENZO

I turned into the driveway, blissfully unaware that I was about to come face-to-face with my wife who was on her way out…alone.

"Lorenzo, that's Ana." Red cleared his throat.

"Thanks for the update, Red," I snapped, my eyes meeting hers through the glass as our paths crossed.

"Where are you going?" I called out. Not that she would have heard me, but she had to know that I was pissed off to the maximum.

She smiled at me without a care in the world as she hit the gas, speeding like a damn maniac out of the open gates.

"Turn the car around and follow her," I demanded. Red was already on it. "She knows not to go out alone. What is wrong with her?!"

"Maybe there's a valid reason. You could just ask her, rather than starting a screaming match. Doesn't that sound more logical?" He said, but I wasn't in the mood to hear it.

"I don't give a shit about logic, Red. She continues to defy me over and over. Tonight is the last time."

I retrieved my gun from the seat beside me, slamming the clip into place as Red's eyes met mine in the rearview mirror.

"What are you planning to do?" The worry in his voice was clear.

"I'm not going to kill her." I sighed, relaxing in my seat as he sped after Ana's car. "Inform the men that there will be a meeting when I get home. This won't be happening again. I want to know who fucked up and let her leave."

"I'll make the call."

I watched as we tailed her closely. She knew we were there. Her weaving in and out of traffic confirmed that.

"Meeting confirmed. They'll all be available for whenever you need them."

"Good. She's getting off. Don't lose her," I ordered as she signalled off the freeway.

I didn't take my eyes off her car as she turned into the parking lot of a prestigious restaurant in the heart of town. We pulled into the space opposite her as she shut off her engine.

Watching her practically jump out of her car was somewhat amusing, but not enough to dim the fire that was burning inside. I pulled out my phone and dialled her number. The phone illuminated her face, but as she soon realised it was my number, she rejected the call before shoving it back in her clutch bag.

"Wait here," I told Red, who remained silent.

I exited the car before she had the chance to lock hers.

"Is that how you treat your husband?" I asked.

She paused for a second before glancing up to look at me. "What was the point in me answering? I knew you followed me here." She scoffed with an eye roll.

"What are you doing here, Ana?" I stepped closer to her. She didn't move. "I already told you about leaving the house alone."

"As I already told Emmet, it's something I do annually, and it's none of your business." She challenged me, edging closer. "Now, do me a favour and go back home like a good little boy, and I'll see you later when you've calmed down."

"Excuse me?" *Good little boy, was she taking the piss?*

"Tonight isn't about you. It never will be." She turned on her heel and headed for the entrance.

I grabbed her wrist, pulling her body flush to mine as her hair whipped across the side of my face. The warmth of her minty breath mingled with my own. I had to stop myself from devouring her right there, right then.

"Get in the car. I'm taking you home."

"No, stop being overbearing and demanding. It's getting tiring and, quite honestly, I'm over it." She glared at me. "Tonight is important to me, like things are to you, so stop trying to get in the way."

"Are you on a date?" I asked, already hoping it was the answer I wanted.

"As I said, I'll see you at home." She shoved me away and quickened her pace.

I caught up to her in a heartbeat, her two strides matching my one. I was ready to see what was so important to the demanding little princess.

I stormed off in front of her, confused as to why she so easily let me head inside. I caught her smiling as I glanced over my shoulder, the kind that would leave anyone unsettled.

As I stepped through the door, I noticed the restaurant was pretty much deserted. Only one table was occupied by an elderly woman, who looked like a much older version of my wife.

Ana entered behind me as the woman stood to greet her. She brushed past me, not waiting for my reaction.

"*Moya devochka*." She smiled, holding out her arms to embrace my wife in what looked like the warmest hug possible. Something I had never truly felt from anyone. "You never said we'd have an extra guest tonight." The woman looked me over, her deep blue eyes trying to read me.

"He just invited himself, I guess." Ana laughed. It was so pure it stirred something within me. Something unexpected. "Victor didn't want to join tonight?"

"No. He knows exactly how I feel about him and his decisions right now. He's not welcome tonight." Her voice was cold as she spoke about Victor. "My son has done many things but what he did to you is unforgivable to me, as it would have been with your *dedushka*."

So, this was Victor's mother—Evelina Fedorov. The only woman brave enough to tame Aleksander Fedorov.

I truly admired Anastacia for a second. She looked beautiful tonight. Her face was pretty much bare and natural. Her hair was poker straight, stopping just shy of her waist. She wore sneakers with a fitted dress, something that paired oddly well.

"I take it you're my granddaughter's husband, Lorenzo?" She sidestepped Ana, holding her hand out to me that I respectfully took.

"I am, and I take it you're my wife's grandmother?" I smiled, much to Anastacia's surprise.

"Correct." She stepped back a little, signalling the waiter over. "Please, add another setting."

"No, I don't want to impose." I held up my hands, wanting to leave and wait in the car.

"If you didn't want to impose, you wouldn't have followed my granddaughter here, would you?" she questioned.

"I didn't follow her here."

Lie.

"I don't like liars, Lorenzo, so sit down and see why we do this annually since you can't seem to let her out of your sight for a night." She pursed her lips, and I instantly knew where my wife got her attitude from.

"It wasn't that." I tried my best, but this woman was good.

"My Ana is not a woman you can expect to control. She is a good girl with an enormous heart, something you'll never know if you keep acting the way you are." She lowered herself into her seat. Ana followed her lead, sitting as well.

I didn't want to know or experience the heart that she had. I wasn't bothered about her. I was bothered about one thing only and that was killing her father and keeping her for fun.

"Sit down," she said, her tone authoritative.

I sat opposite her and beside my wife, who seemed to be relaxed despite me giving her a piece of my mind outside a minute ago. But that could have been because her grandmother gave me a dressing-down.

"So, what did he say?" Ana asked, and I knew she was asking about her father.

"Nothing he could say, darling. I made my decision, and you know how final that is." She smiled, sipping her cocktail.

"Sorry, what night have I intruded on?" I asked, feeling out of place.

"Today is the anniversary of my husband's death." Evelina's eyes brimmed with tears that she rapidly blinked away.

"Well, now I feel like a dick for intruding," I said, my voice laced with regret. I ran a hand through my hair, as a wave of remorse washed over me.

"As you should." Ana said from beside me. I couldn't tell if she was joking or being deadly serious.

"Now, now, it's fine. This is usually a family occasion, but with everything that's happened recently, I decided it would just be me and Ana." She reached over the table, taking my hand in her frail one. "For whatever reason, you are family now." She smiled half-heartedly. "But so help me God, if you hurt my granddaughter, I will skin you alive. Don't let my age fool you. I can do what's needed when it comes to her."

I wasn't expecting her to be as bold as she was, but I respected her for that.

"I will admit, though, my husband would have liked you. He

would have had sterner words than me, but he would have approved." She squeezed my hand tighter before continuing. "I know what my son did to your father, and I am truly sorry for your loss, but I hope that marrying my granddaughter isn't some kind of way to get back at him."

Hearing her mention that and Anastacia in the same sentence should have made me feel some sort of guilt, but instead, I didn't know what I felt.

The rest of the meal went smoothly as Evelina spoke about her life as much as she asked about mine. I kept directing the conversation away from myself, not wanting to delve too much into it.

"Let's move on, shall we?" Evelina asked Anastacia, who nodded in agreement.

"Move onto what exactly?" I questioned, genuinely wanting to just head home.

"You'll see since I'm sure you don't want to go home without your wife." She chuckled, clearly getting the wrong idea of how I felt about Ana.

RED and I followed Anastacia and her grandmother until we reached the final destination, which just so happened to be the graveyard. I waited by the car with Red while Anastacia and Evelina made their way to the family plot where Aleksander was buried.

"Bet you felt like a right dick storming in there, didn't you?" Red chuckled. "I can't actually believe you did."

"Now is not the time, Red." I sighed. "I fucked up. I know I did, but I still need to have the conversation with Ana about running off unprotected every five minutes."

"Maybe not tonight, though, yeah?" He let out a deep sigh, knowing I'd do whatever I wanted to anyway.

I noticed shortly after that Evelina was approaching us alone, her face strong and unreadable. There may have been tears in her eyes a moment ago, but you'd never have known that if you didn't see it in person.

"I'll wait in the car." Red smiled at Evelina as she approached. "Goodnight, Evelina."

"Goodnight, young man."

Red settled into the driver's seat, waiting for us to finish.

"I don't know if she ever told you, but they were so incredibly close. She was the apple of his eye." She spoke softly, not taking her eyes off her granddaughter.

"But wasn't that spot reserved for you? You were his wife, after all."

"He adored me, I know he did." She breathed out a big breath, the corners of her mouth turning up as she thought about her late husband. "But he had a special place in his heart for her."

"Is that why he trained her?"

"Partly. Victor was all about Miles, wanting to make him the best of the best, but in my opinion, Miles fell short. He was never the right choice. Victor overlooked Anastacia time and time again, and my husband had enough, so he took it upon himself to train Ana."

"And Victor still focused on Miles? Despite what your husband said to him?" I asked.

"Indeed, Miles was his sole focus. Anastacia didn't really matter. He never thought she was good enough. He never thought she'd be able to replace him. She wasn't strong enough for that job in his opinion." Evelina clenched her fists, the anger getting to her. There was clearly more to that family dynamic than I'd found out previously.

"And what was your opinion?"

"That she could do that job with her eyes closed. There was no one better to lead after Victor, but he was blinded by focusing on his son. He dismissed her without a second thought." She sighed.

"I never knew."

"Of course, you wouldn't know, Lorenzo. She wouldn't have told you." Evelina turned to face me. "That woman brushes everything off. She may put on this mask and armour, but deep down, she's so much more than what you think."

"I'm sure she is." I turned my attention back to Anastacia, who was kneeling beside the grave, her hair blowing behind her in the wind as the moonlight illuminated the tears that glistened on her cheeks.

"I know you aren't innocent in this marriage. I wasn't born yesterday. I know you have some sort of hidden agenda, but trust me, Ana isn't the easy target you think she is." She informed me, and I already knew she wasn't as easy as I expected her to be.

"Red will drive you home, I can get Ana to drive me back."

"Do you have a death wish?" She laughed as the smile finally reached her eyes.

"Is she really that bad?"

"Do you want to find out?" She rounded the front of the car as she replied.

"Good point. It looks like I'll be driving then." I smiled as she disappeared into the passenger seat.

I made my way over to where Anastacia knelt. She quickly wiped her eyes, hiding any sign of upset from me as if wanting to slip that mask back into place. She didn't want to look weak in front of me.

"Are you ready to go?" I asked, hovering behind her.

"Yeah, just give me a minute." She whispered, tracing her fingers across her grandfather's name. "I love you, *dedushka*. You will always be my sunshine," she whispered before letting out a shaky breath. "Let's go."

She rose to her feet, not wanting to look at me.

We didn't exchange words, but that didn't stop me from doing what I did next. I pulled her into my arms, resting my chin on her head as she relaxed into me. She didn't cry. She didn't speak. She just let me hold her. I didn't know what came over me. I wasn't usually comforting, and I never wanted to be affectionate towards her, but seeing her so upset stirred something in me, something I couldn't name.

It might have been the first time we'd actually been that close without wanting to kill one another—or fighting for dominance—and honestly, I should have hated it... But tonight, I didn't.

"Red took your grandmother home. I'll drive us back in your car."

"She told you about my driving then?" she murmured into my chest.

"Something like that, yeah." I chuckled before leading her to the car.

We pulled into the garage. I should have prepared myself for the mouthful I was about to receive regarding my countless offences tonight. From me following her to crashing the meal with her grandmother and finishing off at the graveside. But when she appeared in front of me at the driver's side door, her face was softer than I expected it would have been.

"Thank you for tonight." She breathed. "It was a change, though, seeing a kinder side to you."

"Don't get used to it, Anastacia. I felt sorry for you, that's all," I replied, my tone cold and unbothered.

"For your information, I don't need your pity. I didn't need you to hold me, either," she snapped. "I managed just fine before you." She turned on her heel and stormed towards the house.

Well done, dickhead.

I followed her inside as she walked past my four most trusted men, including Red, who was already back. Their eyes fell on me the second I entered the kitchen.

"My office now." I shot them all a look that told them exactly what I wanted to discuss.

They followed me through to my safe space. Then, the four of them stood before me.

"Now, I'm going to ask this once and I want the fucking truth," I seethed. "Who let my wife leave the house alone?!" I looked at them. They remained silent. I knew exactly who it was, Ana slipped out with his name earlier. "I know damn well it wasn't Red since he was with me, so Emmet, are you going to confess?" I asked.

"Boss, before you put a bullet in my head, let me explain—" Emmet started as his face fell.

"I don't want to hear what excuse you have." I slapped my gun down on the desk as his eyes dropped to it. "You went against my word, the one I have repeated over and over. You let her leave the house alone. You know as well as I do that she's a walking target."

"I'm sorry. She caught me off guard. I—" He cleared his throat. "I called you the second she left, but it went to voicemail. Please forgive me. You have my word, it won't happen again."

"Too right, it won't." I lowered myself onto my chair, not taking my eyes off of Emmet. "Do you think you can defy me? That you can ignore the rules since we're friends?" I questioned.

"No, I was careless and I should have stopped her, I'm sorry." He breathed.

"Consider this your first and last warning." I leaned forward, placing the knife I'd taken from my waistband down on the desk. "Next time, I won't be as lenient."

"Thank you, Boss."

"Does anyone else have anything to confess?" I asked, glancing at the four of them.

"No, Boss." Red nodded, speaking for everyone.

"Good," I responded. "See yourselves out, I have somewhere I need to be." I ordered before leaving the four of them alone and making my way to Ana's room.

I TAPPED on Ana's door but there was no response. Knocking again a little louder, there was still nothing. *Fuck it.* I pushed the door open slowly, trying to be as quiet as possible. I neared her bed, noticing she was tucked beneath the covers. Her hair fanned the pillow as tears stained her cheeks, but for the first time, she looked peaceful. I carefully sat on the edge of the bed, not wanting to wake her. I felt a pang of guilt for what I said to her in the garage.

I pushed the hair from her face, letting my fingers linger on her skin a little longer than I should have.

"I was a dick, I know that," I whispered. "I shouldn't have been, especially today of all days."

There may have been a hidden apology in there somewhere, but she'd never hear it.

I stood and pulled the covers up around her more. She grabbed my hand and snuggled into it as I stilled, unsure on what to do until I finally realised I had to let go. She didn't mean to do it. She was in too deep of a sleep to realise.

"Goodnight, wife," I muttered before stepping away from her.

14

ANASTACIA

As I sat by the lake in the morning sun, I couldn't stop my mind wandering back to last night. Just when I thought there was a little progress made, he slammed on the brakes and was back to being the same dick he was when we met.

My phone vibrated beside me, and I saw Robin's name flash across the screen.

"You're up early." I laughed when I answered. Robin was a night owl. She hated early starts.

She groaned. "Tay's brother is here. You know exactly how he is in the morning."

"Ah, and how is my favourite little man, Jack?"

"Loud and lively." She scoffed.

"Why don't you and Tay bring him over today? I could use some girl time." That was true. I genuinely could. I missed them.

"Won't your husband mind?"

"I don't know. I think he's out today anyway." I danced happily on the inside at the thought of not having to see him all day. "Besides, it's my house too."

"Valid point! We'll be over at lunch?" The idea of getting together must have woken her up because she sounded more excited than she did a minute ago.

"Perfect, I'll see you then." I smiled, hanging up the phone.

I relaxed back on the grass, enjoying the peace and the rippling lake.

"Mornin', A." Emmet beamed as he sat down beside me.

"Morning." I smiled, until I remembered he was the one who let me go last night, and that wouldn't have gone without repercussions. "I'm sorry."

"Don't apologise, A." He responded, his grin a breath of fresh air. "It ain't your fault, you just want to live a little, and hey, I don't blame ya."

"But didn't Lorenzo have something to say about it?" I asked.

He gently nudged his arm into mine. "Lorenzo has been my mate for a long time, and I wouldn't change that, but at the end of the day, he's also my boss. I let him down."

"I should have stayed." I sighed.

"Nah, Red told me what was so important, so I'm glad you didn't ."

"Why is he such a dick though?"

"You've grown up with men like Lorenzo, A. You know how much pressure they have on them." He responded, his lips twisting into a smile at my previous question.

"So, you agree? He's a dick?" I laughed.

He jumped to his feet. "I have to meet him and the guys. Please stay home today," he pleaded, clasping his hands together as if begging me to listen.

"You have my word. Besides, the girls are coming over."

"Well, have fun then." He held up his hand in a wave before retreating towards the house.

Why couldn't Lorenzo be as nice and easygoing as them?

As I sat outside by the lake with Robin, Tay, and Jack, I finally felt as though I was back at home. Even though this was anything but a home right now. It was a damn prison.

"Ana, why is this house so big?" Jack asked as he stared back at it. "Does one man need such a huge house?"

"No, others live here, too." I ruffled his hair as he looked up at me.

"Cool. What are they like?" he pried.

"Everyone is friendly." I crouched down to his level. "Although, one is a little mean."

"I'll knock that meanness right out of him!" he growled as he balled his fist.

"Yeah, I don't think so," Tay warned, shooting him a look he knew all too well.

"You're mean, too." He stuck out his tongue before he ran off to explore.

Jack was Tay's little brother. He was nine years old and a bundle of energy. But he was adorable and loved to spend time with the three of us.

The girls turned their attention back to me. As if they were trying to read me, and it filled me with dread. I knew they wanted me to gush about Lorenzo and say how amazing he was but I couldn't... He was a dick through and through, and even if I lied, nothing would change that.

"So, spill! How's married life?" Robin quizzed, sipping her lemonade.

"Honestly?" I sighed. "There is nothing to spill. It's awful."

"Really?" Robin's mouth dropped open, clearly not expecting that answer.

“He’s vile. I despise the man, and I wish I killed him when I had the chance.” I admitted.

“Now, I would have paid to see that.” Tay giggled as Robin narrowed her eyes at her.

Robin was a real believer in true love, so me not falling head over heels for Lorenzo wasn’t on her cards.

“To be honest, his attitude at the club was disgusting, acting as if he owns you.” Tay tutted. “No amount of free drinks will make up for his behaviour.”

“I know he didn’t exactly win us over with his first impression, but the more I think about it, the more I think he was just being protective of his wife.” Robin swooned. Fuck, she really loved herself a fairytale.

“There’s being protective and then there’s being whatever the fuck he was.” Tay scoffed with an eye roll.

“Alright, but maybe we should meet him properly before we judge.” Robin threw the suggestion out there as if I’d want that.

“All I’m saying is that man needs to do a lot of work before he becomes worthy of our girl.” Tay picked at her nail polish as she expressed her opinion.

“It’s just that this marriage isn’t what I pictured for myself. I never dreamed of marriage at all. I can’t even imagine loving someone like him.” I groaned, flopping down onto the grass.

The girls laid down on either side of me, most likely understanding my mixture of sadness and annoyance at the situation.

“And what if all we ever do is play this stupid game of cat and mouse until we kill one another?” I asked, covering my eyes with my arm.

“Well, let’s just hope you’re the one that kills first.” Tay winked as she rested her hand on top of mine.

“Ana!” Jack shouted as he bounded up to us. “Can you show me where the bathroom is?”

“Of course, I can. Come on.” I pushed myself to my feet as he slid his hand into mine.

I led Jack into the kitchen as a flash of red hair caught my eye.

“Hey, Ana, who’s this little guy?” Red smiled from the garage doorway.

“This is my friend's little brother, Jack.” Jack waved excitedly and stared at the colour of Red’s hair.

“Nice to meet ya, Jack. I’m Red.”

“Like your hair, I get it.” He giggled.

“Exactly, it’s cool, huh?” Red patted the bun that sat on the top of his head and laughed as Jack nodded his head with enthusiasm.

“Ana, do you think my mom would let me do that?” he asked, his deep hazel eyes staring up at me.

“Hmm, maybe when you’re older.” I ruffled his hair as he pumped his fist in happiness.

“Right, I’d better get going. I got sh—I mean, *things* to do.” Red let out a relieved sigh that he caught himself from cursing.

“I love him!” Jack beamed. “Now, where is the bathroom?”

“It’s just down this corridor. Count five doors, and you’ll reach it.” I pointed him in the right direction.

“Got it! Wait here for me!” he said sweetly before hurrying off to count doors.

I sat on the bottom step of the stairs, picking at the frayed knees of my jeans. The afternoon with the girls was exactly what I needed. I knew they had different opinions of Lorenzo, and that was completely understandable. They didn’t know him, and I hoped they’d never truly want to, either.

“Ana?” Lorenzo appeared before me, catching me off guard. He must have been holed up in his office since returning home.

“Lorenzo,” I replied, matching his tone.

“Why are you sitting there?” he quizzed, looking genuinely confused.

"I'm just waiting for Jack." The second I opened my mouth, it dawned on me that Lorenzo didn't know who Jack was.

"And who the fuck is Jack?" he quizzed, his brows furrowing more with each word.

"That's me. I'm Jack." An overly confident Jack piped up from behind Lorenzo, causing his face to drop when he realised Jack was, in fact, a child.

Lorenzo turned. He stood beside me as he came face-to-face with an adorable little boy who flashed him a smile.

"You know you just said a swear word, right?" Jack scrunched his nose, looking exactly like Tay when he did. He furrowed his brows, challenging my husband.

"I just said a what?" The look on Lorenzo's face was priceless. I had never seen him look so surprised and confused all at once.

"A swear word... You know, a really bad word." Jack's face relaxed a little, amused that Lorenzo didn't understand.

"Well, forgive me, little man. I am sorry." *Holy shit, did he just apologise?* I never thought I'd see the day.

"Do you have ice cream?" Jack asked with a sweet smile.

"I do, why do you ask?" Lorenzo crouched down onto the balls of his feet, his lips lifting ever so slightly at the corners.

"Well, I can forget the swear word if I can have some ice cream?" he whispered close to Lorenzo's ear.

"Alright, you've got yourself a deal." He held out his hand that was decorated with a variety of scars. "How many scoops?"

"I was thinking of nine. You know, because I'm nine."

"Well, I didn't know that, but I do now." Lorenzo chuckled as Jack shook his hand.

They wandered through to the kitchen together while I followed behind.

Had someone asked me this morning how I would have envisioned Lorenzo today, I would never have pictured him like this. His crisp white shirt was rolled up to his elbows as he scooped endless flavours of ice cream into a sundae dish before decorating it with sprinkles and a chocolate flake.

“There you go, little man.” He slid the ice cream over to Jack, whose eyes lit up with delight.

“Woah, Ana, look! He added sprinkles. I like him.” He fist pumped the air before devouring his first spoonful.

"It's a good job she's married to me then," Lorenzo quipped with a mischievous grin, his eyes twinkling with humour.

“Yes! Good pick, Ana!” Jack hopped off the stool, heading back out to Tay.

I turned my attention to Lorenzo. He cocked his head to the side, watching me silently.

"I never knew you were such a softy," I teased, batting my eyelashes dramatically. My voice was light and filled with mock surprise.

“That’s because I’m not.” He scowled, muttering something else under his breath.

“Mhm, then explain to me why you melted faster than the ice cream did when Jack came around.” Winding him up came all too easy. “That was after you knew he was a child.” I laughed, barely holding it in.

“What was I supposed to think? You didn’t exactly make it clear, so I thought—”

“You thought, what? That I’d bring another man into your house? Thought I’d fuck someone else under your roof?” I scoffed, my anger levels rising.

“No, but—”

“But nothing.” I cut him off. “You should know by now that if I wanted to fuck someone, I would do it far from here.” I glared, crossing my arms across my chest.

“Don’t repeat that, Ana.” He stepped towards me, closing the distance between us. “No other man will ever have you, will ever call you his, and I’ll make sure that no other man’s name will ever leave those perfect lips." He gripped my chin between his thumb and forefinger.

"Or what, Lorenzo. What would you do?" I egged him on.

"I'd torture the bastard slowly and painfully before killing him," he whispered. "All before bringing the bastard back to do it all over again." A sinister smile played on his lips. "Do you really think I'd ever let a man walk free for looking at what's mine?" His tone was as impassive as his face was.

"No, I don't," I retorted.

"Good girl." He pulled me into him, his cock pressing against me. "Do I scare you, Ana?"

"No, you don't scare me," I whispered. "You should know I don't scare easily."

His lips brushed against mine. My breath hitched in my throat as the warmth from his mouth kissed my skin.

"Boss." Emmet's thick English accent came from the doorway, shattering our moment. "Sorry to interrupt, but we need to finalise tonight's shipment. Are you good to go or do you need a minute?"

"He's good to go. We're done here." I slapped Lorenzo's hands away from me. He groaned, showing me just how pissed off he was.

"Don't leave the house," he ordered, already turning back into his usual self.

"I won't. Anything to please his highness." I bantered with an eye roll before retreating back outside.

NIGHT HAD FALLEN and there was no sign of Lorenzo or any of the guys yet. I was thankful, to be honest. A quiet night to myself was what I needed. I poured myself a glass of pinot noir and curled up on the sofa to enjoy my guilty pleasure, *Mamma Mia*. A movie I used to watch with my mother.

I drifted off to sleep after a while, waking up to a loud bang on the front door, a full glass of wine, and the rolling credits. A message flashed on my phone as I rubbed my eyes. Chad's name appeared when I picked it up to check.

Open the door, Ana. I'm outside.

Why the fuck was he here?!

Glancing at the time, I realised it was just after midnight. Surely, whatever he wanted could have waited until morning. I was unaware of how he even got through the gate. Lorenzo had given strict instructions about Chad to everyone on his team.

I made my way to the front door, wearing nothing other than an old pair of sweats and an oversized T-shirt, one I wasn't even sure was mine. I pulled the door open, coming face-to-face with my childhood friend, who looked nothing like he usually did. His clothes were dishevelled, his dirty blonde locks were a mess, and his bright eyes lacked their usual spark.

"What are you doing here? It's late," I snapped, keeping the door ajar.

"Wow, what did I do to deserve that greeting?" He asked.

"It's just late, that's all. I wasn't expecting anyone."

"I know, and I apologise." He sighed.

"And what if Lorenzo would have been here?" I asked, looking over his shoulder to check no cars were coming up the drive.

"I just needed to see a friendly face, Ana."

"What happened?" I questioned, the worry in me taking over as he seemed to carry the weight of the world on his shoulders.

"Can I come in?" he asked. The worry I felt switched to unease.

"I don't think that's a good idea, Chad. No one's home." That wasn't a lie. I was alone, and even though Lorenzo was a complete dick, I knew he wouldn't appreciate Chad being with me in his home or anyone else for that matter.

"So, what? You can't have friends over now?" He tutted, rolling his eyes with a hint of sarcasm.

"Of course I can, but you two don't see eye-to-eye, and I don't think he'd appreciate—"

"Since when are you bothered about what he'd appreciate?" He cut me off mid-sentence and slammed his flattened palm against the door.

"Since I have to live with the man." I defended him—to an extent.

"I've had a shit day with your father. I'm sorry." He apologised, backing up slightly.

"That doesn't mean you can take whatever happened out on me, so you will stand there and calm down,"

"I'm calm, Ana, but your father has hired another man to work alongside me," he seethed. "Does he not think I'm capable of doing my job?!" He ran his fingers through his hair before fisting them at his sides.

"Do you honestly think I have a say in anything that man does? Look at what he did to me, Chad!" I sighed. "Look, he's a heavily targeted man, and if he requires more protection, then that's his decision." I rubbed at my temple, getting tired of this conversation.

"I get that, I do, but—"

"But nothing. He took you in when you had nobody else. He gave you the clothes on your back, he feeds you, and pays you a hefty sum. If you don't like that, then you know what to do." I'd had enough. I was irritated, and ready to go to bed.

"Ana, please. The house isn't the same since you left. I miss you." His eyes glistened with tears, and I felt a stab of guilt in my gut. He reached for me, but I stepped back slightly. Something I had never done before, but tonight, it felt different.

"Well, sometimes things change and that's what happened to me." I said. "Listen, Chad, no disrespect, but I think you need to leave."

"Really? You want me to leave?" He seemed taken aback, but I no longer had the patience.

"Yes, I do. Listen, you're my friend and you have been for many years, but you're only here to talk about what happened with my father. You know I don't involve myself in his business. I was never fucking allowed, and after what he did to me recently, I don't give a fuck about who he hires and fires."

"You're right, I shouldn't have come over here to complain." He smiled half heartedly. "We'll catch up soon, right?" he asked with a glimmer of hope in his eyes.

"Yeah, soon," I whispered, unsure of how true that was. "Remember, though, tomorrow is a new day and my father sees you as family. No new team members are going to change that."

"Yeah, I know. Goodnight." He waved softly before heading to his car. I closed the door behind him.

Finally time for bed.

I made it halfway up the stairs when the door almost swung off its hinges. I didn't need to turn around to know it was Lorenzo. I could hear his expensive shoes clicking across the marble as he stormed towards me.

"What was he doing here?" he asked, his tone demanding as usual.

I kept my back to him, not wanting to turn around. I didn't need to.

"Good evening, dear husband," I teased, playing with fire.

"Don't get smart with me. Why was he here?" His voice rumbled through me.

"How did you know he was here?"

"It doesn't matter how I knew. Now, answer my question," he demanded as he took two stairs at a time to get to me.

"He came for some advice from a friend, that's all." I let out a slow and steady breath. "Because despite what you want, that's what I am—his friend."

"I don't want him in my house, especially when you're dressed in my clothes!" He grabbed the hem of the T-shirt between his fingers, yanking it to make his point clear.

"Grow up!" I seethed. "Firstly, I didn't know this was your T-shirt, and secondly, he didn't come inside! I didn't allow him to!" I snapped, not in the mood for his shit anymore.

"Why do you insist on lying to me? His smug face said it all when our cars passed outside." Even with him fuming, I couldn't help but breathe him in. His shirt was untucked and unbuttoned. Blood stained the white material of his rolled-up sleeves as it tightened around his arms.

Now is not the time to admire him, Ana.

"Wow, you can tell everything just by his face? Don't you think that's what he wanted? That this," I used my fingers alternating between us, "is what he wanted?" I pinched the bridge of my nose, feeling somewhat defeated. "I know what happened." I glanced to the bottom of the stairs as Red, Emmet, and Gino joined us. They were all wearing worried expressions at what one of us would do.

"Yes, you do." He backed me against the wall, my hip bumping into the glass table that housed a beautiful antique vase, sending it tumbling to the floor.

He quickly stepped away from me with his hands raised as if in an apology. Guilt flashed across his face as he seemed as though he instantly regretted his decision.

But it was too late for him to regret anything.

"You can believe what you want to believe." I sighed.

"I can see it in your eyes." He continued, and I didn't have a clue how he could see anything right now, his eyes were glassier than the damn window.

"I hope you also see how much I fucking hate you. Because I do hate you. With everything I am, I hate you. You're unlovable. I'd be out of my mind to ever want someone like you." I pushed his chest but all he did was stand there.

"You don't hate me, Ana."

"Put those hands anywhere near me and I'll feed you your own dick." I sidestepped him, the smashed vase crunching beneath my feet as I darted down the stairs.

"Red, can you drive me—" I paused, wanting to say home but I didn't have one anymore. "Anywhere but here?"

"Ana..." He wore a look of defeat as he spoke, like I punched him in the gut.

The three of them looked at me, unsure of what to say, too torn on whether to stay loyal to Lorenzo or help me.

I knew who they'd pick. I was nothing to any of these men in this house. Especially not the one I was forced to marry.

"Don't you dare drive her anywhere, Red," Lorenzo called from the stairs. "She's not leaving."

"Ana, I'm—" Red started, but I cut him off.

"It's fine. He's your friend and your boss." I nodded, accepting it. "I don't need his permission to leave, I don't need a chaperone either."

I let out a steady breath as I walked through the kitchen towards the garage.

"You've got another thing coming if you think I'm going to let you walk out of here." Lorenzo was on me in seconds, his large, calloused hands grabbing my waist and turning me to face him. "Did you sleep with him?" His chest heaved as he spoke.

"If I wanted to fuck him, I'd have done it when we lived under the same roof." His hands gripped me tighter as I continued. "But you know what? I was taught to never give myself to anyone other than my husband, and I obeyed that rule. But now, being here with you, makes me wish I hadn't." I shoved him away from me, not wanting him near me. "Now, I can either walk out of here alone, or Red can take me where I want to go, but I will not stay here with someone who doesn't believe me."

"Red, take my wife where she wants to go, if that's what she truly wants." Lorenzo had given up the fight, even if it was just this once.

"Will do." Red responded, following me out of the door to the garage.

I left that kitchen and never looked back. I would never give him the satisfaction.

I would never allow anyone to break me.

Especially not that bastard.

15

LORENZO

I watched my wife walk out the door, and I did nothing to stop her.

What the fuck was wrong with me?

Of course I believed her, but I let my mouth run away with me just as it always did. I vowed to myself to never feel something for her, never let her see the man I once was, but in doing so all I managed to do was push her away and fuel her hate for me.

I used to be sure that's what I wanted, but now I'm having second thoughts.

No, scratch that, I was sure, she was Victor's daughter, that was all. I had my plan and I had to remain focused enough to execute it.

"What the fuck is wrong with you?" Gino's angry tone cut the silence.

I already knew I was a class A prick. I didn't need a lecture from him and Emmet.

"The way you spoke to your wife was uncalled for. I get you don't love her, perhaps you never will and that's fine, but she isn't some cheap whore and you know it."

I did know it. She was a fucking goddess. One someone like me would never deserve, so why try?

His words hit me like a ton of bricks, and he was right.

"Remember you work for me, Gino. Not my wife,"

"Lorenzo, I get it, alright? You want to kill her father, but why do you feel the need to keep hurting her?" Gino asked. "And I don't mean physically, I mean verbally, sometimes you don't realise how much words can hurt someone."

"I don't know, okay? Maybe it's because I'm a heartless bastard who has never felt anything other than pain for years. And that was because of her father."

"Exactly, her father. Not her." Emmet responded, finally joining the conversation. "She won't even go back to the Fedorov house tonight. Do you care where she's going?"

"Of course I care." I rubbed at my temple. "She's my wife."

"Yeah, you sure know how to show it." Emmet scoffed.

I chose to ignore his comment, mainly because of course, he was right.

My phone vibrated in my pocket, and I knew it was Red, updating me on Ana.

"Red, where is she?"

"At the graveyard." He replied, his tone clipped and distant. "She has nowhere else to go, Lorenzo. Not once did she ask me to drive her to Victor's."

I could picture Ana kneeling beside Aleksander's grave, thinking I was a damn monster, and she wasn't wrong. I was and I always would be.

"How is she?" I asked, softer than before.

"How do you think she is? She's sitting in a fucking heap beside his grave. She's fucking shivering. Shall I continue?"

"No, don't. Just send a couple of men to keep an eye on Chad. I don't trust him."

"Just like you don't trust the woman who is supposedly your wife." He hung up before I had the chance to respond. Before I had the chance to ask him to bring her home.

"Well, where is she?" Gino asked, pouring himself a whiskey.

"Out."

"Where?" Emmet questioned. It was clear as day that my two most loyal men were worried about her. The same men I told not to speak to her or make her feel welcome, yet they did the opposite. I guess they had a bigger heart than I did. Hell, did I even have one at all.

"I'm going to bed," I muttered.

But I didn't want to go to bed, I wanted to go and find my wife. But I couldn't, I would be the last person she'd want to see, probably always would be.

Tonight, I should have gutted a traitor. I should have finally made him sing like a canary. But the second I got the call that Chad was allowed past the gate, I flew home like a bat out of hell, forgetting everything and anything in that moment. Thinking that bastard was with my wife caused something inside of me to snap.

I shouldn't have felt anything, yet I did. I just couldn't explain what.

Tonight had been a shit show... A real fucking shit show, and I was done with everything, including the guilt that crept in about Ana.

I STUBBED out my cigarette in the ashtray on my desk. It had been eight fucking hours since Ana left. Red informed me she was safe but didn't disclose where. I wasn't sure if he felt the need to keep her safe. Whether he was protecting her from me was unknown.

"Lorenzo." There was a soft tap at the office door, which was accompanied by the voice of my mother.

"Yeah?"

She took that as a sign to enter. The second she stepped inside, my eyes found her face, and I knew something was off.

"What do I owe the pleasure of such an early visit?" I rubbed at my temples, squeezing my eyes shut.

"Oh, I just came to see my daughter-in-law, actually." She remained expressionless. There wasn't even a hint of her usual smile. Although, she didn't feel I deserved one these days.

"She's not here." I lit another cigarette, wanting to be on my own.

"I know she's not here, Lorenzo," she snapped, slapping her palm on my desk. "She stayed the night at my house." She narrowed her gaze at me, and my heart stopped for a split second.

"Your house?" I whispered, taken aback as to why Red would have dropped her off there.

"Yes, my house." She snatched the cigarette from my lips and stubbed it out. "Red brought her to me. She had nowhere to go because my son, the one I raised to show at least a little compassion, let her fucking walk out at one in the morning!"

"She had another man in here." I muttered, standing slowly.

"No. She didn't and you know it." She shoved her finger towards me. "You... I am disgusted with you," she seethed. "That woman felt as though she couldn't even go to her own father because of what he did."

"Okay." I shrugged, wanting her to leave. I already felt guilty enough, I didn't need her rubbing salt in the wound.

"Wow. Your father drained any compassion you once had and you let him." She sighed. "You should have seen the state of her when Red knocked on my door, but then again, you don't care."

"Where is she now?" I asked.

"At mine, asleep." Her voice turned calmer, but she was still pissed with me.

"You left her alone?"

"You have no room to talk about leaving her alone, Lorenzo." She turned her back to me. "Red is there, guards are there, and as will I be by the time she wakes up."

"So, you're going to run to the daughter of a man who killed your husband?" I asked as she turned around and backhanded my cheek.

"Watch your fucking mouth," she screamed. "Anastacia is innocent in all this, yet you want to hurt a good woman, and for what? For your pride? For revenge over something she had no clue about?" She stepped closer to me, jabbing her finger at my chest. "You might think you can break that woman, but mark my words, you won't. So, either sort yourself out and give it a real chance or let her go." That was her ultimatum? Really?

"Shut the door on your way out," I ordered, turning away from her.

"Kill her father. Make yourself feel better or superior, but in the end, you'll have nothing. She will leave you, and I'll help her," she threatened, and I knew she wasn't bluffing. "You're just like your father." She sighed. "And unfortunately, that's not a compliment."

I knew it wasn't a compliment, he was nowhere near an angel.

"If you want an update on your wife, I suggest you call Red, because you'll get nothing out of me." She slammed the door behind her, leaving me with nothing other than my fucked up thoughts.

THE DIMLY LIT warehouse reeked of sweat, blood, and the acrid smell of fear. I stood before Ryker, rage surging through me as his head drooped forwards, his chin hitting his chest.

The poor son of a bitch was bound to a chair in the centre of the room. He was a mess of bruises and blood. A beautiful sight. His once proud frame was slumped, his defiance the only thing keeping him alive. I leaned into him, my face inches from his. "Still not going to talk, huh?" I teased my blade between my fingers as his eyes met the steel. "You think you can cross me without consequences?"

Gino and Emmet grinned like hyenas from behind me, Ryker's blood staining their hands.

"So, tell me, who paid you to do me over?" I trailed the blade across his chest before sinking it into his skin. The tear of flesh echoed the warehouse, and it was the most beautiful fucking sound.

"Fuck!" Ryker roared through the pain, his chest heaving as his breathing turned ragged.

He refused to break, refused to give me the names I wanted, and the satisfaction of hearing him beg. "Talk, you piece of shit," I bellowed, slamming my fist into Ryker's gut. His body convulsed against the restraints as he gagged. "Do you really think silence will save you?" I hissed. "You're already a fucking dead man. You just don't know when it'll happen." I glanced back to Emmet who strode over with his burning cigar in hand. "Last chance, Ryker."

"Just kill me," he spat, as crimson red saliva trickled down his chin.

Emmet pressed the cigar into his cheek as his skin sizzled beneath it, causing him to cry out in agony.

"Be a good little boy and tell us who paid you, or we'll be sure to make your end slow and painful." Emmet sent him a sly grin, patting his wounded cheek with joy.

"Go to hell! All of you!"

My patience wore thin. This fucker had stayed silent for days. I slowly sliced a layer of skin from his back as he cried out for me to stop.

"P-please... Don't," he sobbed.

"You've changed your tune." I chuckled. "I won't stop until you look like a fucking jigsaw." I rounded him, holding up the piece of freshly cut flesh in front of his face. "Sure you don't want to speak?" There were no words, just the sound of gagging before he vomited down his front. "You know, I thought you could stomach a lot more than this. You disappoint me." I turned my attention to Emmet who was happily watching from the corner. "What about you, Emmet, don't you agree?"

"I expected a lot more from a man who, just a few days ago, was trying to do you over." Emmet sighed.

"Now, where should I go next?" I pondered as I placed the bloody knife against my lips.

I trailed my blade along his side as I sliced off another layer of his skin. My ears welcomed his screams. I tossed what was in my hand over my shoulder and sliced another piece from his chest.

"Please," he begged.

I spun my blade between my fingers as I toyed with him a little more. "I'll tell you what, I'll give you a choice of where you want me to cut next."

"Nowhere! Please, nowhere!" he pleaded.

I continued slicing off parts of his skin until he passed out. Blood soaked his khaki pants, and his body was painted red. I stepped back to admire my handiwork. Just as expected, he looked like a jigsaw puzzle.

"Creative," Emmet joked as he elbowed my arm.

"You know, I agree." I slid my knife into my waistband before turning to the guys.

"What do you want me to do with him when he comes back around?" Emmet asked as he lit another cigar, the smell of smoke filling the air.

"Whatever you want. I'm done with the bastard. You two dispose of him in one of your fucked up ways."

"You got it." Emmet winked.

"And then prepare the space for tomorrow. You know who's next." I smirked.

Victor.

I PULLED into the garage and instantly clocked Red's car.

Ana was home.

"Boss." Red nodded in greeting as I entered the kitchen. He could barely even look at me, and who could blame him?

"Where is she?" I asked, my tone sharp and cold.

"Asleep." The one word responses were an indication of how he felt.

"Be ready tomorrow," I told him. "You know the plan inside out. Make sure you lure the bastard to where I need him. I don't give a shit what you have to say to get him alone but you do what's requested of you."

"And what will you do to Ana?"

Ignoring his question, I asked my own. "Did she say anything?"

"No, she barely said anything all day."

"She'll have plenty to say tomorrow." I smiled, thinking about finally putting a bullet in her father's head.

After years of waiting for the perfect moment, it was finally here.

16

ANASTACIA

I barely slept last night, still unable to get the argument Lorenzo and I had out of my mind. I had nowhere to go. I would have slept beside my grandfather's grave if it wasn't for Red taking me to Carmella's house.

She did more than I ever expected her to. For the first time, I felt numb, unable to fathom what had happened or why he wouldn't believe me—the woman who was supposed to be his wife or so he kept reminding me.

Carmella tended to me, and despite me saying I didn't need anything, she didn't take no for an answer. She took care of me, something my own mother hadn't done in a while and forgot how to do. I found a safe space in Carmella's home. I found someone who treated me as her own.

"He hasn't always been this way." Carmella sighed, handing me a photo of Lorenzo when he was a boy.

His boyish grin beamed up at me from the frame. My eyes fell to the two who sat beside him, Carmella and Franco. Looking at Franco was like looking at my own husband. Lorenzo was the spitting image of his father. It was clear he took a whole lot more from him than looks.

"He used to have a heart. He used to care, but the day he lost his father that changed, and I'm so sorry you're caught in the middle of everything. You don't deserve to be." She wrapped her arm around me, something I wasn't used to. The only people I ever felt that love and affection from were my grandparents.

"How could they do that to me? How could Lorenzo even suggest such a thing?" I let a tear escape and, for the first time, felt as though I was letting go. Something I hadn't done in a long time. I didn't need to scream or shout to let it out. I just needed to open up a little.

"I don't know but perhaps give it some time. He might surprise you." She smiled, but I wasn't sure if she was trying to convince me or herself. "Why don't you get some sleep? Everything will seem better in the morning."

"I don't think anything will ever look better, Carmella." I sighed, pulling the covers up around my chin.

"You never know. For now, get some rest. Red and I will be downstairs if you need anything."

She flicked off the light, and I fell into a deep sleep until Lorenzo haunted each and every dream.

"MORNIN', A," Emmet greeted as I entered the kitchen.

"Morning." I glanced around quickly. "No Lorenzo this morning?" I asked.

"Nope, but let me introduce you to the next best thing." I heard a voice from the garage door. One I never heard before.

"A, meet Nicolo, Lorenzo's cousin," Emmet said, nodding towards the new arrival with a welcoming smile. Nicolo strolled over to where we stood by the island, his footsteps softly echoing on the tiled floor. He was a tall man with dark, wavy hair that framed his face and intense brown eyes that seemed to take in every detail of the room. He couldn't have been much younger than Lorenzo. Maybe mid twenties. His presence seemed commanding yet approachable. The aroma of freshly brewed coffee was already enough to brighten my morning.

"It's lovely to meet you, Anastacia. My aunt has told me so much about you." He kissed both cheeks before gripping me tightly in a hug.

"I'm so sorry I can't say the same." I breathed, taken aback by his gesture.

"Get your hands off my wife."

And there he was, like clockwork. *My so-called husband.*

Nicolo released me as he turned to face Lorenzo, whose face was a vision of rage. "Alright, cousin, nice to see you!"

"Nice to see me or nice to put those grubby hands all over my wife?"

"Oh, calm down. There's no need to get so territorial," he teased. "From what I understand, you seem to keep messing up, am I right?" Nicolo was skating on thin ice, though he didn't seem to care.

"Keep talking and I'll slice that tongue right out of your mouth," Lorenzo snapped.

"If you'll excuse me, I need to..." I pondered for a second. "Actually why lie? I just don't want to be anywhere near my bastard husband." I turned to Nicolo, capturing his attention. "It was nice to meet you, Nicolo. I guess I'll see you around."

I barged past Lorenzo, who, of course, was hot on my heels before I had time to stop him.

"Ana." His voice was firm as he spoke my name, causing me to stop in my tracks for a moment.

"You should catch up with your cousin and get away from me. I'm here because I have to be, don't think it's because I want to be."

"Listen—"

"No, Lorenzo, the time for listening was the other night, and you blew it. You fucked it up and let your own mother pick up the pieces." I spun around to face him, slapping his chest as hard as I could. "Did you think I would run home to my father? Or stay here while you belittled me? I had nowhere, but deep down, you knew that, and you let me walk out."

"Ana—"

"You know, I thought that maybe, just maybe, whatever this was could work, but now? Now I want nothing to do with you." I turned away from him as he exhaled a sharp breath.

"Ana, I believe you." He sighed. "I believe nothing happened."

Wow... that must have hurt him to admit.

"The time for believing me is long gone."

"Just stop for one minute." He rounded me instantly, his hands cupping either side of my neck. "Give me one more chance."

"You never had a chance to begin with." I didn't know how true that was, but I said it regardless.

"I messed up. I hold my hands up to that." He pulled me closer, not letting go of me. "Be ready tonight. I have a surprise."

"Lorenzo—"

"Be ready at eight."

He disappeared, leaving me no choice but to do as he asked. I had no idea what he had planned, but knowing him, it wouldn't be something romantic or even remotely nice. I'd do exactly what I was taught. I'd keep my guard up and never let someone in who could weaken me.

Lorenzo Ricci would never become my weakness.

He would never become someone I relied on.

And he'd certainly never become the person I'd love.

As I reached the car, I noticed it was just Lorenzo. No driver, no bodyguards, and none of the usual crowd. Every instinct told me to turn around and let him go wherever he wanted to alone but I didn't. I forced a smile, one I hoped looked natural. His charm was as polished as the damn car but it didn't fool me. It never would. I had no intention of letting my guard down tonight, not even for a second.

"You look beautiful." His voice was as smooth as velvet, and his eyes swept over me, lingering just a moment too long.

"Compliments will get you nowhere, Lorenzo, so just start the damn car and take me to whatever it is you have planned." I slid into the passenger seat, not giving him the satisfaction of looking at him.

We started the drive in silence but that was short-lived because he decided to speak a minute later. "I thought we'd go somewhere private," he said with a smirk. "Somewhere we can talk without interruptions."

Private...

The word didn't sit right with me. Something about it was off. I knew he wasn't the type for a quiet dinner and a moonlit stroll. No. He was fucked up. His kind of private was no doubt the complete opposite of mine. He always had an agenda, always seemed to be playing some sort of game, and I was determined to not be his pawn.

The car slowed to a stop as I glanced out of the window. He'd driven us to an industrial area far from town.

Somewhere remote and secluded.

He opened the door, his hand brushing mine, but I refused to take it. "I can get out of the car myself," I snapped. "Just tell me why you've brought me to a shit hole like this."

"Alright, you caught me. I need your help with something."

"Of course you do. Just as I thought, you have a hidden agenda." I scoffed, shutting the car door behind me.

"This way," he insisted, his voice a hushed murmur as he gestured with a slight nod of his head, guiding me through the narrow alley towards the looming silhouette of a large, dimly lit warehouse. Shadows clung to the building's corrugated walls, and the faint hum of machinery buzzed in the distance, adding an eerie undercurrent to the silence that enveloped us.

As we entered the building, I glanced around, and it was clear many people had died here. Blood stained the floors and walls, the stench enough to knock even the strongest stomach sick. I wasn't scared. But with each step I took, I felt uneasy, something screaming at me from the inside that told me to go back to the house. But right then, fear was the last thing I wanted Lorenzo to see.

"Here we are." He smiled, but it was so fucking sly and cocky.

As we turned the corner from the corridor I realised why we were here and why he looked like a cat who got the cream. The hairs on the back of my neck stood up as I spotted the single chair in the vast and empty space.

"Surprise." He chuckled, closing the door with a click behind me. "I thought you and your father could use a little heart to heart, reconcile perhaps."

"What's your plan, Lorenzo?" I asked, not letting my mask slip no matter how much my father stared at me. Chains bound his wrists to the arms of the chair, blood trickling down his fingers as the rough metal bit into his skin. The man who raised me sat there bloody and bruised, but fuck, he sat prouder than ever. Not letting Lorenzo or anyone else faze him. "Let me guess, you want to kill him, and for me to watch?"

"Wow. Ding, ding, ding." He laughed, and it took all I had not to smash his damn face in. "Are you surprised though?" he whispered, leaning into me as his lips brushed my ear.

"Nothing you do could ever surprise me. You're a sick and twisted bastard, I expected nothing less." I retorted. "You deserve to rot in hell alongside your father," I sneered, shoving him away from me.

He pulled my body flush to his, his eyes burning with anger.

"Repeat those words again, and I'll end you the same way I'm about to end him."

"Do you really think you could pull the trigger on me if it came down to it? Because I know you wouldn't. You don't have it in you, Ricci." My lips curved up into a cruel smile as I spoke.

"Don't question what I can and can't do, Ana. You'd be surprised." He dipped his head, running his tongue along my neck, his grip never loosening on my waist. "I'm going to make sure you watch as his life drains away. You're going to listen as he chokes out his final words to you. You're going to hear, see, and feel everything I felt."

"His final words would be to his golden child." I glanced over my shoulder as my father before giving Lorenzo my attention once more. "And in case you haven't yet guessed, that's never been me."

He stood quiet for a second, as if working out his next move.

"What? Did you think his golden child was me?" I cackled. "Poor, poor Lorenzo." I slapped his hand away from me, unable to control my amusement. "If you wanted to hurt or upset one of my father's children, you should have picked my brother. He's the easily broken one."

He reached for his waistband, the cocking of the gun cut through the silence as my father remained expressionless, barely able to look at me.

"Do you not wish to plead for your life, Fedorov?" Lorenzo laughed, directing his question to my father.

"We never plead, Lorenzo. I thought you'd have gathered that already." I scoffed. My heart froze the second he aimed the gun at my father's head. Right between his eyes. My father's gaze dropped to mine as if to say goodbye, but I had other plans. This wasn't how tonight was going to go.

I would run the show, not Lorenzo.

Something inside me snapped. Without thinking too much, I lunged, snatching the gun from Lorenzo's grip. My movements were swift and somewhat desperate, but my aim was steady and remained unmatched. With a sharp crack, I fired, the bullet tearing into my father's shoulder.

For the first time ever, Victor looked proud.

So fucking proud.

He knew that no matter the outcome of tonight, Lorenzo wouldn't break me. He wouldn't see me cry or fall apart like he wished. Lorenzo's eyes widened ever so slightly, and for a moment, neither of us moved. We were frozen in the moment, my arm outstretched, the gun still aimed at my father while Lorenzo stared at me in disbelief.

"You shot him... You shot your own father?" he stammered, his voice nowhere near as confident as it was previously.

My eyes dared him to underestimate me again. "I'm not the puppet you thought I'd be," I said, my voice low and emotionless. "And neither is he." I cocked my head towards my father who watched the pair of us intently.

Lorenzo's face twisted in anger, but there was something else there too. Respect or fear but I'd never know which. He'd never give it away. "You're full of surprises, Ana."

I was and I would continue to be. My grandfather taught me too damn well to succumb to someone like Lorenzo Ricci. He always said that no matter how scared you felt inside, you had to push it aside, slip on that mask, and let it remain there until you were ready to remove it. That's why I shot my father. I knew it would injure him but wouldn't cause any lasting damage. It was just enough to show my so-called husband who he was messing with.

"This isn't over," he snapped, snatching the gun from me.

"For tonight it is," I told him, having the upper hand with no plans of letting it go. "I suggest you call Red to drive you home because I am taking my father in your car." I sneered, grabbing the key off of the table that held an array of torture devices. "Have fun, did you?"

"Not enough." He scoffed, his eyes narrowing at me. "I will kill him, Ana. That's a promise."

"Then go on. Be my guest." I stepped to the side as he watched me with confused eyes. "The target is there, so what's stopping you?"

For once, he seemed lost for words. He clutched the gun in his hand, and I could practically see the wheels turning in his head.

"Lorenzo, if you thought I was brought up to be a yes, sir, no, sir, kind of woman, you're wrong. I was taught that, no matter the situation, to never show any signs of weakness. So, if you want to kill my father, go ahead, but you won't get the reaction you want from me." My voice was cold as I returned my attention back to my father.

"His days are numbered," Lorenzo threatened as I unlocked the chains around Victor's wrists, the welts and cuts seeping and sore.

"Somehow, I doubt they are," I challenged as my father pulled himself up. I didn't offer help or assistance. He could manage well enough on his own. "Unless you're planning on putting that bullet in my back, I suggest you put the gun down." My voice was steady and calm, but my heart hammered against my ribs.

"Take that fucker home," he instructed, his voice nothing more than a hiss, his words laced with hatred.

"Wow, I never thought I'd see the day where Lorenzo Ricci lets his wife call the shots on who lives and who dies." My father cackled, the sound grating and unhinged.

Lorenzo stood there silently. He didn't flinch at the words my father threw at him. His face was a mask of stone, his eyes cold and unreadable. I glanced at him briefly, my stomach twisting with fear and something else I couldn't quite work out. Without hesitation, Lorenzo raised the gun, his movements deliberate and precise. He fired the remaining bullet into my father's hand. It tore through flesh and bone before exiting as quickly as it had entered.

The warehouse erupted in a cacophony of noise—my father's scream, the echo of the gunshot, the clatter of the gun hitting the floor as Lorenzo dropped it, and the sound of my breath catching in my throat. I glanced at my father's hand, and as expected, it was a mess of blood and shattered bone.

"You didn't have to do that," I snapped.

Despite feeling slightly satisfied that someone was able to hurt my father and bring him and his ego crashing back down to earth, it still stirred something in me to see him broken and bleeding.

Lorenzo said nothing. He simply tore his gaze away from me and walked out, leaving a mess in his wake. I hated myself for watching him go, but for some reason, I couldn't stop. It wasn't until he was fully out of eyesight, and I heard my father's hiss, that I turned my head.

"You should have known better," I scoffed, reprimanding him for acting so careless. "You should've known he wouldn't hesitate."

My father looked up at me, his eyes wilder than before as he scoffed at my words. "I see it now. He wanted to use you to get to me. All he'll ever do is use you, just like I did to get what I wanted."

His words should have hurt. Fuck, they should have cut deep, but I felt nothing... Absolutely nothing. His words glided off me like water, and it felt good not to feel a damn thing. I was done being a pawn in their games. In anyone's game.

I retrieved a knife from the table of tricks as my father swayed slightly from blood loss.

"You know, I used to look up to you, wanted to be like you. I basically wanted to be you." I scoffed. "But now, now I see I'm already better than you ever were, are, or will be, and that kills you inside because you already know that." I pressed the tip of my knife into the gunshot wound on his shoulder, his sharp inhale pleasing me. "You may have all used me to get the upper hand in your game, but it ends now. For both of you." I pushed the blade in deeper, watching as the blood soaked through to his shirt. "You can make your own way home."

I threw the knife to the floor with a clatter before turning on my heel and disappearing into the cool evening air.

I was done.

Done with being a Fedorov.

Done with being a wife.

And done with being a fucking Ricci.

17

LORENZO

The dim glow of the bar's neon sign cast an eerie red hue over the street as I strode inside, heading straight for my office.

Red, Gino, Emmet, Nicolo and Finn sat huddled around the main table, sharing laughter, cigarettes, and whiskey. As they caught sight of me, they instantly knew something was off. Maybe the fact that I wasn't smiling gave me away. Their laughter stopped short, and they watched me with unease and curiosity.

"She shot him. She fucking shot him," I announced, dropping into the chair at my desk. I scanned their faces, their eyes wide with shock and mouths slightly agape. They processed the gravity of the news. The room filled with a heavy silence, the weight of my words hanging in the air like a storm cloud. "Anastacia, the woman I was so sure would break, shot her own father in the shoulder. Sure, there was no intent to kill, but she wanted to harm him. She wanted him to feel the pain she felt when he practically handed her to me." I sighed, running my hand through my tousled hair.

"Wow, she's badass." Nicolo clapped his hands together in delight, clearly wanting a black eye or worse.

"Shut up, Nic. You've known her less than twenty-four hours, you don't get an opinion."

Red's scarred face twisted in a grimace as he leaned forward, his elbows resting on the table. "We told you repeatedly that she was different. She's got a backbone. You can't just bend her to your will, and you know that."

My jaw clenched, anger bubbling just beneath the surface. "You were right," I admitted, my tone bitter at the fact I was wrong. "She's not easily breakable. She proved that tonight and every other time I've tried to control her." I paused. "I thought—I don't know what I thought I could do to her, but it's clear what I had planned will never happen. She's untameable and, most certainly, unpredictable.

"Maybe it's time to let her go," Gino suggested, his voice casual. His words carried a weight. "Some people aren't meant to be caged. No matter how much you want them to be."

My head snapped up as I succumbed to my anger. "Let her go?! Let her fucking go?! Do you hear yourself, Gino?!" I snapped. "She's mine. She's my wife."

"Alright, maybe it's time you reevaluate the whole plan, situation, whatever you want to call it." Emmet smiled, hoping to be the one to get through to me.

"Enlighten me. What would you do?" I questioned Emmet.

"If you want to kill Victor, go for it. By all means, have fun, but forget about tryin' to hurt her." He sighed. "Maybe try to give your marriage a go. Stop tryin' to own her and let her be your—"

"Don't say it." I narrowed my eyes as he continued.

"Let her be your equal." Emmet spoke confidently as if he knew he was saying the right thing.

"She'll never be my equal,"

Red echoed Gino's words from earlier. "Then let her go."

"No. That woman will never walk away from me. I won't let her." I stood, slapping my palms on my desk. "Let's go home. I'll deal with the fallout tomorrow."

"With your wife or her father?" Nicolo asked.

"I don't give a shit about the fallout with Victor." I didn't mention Ana, and of course, it didn't go unnoticed.

"Maybe try and talk to her. Make her understand your reasons for doing what you did," Red suggested, sounding too damn hopeful.

"Let's go," I ordered as they jumped to their feet.

THE DRIVE back to the house was a blur. I shut myself off to everyone, not wanting to hear whatever else they had to say. For the first time, my mind raced with thoughts of Anastacia. Her defiant gaze, her sharp tongue, and the way she always seemed to slip through my fingers no matter how tightly I gripped.

The second Red parked the car, I strode inside, my footsteps echoing against the marble. Maybe Red was right. Maybe I had to tell her everything and explain my reasons. Before I had time to second guess everything, my feet led me to her door, ready to help her understand.

I pushed her door open, instantly feeling as though something was off.

The room was empty.

Not just of her presence but of everything.

I flung her closet doors open, my blood boiling as I noted her clothes were gone. There was no trace of my wife in this room anymore. She'd taken everything. It was as if she'd never been in here at all.

All that was left was her wedding ring on the bedside table.

Rage surged through my veins as I stormed out of the room, marching straight to the office as I summoned my men. "Get in here, now." I demanded, my voice cutting through the silence.

They came running in after me, their faces twisted with confusion. "Check the cameras," I ordered, barely regaining control. "I want to know exactly when she left, how she left, and where she went."

As I paced the floor, Red rapidly pulled up the footage, his fingers flying over the keyboard on my desk. As the screens flickered to life, there was nothing. Nothing at all. No movement from her whatsoever. It didn't even show her coming home.

"How the fuck is that possible?" I queried, my fists clenching at my sides. "Everything from her room is gone. It's as if she was never here."

Gino stepped forwards, his voice remaining as calm as possible, but it was clear he was worried. "She's gotten around those cameras before, she could have done it again."

Finn exhaled as he burst through the door. "Nobody saw her enter or leave."

"She must have had help. I've been away from her for an hour tops. She couldn't have managed all this alone." I smashed my fist into the desk, my knuckles cracking as they hit the wood. "Find her," I snarled. "I don't care what it takes. Bring my wife back to me."

"Already on it," Emmet assured as he exited the room with everyone except for Red.

"On me, Red. We're paying the Fedorov's a visit." I had no idea why I thought she'd be there, not after what happened tonight, but I'd give it a go.

RED SPED towards Anastacia's old home, the tires screeching with every turn. I knew he, along with some of the other men, had grown close to her. They developed a soft spot for her despite my warnings.

"Do you really think she left?" he asked.

"That's the only explanation, Red." I muttered. "If she thinks she can walk away from me, she's wrong."

"We'll bring her home. No matter where she is, we'll find her." He sounded so sure, so confident in his own words.

Once we reached Victor's house, I barely waited for the car to come to a standstill before I exited and raced up the steps to the door. My fist collided with the glass. It opened within seconds. The guards at the gate had probably announced our arrival.

"What do you want?!" Florence snarled. "You've done enough damage tonight," she hissed, her voice trembling with anger.

She wasn't as strong as Anastacia.

Anastacia's voice never trembled, never faltered, no matter how scared or angry she was. Florence's eyes narrowed as she watched me intently.

"Where is she?!" I demanded. "My wife doesn't belong here anymore."

"You shot her father. You could have killed him, and now you have the nerve to come here shouting your demands?"

"Where the fuck is she?" I bellowed as Red appeared beside me.

Victor finally showed his face. "She's not here." His hand and shoulder were stitched up and bandaged tightly. "I haven't seen her since she left me in that warehouse."

She left him? She didn't care enough to get him home safely? Wow... I really did underestimate her.

"What do you mean she's not here?! I'm not in the mood for your games, Victor." I glanced around, not sure what the hell I was looking for. "She has to be here."

"My own daughter shot me, Lorenzo. Do you really think she'd come back here?" Victor questioned. "If she left you then that's on her own accord."

"Fuck off, Victor. She hasn't left me." I didn't know why, but I was certain she'd never truly walk out on me.

"Maybe she's at your mother's?" Red suggested, already calling her number.

"Lorenzo, my daughter knows what she does and doesn't want. If she chose to leave you, we had no hand in that." Victor responded. The lack of care and worry was apparent.

"Do you not care where she is? Would you only care if it were Miles?" I asked as I caught Red's gaze. He shook his head.

She wasn't with my mother either.

"Do you want me to look for her, Victor?" Chad piped up from behind him at the door.

"No, she's just throwing a tantrum and wanting attention. You won't waste your time," Victor snapped, stepping in front of Florence. "You used her to get what you wanted."

"As did you. You can pretend you're innocent in all this, but you're the worst." I scoffed, turning my back to him and readying myself to leave and turn the whole damn city on its head for her.

"You're just like your father. Use and abuse, take and betray," he spat before slamming the door behind him.

I was about to storm up the steps when Red's voice stopped me, bringing my thoughts back to my wife.

"She's not at the graveyard. She's not at your mother's. She's nowhere, Lorenzo." Red sighed, making his next call.

"I don't want to hear it. She didn't just disappear. Call every hotel, every hospital. Leave no stone unturned, do you understand?"

"You almost sound like you care."

"Not now, Red." I turned to face the house. "I will not lose someone else because of Victor Fedorov."

18

ANASTACIA

My eyes slowly fluttered open, and I was immediately assaulted by the overpowering stench of rot and decay, a vile and putrid odour that seemed to cling stubbornly to the back of my throat. Attempting to shift my position, I quickly realised that my wrists and ankles were tightly bound to a rickety wooden chair, positioning me right in the heart of a grimy, clearly abandoned room. The coarse rope dug painfully into my skin, leaving raw, bloody marks as I struggled against it. For a moment, I squeezed my eyes shut, before forcing them open once more. That's when I saw it. The walls were plastered with pictures of me, covering every inch like a horrific, personal wallpaper. A chill raced down my spine as I realised the unsettling truth: this person had been disturbingly close, even watching me as I slept.

If this was some fucked up game from the man who called himself my husband, I swear I'd kill him.

The sound system, ancient and crackling, blared my own voice on an endless loop. My conversations with family, snippets of laughter, and whispered inside jokes with friends ricocheted around the room, creating a warped symphony that seemed to taunt me with each echo. It felt as though my entire life had been meticulously dissected and cruelly put on display for an invisible audience. My eyes darted frantically around the dim, oppressive space. Cobwebs, like ghostly veils, dangled from the rotting ceiling, swaying gently in the stale air. The threadbare carpet beneath me was stained with dark, ominous patches of blood, and the windows were heavily boarded, allowing only the faintest slivers of light to seep through. My mind raced wildly, struggling to piece together the fragmented memories of how I had ended up trapped in this nightmarish hellhole.

And then it hit me like a wave. I remembered.

I'd just returned home, feeling drained over everything that unfolded at the warehouse when there was a bang on the front door. Upon opening it, I found three men, their faces hidden behind masks.

"Who the fuck are you?" I snapped, showing no weakness.

But that wasn't enough. No matter how strong I was or how calculated the movements were, the second I reached for my knife was the second everything went black.

The creak of the door jolted me back to the present, as a shaft of light from the hallway cut through the room. The same trio of men entered, their presence as unsettling as before. Their faces were obscured by masks that left only their eyes visible, eyes that shone with a disturbing delight at seeing me awake. Each of them was tall and lean, their frames exuding a wiry strength, and their movements were slow and deliberate, like those of predators closing in on unsuspecting prey. My heart pounded in my chest, a frantic drumbeat that clashed with my outwardly defiant expression. Their voices, deep and gravelly, whispered amongst themselves, carrying a familiarity that gnawed at the edges of my memory.

"If it isn't Tweedledee, Tweedledum, and the third wheel," I taunted, my voice steady despite the small amount of fear that ate away at my insides. I knew better than to show weakness, especially to lowlives like these. I knew how to withstand torture, no matter who it was at the hands of.

The man in the middle stepped closer, his leather-gloved hand curling into a fist at his side. “You think you’re so funny, don’t you?” he snarled.

“I mean, do you want an honest answer, dickhead?” I smirked.

His eyes narrowed behind his mask as his fist collided with my jaw, sending my head snapping to the side.

Son of a bitch!

It was at that moment that I knew this wasn’t one of Lorenzo’s games. I couldn’t imagine he’d allow someone to hurt me like that, but then again, I didn’t know him at all.

Pain exploded through my skull, but I refused to let them see me wince. Instead, I laughed. A defiant, mocking sound that filled the room. “Is that it?” I teased. “That’s your best shot?”

The other men exchanged a glance, their eyes darkened with anger as I glared at the bastard in front of me. I didn’t know if they had orders to hurt me or if they had to refrain from it, but I loved adding fuel to the fire.

The man on the left stepped forward, his fist crashing into my stomach. I gasped as my body convulsed, the air knocked from my lungs. I doubled over for a second, trying to compose my breathing, but no matter the pain I felt, I refused to cry out.

“Stop it,” the third man hissed, warning the others. “We were given strict instructions not to hurt her.”

But there was no point. The two who stood before me didn’t listen, and it was clear they didn’t care about the orders they were given. The man who punched me in the jaw fisted my hair, yanking my head back so my eyes were forced to meet his beady ones. “You think you’re better than us, don’t you?” He sneered, his breath hot on my face as it travelled through the fabric of his mask. “You think you can run that pretty mouth and get away with it?”

“You’re nothing. You’re just one of the lapdogs. You’re nothing special,” I said, already knowing what would come next. “You’re pathetic.”

His fist slammed into my face again, but that wasn't enough. He landed another blow, splitting my lip. Blood trickled down my chin. My vision blurred, but I refused to close my eyes. I refused to give them the satisfaction of seeing me break.

"That's enough! Fuck!" the third shouted yet again, trying to regain control of the situation.

The other man finally stopped, his chest heaving as he caught his breath. My body slumped in the chair as my head lolled to the side. Blood stained my skin as bruises bloomed across my skin. I might have been a mess, but my spirit was unbroken.

"You took it too far. He's going to be pissed," the third muttered, but the damage was done.

"I hope he puts a bullet in your head." I coughed. "And if he doesn't, I fucking will." I laughed sarcastically to piss them off, which earned me a backhand across my cheek.

"Get out. Now," the third demanded as he shoved one and two out the door.

I listened to their footsteps as they echoed down the hallway. And then, I finally gave into the pain I was feeling.

My body ached with every breath, but I was far from defeated. I would survive this just as I did everything else. I let my mind wander, thinking of ways to escape. This was just another challenge to overcome. I had made it through worse.

Being married to Lorenzo was one.

I succumbed to exhaustion, my eyes closing and blocking everything out except the soundtrack of my voice and the many questions that raced through my mind.

Who was the bastard who wanted me here?

Would Lorenzo even look for me or was I just a loose end he no longer needed?

I had so many questions and for the first time, I had no answers.

A SUDDEN, shocking splash of ice cold water jolted me awake. I gasped as my eyes flew open to meet one of the three masked faces. This time, he was alone, and I knew exactly which one it was.

His breath smelled of cheap vodka and cigarettes, making my stomach churn. He loomed over me, his bulky frame blocking the faint light from the single bare bulb hanging overhead. His fingers clenched the bucket handle as the remnants of water sloshed around at the bottom.

"Wakey, wakey, princess," he sneered. "I think it's time to play some more, don't you agree?"

"How about we play fetch? Do you have a ball?" I teased. "You know, since you're pretty much a lapdog."

His hand shot out, his fingers curled into a fist as I braced myself for the blow, my heart pounding against my ribs. But just as his fist was about to connect with my cheek, a loud crash echoed in the room. And just like that, he froze.

"Get the fuck out," a deep voice boomed from the doorway, masked man number three coming into view.

He was taller and broader than the others. He strode into the room, shoving him aside.

"Boss didn't want a hair on her head harmed and look at her," he snarled. "She's a mess!"

"Wow, thanks for the compliment." I said, letting my head fall back as the ice water dripped down my front.

He never took his threatening eyes off me as he exited the room. Slamming the door behind him, I was left with the man who seemed to call the shots. He approached me, carrying a tray of something vile looking.

He set the tray down beside me. I cast my gaze downward, clocking what was on it. Stale bread, a chuck of cold meat, and a bowl of what looked like watery soup. I clenched my jaw, trying to suppress the rising urge to gag. He grabbed the spoon, scooping up a mouthful of soup. Before I had time to react, his gloved hand cupped my chin, forcing my head up.

"Eat," he commanded, his breath warm against my cheek.

My eyes narrowed, defiance sparking within me. No matter how hungry I was, I would never eat something they prepared. I refused to open my mouth, as he growled in frustration, his grip tightening on my chin.

"Why can't you just do as you're told?" he asked with a sneer, unable to keep his cool.

In one swift movement, I bit him, clamping down hard on the flesh between his thumb and index finger. He yelped, letting a sharp intake of breath escape him. He jerked his hand back, but I held on, my teeth sinking in deeper.

"Bitch!" he bellowed, the spoon clattering to the floor as he pried my mouth open. He stumbled back, cradling his hand as his mask slipped slightly.

"I was trying to help you," he spat. "I was trying to keep those animals away from you. I was protecting you for my boss."

"I don't need your protection," I hissed. "I don't need anyone's protection."

"Not even your husband's?" He laughed. "Poor bastard thinks you've left him." He leaned into me, his mouth beside my ear. "But that's a story for Boss to tell you, and boy, did we execute the plan to perfection." He broke the stare first as I tried to understand what he meant about Lorenzo thinking I'd left him.

"He'll find me, you know." I sounded so damn certain, but I was anything but.

"Sure he will." He scoffed. "But until that *doesn't* happen, eat something," he said, picking up the spoon that was decorated by lint and whatever else lived in the carpet.

"No."

"Suit yourself." He turned his back to me before pausing for a second. "He won't come, Anastacia. Remember, you were nothing but a pawn in his game. Boss had us save you. You should be thankful."

And with that he was gone, leaving the stale food out of reach as his words played on repeat like a broken record.

He won't come, Anastacia.

How he said my name was so familiar. Almost as if I'd heard it a thousand times. I racked my brain over and over until it dawned on me...

He worked for my father.

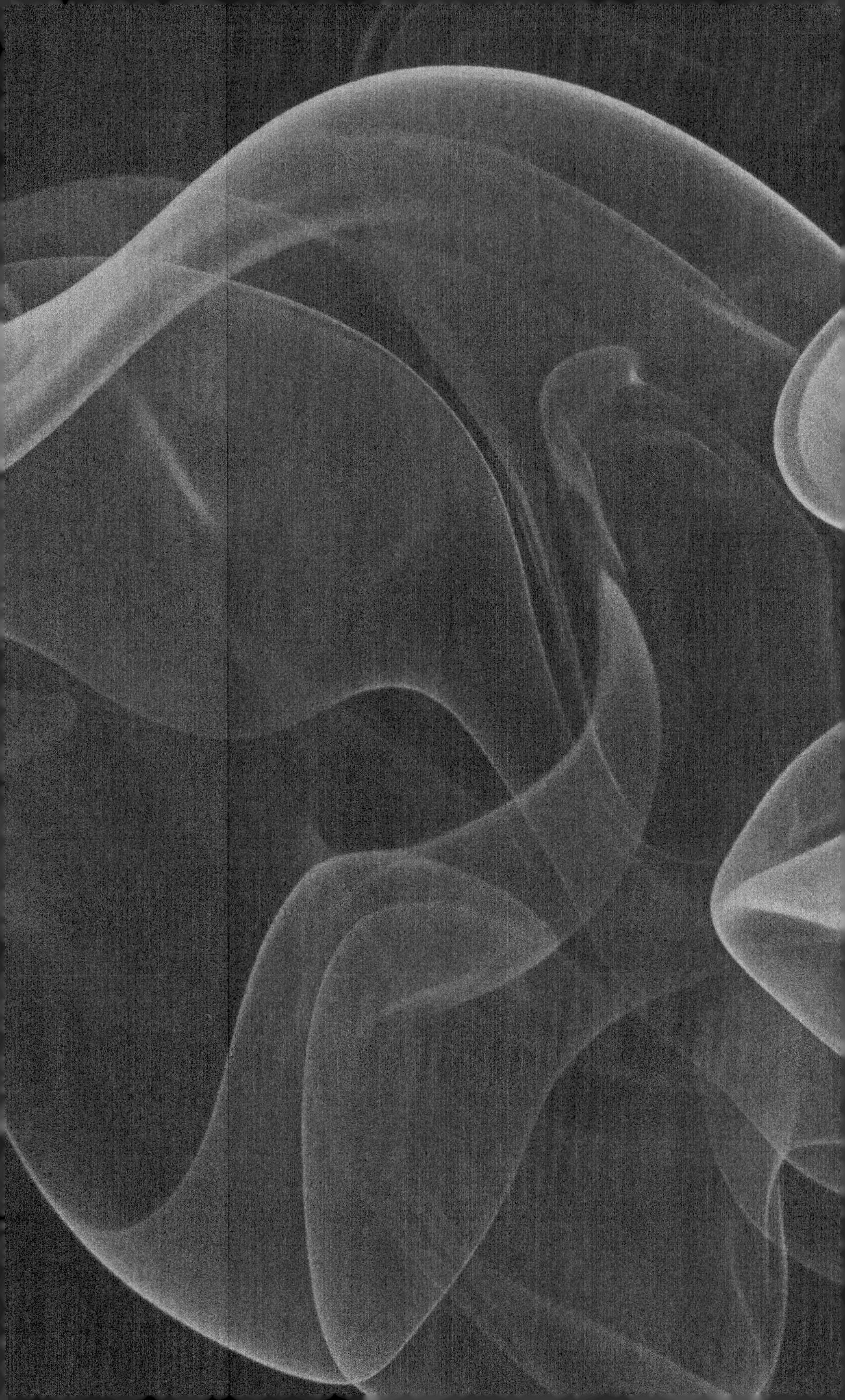

19

LORENZO

It had been a week.

A whole fucking week since I last saw my wife.

The dim glow of the security monitors illuminated the desk as I scoured the CCTV footage for the umpteenth time. I'd lost count how many times I watched it over the past week, looking for something that wasn't there. I'd torn apart every inch of her room, even every inch of mine. I'd had the grounds searched repeatedly but there was fuck all.

She wasn't the type to just walk away. She'd shown that on many occasions. I tightened my hold on her dainty wedding band that my hand housed as I rewound the same footage. Maybe I had missed something. There had to be a crack, a glitch, a fucking clue.

"Renz, I think it's time you stop." Nicolo sighed as he entered the office. "There's nothing on there."

"There has to be something, Nic. Something I've carelessly missed." I pinched the bridge of my nose, frustrated and borderline angry.

"Listen, how well do you know that guard at the gate? Kip, I think his name is," Nicolo asked, tapping his index finger against his lips.

I may not have seen Nicolo much, or even spoken to him, but he had always been a good judge of character. "He's been with us a good couple of years, why?"

"He's been acting strange this past week. It's clear he's on edge whilst trying to hide something," he muttered. "Something's off with him."

My head snapped up, my eyes locking with Nicolo's. "Define off."

He shifted his weight as his hand rubbed the back of his neck. "He's jumpy. Keeps looking over his shoulder. His drinking has increased at all hours of the day like he's trying to drink away guilt. I could be wrong, but he seems sloppy, and I know you don't employ sloppy." Nicolo had watched the team undetected for the past week at my request. There had been nothing to report until now.

I knew exactly what had to be done. I'd make him speak, I was damn sure of it.

"Bring that fucker to the warehouse," I demanded. "I'll meet you there."

"Gladly."

I STROLLED INTO THE WAREHOUSE, the same one I'd last seen Anastacia in. Kip was already there. I expected him to be in the same chair Victor was, but I was welcomed by a completely different sight.

Red had chained him to the ceiling, his head hanging limp as his body swayed on his tiptoes.

"Chair not good enough for him, huh?" I chuckled, flicking my cigarette onto the floor.

"Course it's not. He knows something about our Ana." Red sneered. "Gino was the one who said I couldn't hang him yet."

"Feel free after we get the information we need." I gave him the green light to end the bastard if he was involved in something he shouldn't have been. I approached Kip, as he struggled to look at me.

That wouldn't do

I fisted Kip's hair, forcing his head back as he gasped. "Wake up."

"Boss," he croaked, his voice trembling already. "I didn't—"

I didn't give him a chance to finish. I gripped his neck, squeezing just enough for him to still be able to talk. "Where is my wife, Kip?" I demanded with a storm brewing in my chest.

"I don't know, Boss. I swear—"

"Wrong fucking answer." I tightened my hold on his neck, the chains rattling from above as he thrashed beneath my hand. "Don't lie to me." I pulled my knife from my waistband, holding it against his cheek. "You were the last person to see her. You're the last link," I growled.

He whimpered as my blade sunk slowly into his flesh. "They blackmailed me. I had no choice," he cried.

"Who?"

"I don't know," he choked, but my grip remained the same. "The men who came to the house wore masks, all three of them." He struggled against my hold, but I didn't care. "The one who blackmailed me wasn't there. I've never seen him."

"And you just watched them take her?!" I sliced my knife from his cheekbone to the corner of his mouth in one swift move.

"I was blackmailed." He swallowed hard.

"What did they have over you? What was so fucking bad that you failed at your job? That you let them take my fucking wife?!"

"I m-messed up!" he spat, blood spurting from his mouth and onto my shirt. "I was skimming off the top of your shipments, making extra money of my own."

"And now my wife is paying the price for your stupidity?!" I drove my blade into his shoulder, his piercing cry filling the room.

"They told me they'd hurt her if I didn't cooperate. They promised if I just let them go, she'd be safe," he whimpered.

"And you're sure of that, are you? You're sure they haven't harmed a fucking hair on her head?!" I was past angry, my blood boiling at the thought of Ana being hurt in any way.

He sniffled. "They promised."

The prick was a mess, a mixture of blood, sweat, tears, and who knows what else.

"Oh, they promised, did they?" I growled. "Well, that's alright then, as long as they promised." I removed my blade from his shoulder, sinking it into his stomach next. "Are you that stupid?"

"I'm sorry. I—" He yelped, the pain radiating through him. "I l-looped the footage to make it look as though she dodged the cameras or as if she never came home."

"And her stuff?!" I asked, unable to remain calm at what he was telling me.

"They took it all. Made it seem like she upped and left."

Images of three masked bastards in my wife's room, touching every single one of her belongings played in my mind. The thought of killing each one of them spurred me on.

"Red, hand me that cigar cutter," I demanded, holding out my hand to Red as he placed the cutter into my palm. "You betrayed me, Kip." I slid the cutter down his pinky finger. Right down to the second knuckle as I clamped them just enough to bite into his skin. "You let them take what's mine."

"I'm s-sorry, Boss," he sobbed. "I'm so sorry." His eyes filled with more tears, but I had no sympathy, no guilt. I felt nothing.

"Tell me everything. Every word of every single conversation. I want every detail," I ordered.

"I don't remember." His voice trailed off as blood seeped out of him.

I clamped the cutter down on his finger, slicing it off before he could anticipate it happening. "Every single time you don't remember, you'll lose a finger, and then I'll move onto toes. So I suggest you think hard."

"Please, don't... I can't remember every detail. Please," he pleaded.

"Losing fingers and toes doesn't seem to be motivating you as much as I expected." I pondered before knowing what to do. "Red, you continue cutting one by one." I handed Red the bloody cutter as he stepped towards Kip with a sinister smile.

I retrieved the blowtorch from Finn's hand. He held it like he already knew what I had in mind. It flicked to life in my hand as I admired Red cutting off Kip's third finger, his screams piercing through me.

"I don't think he's going to take all ten." Red muttered before cutting off the fourth finger, leaving just the thumb left on Kip's right hand.

"O-one had a s-snake tattoo on his n-neck," he panted through the pain, only just managing to get his words out. "It was burned o-off."

"And the others?" I asked, trailing the flame over his forearm as the flame deliciously licked his skin.

"Fuck!" He screamed through the pain. "I d-don't know. N-nothing was v-visible," he said, trembling through ragged breaths.

"Where is she, Kip?" I asked, giving him one last chance.

"I d-don't know. T-they didn't g-give any information on t-that."

"Then it looks like I have no use for you." I threw the torch to the floor, pressing my blade to his neck. "You should have paid more attention."

I was about to slice his neck clean open when my phone vibrated in my pocket. "Red, keep cutting until I see who is interrupting."

Pulling it from my pocket, I swiped open the message from an unknown number. I read them, and they were enough to send me over the edge.

> Ah, Lorenzo Ricci, it looks as though you now know your wife didn't leave you. But maybe it's a blessing in disguise that she's no longer yours since you never truly wanted her anyway.

Another message appeared on the screen, but this time there were no words. It was an image. An image of my wife.

Bloody, beaten, and bruised.

Her hair hung around her, limp and matted with blood. Her wrists were bound so tightly, I could see the damage on her skin. Her lip was split in two places, and her eyes were barely open.

> She's a defiant little thing, though, I have to admit. She never wants to do as she's told, but don't worry, we've taken great care of her.

Taken great care of her?! Look at her! My heart pounded like a drum in my chest, each beat echoing with an intensity that was foreign to me. An unfamiliar fire ignited within me, a mix of rage and helplessness that surged through my veins. I could feel the heat rising in my face, my breath coming in short, sharp bursts. Every fibre of my being screamed for justice, a fury so intense I could almost taste it.

> She doesn't belong to you anymore.

> Don't bother trying to find her. She's his now.

"Motherfuckers!" I roared, gripping my phone tightly as the messages stopped. All eyes landed on me, including Kip's.

"Mate, what is it?" Gino questioned, snatching the phone from my hand. It took him a split second to scan the messages. "Shit."

"Who the fuck has her, Kip?!" I demanded. "This isn't a game anymore! They've hurt her, beaten her to within an inch of her life," I seethed.

"I-I don't know," he whimpered. "I'm s-sorry." His apology was useless and pathetic, one I didn't wish to hear again.

I didn't give him a chance to say anything else. I strode back to where he hung, not thinking twice as I sliced my blade across his neck, making one clean, perfect cut. He spluttered for a few seconds before his head drooped. "Get rid of him," I said. Red and Finn were more than happy to oblige. "Meet me at the house once it's done."

"Where we off to?" Gino asked as he followed me out of the warehouse.

"Victor's."

I STRODE up the steps of Victor's house, not stopping until I hammered on the door. Within minutes, Florence appeared, pulling it open, her smile fading the second she saw me.

"Where is he?" I asked, not in the mood for pleasantries.

She scowled. "I don't see how that is any of your business, Lorenzo."

"I won't ask again, Florence,"

"His office." She sighed. "Is it about Anastacia?"

I didn't answer. She didn't deserve to know. They didn't give a shit before, so why now? I stormed down the corridor towards Victor's office. It was about time he realised all this happened because of him.

I kicked his door in, four pairs of eyes honed in on me, including his.

"Ricci, you seem to have lost your manners." Victor scoffed, sipping his whiskey, the cigar smoke from the ashtray surrounding him.

My eyes scanned the men as their eyes darted between Victor and me. And, of course, Chad was there.

I slid my phone across Victor's desk, ignoring his last smartass comment. It took him a second to realise what he was looking at, but then the penny dropped. He was looking at his daughter. His fingers tightened on the phone, his face falling as he took in all the details.

"Still think she's seeking attention?" I questioned, snatching my phone back from his bandaged fingers.

"I'll help you find her," he said quickly and without hesitation. "Whatever it takes, I'll—"

"Shut up, Victor," I snapped, cutting him off. He flinched, something I had never seen. Chad stood to interject, but I didn't even warrant him with a glance. "You can sit the fuck down, too. This has nothing to do with you, you useless piece of shit." I slammed my fist on Victor's desk. "You thought she was craving attention and being dramatic."

Victor opened his mouth to protest, but I cut the bastard off, yet again.

"You didn't want to help before, and I most certainly don't need your help now," I sneered. "You've done enough damage already."

"I've always tried to protect her! How the hell is this my fault?!" He stood, his chair tumbling to the floor.

"Maybe you need to take a good hard look at who you employ then, Victor, since one of the men that took her had a snake tattoo on his neck. Fair enough, it was burned off, but that's your mark. *Your* fucking mark, Victor!"

"That's absurd!" It was clear he was in denial, his face a picture as if he couldn't believe anyone on his team, past or present, would betray him.

"There's nothing absurd about it. Someone you banished took

my wife as some sort of vendetta against you," I sneered. "You haven't made one move since seeing Anastacia's photo," I said. "Actually, that's a lie. You stood up. Well done, father of the year." I clapped my hands in a sarcastic gesture as his eyes narrowed. "You really don't care about her, do you?"

"And what? You do?!" he spat. "You don't care about my daughter."

I pulled out my gun and held it to his head, right between the eyes, not backing down. "I will find my wife without your help, Victor," I could feel Chad's gun pointed at my back. Victor gave him orders with his eyes to lower it. "When I find her, and trust me I *will* find her, you will stay away from us both." I informed him.. "Don't make me regret not pulling this trigger tonight."

"You can't keep me away from my daughter."

"I can and I will. You're only bothered about yourself." I tucked my gun back into my waistband and turned to leave, not wanting to spend another minute with him.

"I won't stay away from her," he called from behind me as I paused at the door.

"Yes, you will. Otherwise, the next search will be for your body."

I exited the house, not stopping to speak to Florence who stood there unaware of what was going on.

"Boss." Gino nodded. "How'd it go?"

"Victor is a waste of time and space. We don't need him." I slid into the passenger seat.

"Then what do we need?" he asked.

"I need to find my wife and bring her home."

"And then?" he pressed.

"And then I'll be the best person I can be for her." Finding her would be my turning point.

"Well, it's about damn time." Gino smiled as he relaxed into the driver's seat.

It *was* about time. I didn't know if what happened had knocked some sense into me or whether she had slowly wormed her way in, but I'd been an absolute bastard to her. Sure, she wasn't innocent in all this either, but she never wanted this marriage. She never even wanted me, and of course, I made everything a thousand times worse just by existing.

Anastacia Ricci was the only person who I knew could save me. And just as well, I would be the one to save her.

20

ANASTACIA

I didn't know how long I had been in this hellhole for, but it was long enough to not want to look at the stupid photos on the wall or listen to that ridiculous soundtrack of my voice and laughter. My body ached from the bruises I received from those masked fuckers, but no matter how sore I was, my spirit remained unbroken. My grandfather's voice echoed in my mind repeatedly. *Pain is temporary, Moy voin. It's what you do with it that defines you.*

The door creaked open, and my eyes adjusted quickly to the bright light that streamed in. My gaze locked onto the silhouette of a fourth man. I knew he was new because he was built smaller than the others. He was careful with his moves, something the other three weren't.

There was something incredibly familiar about the way he moved. About the way he tilted his head. Even the confidence in his stride. He stepped fully into the room, his mask concealing his identity.

"Still holding out?" His voice was deep, laced with malice. A shiver ran down my spine. "Your dear *dedushka* would be so incredibly proud," he taunted. I did tell them to behave, but it looks like you were the one who didn't. You brought this on yourself." He waved his hand up and down my body, blaming me for the beatings I had received.

"You're nothing but a coward," I sneered, keeping my voice steady. "Hiding behind a mask is really brave, isn't it? Are you afraid?" I chuckled, no longer caring how many punches or kicks I took.

He laughed, a low, guttural sound that seemed to reverberate through the room. He stepped closer, and his shadow loomed over me. "Me? Afraid? I'm not the one captured and tied up like this, am I?" He paused for a second. His gloved hand reached out, stroking my cheek. My body stiffened as his leather-clad fingers caressed my cheek.

"Then take it off," I demanded. "If you're not afraid then show me who you truly are instead of hiding behind a piece of fabric."

He hesitated for a moment, his gloved hands hovering in the air between us. "Fine, but say please first."

"Get fucked." I scoffed, fighting against the rope that restrained me.

"You always did have a dirty mouth, didn't you, Anastacia?" he purred, and it hit me. I knew that voice. The way he said my name was distinct, and I instantly felt sick. I knew but I couldn't get my head around why.

With a dramatic flourish, he pulled off his mask, revealing a face that made my heart stop as he confirmed my suspicions.

"C-Chad," I whispered, my voice barely audible as my breath hitched in my throat.

He smirked, his eyes glistening with triumph. "Surprise." He leaned in closer, his breath hot against my ear. "Didn't you realise how I watched you, Ana?" He grazed my earlobe with his teeth, making my body go rigid. "And not just because your father asked me to. I did it because you were mine in my mind long before you were mine in the flesh." He pulled away, and bile climbed my throat.

A knot tightened in my stomach, twisting and turning as if it had a life of its own. My heart raced, and a cold sweat prickled my skin. I clenched my jaw and took shallow breaths, desperately trying to steady the tremor in my hands and calm the rising tide of disbelief that threatened to overwhelm me. He was my father's right hand, a man who I called my friend. But he wasn't really. He was just a stranger. A monster cloaked in familiarity.

"This room," he continued. "It's a shrine to you. The photographs on the walls? I took them. Every whisper in that soundtrack? Your voice—that I recorded over the years. I've crafted this space just for you, Anastacia. A place where you're mine and mine alone."

"You're sick," I stated, the rope biting harder and deeper into my flesh. "Lorenzo—"

"Lorenzo isn't coming for you." He laughed, resting his hands on the arms of the chair beside mine. "He's already moved on and found himself a new toy to play with. You're yesterday's news. But not to me. To me, you're everything."

"You're lying." My heart pounded in my chest, but I refused to let him see the fear I suddenly felt. "Lorenzo would never—"

"Never what?" he interrupted. "Never forget about you? The woman he used as the main pawn in his game with your father? Never find someone else?" he spat. "Open your fucking eyes. His world won't stop because you're trapped in here." He cocked his head to the side. "Lorenzo thinks you packed your stuff and disappeared. We made it look as though you walked out on him. Even left your ring on the side table, too."

I glanced down at my ring finger, and of course, it was empty. They did a number on the pair of us. They tried to make Lorenzo believe I'd give up so easily. I didn't know if he did believe it. I just had to hope he was clever enough to know I wouldn't have walked out. That, no matter how shitty our marriage started out, I wouldn't have given it up without a fight, because deep down, it could work... We just had to make it.

I closed my eyes, shutting out his words and presence. I couldn't look into those emerald green eyes I had looked into many times before. I felt him lean into me, his obsession becoming a suffocating weight. He traced his tongue along my cheek, leaving a wet path in its wake as his thumb brushed roughly across my lips. I shuddered, my body recoiling from his touch, but the bastard held me firmly in place.

"You are mine now," he whispered. "I'm going to make you see that, whether you like it or not."

The room seemed to close in around me as his words echoed in my mind. As the air became thick with his scent, his voice, and the weight of his gaze. My mind raced as my grandfather's words kept repeating in my head. For the first time, I didn't know if I could endure this. Chad's obsession was a different kind of torture. It was relentless, psychological, and inescapable.

"Who are they?" I asked, referring to the three masked men.

"Men you know. Men your father banished and were made to feel as if they were nothing." He paced the room. "Men who are taking their anger out on you rather than him."

"More cowards then." I said. "Can't go up against someone untied and able?"

He stopped before me, his backhand colliding with my face as I fought against the force. I managed to keep my head upright. He stepped back as I let out the breath I held. "We will see how long your defiance lasts." His voice was cold and distant. "I hate to hurt that pretty face, but I'll allow it until you see sense."

"You may as well have them beat me to death then because I'll never give myself to you," I bellowed, my throat hoarse from refusing the food and drink they had offered me.

"I will never let it get that far, angel." He strummed his finger against his lips. "Until then, I'll leave you to enjoy your stay here. This room was made for you, after all."

"I'll never be yours, Chad."

He was on me in seconds, his hand gripping my throat as I fought against him. "You *will* be mine. You already are. You just need to see it." He tightened his hold as I tried to swallow. "Now, I need to get back to playing the perfect right-hand to your father. We wouldn't want him to suspect something amiss."

I managed to free myself from his hold as I reared my head back, head butting the bastard in his nose. Blood spurted on my skin, but all I did was smile as I watched him clutch his face.

"You'll regret that, Anastacia!" he cried out before storming towards the door.

"I'll never regret anything." I scowled.

The door slammed shut behind him as my breath suddenly came out in ragged gasps. The soundtrack continued its endless loop, my own voice and laughter haunting me from the speakers. I tried to block out the images, the sounds, and the memory of Chad's touch.

I couldn't shake the feeling that this was just the beginning. His obsession was a fire, and I was the fuel. I had no idea what he had planned next, but one thing I was sure of was that I would never make it easy for him.

Pain is temporary, Moy voin. It's what you do with it that defines you.

I would endure.

I would survive.

And one way or another, with or without Lorenzo's help, I'd find a way out.

I'd escape.

21

LORENZO

The rain hammered against the windows of Anastacia's bedroom, mimicking the relentless storm that raged inside me. Days had bled into nights as I scoured the city for traces of Ana. It took this happening for me to realise that her presence was more important to me than I ever knew. Her laughter, her scent, the way she occupied every room with a smile—until she saw me, anyway. But I missed her. There was a dull, painful ache inside of me, one I had never felt before. Everything was just so damn empty.

"Lorenzo!" Nicolo called from the kitchen.

I exited the room, making my way to where he stood, drenched and disheveled, his usual composure shattered.

"Any news?" I asked, feeling somewhat hopeful.

Nicolo shook his head. "Not about Ana, but Chad... He's got a nasty cut across his nose. A deep one, too, and I know that isn't Victor's style."

"What are you suggesting?"

"Finn and I have been tailing him. Something just felt off when you mentioned him and how he was with Ana." He sighed.

"Carry on. I don't have all night, Nic," I told him. I loved the guy, but boy, did he take forever to get to the point.

"He's been disappearing in the middle of the night. At times when Victor won't notice him gone. It's as if he has his own agenda."

My mind raced. I knew he was a snake, but this... This was some next level betrayal, obsessive shit.

"Did you follow him?"

"We started to but we didn't want him to catch on. Not yet, anyway." He lit a cigarette, pouring himself a whiskey.

"Right. I want you to rig his car with one of the best tracking devices you can build," I nodded, knowing he could do it with his eyes closed. "If it means no sleep, so be it. I need her home, and I need Chad finished if he's involved."

"You have my word." Nicolo smiled.

"I need you to go undetected. Follow him closely until you can get to his car. If he catches on, he could do something to Ana."

"I promise he won't know a thing." He finished off his drink and headed to a hidden room at the back of the house.

I'm coming, Ana.

That's a promise.

***

Two nights later, we followed the tracker's signal that brought us to a secluded, abandoned house that looked as though it would blow over in the bloody wind.

"What if she's not in there?" Red asked, carefully getting out of the car.

"She is. I have a feeling." I drew my gun from my waistband as we slowly made our way up to the house, broken glass crunching beneath our feet.

"The door's open," Nicolo whispered as we noticed shadows dancing on the walls inside.

We slipped into the abandoned house, our footsteps silent despite the creaking underfoot. My heart pounded in my chest, a relentless drumbeat of fury and dread. I could feel the weight of every passing second. I could only hope Ana was here. All signs pointed right here. The thought of her in this godforsaken place sent a spike of adrenaline through me, sharpening my senses.

My men moved with practiced silence as they scanned every corner. Each movement they made was fluid and deadly, and I trusted them implicitly with helping me bring my wife home.

The first masked man appeared from the shadows, his breath visible in the cold air. Red grabbed him with a sharp, swift move, pressing his body against the rotting wall beside us.

"Where's my wife?" I demanded as Red's hold on his neck tightened.

"I don't know who your wife is." He chuckled sarcastically, and it was at that very moment I knew she was here. *Thank fuck.*

"Wrong answer," Red sneered as he sliced his neck open with ease and grace.

We watched him slump to the floor as heavy footsteps came from our right. "Mate, stop messing around, where are you?" the second masked prick called as he appeared in the doorway. "Shit," he gasped.

I pulled the trigger the second I saw him, precise as it pierced his skull right between the eyes. The third was next. He tried to retreat, tried to warn whoever else was hidden in this shit hole, but Gino was fast. He was already on him, his grip like iron around the man's neck. One quick snap, and it was over.

"This way," I directed as we headed down the corridor.

We reached a door that was ajar. Hushed, harsh words came from inside, and I recognised the voice instantly.

"He's not coming for you, Anastacia."

Chad.

I kicked the door open, and his body stilled, sensing we were behind him and not his men.

"Get away from my wife," I warned as my eyes landed on Ana.

Her petite frame was bound to a chair in the middle of the room, her body a canvas of blood and bruises. Her hair hung limp around her shoulders, matted with crimson. Her once vivid blue eyes were barely open, clouded with pain and exhaustion. The sight tore at my insides, a raw, aching wound threatening to consume me.

Chad fisted her hair, forcing her head up before pressing a knife to her neck. A sick and twisted grin played on his lips. His beady eyes shone with malice as he pressed the blade into her skin. "She's mine, Lorenzo," he sneered. "You'll never have her again."

I tightened my hold on my gun, but I had to tread carefully, especially with Ana in danger. I kept my eyes trained on her and the knife that was pressed to her throat. "One step, Lorenzo... That's all it will take for me to end her life. I love her enough to take her away from a monster like you." He released her hair and caressed her face.

I knew I had to act fast and be clever. There was no other way. My eyes flicked to Red in a silent plea. He nodded inconspicuously, his fingers already moving towards the trigger. Chad was too focused on me and Anastacia to pay attention to what Red was doing.

Anastacia's eyes met mine once more as her lips parted slightly. She had no strength left, and I knew she usually had bags of it. I had no idea what those bastards did to her, but I'd find out from Chad's mouth when I tortured him to within an inch of his life.

In an instant, the room erupted. Red's shot was a thunderclap in the confined space, the bullet tearing through Chad's shoulder. The knife clattered to the floor as he howled in pain, his grip on Anastacia loosening instantly. Gino crossed the room in three long strides, grabbing Chad's injured shoulder, his fist connecting with his jaw in a brutal, satisfying crack.

"Get him out of here," I ordered as Emmet and Gino removed him from the scene.

The room fell silent, except for one sigh of relief from Anastacia. I dropped to my knees in front of her, my fingers working the ropes that bound her wrists and ankles. The material had bitten into her skin, leaving deep, red welts in their wake. I couldn't help but wince at the sight. "I'm here, Ana," I whispered, trying to remain calm. "I'm right here, and I'm never leaving you again." I pulled her broken body into my arms as she flopped against my chest. I could sense the steady yet weak beat of her heart as I cradled her.

I was going to kill that motherfucker.

"I d-didn't think y-you'd—" she stuttered.

"Didn't think I'd come?" I stroked her hair as Red draped his leather jacket over her. "Of course I'd come. I never stopped looking for you."

She nodded her head slowly as she closed her eyes, giving into exhaustion. I didn't know when the last time it was she slept or ate. I didn't know anything. I glanced around the room, her pictures decorating the walls making me sick. Chad had an obsession with my wife, an unhealthy one, and I was going to make him pay.

"Finn, Nicolo, check the rest of the house," I ordered. "I want the heads of the three masked bastards out there sent to Victor." I wanted him to see exactly who had his daughter. "Once you're done, burn this shit hole down," I forced out, scooping Anastacia off my lap and into my arms. I cradled her against me as her head rested on my shoulder. "Red, start the car and call Thomas. I want him waiting when we arrive."

"On it."

I carried her through the corridor towards the exit. The weight of her in my arms was a comfort, a reminder of her existence and strength. Her breath was warm against my skin, but her trembling never stopped as she released silent sobs. "Shh," I murmured against her hair. "It's okay, I've got you. I'm not letting go." I kissed her head gently, reassuring her that I was there.

My most trusted men flanked us in a silent promise of protection until we reached the car. I settled her into the backseat, sliding in beside her, and pulling her as close to me as humanly possible.

"How is she?" Red asked from the front seat.

"I have no idea, Red." I sighed. "I need Thomas to check her over to know." I cupped her head, keeping her as still as I could as Red started off down the bumpy side roads.

"What are we doing about him?"

"Chad will get exactly what he deserves. But he can wait. Tonight I need to make sure my wife is okay. I don't want anyone to disturb me or her, you got it?"

"You think Victor will try and see her?" he questioned.

"After receiving the heads and news of Chad, yes, I do. But keep him away. I need her to rest." I glanced down at her, the sight of her caused my heart to ache.

"You don't need to worry. We'll do whatever's needed." He nodded as he focused on the road ahead.

This woman had gone through more than I could imagine since marrying me. The mental abuse I gave her on a daily basis was eating me alive and now this— the physical torture she endured. There was nothing I could possibly say that would ever make up for what I did. I didn't even know if she'd want to hear me out but I would try. I wouldn't stop trying until she listened, until she forgave me, and until she accepted being my wife because she wanted to be, not because she was forced to.

I had never tried before, but I was willing to try now. Willing to do anything to make her see that I was a man worthy of her.

As we entered the house, Thomas, the family doctor, was already waiting. His eyes widened at the sight of Anastacia in my arms, his expression a mix of concern and professionalism. "Take her upstairs," he instructed, his voice steady but laced with urgency. I nodded, my grip tightening around her as I hurried up the stairs towards my bedroom.

Once there, I used one hand to pull back the covers, placing her under one of the thinner sheets. Thomas appeared at my side, taking a good look at my wife.

"You may stay or leave. It's your choice." He nodded as I stepped aside to let him get to her.

"I'll stay. I promised I wouldn't leave her again." I pulled the armchair to the side of the bed, settling into it without letting my gaze leave her.

Thomas worked swiftly and gently as he examined Anastacia. When he lifted her shirt, I saw more bruises covering her ribs, stomach, and waist. I felt sick and tried my best to suppress my rage. Despite being asleep, her brows furrowed. She winced with every bruise that he touched.

"Her rib is broken," he muttered, his gaze flicking to me. "I suspect her jaw has a minor fracture. You can bring her to the hospital for an x-ray. Other than that the rest are bruises, but she'll need rest. A lot of it."

"Trust me, she'll get it. Whatever she needs."

Thomas nodded, handing me a bottle of medication. "I'll leave this for her, along with some instructions for her care. Keep her as still as possible, no matter how much she protests."

"You have my word." I nodded, "I'll arrange to bring her into the hospital too."

"Good." He smiled softly. "And Lorenzo, don't beat yourself up about this. She's safe because of you." He patted my shoulder. I had known Thomas since I was a boy. He looked after every cut, scrape, and wound I had.

"She was also taken because of me. I should have come straight to the house the night I let her father live, but I didn't, I went for a drink. One I didn't even have. I wasn't here when she needed me." I sighed, pinching the bridge of my nose.

"But you're here now. That's what matters. Take care of her."

With a final glance at Ana, he was gone, leaving me alone with the woman who turned my whole life on its head.

I sat beside her, gently brushing my thumb over her bruised cheek as her pained expression softened and relaxed. I took her hand in mine and caressed her bare ring finger.

"I'm so sorry, Ana," I whispered, taking her wedding band from the side table, but before I could put it back in its rightful place, a commotion erupted downstairs.

My head snapped up, my body coiling like a predator. I rose to my feet, leaving her side for a split second to investigate. The sound of Victor's bellowing voice reached me first, the man's fury vibrating through the halls.

"I want to see my daughter!" he roared. I rounded the corridor, catching sight of him from the top of the staircase. His frame blocked the entrance to the foyer, his men scattered behind him like discarded toys.

"You go. I'll watch Ana." Nicolo nodded as he joined me at the top of the stairs.

"Don't take your eyes off her," I ordered before making my way towards where Victor waited for me.

"I suggest you keep your voice down," I hissed as I reached the bottom of the stairs, his eyes narrowing in on me.

"You killed three of my best men," he spat.

"You mean, the men you banished? The ones that *used* to be your best men? Or the ones who kept your daughter locked away and tied up like she was nothing?!"

"Where is she?" he demanded, but he had no right to demand anything.

"She's safe. Unlike Chad, who will pay a heavy price for what he did to her." I stepped closer to him, my voice dropping to a dangerous whisper. "Let me make myself clear, Victor. If you think I'll ever disclose Chad's location to you, then you're out of your mind.

The only one who will kill him is me. Or my wife, if that's what she wishes. You are not part of this."

His chest heaved, his pride faltering. "I'm her father! I have a right—"

"No, you had a right once but not anymore," I interrupted. "Did you know about Chad's games?"

"I swear I didn't know what he was up to,"

"Did you know he had photos of her? Hundreds of them were plastered all over the walls. Did you know he let those men you claimed to once be the best assault her until she was covered in bruises?" I leaned into him. "Of course you wouldn't, because you don't give a shit about anyone other than yourself."

I knew he had no clue what they'd done to her. I only just found out, but that didn't stop me from losing it. I used to think that the second he agreed to my deal was the second he stopped caring about her, but I was sure he never truly cared about her to begin with. I may have told him to stay away, but as her father, he could have gone against my word and started a search himself.

"Get out of my house, Victor," I had calmed down a little, I realised there was no point in losing it, he wasn't worth it.

"No, I want to see my daughter," he shouted at the top of his lungs.

The man to his right stepped forward, raising his gun as if to threaten me, but I wasn't born yesterday. I noticed every clumsy movement he made. I raised my weapon faster, the gunshot echoing the walls as the bullet ripped through his kneecap.

"I'm giving you one more chance to choose: leave freely or in hacked up pieces." I kept my gun raised as he took less than a second to decide.

"This isn't over, Lorenzo. I will see my daughter. You can't keep me away."

"Believe me—I can and I will." I turned my back to him, my eyes locking with Red's. "Show Victor and his men out. They aren't welcome in my house."

"Boss." Red nodded, already carrying out his task.

I wasted no time in racing back upstairs to Anastacia, who was still asleep. I settled into the chair beside the bed, picking up the ring to continue where I left off. I slid it back onto her bare finger, dried blood still staining her skin.

"I'll be better for you," I whispered, kissing her knuckles. "I swear it."

"L-Lorenzo?" she mumbled, her voice thick with sleep.

"Shh, I'm here, go back to sleep." I stroked her hair as she turned to face me, letting sleep overcome her yet again.

I pulled my phone from my pocket, calling the one person I knew would be able to help me.

"Lorenzo, thank God!" my mother cried from the other end. "Please tell me you found her."

"I did. She's here...but I need you."

"I'm on my way." She hung up the phone, stopping what she was doing to come to my aid, just as she always did.

22

ANASTACIA

After what felt like a lifetime of sleep, I finally began to come around. My body throbbed and ached all over, and I dreaded seeing how I looked after that ordeal. With every ounce of strength I had left, I forced my eyes open, the soft lighting of the bedroom making it easier to come around.

Of course I was in Lorenzo's bedroom and not my own. It was a stark contrast to mine, enveloped in shadows and simplicity. The walls were painted a deep charcoal, absorbing the light and giving the space a cozy yet mysterious ambiance. Sparse furnishings adorned the room, with only a sleek, black dresser and a minimalist wooden desk standing against the walls. Heavy, dark curtains hung over the windows, keeping any unwanted light at bay.

I turned my head carefully as pain surged through me, almost taking my breath away. My gaze landed on Lorenzo, he rubbed his eyes wearily as he sat perched on the edge of the chair, hunched forward, not realising I'd woken up. His hair was disheveled, and the stubble on his chin was more pronounced than usual.

"L-Lorenzo," I whispered, my throat dry and raspy.

"Ana," he breathed, his eyes brightening instantly as he looked up at me. "How are you feeling?"

"I'm f-fine," I lied, unsure whether he believed me or not.

I didn't want him to see my weakness. Not after everything. I had to put on a front. I had to show him I wasn't going to let them break me, despite the days of torture, beatings and endless hours of fear and humiliation that still clung to me like a second skin.

"Don't lie to me, please." He sighed, pleading with me, but I couldn't let him in. I couldn't let him know how I felt on the inside. It was bad enough he had to see the outside.

"Honestly, I'm just sore, that's all." I glanced down at my wrists, and I wished I hadn't. Angry red marks encircled them like tight bands, a vivid reminder of the struggle. The sight made my stomach twist into knots, nausea rising as I quickly looked away.

Lorenzo's brow furrowed, his lips pressing into a thin line as regret etched onto his face. "I'm so sorry I didn't find you sooner. I tried everything to find you," he whispered, his voice thick with guilt.

He retrieved a bottle of water on the side table, bringing the straw to my lips to help me drink. "It's okay. You thought I walked out on you." I touched his hand, trying to soothe away his guilt in some way.

I painted on a fake smile as the recent events replayed in my mind—the soundtrack of my voice, the hundreds of photos, and my own whimpers when I was alone. I didn't know how long it'd take for me to forget all of that, but if I had to guess, it wouldn't be anytime soon.

I thought that day was the end for me. Chad was completely unhinged, talking about how we'd have one another in the next life as we weren't meant to be together in this one, but when Lorenzo stormed into that room, I knew that everything was going to be okay, and I would have another chance at life. A do-over at being happy.

"I knew you never walked out on me, Ana. We all knew it." He squeezed my hand. "My mother is here to help get you cleaned up. I didn't think you'd want me to offer my services for that so soon." His worry and care was something I had never seen with him before. It was as if the current events had changed him a little. Sure, we still had plenty to discuss, but right now, I couldn't think about anything other than recovering.

Carmella appeared at the door, making her way over to us. She placed her hand on Lorenzo's shoulder. Even if she was shocked and horrified by my appearance, she hid it well as she offered me the kindest smile without an ounce of pity.

"Come, *mia cara ragazza*." Carmella smiled, her voice soft and patient. "Let's get you cleaned up." She helped me up with gentle hands, walking beside me towards the ensuite. "Son, you go and make yourself and Ana something to eat, I'll look after her."

"I'll be right downstairs." he said, his voice wavering slightly in a way I hadn't heard before. There was a tightness in his words, as if he was hesitant to leave.

"Lorenzo, don't worry, I've got her until you're back." Carmella closed the bathroom door behind us before turning on the faucet.

Steam slowly filled the bathroom as she turned to face me. "I'm going to remove these clothes, okay?" She asked as I nodded in response.

She slowly removed the tattered material that remained on my body, and I felt embarrassed.

"I'm sorry you're having to do this, Carmella," I whispered, my voice getting lost within the running water.

"Don't you dare apologise to me. You are just as much family to me as my son is." She cupped my face as I continued to fight back the tears.

"I think he needs some sleep..." I changed the subject, not wanting the attention on me any longer.

"He'll get some sleep now you're home. He was worried sick about you, *mia cara ragazza*." Hearing those words erased all the ones

Chad had said about him finding another woman. "Come on, in you get."

She took my hand in hers as I let the warm water envelope me. I sank beneath the bubbles. A wave of relief washed over me as Carmella's hands started cleaning away the dried blood, carefully making sure not to press too hard on my fresh bruises. She hummed softly, a sweet melody that filled the silence and calmed my racing mind. I suddenly felt safe for the first time in this house.

After lying in the water until it cooled, Carmella helped me out and wrapped me in a thick, warm towel.

"How are you feeling?"

"Better, but I'm okay. I probably look worse than I feel," I lied yet again.

"I can tell you're not being truthful, I can see it in your eyes. Believe me, Lorenzo will catch on sooner rather than later." A smile tugged at the corner of her lips as she helped me into a soft cotton dress.

After she brushed and dried my hair, I felt a little like myself again, despite the cuts and bruises. Seeing my reflection in the mirror for the first time since returning home was unsettling; the image staring back was far from comforting. I was taken aback that Lorenzo could look at me without wincing, given the stark evidence of my ordeal etched across my face.

"I'm going to go back to my bedroom," I whispered, already halfway out the door. I didn't know if that's what I really wanted, but I needed to be alone. I needed to shut myself away from everyone and everything, and I thought there was no better place to do so.

"I'll go and check how Lorenzo is doing in the kitchen. You go and get some rest."

I nodded before making my way to my room.

I TOSSED and turned as sweat drenched the sheets beneath me. Vivid images haunted my dreams. I couldn't escape from them.

"He's not coming for you, Anastacia. You should know that." Chad's voice echoed through my nightmare. "He's got a new toy to play with." His words sliced me like daggers even though they weren't real anymore.

"Please, Chad... You don't need to do this..." I pleaded, hoping whatever friendship we had would snap him out of his vile obsession.

"I do, Ana... He can't have you. He doesn't want you, but I do, in this life and the next." His fingers brushed my skin like spiders crawling across my flesh.

Suddenly, the memories of my dream shattered, jolting me back to the present as my heart pounded against my ribcage, my breath coming in short, desperate gasps. For a moment, I had no idea where I was. My mind was still trapped in the horror of my nightmare. I glanced around my room. It was bare. All I could imagine were the three men trampling around in here, making it look as though I left.

My body shook uncontrollably as I wrapped my arms around myself to try to hold the pieces of my shattered composure together.

I've got to get out of here... Coming in here was a bad idea.

I got out of bed and pulled the bedroom door open, not wanting to be here any longer as I hurried past Nicolo and Red who stood as protection outside my room.

"Ana, are you okay?" Red called after me, but I didn't stop as my feet led me to Lorenzo's room.

I slipped inside, seeing the room empty. I felt as though wherever I went, I couldn't escape. The phantom pains of their blows remained, the sharp sting on my face, ribs, and stomach lingering. My nails clawed at my skin as if trying to rid myself of the memories.

I locked the ensuite door behind me before flicking on the cold water in the shower, hoping to wash everything away. The icy water rained down on me, soaking through my clothes and clinging to my skin. I slid down the wall, letting the spray drown out my sobs.

I remembered the room. The rotten walls adorned with photos of me, each one a haunting reminder. I remembered the voices, the sinister laughter, the pain... I remembered everything.

"Ana?" Red's voice called out from the other side of the door, but I couldn't respond. My sobs cut off my words as I pressed my hand to my mouth, trying to muffle the sound. "Ana?! Please open the door," he called again, his voice filled with concern.

They don't care about you, Ana... But I do.

Chad's voice embedded itself into my mind as I closed my eyes, violently shaking my head, trying to block him out.

Oh, Ana, you know I'll always be here. Your husband can torture and kill me, but you know I'll live on in your mind.

"Go a-away... Please..." I pleaded through ragged breaths.

"Ana?" Red shouted again, managing to interrupt the unwanted voice. "Fuck!"

I felt small, vulnerable, and alone.

Wondering if I'd ever forget and be the woman I once was.

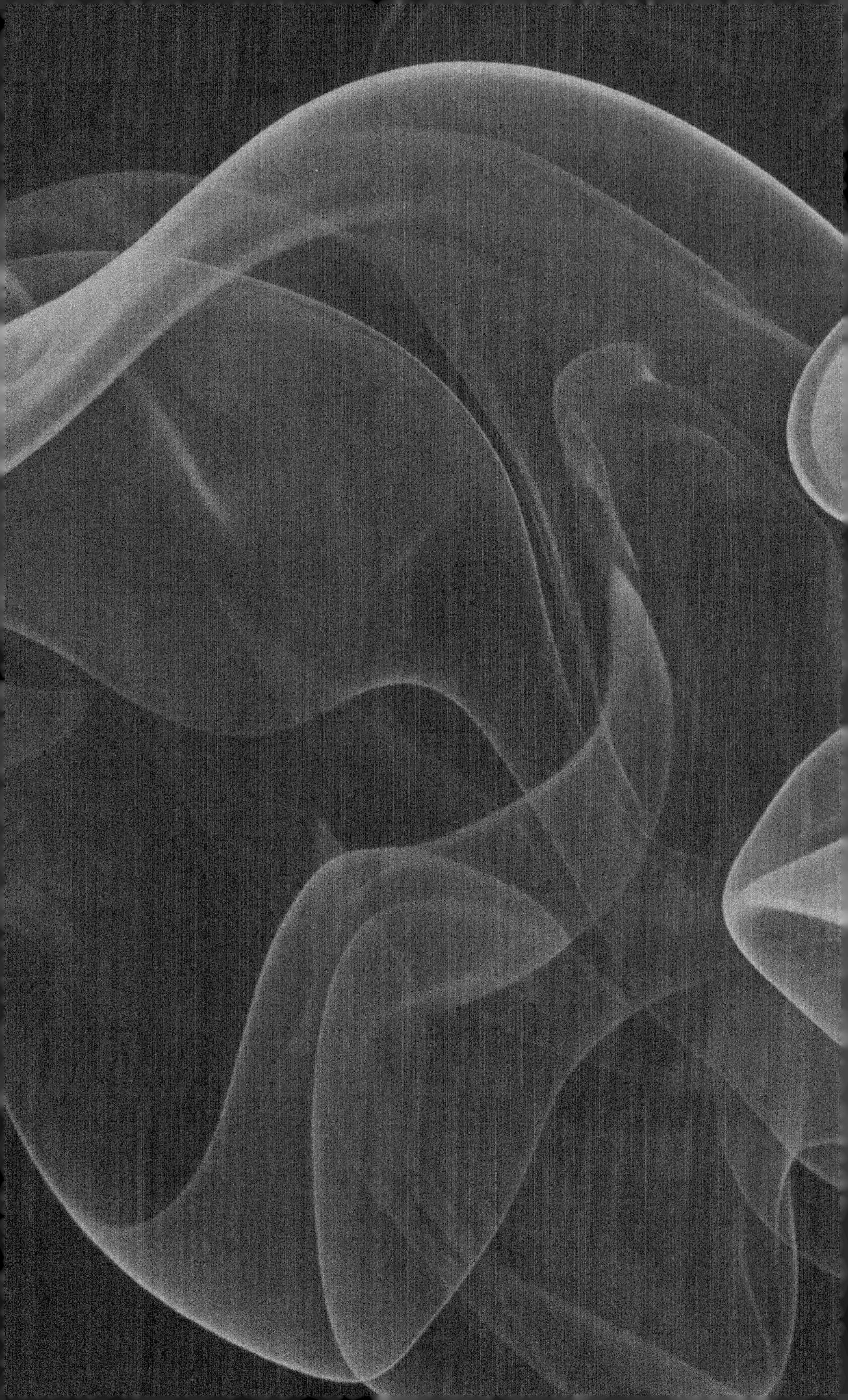

23

LORENZO

The scent of garlic and basil mingled in the air as I added the finishing touches to Anastacia's dinner, wanting to make sure she ate something to regain her strength. I had gotten used to seeing my wife with such fire and that spark I'd grown to enjoy. Seeing her the way she was now killed me inside. Although she said she was fine, I knew she was anything but.

I planned on making Chad pay for what he inflicted on Ana. I wouldn't rest until he was tortured, killed, chopped up, and disposed of. However, he could wait until Ana was better. She would be my sole focus before anything or anyone else.

"Boss!" Red burst into the kitchen, his expression uneasy. "Ana's locked herself in your ensuite. She won't open the door." He seemed panicked, rightfully so.

The dishes clattered on the tray when I dropped them. I was ready to race up the stairs. "Red, finish that for her. She needs to eat." I instructed as I hurried out of the kitchen, doubling my strides until I climbed the staircase and reached my bathroom.

"Ana, open the door," I called out, but there was no response. I pressed my ear against the cold wood, only hearing the sounds of running water. My mind raced with possibilities of what was happening behind the locked door, each one more terrifying than the last. Desperation clawed at me, and I felt a deep, unwavering need to be by her side, to be her comfort and support, whether she realised she needed me or not.

Without hesitation, I kicked the door in as the wood splintered beneath the force. The room was a stark contrast to the warmth of the kitchen as my eyes automatically fell on the shower. My heart stopped. There was my wife, crumpled on the shower floor, violent sobs leaving her.

My heart clenched in my chest as I crossed the room in two strides and entered the shower stall with her. I dropped down beside her, the ice cold water coming down on me. Her body trembled, and her lips were blue.

"Ana," I whispered.

"I c-can still f-feel—" She struggled to breathe through her tears as she clawed at her skin. I realised she was trying to scrub herself clean, trying to erase the abuse of Chad's men.

"Stop. Please, stop." I took her hands in mine, pulling her drenched body into mine as I shut off the water. "I'm here. Nobody will ever hurt you again." I shushed her, holding her close, not letting her feel as though she was alone.

I never thought I'd ever see her so vulnerable. There might have been a time I would have loved to see her broken, but seeing her this way made me realise it was never truly what I wanted. All I ever truly wanted was her, I was just too stupid and closed off to see it.

I held her tightly, pressing a kiss to her temple. "I'm sorry, so fucking sorry," I whispered into her hair, but she didn't reply.

I didn't know how long we sat there for, but it was long enough that my embrace stopped her shaking, stopped her clawing at her skin and calmed her breathing.

"I'm going to take you out of here, okay?" I said gently, which was new for me. I had stepped into unfamiliar territory and realised she'd be the only one I'd ever do that for.

She replied with a nod. I scooped her into my arms. "Please stay with me tonight, in this room or yours, but I don't want you to be alone." I set her down on the edge of the bed and retrieved a towel.

"Can I stay here? I don't feel safe in there..." she whispered, tears welling up in her eyes again.

"We can." I cupped her face, wiping the tear that fell with the pad of my thumb. "We can stay anywhere you want." I placed the towel on the bed, her eyes meeting mine. "I need to get you out of this dress, okay?"

She nodded, looking away from me. "Okay."

She raised her arms as I slipped off her dress, goosebumps covering her bare skin. My eyes dropped to the bruises that covered all parts of her and my blood simmered beneath the surface. My wife took everything they gave her, and it made me sick.

What sort of fucking person could hurt her like that?!

I composed myself internally, not letting my inner rage rattle her. I replaced her lace lingerie with a pair of my boxers before covering her with one of my T-shirts that drowned her slender frame.

I lifted her onto the vanity chair as she watched me with wandering eyes. "What are you doing?" she asked, a little of that spark I enjoyed rearing its pretty head.

"You can't exactly sleep with wet hair, can you?" I smiled, retrieving and holding up the hairdryer my mother left earlier. "So, if it's alright with my wife, I'd like to dry her hair."

And there it was, the first smile I'd gotten since she'd been home.

The first of many.

I LAID BACK in bed as Anastacia nestled into the crook of my arm. This was new for me, and to be honest, I kind of liked it. Her hair decorated the pillow beside her as her head rested on my chest. It must have sounded so cliché, but she fit perfectly against me. Almost as if she was the missing piece of the puzzle. Maybe what happened between our fathers was meant to happen, maybe it was fate's messed up way of making her mine.

My T-shirt had slipped slightly, allowing me to trace patterns on her bare shoulder, my touch gentle yet possessive.

"Ana, tell me what happened," I whispered as I felt the warmth of her breath on my chest. "I need to know."

I felt her stiffen slightly as her eyes flicked up to meet mine. "Just a few punches, that's all." Her voice was steady as her lips turned up into a soft smile.

"That's all? You say it as if it's nothing." I sighed.

"The punches were as hard as the ones Miles gave me as a kid during play fights. It's no big deal. Just drop it," she said sternly while smiling.

I knew she wasn't telling the truth. All the telltale signs were there, but I couldn't push it. I wouldn't, not now, anyway. She'd tell me more when she was ready.

Her eyelids fluttered shut, and her lips parted slightly, releasing a soft breath. She looked so serene lying against me, her face a picture of tranquility, that for a fleeting moment, I almost forgot the depths of my own failings—the harshness, the mistakes I'd made with her. Yet, the weight of those memories was something I'd never be able to shake off. Her breathing gradually settled into a gentle rhythm as she slipped into the realm of dreams. And what did I do for most of the night? I watched her, my eyes tracing the delicate contours of her face, refusing to surrender to sleep myself, in case she had a nightmare or needed me for any reason.

I had been mistaken about my wife. To outsiders, she might have appeared as nothing more than a mafia princess, with her poised demeanour and elegant attire. I, too, had been guilty of underestimating her. But she was so much more than that superficial image. Beneath her refined exterior was the heart of a warrior, fierce and unyielding. Many, myself included, had failed to protect her, but that was a mistake I vowed never to repeat. As long as there was breath in my body, I would ensure she was never left unprotected again.

My arms tightened around her, simply holding her close, hoping I'd be the one that helped her sleep soundly.

"Maybe one day you'll forgive me for the bastard I was," I whispered, placing a kiss on her head as she stirred a little. "I'm sorry it took that ordeal happening to realise just how special you are and how amazing our marriage can be." I knew she couldn't hear me, but that didn't stop me from saying it out loud for the first time. I'd make sure I'd repeat it as many times as she needed to hear it.

I LEFT Anastacia asleep the following morning, but not without leaving her a note to let her know I'd be in my home office all day. Gino rearranged my meetings and Red slaughtered anyone that wasn't happy about it.

"Boss," Finn started. "Can I just say you seem different this morning?" He smiled. "Would that have anything to do with your wife being home? And the fact that you're no longer wanting to kill one another?"

"Not that it's any of your business, Finley, but I do feel a hell of a lot better since we found her." I relaxed back in my chair, waiting for the next comment or question.

"How's she doing?" Red asked, settling into one of the chairs opposite me, his voice laced with concern. He hadn't told anyone what had happened last night. The only ones who knew were myself, Red, and of course, Ana.

"She says she's alright, but I know it won't be easy to overcome." I sighed. "She won't even tell me what they did... What that little prick did," My stomach churned, and my chest tightened, thinking about Chad's hands touching her. "But listen, I'm thinking of taking her to Sicily for a long weekend, just the two of us." I strummed my fingers on the desk as they failed to hide their amusement and excitement. I hadn't quite worked out which it was yet.

"Finally!" Emmet beamed, lighting a cigarette.

"I don't want us to be disturbed, alright? I will deal with Chad when we get back, but until then you all keep him alive," I ordered.

"Boss," they all said in unison.

"You can all go. Except you, Red. I need a word."

Red remained where he was as the rest of the team exited the office. He shot me a glance, already knowing I planned on asking him something.

"What do you need, mate?" He leaned forward, resting his forearms on his thighs.

"I need you to see if Anastacia will open up to you." I leaned back, closing my eyes for a second. "She told me she took a couple of punches, but I've seen her body, Red. It was more than a few that did that to her."

"Please tell me you're not thinking what I think you are." His eyes narrowed as he spoke.

"No, I—Fuck, I don't know," I seethed. "She'll open up to you more than she would with me. You have a great relationship with her, and I know that's my own fault."

"How about you forget the past and just worry about the present and the future." He smiled. "Take her away, talk to her about why you did what you did, lay every damn card on that table, and see what happens." He blew out a mouthful of smoke from his cigarette.

"Let her in. Let her see that you're actually a genuinely nice guy and she just might surprise you."

"Me? Genuinely nice?" I scoffed.

"I've known you for a very long time to know that you are. Taking the Don title as early as you did may have changed parts of you but don't let it change what you used to want."

"And what did I want?" I asked, forgetting what I used to feel and desire before the vendetta clouded it all.

"You wanted to have a life like your parents had, a wife who was your equal, and children who ran to you as soon as you came home, just like you did with your father." The mention of my father left a bitter taste in my mouth.

"My parents' marriage wasn't the best, Red, and you know that." I said. "My mother deserved so much more."

"Just like Ana does." He smiled, loving the fact he was right.

"I know that." I knew she deserved the whole world and more. She deserved a husband that worshiped the ground she walked on. A husband that would burn the world for her. A husband that treated her as though she was the only person in the world.

"We'll handle everything here. You take her away for a few days and forget about everything else." He slapped his thighs as he stood, readying himself to leave. "I'll try and speak to her, but I can't promise anything, mate."

"I know." I nodded in agreement and thanks as he left me alone with my thoughts.

My parents' marriage had once been amazing. My father idolised my mother. Made her feel as though she was everything, but over time he slipped up on many occasions. He slept around, not caring whether she knew or not, and made her feel as though he was her keeper. Like she was no longer his equal.

Him being Don was his life. We never seemed to come close in importance or matter as much as that did. I should've hated the man but I couldn't. I wanted him to set my mother free in the end but not in the way it happened. Despite the humiliation and upset she felt when he fucked other women, she was still heartbroken from his death. I think the only reason I wanted to avenge him was because he was my father, nothing else. I didn't want to seem weak, didn't want people to think I let it slide. But being here now, I wasn't sure what I wanted anymore.

I wasn't sure if Victor was telling the truth about my father or if he was lying to save himself, but I'd find out. I always did. If my father did in fact betray his best friend, he hid it well.

"Lorenzo?" I glanced up, seeing Ana standing at the door, watching me with gentle eyes.

"Ana." I pushed back my chair, patting my knee. "Come here, wife."

"I wasn't sure I'd hear that again..." She sighed but quickly smiled to cover the frown that almost graced her face.

"What? Me calling you wife?"

"Yeah... That." She crossed the office. I was so sure she'd sit on the desk opposite me, despite my gesture. But she didn't. She perched herself on my knee, her eyes meeting mine.

"So, why aren't you in bed? Thomas said you needed rest."

"Lorenzo, I can't lie in bed all day. I'll drive myself mad," she complained. "Besides, I wanted to see what it is that you do holed up in here all day."

"Well, actually nothing today." I leaned into her, my hands resting on her thighs as a familiar discomfort settled in my chest at the sight of her bruises.

"It's fine," she reassured me, but it wasn't fine. It was anything but fine.

I paused for a second, looking at her and remembering how she looked last night in my arms. So peaceful and strong, yet with a hint of vulnerability. I sacrificed a lot with her for vengeance. Revenge didn't seem so important anymore.

"Lorenzo... I need to know, do you still want to kill Victor? Or are you ready to let it go?" she asked with no emotion. It was as though the love she had for her father was slipping away and all she wanted were answers.

I took her hand in mine, letting my thumb trace circles on her palm. "I don't want to think about our fathers right now," I said gently. "I just want to focus on us, and our marriage. The rest can wait."

"And I get that, I do, but we need to talk about your thirst for revenge. There are things you don't know, things I overheard all those years ago, things I think you deserve to know." She sighed as she brushed away the hair that fell across my forehead.

"Not right now, though." I leaned into her, capturing her chin between my thumb and forefinger. "Right now, I want to kiss my wife."

Her cheeks blushed a soft rosy pink, adding a warmth to her complexion. Her lips parted ever so slightly, as if silently granting permission, a subtle invitation to draw me closer. I leaned in and pressed my lips against hers, feeling the electric connection as our tongues danced and intertwined with a fervent intensity. She let out a breathy moan, a gentle melody that resonated against my lips and sent a shiver down my spine.

Her fingers wove through my hair, pulling me closer with an urgency that matched the rhythm of my hands as they trailed up her back. I could feel the rapid drum of her heartbeat against her chest as I deepened our kiss, savouring every moment. Her tongue danced with mine, a tantalising stroke that left me lost in the intoxicating taste of her, the warmth of her embrace, and the gradual surrender she offered so willingly. My teeth gently grazed her lower lip, eliciting a soft, breathless gasp—the most exquisite sound I had ever heard. I desired her before, but never like this. My hands glided down to her ass, and she whimpered into my mouth, a sweet, soft sound that resonated deep within me.

"I'm taking you away, wife." I smiled as I reluctantly pulled away, resting my forehead against hers.

"Away? Where?" she gasped, the excitement on her face enough to tell me I made the right decision.

"That's a surprise for now."

Only me and my most trusted men knew the location. I'd tell Anastacia soon enough. After all, we were going somewhere that was hers. Somewhere that was ours.

24

ANASTACIA

I RELAXED DOWN BY THE LAKE, LETTING THE EARLY EVENING SUN KISS MY SKIN before it set. I was at peace out here, and to be honest, I needed it more than I thought I would.

Being in that room with just a dim light overhead had only made me crave this even more. I had no idea if I'd ever forget what happened in that house, but all I knew was that I had to try.

Chad's face still haunted me every time I closed my eyes. The smugness in his smile as he leaned over me, thinking he was untouchable when, in reality, he was a coward.

"Hey." Red interrupted my thoughts from behind me. "Mind if I join you?"

I turned slightly, offering him a faint smile. "Of course. Sit down." He lowered himself onto the grass beside me, his frame much larger than mine. "How you doing?" he asked, his voice sincere and gentle.

"Never better." I forced a smile, gritting my teeth in hopes he'd believe my lie like Lorenzo did.

Who was I kidding? Lorenzo didn't believe me.

"Ana, you know that's bullshit. You can talk to me, you know?"

He sighed, nudging my shoulder with his carefully. "What happened?"

I thought about brushing the question off and pushing it to the back of my mind, but what good would that do? Letting out a slow, steady breath, I turned to face Red.

"They knocked me about as you can see from the bruises." I traced the bruise on my shin, flinching as I remembered what it was like for a masked man's boot to come down on my leg. "And Chad... That sick bastard tried to kiss me," I admitted. I noticed Red stiffen beside me. "I-I pushed him away though. I wasn't going to let him near me, Red." I trembled.

"Ana—"

"I didn't eat or drink what they offered. I couldn't stomach it, no matter how hungry I was. I know I needed the strength to fight against them but I just couldn't." I met his gaze, one that wasn't filled with pity or sympathy. "Moments before Lorenzo and all of you found me, I was slowly giving up. I didn't think I'd see him again."

"I'm guessing you mean Lorenzo?" He asked.

"Yeah, but he's not so bad. You were right."

"I usually am, Ana." He puffed out his chest playfully. "But in all seriousness, Lorenzo barely slept. It wasn't because he couldn't. It was because he didn't want to. He had no plans of resting until he brought you home. I have never seen him so focused and determined before, and I've known that man a long time."

Hearing things like that about Lorenzo stirred something within me. Something I had never felt before. And I had to admit, I liked it.

"Chad's face haunts me, Red." I sighed, not wanting to close my eyes.

"He's getting what he deserves, Ana. We'll take good care of him until you and Lorenzo return from your long weekend away."

"About that... Where is he taking me?" I smiled, hoping my puppy dog eyes would work in my favour.

"Nice try but those eyes won't work on me. My lips are sealed," he joked, pretending to zip his lips closed.

"Was worth a shot, I guess." I smiled genuinely, finally feeling like it was possible that I'd get back to feeling like myself sooner rather than later.

"Ana, before I go, can I ask you something?"

"Sure, shoot." I waited, wondering what he wanted.

"Why won't you speak to Lorenzo about what happened?" he asked.

"Because..." I whispered. "I don't want him to see me as weak, like I couldn't take it."

"You're anything but weak, and Lorenzo knows that. He just kept thinking they—"

"No, no! Nothing like that happened." I gasped, shaking my head at the thought.

"Thank God." He breathed, as relief flooded his face. "If you want my advice—talk to him and let him in, even if it's just a little." He nudged my shoulder once more before standing up to leave me alone. "I think you two will have a kick-ass marriage, but the pair of you need to take the gloves off and just let go with one another."

I nodded in agreement as he walked towards the house.

Maybe he was right. Maybe our marriage could be kick-ass. Who knew what the future held, but I did know I wanted to stop fighting and get to know who my husband really was behind the mask he wore.

Lorenzo gently ushered me up the sleek steps of the private jet he had meticulously arranged, insisting with a playful grin that this was, in essence, a belated honeymoon and that every detail had to be perfect. The polished exterior of the aircraft gleamed under the sunlight, as we stepped inside.

"You look absolutely beautiful today, by the way." His compliment sent an unexpected flutter through my stomach as he admired my outfit.

I had chosen a cream midi dress, its fabric soft and flowing, with a pleated skirt that swayed gently with each step. The dress was the perfect blend of comfort and style, effortlessly elegant, and suited for wherever we were heading.

He gently grasped my hand in his, guiding me toward our luxurious seats arranged opposite one another. I had flown on jets with my family before, but this experience was something entirely different. The cabin exuded an air of luxury, with its sleek, polished surfaces and soft, ambient lighting that created an intimate atmosphere. The faint hum of the engines was a comforting backdrop to the lavish surroundings.

"Mrs. Ricci, good morning and welcome aboard." A young man approached us, keeping his eyes locked on me, and ignoring Lorenzo which I knew wouldn't go down well. His eyes flicked from my eyes to my body and back up again.

Lorenzo's hand tightened around mine, his knuckles whitening. I couldn't deny that I felt a surge of pride at the possessive gesture. My husband's protective nature was already on high alert on a normal day. I was sure it rocketed higher at the notion of another man checking me out.

"If you want to keep those pathetic, beady little eyes from being ripped out of your skull, I suggest you stop mentally undressing my wife,"

"I was just—"

"I know exactly what you were doing, I wasn't born yesterday," Lorenzo sighed. He fisted the man's uniform, walking him backwards towards the open door. "Fuck off, you're not needed."

"But I—" he stuttered as Lorenzo gave him a sinister smile.

"You have two choices because I'm in a pretty good mood today." He looked back at me as if I was the reason. "You can either walk down those plane steps yourself or I can throw you down them. You choose."

I had never witnessed someone bolt away with such urgency, nearly stumbling over his own feet in his frantic attempt to escape. Lorenzo turned to face me as a smile played on my lips.

"And now what do you plan on doing about having a flight attendant?" I tutted with a playful eye roll. "We only had him."

"We don't need anyone else. I'll take care of your needs, wife." He leaned into me, bringing his lips to my ear, as the warmth of his breath skating across my skin like a warm summer's day. "You can have whatever you desire."

"Who is this man, and what has he done with my husband?"

Lorenzo's hands wrapped around my waist, pulling my body flush to his. "Think of this as part of my very long road to being forgiven."

"Lorenzo—"

"Ana, it took me too long to realise and appreciate what and who was in front of me." He pressed his lips gently to mine. "I'm done with wasting time. I want to change for you, and for us. I want to be the husband you deserve and admire." My stomach fluttered as if filled with a thousand butterflies, and I could feel the heat creeping up my neck to my cheeks, painting them a soft shade of pink. His words resonated deep within me, sending a wave of warmth through my entire being. "Let's sit down," he suggested, gesturing towards our plush leather chairs, "so we can get going."

I sank into the chair opposite Lorenzo who never took his eyes off of me. That man had changed in the shortest amount of time, but I didn't overthink it. I was done second guessing everything. I was done with the past, and only looked forward to what our future held.

The plane ascended smoothly, the world below shrinking as we soared into the clouds. I settled back into the plush seat, enjoying the view and the peace that consumed me. I turned to Lorenzo, whose eyes were firmly locked on me.

“Do you want champagne or something softer? Stronger perhaps?”

“Do you know what I really want, husband?” I purred, uncrossing my legs.

“Enlighten me,” he murmured, resting his index finger gently to his lips.

“I want you on your knees for me,” my voice a soft, inviting whisper that lingered in the charged air between us.

His eyes darkened like storm clouds gathering on the horizon, his pupils dilating with an intensity that sent a shiver down my spine as he fully grasped my request. Silent as a shadow, he moved with graceful swiftness, dropping to his knees before me. His hands found my thighs, their grip firm yet possessively gentle, a mixture of strength and tenderness. As he parted my legs with deliberate care, it was as if the world narrowed to just the two of us, exposing me to the depth of his burning, ravenous gaze.

“Tell me, now that I’m on my knees, what do you want?” he growled against my skin.

“You know exactly what I want, so why keep us both waiting?” My voice was steady despite the throbbing need between my legs. “I want you to make me come.”

The man didn’t hesitate. His hands slid up my thighs, pushing my dress up to allow him the access he needed. “Is there a reason my wife decided against panties today?” he asked, his breath warm against my already sensitive clit.

"I think that's enough questions," I said, my voice carrying a playful yet commanding tone. "Now, be a good boy, and make your wife come." His response was immediate—a deep, guttural groan that vibrated against my pussy, a clear indication that my words had struck a chord with him, sparking a mix of anticipation and eagerness.

His mouth closed over my clit, alternating between rough and gentle sucks. The first moan escaped me. “Fuck...”

My fingers gripped his hair with an urgency that bordered on desperation as I pulled him closer. I ground my hips against him, consumed by an insatiable hunger for more. Lorenzo's mouth was an exquisite instrument of precision, every lick, suck, and nip expertly executed, igniting a fire within me that made my body throb with an overwhelming need.

His fingers entered me, curling with precision to hit the spot that sent shockwaves through my body. As his fingers relentlessly worked their magic, his thumb found my clit, rubbing with a tantalising rhythm that drove me to the brink of ecstasy.

"Lorenzo... I-I—" I panted, my body tightening like a coiled spring.

He growled fiercely against my core, a sound vibrating with raw, primal desire. His fingers drove into me with relentless intensity, each thrust stoking the inferno of pleasure that surged through me with unprecedented speed. My breathing became ragged, each gasp a desperate attempt to keep pace with the overwhelming sensations consuming me.

"Come for me," he whispered. "Let me feel you fall apart."

I gripped the edge of the seat as he sucked on my clit, his fingers continuing to curl inside of me, as my moans filled the cabin.

Fuck... The things this man can do with his mouth were out of this damn world.

My orgasm exploded through me, a radiant burst of light igniting behind my eyelids as I squeezed them shut. "God, yes," I moaned, surrendering to his touch as he claimed every ounce of my being. "Fuck!" I cried out, my voice trembling with the sheer force of pleasure that spiralled beyond my grasp. My body arched upward, lifting off the seat, as I clutched his hair with trembling fingers, anchoring him in place while I rode the unrelenting waves of pure bliss.

"You taste so good," he murmured as he slowly removed his fingers.

His hands glided softly over my thighs, leaving a trail of warmth as he placed tender, deliberate kisses on my skin. Each gentle touch seemed to melt away the tension in my muscles, and my breathing gradually steadied, returning to its natural rhythm. Our eyes locked, and a warm, contented smile spread across my face.

"Kiss me, wife," he said. "See how good you taste."

I leaned forward, brushing a gentle kiss against his lips, feeling the softness that invited me closer. The kiss deepened as his tongue slipped past my parted lips, a wave of sensation washed over me as I tasted the unmistakable tang of my own arousal on his tongue, just as he had requested. It was a mix of thrill and vulnerability, a moment that felt both intimate and electric.

My fingers delicately traced the intricate tattoos inked across his chest, their dark designs peeking out provocatively from beneath the fabric of his shirt. As he deepened our kiss, his lips moving with a passionate intensity, he skilfully manoeuvred us without breaking contact. With a seamless motion, he guided me onto his seat, and I nestled comfortably onto his lap, feeling the warmth of his body enveloping me.

"I'm pretty sure we can't sit like this the whole way." I giggled as he rested his forehead on mine.

"And I'm pretty sure we can." He reached out and gently tucked a loose strand of hair behind my ear. His fingers lingered for a moment, and a warm smile spread across his face.

"Will you tell me where we're going now?" I asked, hoping to coax the secret from him.

"Sicily. We're going to Sicily."

THE SECOND I stepped out of the car, the warmth of the late morning sun seeped into my skin. The air was thick with the scent of citrus and salt, a reminder that I was closer to the sea than I had ever been.

Lorenzo appeared beside me, his presence tall and commanding. He hid his eyes behind dark sunglasses, and his hair was tousled from the gentle breeze. He took my hand, gripping it firmly as he led me up the steps to the house.

"Welcome to our home, my beautiful wife," he said, his voice deep and laced with happiness. "I bought it for you. For us. Think of it as a belated wedding gift."

He bought us a house? And not just any house, but a breathtakingly gorgeous one perched off the sun-drenched coast of Sicily. I couldn't wrap my head around how he could go from wanting to kill me one minute to treating me like the queen of his world the next? Maybe he never truly hated me at all. Maybe he just wanted me to believe he did.

"Lorenzo, that's too much—" I began to protest, but he interrupted me with a smile that sent a gentle rush through my veins.

"Nothing is too much," he said, his eyes twinkling with mischief and his smile turning more playful by the second. The air seemed to hum with excitement as he added, "Now, let me carry you over the threshold. It's tradition, after all." His voice was warm and inviting, a hint of laughter in his tone, as he leaned forward, ready to sweep me off my feet.

And that's exactly what he did. With an effortless motion, he swept me into his arms, his strength undeniable as he cradled me securely against his broad chest. I couldn't help but giggle, a light, playful sound escaping my lips, as he carried me over the threshold of our second home. The scent of pine and fresh paint welcomed us as we crossed the doorway. "You're a little late with this tradition, aren't you?" I teased, as my fingers gently threaded through his soft, tousled hair, feeling the warmth of his skin beneath.

"It's better late than never," he replied as he set me down on the floor as I took in the sights around me.

The soft, cotton-coloured walls were beautifully adorned with an array of hand-painted pictures, each brushstroke capturing a unique story. Golden sunlight streamed generously through the large, arched windows, casting mesmerising patterns on the polished stone floors. Plush sofas surrounded an intricately carved coffee table, and I could already imagine the evenings sitting there, watching the sunset through the windows. My heart swelled with a mixture of awe and gratitude, overwhelmed by the beauty and serenity that enveloped me..

"I'm going to grab the luggage from the car and take it upstairs. You head up and get some rest or take a look around. Whatever you want."

He kissed my cheek and headed back out to the car, leaving me to explore the upstairs until he joined me. I made my way up the winding staircase, wandering the corridor until I reached the master bedroom. Like downstairs, the walls were a soft cotton colour. Instead of sofas littering the space, a four-poster bed, draped in sheer white fabric, graced the middle of the room. I padded over to the window that overlooked the beach and our private pool. When I opened it, the cool breeze kissed my skin with promise. The view was breathtaking, and I already knew I'd lose myself here.

"That view is what sold me on the house." Before I could even turn around, Lorenzo had already moved swiftly across the room, his footsteps silent on the wooden floor.

"I can see why."

He gently swept my hair over my shoulder, the strands slipping like silk between his fingers, before leaning in to place tender, lingering kisses on my bare neck. His breath caressed my skin, as each kiss seemed to ignite a delicate spark, leaving a trail of tingling warmth in its wake.

"You took my breath away from the very first day." He whispered, the sincerity of his words stronger than ever. He meant it every single one.

"You hid that well," I said, feeling the heat rise to my cheeks.

"Unfortunately, I didn't even truly let myself see you. I was too blinded by revenge to see what was right in front of me, and I regret that." He sighed, resting his chin in the crook of my neck. "Please, forgive me."

"I don't agree with what you did, Lorenzo. I can't deny that, but I know you went through some shitty things, and believe it or not, I understand the need you had." I turned to face him as he wrapped his arms around my waist. "If you want to sever the alliance with my father, then I support that. I will stand by your side as your wife should, but I will not support your desire to kill him. I can't stand here and say my father and I have a good relationship, because we don't, but you need to hear his side of the story before you decide anything else."

"Fuck," he groaned, resting his forehead on mine. "I know I do. I just—"

"You just worry that he's not the man you thought he was, right? You don't want to think he could have betrayed the man he called his best friend, do you?" I cupped his face, letting my thumb brush over his scar.

"I already know he was no saint. He was far from it. I guess I just don't want to hear it from someone else." He closed his eyes for a second, as if he wanted to erase the thoughts from his mind. "I will hear what Victor has to say, but not right now. Now is about earning your forgiveness, and to show you that I deserve it."

"I better make you work for it then."

"I'll beg on my knees, if that's what my wife wants." He rasped, his arms tightening around me.

"I've already had you on your knees once today, and I plan on seeing you on them later, but for now I have another idea."

"Name it. I'm good with whatever." His eyes lit up as he spoke, enjoying the moment rather than dwelling on the past.

"Let's go swimming."

25

LORENZO

I stood on the stone patio, captivated by the sight of my wife gracefully descending the steps into the shimmering pool. Each step she took was a dance, her hips swaying with an entrancing rhythm that held my gaze. Her hair flowed down her back in soft waves ending just above the delicate ties of her barely-there bikini. The tiny garment clung to her body, the thin fabric offering little disguise for the way her nipples responded, tightening against the cool embrace of the water as it slowly enveloped her body.

Holy fuck, she was a vision.

I stalked her every move, my gaze relentless as I thought of ripping that bikini off her body and claiming every inch of her on the edge of the pool. The water lapped around her waist before she submerged herself completely, all of her disappearing beneath the surface.

When she came back up, droplets clung to her skin, highlighting the curves of her breasts. Shaking her hair back, her piercing blue eyes locked onto mine with a challenge in her gaze. "Aren't you going to join your wife?" She smiled with playful innocence as droplets trickled past her lips.

I peeled off my shirt as her eyes dropped slightly, breathing me in. "My eyes are up here, you know?" I chuckled.

"I know where your eyes are, but right now, I'm not interested in those." She winked, and I had to admit, it felt good to have her back. I missed her banter and witty comebacks. No matter how much I expressed that I hated the way she spoke to me, or the way she acted, I never truly did. I used to silently and secretly love it. I could easily go as far as saying that it was the best part of my day.

I stepped into the pool as the water cooled my heated skin. She watched me approach, never tearing her gaze from me. Her breath quickened as I closed the distance between us, commanding her attention.

I never understood what people meant when they said they were drawn to someone. It never made any sense to me. That was, until now.

Seeing my wife standing in the glistening water as the sun reflected around her caused something to stir within me, something different and new, something I wanted to feel for the rest of my life. I didn't just want it. I *needed* it.

"I think you might be trying to put me into an early grave." I pointed out, my voice breaking the silence.

"It wouldn't be the first time, would it?"

I gripped her hips, pulling her flush against me as the water swirled around us. "No, it wouldn't, although I can't say I truly minded all the times you've tried." I brushed my thumb across her lower lip, removing the droplets that clung to her skin. "Fuck, you're so beautiful."

"I bet you never thought you'd compliment me, did you?" she whispered, before pressing a kiss against the pad of my thumb.

"I've done many things recently that I never thought I'd do." I cupped her ass as she let out a squeal of delight.

"You know, I've never been kissed in a pool before."

"Come to think of it, neither have I." I inched my lips closer to hers as the smell of her perfume hit me like a wave.

"Maybe we should change that then," she whispered in that seductive way of hers, making my cock twitch.

My lips crashed against hers, hungry and demanding as she parted her lips and allowed me to deepen the kiss. My tongue clashed furiously with hers, tasting and claiming her as she moaned softly. Sliding my fingers down her sides, I traced imaginary patterns on her skin as her breath hitched.

Without hesitation, she locked her legs around my waist as the water surged and swirled around us. The moment my cock pressed against her pussy, she unleashed the most intoxicating moan, a sound that seared into my soul and reverberated through my entire being. In that instant, I was certain that her desire matched the burning intensity of my own.

"Lorenzo..." she breathed against my ear, my skin prickling as she spoke. "I need you,"

"You're going to have to be a little more specific, wife," I growled, already knowing exactly what she meant, but I needed to hear those delicious words leave her mouth.

"I need you to fuck me," she whimpered as my cock teased her clit through the restraints of our swimwear. "Please."

And there it was—seven sweet words.

"There's no going back after that." I whispered, already making my way to the pool steps.

"As if there ever was, anyway." She blushed before sucking on my neck. *Fuck...*

With powerful strides, I carried her out of the pool, water dripping from our entwined bodies as I strode towards the house, not stopping until I reached our bedroom.

"Are you sure?" I asked, not wanting her to get lost in the heat of the moment and regret anything afterwards.

"I've never been more sure of anything."

I gently dropped her feet to the floor in front of me, not taking my eyes off of hers. The sunlight peeked through the blinds, casting a soft glow over her skin, highlighting the way her chest rose and fell with anticipation.

"You're mine, Anastacia," I murmured, my voice rough with desire, my words a statement of fact, a declaration. "Every fucking inch of you is mine." My fingers brushed the strap of her bikini top as my touch sent goosebumps over her skin.

"Prove it," she challenged as I dropped her top onto the floor.

I laid her down on the bed as I loomed over her, my eyes roaming over every inch of her body and taking in every detail, every freckle, every fucking inch of exposed skin. She reached up, hooking her fingers in the waistband of my swim shorts, pulling me closer to her. My hands rested on either side of her, caging her in.

"I plan on it." I smirked, my lips brushing hers in a kiss that cemented my promise.

My mouth left her lips, leaving a trail of kisses along her jawline, down her neck, and across her collarbone. With each kiss, she let out a sweet moan, making my cock twitch with need. My hands moved with purpose, my fingers teasing the ties on her bikini bottoms before I parted her thighs. She gasped softly, her breath catching as she revelled in my touch.

I lingered, deliberately drawing out every second, my lips and tongue exploring every sun-kissed inch of her skin with a feverish hunger. It tasted faintly of sweat, electrifying and pulsing with life beneath my touch. *Fucking incredible.*

I slid the piece of fabric from her, leaving her exposed, vulnerable, and yet, somehow, more powerful than ever before. My cock ached as I took in the sight of her naked body, wanting to explore every single inch of her. Her breathing quickened the second I dropped to my knees between her legs.

I was about to lose myself in my wife, enjoying her pussy with my mouth and cock until she physically couldn't take it anymore.

"Spread your legs more for me," I ordered, my voice laced with a commanding edge.

She obeyed without hesitation, her legs falling open instantly. My lips twisted up at the corners, seeing how wet she already was for me. "Good fucking girl. Already wet for your husband." I dipped my head, stroking her clit with my tongue as she gasped at the sensation.

"Fuck..." she moaned, her fingers tangling in my hair and holding me close. She wanted all my attention fixed on her.

I slid my fingers inside her, curling them in a way I knew she loved. Her fingers tightened, my scalp burning beneath her hold, but I welcomed it.

Craved it.

Loved it.

I flicked the tip of my tongue over her clit with deliberate precision, teasing her until she writhed beneath me, her body a live wire of need, arching desperately to draw closer, to feel more. Each tantalising stroke of my tongue sent tremors coursing through her frame, a symphony of shivers. I couldn't deny the intoxicating power running through me, feeding off every quiver and moan.

"Lorenzo... I—" she whimpered, her voice a desperate plea. "Please."

I hummed against her pussy as I heard her beg for her release, something I wasn't going to give her...yet.

"Such a pretty little cunt." Her pussy clenched around my fingers, her body betraying just how much she enjoyed the harshness of my words. I devoured her clit, her moans of pleasure ricocheting off the walls. "You're going to come and then take my cock like a good fucking girl."

"Please..."

"I love to hear you beg," I growled against her.

"Please..." Her voice trembled, each syllable a desperate plea. Her perfect mouth formed the word, imploring with a raw, aching urgency that cut through the air like a knife, every fibre of her being begging for salvation.

If I died to that sound, I'd die a happy man, that was for sure.

"Not yet, wife. I'm not done with you," I chuckled, the rumble vibrating against her sensitive flesh.

My tongue delved deeper, working alongside my fingers, teasing her to a point of no return and pushing her closer and closer to the edge. Ana was a mess of writhing limbs and incoherent moans, her body a symphony of pleasure and need. I knew she couldn't take much more as I nipped her clit.

"Fuck," she cried out, breathless and in need of more, as I thrust my fingers inside her pussy. I sucked her clit into my mouth, my tongue flicking against it in a relentless rhythm. "Please, Lorenzo."

"Come for me," I growled against her pussy. "Fall apart for me."

Those words were all she needed to give me everything I wanted. Her body arched into me as her orgasm ripped through her body. She fisted the sheets as she convulsed. I didn't stop, not until I drained every last drop from her.

"Lorenzo," she moaned, her breathing ragged as she struggled to get more words out.

I locked eyes with her, our gaze electric as she observed me teasingly flick my tongue across her clit one last time before rising to peel off my swim shorts. Her eyes widened, a mix of surprise and anticipation etched on her face at the sight of my cock. Even though she had seen it before, I could sense a whirlwind of questions swirling in her mind. I joined her on the bed, my presence looming over her petite frame.

"Tell me what you need," I whispered, bringing my lips to her ear.

"You. I need you," she whispered, her voice quivering like a fragile leaf in the wind.

My body enveloped hers as her icy blue orbs implored me with a silent, urgent plea. "You have me, wife. You'll always have me," I said, my voice a soft promise in the quietude that surrounded us. My lips grazed hers tenderly, a feather-light touch that spoke volumes, while my hands found their place on her hips, fingers curling around them with a gentle yet firm grasp, as if anchoring us both in the moment.

"Then fuck me... Please," she whimpered as I teased her lower lip between my teeth.

Her body quivered beneath me as I aligned myself at her entrance. The searing heat of her pussy was an intoxicating invitation, urging my cock forward with a relentless hunger as I pushed insistently against her core. Her breath caught sharply, a gasp of desire escaping as the head of my cock entered her slowly, the cool metal of my piercing sending shivers through her as it brushed her sensitive clit. Her eyes locked onto mine, burning with passion, a silent yet fervent approval that fuelled the fire between us.

This was more than sex to me, more than just fucking her. This was me showing her that, no matter what happened or what was thrown at us, she was mine.

With a fierce, deliberate thrust, I drove my cock into her, feeling her pussy stretch and envelop me as those intoxicating whimpers escaped her lips. My piercing teased every inch of her tight, slick pussy, and damn, she was tight. I plunged deeper, filling her utterly as she gasped, the sound echoing like a siren in the room. Her nails raked down my back with a fiery urgency, and her legs clamped around my waist with unyielding force, locking me in with primal intensity. I lived for it.

Lived for her.

"Relax for me, Ana," I instructed as her eyes softened, and a smile played on her lips.

She obeyed my every word, her body surrendering as I began to move inside her. My thrusts were slow and controlled, a careful restraint to ensure I didn't lose myself completely for her first time. Yet, with every thrust, an overwhelming torrent of ecstasy coursed through me, as her tightness gripped me with an irresistible force.

"You feel so fucking good," I moaned against her ear as hers joined mine in a beautiful symphony. "So fucking perfect."

She tilted her hips, meeting my thrusts as her nails raked down my back. My skin burned, but I craved it. It took everything I had not to flip her over and fuck her with no control. Right now, it was all about going at her pace.

As if she knew what I wanted, she captured my face in her hands. "Lorenzo..." she whispered. "Harder." That one word was all I needed.

I obliged. Of course I did. My thrusts became more urgent, more relentless, as she relaxed and fully let me in. "Fuck," I breathed as her pussy squeezed my cock. I was lost in her and the way she commanded me with nothing more than a word.

She arched into me, her breasts pressing into my chest as I gripped the back of her neck, slamming my lips against hers. I could feel how close she was, her pussy giving her away as I filled her to the brink. "Look at you, taking my cock like a good girl," I purred against her mouth as she moaned into mine.

"Lorenzo," she panted. "I'm close."

I kissed her with a hunger that left us both breathless. My tongue invaded her mouth as I slammed into her pussy, stealing everything from her. Our bodies collided in a heated embrace, her moans filling my mouth as she fought for breath.

"Does my wife want to come?" I managed through heaving breaths as sweat trickled down my forehead.

"Please... Please let me come," she gasped as I sucked on her neck.

"Is that what you want?" I thrust inside her again as she let out a cry of pleasure, and I revelled in it.

"Yes."

"Then come for me, wife. Come all over my cock," I ordered, knowing that the second she came, I would, too.

With a cry that was a fierce blend of ecstasy and surrender, she erupted. Her body convulsed beneath me, every muscle tense and trembling, her core pulsing violently as I seized the orgasm she gave me.

"Fuck, yes," she whispered, her voice unable to come out any louder.

An overwhelming surge of ecstasy tore through my body like a tidal wave. "Ana, fuck!" I cried out her name, my voice cutting through the symphony of her moans.

I pressed my face against her neck, consumed by the sensation as I released into her, my body convulsing violently with the intensity of my climax. It was an indescribable high, a euphoric peak that left me feeling invincible, and I was desperate to remain suspended in this blissful state forever.

"Are you okay?" I asked, stilling inside of her.

"Never better." She pressed her lips against mine in confirmation.

"Did I hurt you?"

"No, you didn't hurt me, Lorenzo." She smiled. "It was perfect."

For a moment, we laid tangled together, our bodies damp from sweat, our hearts pounding in unison as our breathing began to return to normal. I relaxed beside her, pulling her close as my fingers trailed across on her skin.

"You continue to surprise me, Ana." I murmured as she turned her back to me, snuggling into my embrace as the breeze from the window kissed our naked skin.

"I could stay like this until morning."

"Unfortunately, that's not an option. I'm taking you out tonight." I planned on making memories with her from the moment we stepped on that plane to come to Sicily. And I didn't plan on stopping for the rest of our lives.

The evening air was warm, carrying the faint scent of blooming jasmine as we walked hand in hand through the cobblestone streets. My gaze repeatedly drifted over to her, the glow of the street lamps illuminating her skin. She'd chosen a fitted, deep red floor-length dress that accentuated her body. Her lips were painted the exact same shade to match, and they curved up into a soft smile when she glanced up at me, making my heart practically stop.

I had never experienced anything quite like this before, nor had I anticipated such a feeling. There was no adrenaline-fuelled rush, no fiery excitement coursing through my veins—just a serene fullness, as though every part of me had finally come to rest. Her hand in mine wasn't a jolt of electricity; it was a steady anchor. She didn't need to utter a single word, her very presence felt like an unspoken promise I hadn't realised I was longing for.

If the men or my mother would have said I'd be here with Ana, falling head over heels, I'd have laughed because it seemed near impossible. *But not anymore.*

I hated the fact that it took that bastard Chad taking her for me to realise that she was actually important to me. She was the only person I wanted to let in. The only person that saw me for me. The only person besides my mother that I'd give my life for.

Her blue eyes met mine, sparkling with a mixture of excitement and contentment, something I never thought I'd see, let alone be the reason for.

"Here we are." I smiled as we stopped outside a small, family-owned restaurant. I chose this place on purpose because it was a spot I frequented as a child. Long before my life changed to what it was now.

"Oh, Enzo, it's perfect," she murmured, her nickname catching me off guard.

"Enzo?" I questioned, unable to hide my amusement.

"Yeah, just trying it out, don't you like it?"

Like it? I loved it. No one other than a very select few called me Enzo, and even then, it was extremely rare.

"Keep trying it out and we'll see." I winked as I squeezed her hand tightly.

As I turned my attention to the restaurant's entrance, I was welcomed by an elderly couple I hadn't seen in a while. "Welcome!" The woman, who was actually my grandmother, smiled and held out her arms to me. "Lorenzo, my boy, it's been too long."

I embraced her as tears sprung to her eyes.

"*Lo so, Nonna.*" I sighed. "*Troppo a lungo, mi sei mancata.*" I spoke in Italian, something I knew my grandparents were proud of.

"*Risparmia un po' d'amore per il tuo Nonno.*" My grandfather chuckled, holding out his arms to me as he pulled me into him with a firm pat on the back.

"This must be..." My grandmother, Silvia, gasped as her eyes fell to my wife.

"*Nonna*, this is Anastacia, my wife." I hadn't even finished my sentence before she wrapped her arms tightly around Ana, who was smiling ear to ear.

"It's so lovely to meet you, Anastacia, dear." She stroked her hair, welcoming her like the family she was. "I've heard all about you from our daughter, Carmella." She led Ana to our reserved table as I watched on with a smile I couldn't hide.

"How have you been, son?" My grandfather, Elio, asked.

"Good. Really good, actually." I turned to face him. "I guess you'll meet her properly when *Nonna* lets you," I teased.

"You know her all too well." He chuckled. "You seem happy. That's all we ever wanted for you, especially since..." He paused, unsure if he should continue.

My grandparents weren't fans of my father. In their eyes, he was never good enough for their only daughter. The more I thought about it, the more I realised they were right. He wasn't good enough for her.

He tried at first. Brought her home frequently even when they had me, but after a short period of time, he stopped. He wouldn't allow her to leave and visit alone with me. Maybe he thought we wouldn't return. Fuck knows what went on in that man's head. I visited when I was old enough, but after my father passed away, my time was limited and unfortunately, seeing them and spending time in Sicily was one of the things I had to give up.

"I plan on being out here a lot more, especially since I bought a house for us here."

"Well, your *Nonna* will love that. She seems to have taken to your wife." He nodded towards them as she was already pouring Ana a limoncello. *God, was she trying to get her drunk already? It had only been five bloody minutes.*

"Lorenzo, come over here," Ana called. I found my feet already moving towards her.

"She's a keeper, especially if she makes you smile like that." Elio said loud enough for me to hear as he slapped his palms together in delight.

He was right. She was a keeper, and I didn't plan on letting her go, not even for a second.

26

ANASTACIA

I sat opposite Lorenzo on the quaint, wooden table that was covered with white linen. An old wine bottle decorated in old wax that housed a single candle sat atop it as well.

"This is... perfect," I whispered, taken aback by how special tonight had been so far. I glanced up at my husband who wore a rare, genuine grin. "I like it when you smile."

"It's a good job I have plenty to smile about then, isn't it?" He took my hand across the table. "I'm sorry. I know my *Nonna* is full on. They just wanted to meet you."

"I don't mind. It's actually quite nice. I haven't felt love from my family like that in a while." I hid the way my voice wobbled, pushing my parents to the back of my mind, not wanting to think about them.

"My family is yours now, and I promise we can visit Sicily whenever you want. If it means I get to see you happy, then just say the word, and I'll drop everything and make it happen." He sipped his whiskey with a mischievous glint in his eye. "Besides, it'll be nice to bring our children out here."

I almost choked on my wine. I had a feeling he'd want kids. He'd want an heir at some point, but hearing him mention it was unexpected. I had never really wanted children. I had a different vision for my life previously, but I guess things could change for the better, or whatever the saying was.

"How is everything?" Elio beamed, appearing from the restaurant's kitchen, changing the subject of children.

"Oh, Elio, it was beautiful. Bless your hands," I complimented.

"I'll be back shortly with the best dessert you've ever tasted." He grinned, clapping his hands together.

"That's quite the statement, *Nonno*." Lorenzo chuckled.

"You know the exact dessert I'm talking about, so you know the statement is true." He tsked before returning to the kitchen.

"Lorenzo..." I sighed. "Why weren't they at the wedding?" I asked, hoping I hadn't overstepped.

"Honestly, they hate the life I lead, but that doesn't mean they don't love me. They just don't agree." He offered a lopsided smile. "They hated my father, hated the life he dragged my mother into and raised me up in." He let out a deep breath.

"You weren't dragged up. Your mother raised you well. You just went off track a little bit."

He gripped the edge of my chair, pulling me towards him effortlessly as I let out a delighted giggle. Bringing his face close, he rested his nose against mine. "And you're the one getting me back on track." He tucked my hair behind my ear, his fingers lingering beside my jaw. "Anastacia Ricci, you're mine. Do you know that?"

"I had a feeling," I teased as he caressed my face with his knuckles.

"You make me want to be a better man, Ana," he whispered. "You make me believe that I can be."

"You are a good man. You just chose to hide it before." I leaned into him, my lips almost brushing his as a bright flash of white caught our attention.

"I'm sorry, Lorenzo. The moment was just too perfect to miss."

Silvia held a small camera in her hands. Lorenzo couldn't hide his amusement when he glanced over. "This photo will grace our wall alongside our many family photos." She directed her hand to the wall behind us. All the photos were of Lorenzo's family, including Carmella's wedding photo. Although she stood alone, clutching her bouquet, and looking radiant.

"Ah, Lorenzo, look at you!" I pointed at a photo of my husband as a small boy beside his grandparents. He was elbow deep in dough with a cheeky smile.

"He was full of mischief as a boy and into everything." Elio chuckled, as he admired his grandson.

After dinner, we said our goodbyes, promising to spend more time together before we returned home. I never felt so welcomed before, and I was honoured that I got to meet them and learn more about Lorenzo as a boy.

"So, where to now? Home?" I asked as we stepped back into the night, the warmth of the evening wrapping around us like a blanket.

"Most definitely not." He led me through the side streets back to the main square where the city was alive with music and laughter. "If you'll give me one minute."

Before I had time to answer, he stepped up to a small flower vendor, purchasing a single red rose. "I know it's not much, but I couldn't resist." I accepted his gift as I admired the beauty between my fingers.

"It's perfect, absolutely perfect." I blushed, inhaling the fresh scent of the flower.

"That's the first of many, wife." The way he called me that had changed. It was softer with a whole lot more emotion. Before, he just sounded like a menacing robot. "How about some gelato from the best shop in Sicily?" he asked, already guiding me across the cobbled street to the vibrant storefront.

"As long as we don't have to share," I teased, noticing the array of flavours in the see-through freezer display.

"So you'll share the rest of your life with me but not your ice cream?" He gasped, a playful tone lacing his voice.

"Mhm, that's correct,"

"What flavour do you want?" he asked, his hand never leaving mine.

"You know what—surprise me."

"I love a challenge." It was true, he did.

And he lived up to that challenge, picking my favourite flavour without even knowing.

We headed back outside, strolling alongside one another. "So, how's the lemon?" he asked before spooning a scoop of pistachio gelato into his mouth.

"Really good. You want to try some, don't you?" I questioned, holding out the spoon to him.

"Go on then. Let me see if it's better than mine."

"Close your eyes and open your mouth," I replied, watching as he did what I asked of him.

I scooped a dollop of ice cream onto my finger and smeared it on the tip of his nose. Unable to hide my laughter as he opened his eyes in surprise.

"You're going to regret that, Mrs. Ricci," he warned, his voice low and seductive. He said it in a tone that made my stomach flip before he erupted in laughter. I had never seen him so carefree and relaxed. It was a side to him I wanted to see more often. He wiped off the ice cream with his thumb before popping it into his mouth. "I think yours might be better than mine."

"Hands off, Ricci," I rolled my eyes with a smile teasing my lips. My gaze softened as I looked at him, feeling something I never thought I'd feel around him—at ease. It was the first time we were relaxed enough that we let our guards down.

"Come with me." He gave me no choice as he weaved us through the crowd with the confidence of a man who owned the streets. I gripped his hand tighter, following him wherever it was he wanted to go. We stopped in front of a jewellery shop, its windows glittering like a treasure trove.

When he led me inside, the air was cool and fragrant, the beautiful jewels bathed in soft, flattering light. The elderly shopkeeper nodded respectfully to Lorenzo before offering me a gentle smile.

"How can I help you both this evening?" he asked warmly.

"I'm looking for something specific." He glanced down at me as his eyes landed on my ring finger momentarily. "Something to match my wife's wedding band." He smiled.

Wait a minute... Was he looking for an engagement ring?

I was happy with my ring. I didn't need something else or an additional band, but Lorenzo didn't seem to do things by halves. Wearing *just* a wedding band didn't seem like an option for him anymore.

"Of course. We have plenty. What's your budget?" he asked as Lorenzo chuckled.

"There isn't one," he replied, causing me to choke on air.

"Lorenzo, I don't need fancy diamonds. We're already married." I blushed, trying to pull him away from the cabinet.

"I know and I went about everything the wrong way, so please, will you let me do this for you?" he asked, leading me to a plush velvet chair in the corner of the room.

I sighed, giving up the fight. It was hopeless, anyway. "Okay, but nothing too expensive."

"You wait here. Let me surprise you, and see if I can get it right the second time tonight." He smiled, cupping my face for a second before returning to the gentleman.

I couldn't see what rings Lorenzo was looking at, and didn't even try to snoop. I'd let him surprise me, he seemed to do well so far. After a few minutes, I saw him point to the one he decided on as the gentleman mirrored my husband's smile.

"An excellent choice, Signor Ricci." He handed Lorenzo the velvet box as he spoke. "The centre stone is a rare oval diamond. It's one of a kind."

Lorenzo strode over to where I sat, dropping to one knee the second he reached me. "What are you doing?" I blushed.

"Everything backwards." His lips split into a boyish smile, and it made my heart flutter. I looked down at the open box, my breath caught in my throat at the sight of the ring. The oval diamond was indeed beautiful, surrounded by a halo of smaller stones. It took my breath away as my fingers trembled and traced the box.

Lorenzo took my hand in his, wasting no time sliding the ring on my finger beside my wedding band. It was heavy, not because of its weight but the meaning behind it. It was as though it was a testament to him changing, to him wanting to be better with and for me. I tore my eyes away from the ring, focusing my attention on Lorenzo who appeared different. He looked like a content man, a man who would do anything for the woman he called his wife.

He remained on one knee, not taking his eyes off of me. "Lorenzo..." I began, unsure of what to say.

He silenced me by his touch alone, his thumb brushing my cheek as his gaze intensified. "You wear a wedding band, I know," he breathed. "But I want you to have this, too. I want to show you and everyone else that you're mine. And that I'm yours." His words were simple, but they carried the weight of a thousand unspoken truths. My chest tightened, and my eyes stung with unshed tears.

Reaching up, I traced the scar on his cheek. "I don't need a ring to know that," I whispered.

"Maybe not." He smiled. "But I do."

There was a clearing of a throat beside us, bringing us back to reality and out of our bubble. "Sorry to interrupt, but would you like your purchase wrapped, Signor Ricci?"

"No, thank you. She'll be wearing it now," Lorenzo replied, rising to his feet before handing his card to the shopkeeper. "Charge the amount to this."

"Thank you. It's beautiful." I whispered, admiring the ring that graced my finger.

"Nowhere near as beautiful as you." He wrapped his arms around me, bringing his lips to mine in a sweet, gentle kiss. "That was cliché, wasn't it?" He chuckled, kissing me one more time.

"Not at all," I responded, mirroring his laugh.

Once the ring was purchased, we said our goodbyes and headed back into the bustling square where live music played. It was incredible witnessing the laughter, love, and secrets of the city.

The scent of citrus from nearby orchards mingled with the aroma of freshly baked cannoli, creating a heady perfume that hung heavy in the air. Strings of twinkling fairy lights criss crossed above, casting a warm, festive glow over the bustling crowd. We drifted over to where the band played, and I couldn't hide how happy I was at that moment.

Lorenzo pulled me into his arms, his hands settling on my hips as we swayed to the music. "What are you doing?" I exclaimed.

"Dancing with my wife like I should have done at our wedding," he said, leaning in closer as I melted into him. I rested my head on his chest, his heartbeat a gentle rhythm against my ear as the rest of the world seemed to fade away.

The music swelled around us, the notes wrapping us in a cocoon of intimacy. His hand moved up to cradle my face, his thumb brushing my cheek. "Let's go home." He kissed my forehead. "I need you all to myself."

Just as I needed him.

***

Lorenzo ascended the stairs with me in his arms, his feet thudding softly against the marble. Once we reached the bedroom, he placed me gently on my feet.I stood before him with longing eyes.

"Lorenzo..." I whispered, my voice thick with desire. "I need you. I need you to lose control with me tonight."

He paused for a second, his eyes darkening as they locked onto mine. I noticed something primal passing between us. Without a word, his hands slid up my arms, setting my body alight with his touch alone. He lowered the straps of my dress down my arms, letting it fall to the floor. It pooled at my feet, leaving me standing bare before him. My breathing quickened as my breasts rose and fell harder than before.

"Are you sure about this?" he asked, his voice a rough whisper as his lips curled into a faint, dangerous smile that matched his hungry gaze.

"I'm sure," I replied, my hands reaching for the buttons of his shirt, pausing to wait for his word.

"Carry on," he growled as I slowly undid each button one by one, revealing the intricate ink that decorated his chest. I tugged his shirt free, letting it fall to the floor before moving to his belt.

As his pants slid down his legs, he kicked them aside, standing before me in nothing but his boxers. His cock was already hard, pressing against the fabric, and I couldn't hide the breath that hitched at the sight. Without hesitation, I dropped to my knees, my hands reaching for the waistband of his boxers. Pulling them down slowly, my eyes locked on his. I took him in my hands, my fingers tracing the length of him.

"Anastacia," he groaned, his voice a warning, but I didn't stop. I wouldn't. I leaned forward, my lips brushing the tip of his cock, my tongue flicking out to taste him. He tasted like pure desire.

I lowered my mouth down his cock, taking him deep. My lips wrapped tightly around him, my tongue swirling as I bobbed my head. Gripping his thighs, my nails dug into his skin as I took him as far as I could. Lorenzo hissed, his hands tangling in my hair, his fingers fisting the waves that cascaded down my back as he guided my movements. "Fuck," he hissed, his voice thick with need. "You're going to make me fucking lose it."

I didn't respond, my mouth too full of him. I sucked him harder, my cheeks hollowing as my mouth moved faster, while my tongue teased the sensitive underside of his cock. His breath came in sharp gasps, his body tensing as he fought for control. But I wasn't giving him any. I wanted him to lose it. I wanted him to let go completely.

"I'm going to come, Ana." His voice was rough as he moaned. "You're going to swallow every fucking drop," he commanded, and I was more than happy to obey. I moaned around him, the vibration sending him over the edge.

With a deep groan, his cock pulsed against my tongue as he filled my mouth with his cum. I swallowed greedily, closing my eyes as I savoured the taste of him.

He reached down, his hand cupping my cheek as his thumb brushed my lips. "Get on the bed."

I obeyed, climbing onto the bed, my body already flushed and trembling. Lorenzo followed me, his eyes dark with desire as he looked down at me. "Turn around and bend over," he demanded. His hands gripped my hips as he pressed the tip of his cock against my entrance.

"Is my wife ready?" he asked, his voice a low growl. "Are you sure you want me to lose control?"

"Yes," I whispered, my voice barely audible as I waited with anticipation.

He thrust into me in one smooth motion, his cock buried deep inside my wet heat.

"Fuck!" I cried out, my head falling forwards as he began to move, his hips snapping against mine in a relentless rhythm, fucking me hard and fast.

His hands gripping my hips tightly, my breath coming in sharp gasps. "Lorenzo," I moaned, my voice breaking as he buried himself deeper, his cock filling me completely. "Harder... Please."

He didn't need to be told twice. His thrusts became more urgent, more desperate. His hands fisted my hair, yanking my head back. "This is what you want, isn't it? You fucking love it, don't you?" he growled, his lips brushing my ear. "You like being fucked like my little slut."

"I do... Fuck, I do," I whimpered as he continued to fill me while I fisted the sheets. "Please..."

"Keep fucking begging, wife, until I let you come," he demanded, his fingers digging into my hip. "You take me so fucking well," he praised.

His cock throbbed inside me as I revelled in everything he was giving me. He was pushing me closer to the edge, and I couldn't hold on much longer. "Please, Lorenzo, please..." I moaned. Pleasure built inside me as I waited for him to let me come. As I waited for his words. "Lor—" I whimpered.

"Come for me," his words were intoxicating, seizing my senses as I surrendered completely to the overwhelming passion he ignited.

With a final, brutal thrust, he followed me and came, his cock pulsing as he filled me with his cum. My moans came out loud and breathless as my body shook, my orgasm ripping through me at record speed, soaking his cock with my arousal.

"Fuck, Ana," he roared from behind me, his fingers marking my skin.

He leaned down, pressing a kiss to my shoulder as his arm snaked around my waist, pulling me up into him. We stayed like that for a moment, our bodies joined as we came down from the high we were riding.

"Are you okay?" he whispered, pulling out of me slowly.

"Never been better." I smiled as he guided me onto my back.

He laid on the bed beside me as I nestled in against him, resting my head on his shoulder. I let my fingers trace that ink on his chest as I watched his breathing steady. His fingers teased my skin as he skated them up and down my back.

“Thank you for today. It’s been something else completely,” I whispered as I started to drift off to sleep.

“I’d recreate it every day for the rest of your life if it meant I got to see you smile the way you did.” He kissed my temple, a moment that was so tender and loving. “Sweet dreams, my wife.”

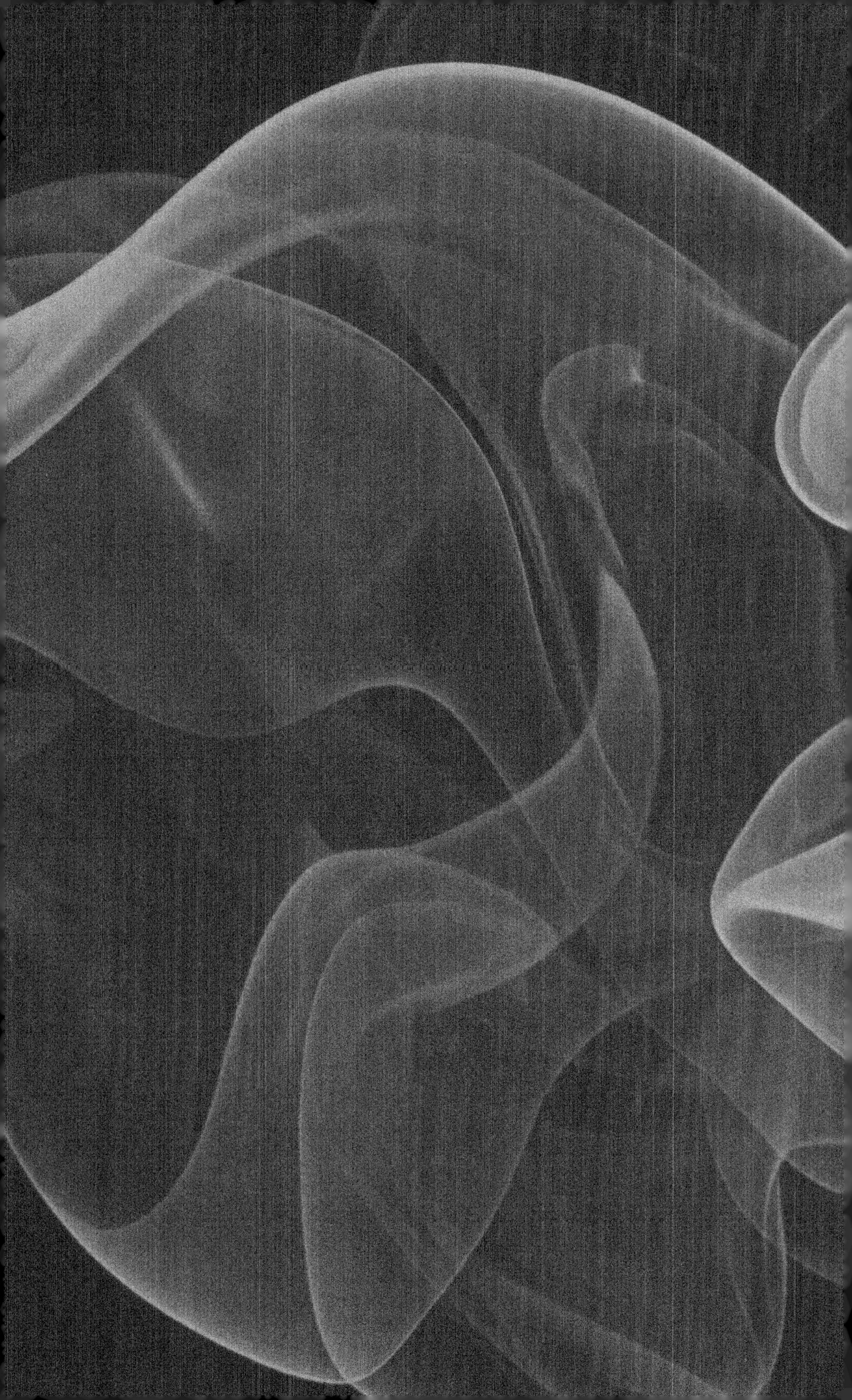

27

LORENZO

We decided to spend our final day in Sicily at a local beach. I wanted to stay at the one behind our house since it was private, but Ana wanted to explore a little. There was no point going against her, she always seemed to win. The thought of returning to reality wasn't one I wanted. I would have rather stayed here with my wife, but I had responsibilities, unfortunately.

"Your drinks, man." The bartender handed me the whiskey and cocktail I ordered.

"Cheers." I thanked him and made my way back to where I left her. My eyes landed on her face as a small, possessive smile tugged at my lips.

But as I drew closer, I realised she wasn't alone.

Who the fuck was this cunt?

Some jumped up little prick with hair as bright as the sun sat on my fucking lounger, leaning in too damn close to my wife. My blood ran cold then hot as my grip tightened on the glasses I held. I tried to control myself since we were in a public place.

My chest tightened as I noticed the smile that graced her face, only it wasn't the one I'd grown used to over the last few days. No, this one was forced and didn't even reach her eyes.

As I neared them, I could hear the fucker's words, smooth and practiced, as he tried to charm her. "You know, you're too beautiful to be alone on a beach like this," he said, his gaze lingering on her lips. "Maybe I could keep you company?" And maybe I could gauge those eyes out of his air filled head. The bleach had obviously seeped into his brain if he thought he had any chance with my wife.

Her smile remained polite, but her body language shifted subtly. She crossed her arms, her gaze flicking towards the horizon. "And you should know I'm not alone," she replied, her voice calm but firm. "My husband will be back in a minute."

The bastard's grin faltered, but he recovered quickly. "Husband, huh? Where is he, then? Doesn't seem like he's doing a very good job of keeping an eye on you." He tapped his finger against his lips. "Or does he not exist? You could just be using the husband line to get rid of me."

My jaw ticked instantly, my blood boiling as if it'd been set alight. *Fuck this.* I strode past his mates who were egging him on, not stopping until I reached my wife. I set the drinks down on a nearby table, my eyes burning into the prick's head. My presence loomed behind him like a giant storm cloud.

The jumped-up twat turned, his smirk fading as he took in my imposing figure. "Oh, you must be the husband," he said, his tone mocking. "Took you long enough."

I didn't say a word. There was none needed. I simply wrapped my hand around his neck, lifting him off the ground with a strength that bordered on terrifying. His eyes widened in shock, his hands clawing at my wrists as he struggled to breathe. My face was a mask of indifference, my voice a low, dangerous growl. "You talk to my wife again and I'll bury you where no one will ever find you," I threatened. "And trust me, I know plenty of places."

The crowd around us went silent, watching the scene with a mix of fear and fascination. Ana rose to her feet, her eyes trying to capture my attention. She knew my temper, knew the darkness that lurked beneath the surface.

"Lorenzo," she called out, her voice stern.

I kept the stranger suspended for a moment longer, my hands like iron around his throat. "Lorenzo, please," Ana pleaded.

With a snarl, I dropped him, sending him stumbling back into the sand. The fucker coughed and spluttered, clutching his throat, his eyes wide with fear. "Mark my words, you little cunt, I'll skin you alive if you come near my wife again." I narrowed my eyes, watching as he scrambled to his feet and fled without a backward glance.

The beach erupted with murmurs, but I didn't care. My gaze locked onto Ana as I closed the distance between us, my movements predatory. I stopped before her. "I'm sorry," I whispered before grabbing her by the waist and pulling her against me with a force that left no doubts about my intentions.

My lips crashed down on hers in a kiss that was anything but gentle. It was desperate, hungry, a declaration of ownership for anyone who dared to watch. My hands gripped her hips as I dug my fingers into her skin. I tilted her head back, deepening the kiss as her eyes fluttered closed, her body melting into mine. Her resistance crumbled under the weight of my need.

I tasted the salt of the sea on her lips, the heat of my anger mingling with the calming nature of my wife. My tongue invaded her mouth, claiming her with a ferocity that left her breathless. Her arms snaked around my neck, her fingers teasing my scalp as she kissed me back with equal fervour.

The world around us faded away—the crowd, the sun, the sand, all of it disappeared as we lost ourselves in each other. My hands moved up her back, my touch rough and reverent, as I pressed myself closer, my body hard against hers. I could feel the throb of her heart beat, the heat of her skin on mine, and the way she needed me.

I finally pulled away, my breath coming in ragged gasps, my eyes searching hers. "You're mine," I growled, my voice thick with possession. "Nobody else's. Never forget that."

Her lips curved into a small, submissive smile. "I could never forget."

I pressed my lips to hers again, softer this time, but no less intense. Cupping her face, I let my thumbs brush over her cheeks as I held her gaze. "Let's get out of here," I murmured. "I'm sick of sharing you with others."

"Yeah, it wasn't my best idea, was it?" She asked, taking my hand.

"Sorry to say, but no, it wasn't."

We walked hand in hand along the sand, leaving the drinks and towels behind along with the whispers of the crowd. I didn't give a shit about the gossip. All I cared about was this woman beside me. She was mine, and I'd make sure the world knew it.

I STEPPED INTO THE KITCHEN, wearing nothing but a pair of sweats after my shower as I clocked Ana standing at the stove. The air was thick with the aroma of garlic and simmering tomatoes, a scent that immediately made my stomach growl. She stood with her back to me, her slender frame bathed in the soft glow of the overhead light. Her ash-blonde hair was pulled into a loose bun on top of her head while her face was fresh and bare. She wore a summer dress, a light blue number that stopped mid thigh.

She smiled over her shoulder. "I hope you're hungry."

"For what, though?" I smirked. I knew she was rolling her eyes without even having to see her face.

I pulled out a stool at the kitchen island, my gaze lingering on the curve of her hips as she stirred the sauce with a wooden spoon.

There was something hypnotic about the way she moved, graceful yet purposeful, as if every action was a deliberate dance to either tease me or turn me on.

I leaned back, crossing my arms over my chest, unable to stop my eyes from tracing the lines of her body. Fuck, she was a vision. The thought of coming home to her daily had changed recently. It was something I looked forward to, and not just for the banter or to get on her last nerve, but to see her and enjoy my evenings with her.

"Is there a reason you're staring at me?" She chuckled, turning to face me.

"Can't I admire my wife?" I winked, resting my arms on the island as I leaned closer to her, inhaling her floral scent.

"You can admire me all you like, just behave until we've eaten."

She turned away from me, reaching up to grab a pot from the highest cabinet. I could have helped her, but then I wouldn't have gotten to see her dress riding up the backs of her thighs as she stretched. My breath hitched as I caught a glimpse of bare skin—wait a damn minute. She wasn't wearing any panties. The realisation hit me like a punch to the gut. It was primal and raw. My heart quickened, and a hunger stirred deep within me.

Without thinking, I was across the kitchen in an instant with only one thought on my mind. I set my sights on Ana who had no idea what was coming. I swept her up into my arms, her soft gasp mingling with the clatter of the pot she dropped. "Lorenzo, what—" she started, her blue eyes widening as I carried her out of the kitchen and into the living room. "The dinner, Lorenzo..."

"Dinner can wait," I growled.

I laid her down on the sofa, my gaze intense as it burned into hers. "You're not wearing anything under that dress, are you?" I murmured against her neck. "You did that on purpose, right?"

Her cheeks flushed, but her gaze didn't waver. "Maybe..." she admitted, her voice low and teasing. "Or maybe I just forgot."

"Is that how you want to play it?" I smiled, planting kisses on her neck.

I didn't give her a chance to respond. I hiked up her dress to reveal the smooth skin of her thighs. "Fuck," I breathed, letting my fingers trace the contours of her legs. I lowered kisses down her body, pushing her dress up around her waist before I buried my face between her legs, inhaling the warm, sweet scent of her. She let out a soft moan, her hands tangling in my hair as I kissed and nipped at her sensitive clit.

"Lorenzo," she whispered, her voice already trembling.

My hands gripped her thighs as my tongue delved into her pussy. She was already wet and ready for me. Her legs fell open, and I knew it wouldn't be long until she fell apart. Her body arched off the sofa as I devoured her, losing myself in her pretty cunt.

"Enzo," she moaned, the nickname she used, causing me to lose my fucking mind.

I traced patterns on her pussy with my tongue, ones that made her squirm beneath me. She dug her nails into my shoulders, and I welcomed the pain.

"Fuck me, please," she begged, grinding her hips against me.

"Don't you want to come this way, wife?" I murmured against her pussy, my cock throbbing against my sweats.

"I want you to fuck me," she whimpered.

With a rough tug, I pulled the only barrier between us off, my eyes meeting hers as I positioned myself between her legs. Her gaze dropped to my erection, her lips parting in a mix of desire and anticipation. "Hard, Enzo, I want it hard," she murmured, her hand reaching down to stroke my cock.

I caught her wrist, pressing it above her head before she could blink, my other hand gripping her thigh as I leaned in. "This pussy is mine," I breathed against her ear. "Every inch of you is mine."

She shivered at my words, her body yielding to mine as I pressed my cock against her tight entrance. With a savage thrust, I buried myself deep inside her, her gasp echoing through the room. She was so fucking tight, her pussy gripped me. I moved with a relentless rhythm, my hips snapping forward as I fucked her just like she wanted.

I grasped her thighs, forcing them around my waist. Her heels dug into my back as she met my thrusts, her body aching and desperate for more.

"Harder. Please." she panted, her voice breaking.

I tightened my hold on her as I pounded into her, my cock sinking deep into her sweet pussy. Her cries grew louder, her body tensing as she neared the edge, and I loved every second.

"You're so fucking tight," I moaned, letting pleasure surge through me like an electric current as I neared the edge. "I need to feel you fall apart. I fucking crave it."

"Then take it," she murmured, her breathing ragged. "Please, take it all."

"Fuck. Come for me,"

Her body convulsed beneath me as her orgasm ripped through her, her body shaking as she screamed my name. "Lorenzo!" she cried, her nails leaving marks on my shoulders. I followed soon after, my thrusts slowing as I buried myself deep inside of her, my release hot and relentless.

"Fuck, Ana," I groaned her name, pressing my forehead against hers as I emptied myself into her, my body jerking from the force of it.

She slowly unwrapped her legs from my waist, her body relaxing. I pulled out of her as the mixture of our arousals trickled from her pussy. Using the head of my cock, I gently nudged the mixture of our cum back into her wet, eager pussy. "Good girl." I pressed a soft kiss to her forehead before brushing a strand of hair from her face. "You're a dangerous woman, you know that?" I smiled.

Her fingers traced the scar on my cheek. "And you're a dangerous man," she replied, her voice laced with affection. "Now, how about we have dinner and go to bed?"

"For round two?" I teased.

"For whatever you want."

I SWITCHED off the car's engine in front of our estate, turning my attention to Ana. "Name a weekend, and we'll go. Whenever you want."

"Thank you. Being there was different, you know? Like I didn't need to think about any of the shit that has happened." She sighed.

"I'll never let anything happen to you ever again," I promised as I took her hand in mine, kissing her knuckles. "Come on, let's get inside. Maybe we can have a nice bath," I offered.

"I thought you were more of a shower man?" She laughed, the smile fully reaching her eyes as if what I said was funny.

"Usually, but I want to see what all the fuss is about." I winked. "Besides, you'll be in there with me. I can't imagine I'll get bored."

As we exited the car, our happiness soon vanished, the weight of reality crashing down around us.

Victor.

I clocked Red first, his body tense and ready for whatever happened next. Victor stood beside him. A man who once commanded a room, now just looked desperate. It didn't suit him. His pleading eyes met my wife's. He'd take anything she would give him.

"Anastacia," he called, his voice hoarse as if he hadn't used it in days. "Please, let me explain everything."

I tightened my hand around hers, brushing my thumb against her knuckles in a silent gesture of support. No matter what she wanted to do regarding her father, I'd always support her decision.

She stepped forward, moving with grace and elegance as she commanded everyone's attention.

"Explain what, Victor?" she asked, her tone cool, calm, and collected. "That you palmed me off for your own gain?" *That wasn't exactly a lie.* " Or that you let me disappear without putting up a fight?"

Victor's face twisted with pain, but Anastacia didn't flinch. She spent too long waiting for this moment, wondering why her own father hadn't come for her while she was holed up in that abandoned house.

"Lorenzo!" he spat. "He told me to stay away." His voice broke slightly. "He said I had to."

"And so what if he did?" she asked, sarcasm lacing her voice. "But you're Victor Fedorov. You could have fought against him. You could have come for me if you wanted to. But you didn't even try. You didn't even want to."

Victor's eyes dropped to the ground, and for a moment, I thought she'd stumble at the first hurdle, but she didn't. It didn't seem as though she was ready to forgive him. Not yet, anyway.

"Just go. You aren't welcome here." Her voice was firm as she squeezed my hand. "My husband told you to stay away, yet you disobeyed him and came here," she breathed. "Now I'm the one telling you to go, and I hope you don't disobey me the same way."

"Me? I disobeyed?! You are my daughter. I have every right to be here," he snapped.

"Shame you didn't think that way when I was missing." She turned to face me. "Lorenzo, let's go inside."

"I'm not done, Anastacia!" Victor spat, his anger rising. Red placed his hand firmly on his shoulder, but Victor shrugged it off aggressively. "Your husband took away my right to kill Chad."

"It's my right, not yours, so I think you'll find he took nothing from you," she seethed.

I slipped my hand around her waist, leading her towards the

house. Victor reached out, grabbing her arm, causing her to stop in her tracks.

"Get your hands off my wife, Victor," I growled as he only tightened his grip.

"Stay out of this, Ricci," he sneered. "This is a family matter. It doesn't concern you."

"That's where you're wrong. Ana *is* my family," My hand clenched into a fist at my side. "You're nothing but someone who's overstayed his welcome. My wife doesn't want you here, and neither do I."

"You used her, remember?" He snickered. "Is that what you do to someone you call family? Use them for your own gain?"

"It's what you did," Words tumbled out with a sharp edge, barely masking the fury that surged within me.

"I did what was needed." He smirked, his cockiness returning with a vengeance. "Anastacia, do you have no pride? The man used you before, and he'll do it again. Are you really that desperate for love? I didn't raise you to be that easy."

I'd heard enough. Without warning, I moved Anastacia out of harm's way before lunging forward, my fist connecting with Victor's nose in a swift, brutal motion. The sound of crunching bone beneath my fist only managed to subside a small percentage of my anger. "You didn't raise her at all, you motherfucker." I shouted, as Victor staggered back, clutching his face. Ana's hand flew to her mouth, but she didn't move. She remained by my side.

"You broke my—"

"Nobody, and I repeat nobody will ever speak about my wife that way again," I snarled. "You have no idea who she really is, or how incredible she is. And you don't deserve to know either. Now, get the fuck off my property." I loomed over Victor. "Leave Ana alone like she told you to. If I ever see your face again, I'll make sure mine is the last thing you'll ever see."

I led Anastacia inside, not looking back to see what Red was doing with Victor. Closing the door behind us, she buried her face into my chest, shocking me as I was sure she'd have kicked off at the fact I kept him away.

"I'm sorry," I whispered. "I kept him away to protect you."

"I know," she said softly. "And you were right to keep him away." She sighed. "All that matters right now is us."

I tilted her chin up with my finger, my eyes searching hers. "Always," I replied. "Just you and me."

28

ANASTACIA

One week later...

"You don't have to do this," Lorenzo reassured me, his voice laced with worry. The authority of who he was hung heavy around us. "Let me handle it."

I shook my head. "I need to see him." I may have sounded calm, but I had a storm raging inside me. "I need him to see me." Tonight, I planned to take back my power. Take back the part of me he thought he claimed.

"Okay, then I'm right beside you." He grabbed my face between his hands. "No matter what, I'll be right there."

His words were all I needed at that moment. They comforted me as much as his touch. My heart hammered in my chest. Not because I was scared, but because I was more than ready to end this and him.

We entered the warehouse, the air laced with the scent of metal, blood, and vomit. Gino, Red, Emmet, and Finn stood in a semicircle around Chad, who was suspended in the centre of the room. His wrists were bound in chains, hoisted above his head, his body a canvas of bruises and cuts. He hung there, broken but defiant.

"I'm back, you snivelling little cunt," Lorenzo sneered as he stepped closer to Chad.

"Fuck off," Chad spat, spit clinging to his chin, making me shudder with disgust.

"Ah, and here I was, thinking you'd be begging for your life." Lorenzo laughed. "But seeing you try and fight back has added a little excitement, a little spice, and I love it. I mean, what fun would it be killing someone who has already given up?" He smirked. "But then again, it won't be me killing you, it'll be my wife." A maniacal laugh left Lorenzo's body as Chad's mask slipped, revealing his shit-scared expression.

I stepped out from behind Lorenzo, Chad's eyes widening the second his gaze landed on me.

"Ana," he croaked desperately. "You came." He tried to smile, but it twisted into a grimace of pain. "I knew you'd come back to me. You're mine, remember?"

Deluded fuck.

My stomach churned at the sound of his voice. But I stood tall, not letting him see any weakness. "I'm not yours," I seethed. "I never will be."

Lorenzo shrugged off his jacket, throwing it over the chair in the corner, never once taking his eyes off of Chad. He kept his guard up in case Chad tried something, not that he could. Chad's twisted, vile voice spoke again, but this time his gratefulness was long gone.

"Oh, is it because you're already his?" He scoffed, his lips twisting into a sneer. "I bet you've already spread those pretty little legs for him, haven't you? Just like you should have for me."

Lorenzo took a step towards him, yanking his blade from his waistband. He pressed the steel against Chad's chest drawing a thin line of blood. "Shut your fucking mouth," Lorenzo growled, his voice a low rumble, causing my body to vibrate beside him.

Chad laughed, a ragged, painful sound. "You can't silence me,

Ricci. You think just by fucking her, you own her? She'll always belong to me and you know it."

Rage surged through me, a fire burning in my veins. I stepped closer to him as Lorenzo remained stoic and strong, letting me take control just as I needed. "Nobody owns me, not even my husband," I breathed. "Lorenzo, hand me the knife." I held out my hand. He placed the blade carefully into my palm.

Lorenzo's hand shot out, grasping my face between his fingers, his touch rough, yet intoxicating. I gasped at the intensity of his hold as my body reacted to his dominance.

He slammed his mouth against mine, his kiss savage and unrelenting. It wasn't a kiss of love or tenderness, but one of ownership, a brutal claim that left no room for resistance. His lips bruised mine, his tongue invading my mouth with a ferocity that stole my breath. My nails dug into his chest as he devoured me, marking me as his in the most primal way possible. "Have fun, wife." He smiled sinisterly, releasing me before he joined the men behind me.

Chad's expression was hurt, yet angry, and I welcomed it, I wanted him physically and mentally feel pain. I wanted him to feel what I felt.

"You're just doing this to hurt me," he screamed, his voice damn near damaging my eardrums.

"I'll show you just how much I can hurt you, Chad," I sneered, watching the colour drain from his face as the realisation hit him hard.

With a steady hand, I pressed the cold steel of the blade against his arm, watching as it effortlessly cut through the layers of his skin. Blood welled up instantly, a crimson river flowing down his forearm. His scream tore through the stillness of the warehouse, a shrill, primal wail that bounced off the concrete walls like the crescendo of a symphony. Each note of his agony seemed to resonate within me, filling me with a sense of liberation. The raw power coursing through me was intoxicating, a dark satisfaction that gripped me and refused to let go.

"Stop!" Chad cried, his body twisting in the chains. "Please, just fucking stop!"

But I didn't stop. I didn't want to. I moved methodically, slicing into his flesh, each cut a reminder of the pain he and his masked men had inflicted on me. Lorenzo watched, his eyes burning with a dark intensity. I bet the fucker was turned on. He always seemed to be, anyway. But he also knew what this meant to me. He knew I needed this.

Trailing my blade across Chad's exposed flesh, his body trembled. "Don't tell me you're scared?" I chuckled.

"I know what you're capable of," he cried.

"That's true. Shame you didn't stay on the right side of me then, isn't it?"

"You're too good for him, Ana." He thrashed against his restraints as I watched him exhaust himself.

"Oh, and I suppose you're perfect for me, are you?" I toyed with the tip of the blade as his eyes flicked between mine and the steel. "How about we play a little game?"

"Fuck you!" He raised his feet from the floor, trying to launch himself at me but it was useless. He had no strength left.

"I see you want to play, lucky me." I winked, patting his cheek as a stray tear left his eye. I didn't know if it was from the pain or if it was from the fact that it was me he was facing. "Question one—how could you and the cowards you call men beat the woman you supposedly love?" I asked, waiting for his stupid response.

"You provoked them, and you provoked me! What did you expect me to do?!" he screeched.

"Okay, squealer, calm down. It's too early for a headache, and if you survive what I've got planned for you, we'll be here a while," I replied, pondering what I wanted to do next.

"I know you're going to kill me, so get on with it," he roared.

The door behind me opened and closed. "Room for one more?" Nicolo beamed, clapping his palms together.

"What the hell is this? Some sort of party?!" Chad tried to crack a joke. How cute.

"If you want it to be," I teased. "How about this, you can be the human piñata." I laughed.

"That's not a bad idea, Ana," Red called from behind. "Save a whack for me, yeah? I want to see what candy falls out."

I picked up a bat from the table beside me. Maybe not a weapon some would choose, but I wanted to have fun. I wanted to make him feel it. Chad's eyes widened. He knew the ideas and thoughts that played in my mind.

"The difference being, we play for body parts, not candy." A sinister smile played on my lips as he let out a pent-up roar.

I ran the bat along his body, pausing at the tip of his shrivelled-up dick. "Maybe I'll start here. What do you think?"

"Get fucked!" he spat, thrashing in his chains.

"You know what, that's not a bad idea." I glanced over my shoulder at Lorenzo who wore a mischievous smile.

"Everyone out," Lorenzo demanded from behind.

The guys hesitated for a moment, their eyes flicking between Lorenzo and me. But in the end, they obeyed their boss, their footsteps echoing as they disappeared into the shadows.

The warehouse fell silent, except for Chad's ragged breathing and the occasional whimper. I felt a strange mix of satisfaction and revulsion as I stared at the man I once called my friend.

Lorenzo stepped closer to me, his presence overwhelming. He grabbed me by the wrist, pulling me toward him with no hesitation. His eyes burned with a raw and primal hunger as he pressed me against the table, the cold metal digging into the backs of my legs.

"What's going through that mind of yours?"

"I want you to fuck me." I whispered, as his teeth grazed my earlobe.

"Right here? Now?" The warmth of his breath caused goose-bumps to decorate my skin.

"Yes."

"You're something else," he murmured. His hands moved to my hair, fisting it tightly as he pulled my head back and exposed my neck. "So beautiful. My wife. Mine."

I felt his cock press against me, his desire palpable. The timing couldn't have been worse, but there was something about tonight that made me need him more than normal, made me crave him wholeheartedly.

Within a split second, he lifted me effortlessly onto the table. "Lie down," he demanded, the softness in his eyes gone.

Chad's screams filled the air, his pleas for mercy ignored. "Stop!" he cried. "She's mine! Anastacia, please, you're mine!" Despite being so close, it seemed as if he wasn't in the same room. I had never been fucked in front of anyone before, but there was something about it that made my pussy ache with need.

"Don't move," Lorenzo ordered as he fetched the duct tape from the table beside us. He ripped enough off to cover Chad's mouth , shutting the bastard up.

"Shut the fuck up, Chad," Lorenzo scolded, patting Chad's cheek in a humiliating gesture. "That's a good boy."

Lorenzo turned his focus entirely on me as he undressed me, savouring each passing second. I was submitting to him, something I vowed never to do, but right then, that had gone out the window. He could take whatever he wanted from me.

The knife in his hand caught my attention as the light reflected off the steel, its blade glinting with a thin sheen of Chad's blood. "Are you ready to play, wife?"

"Yes," I breathed as his lips twisted up at the corners.

"Good girl," he praised, tracing the knife lightly across my collarbone, the cold metal sending shivers through my body. It was a new feeling, something erotic, something I never expected to enjoy.

I bit my lip, a soft gasp escaping me as the blade left a faint red line on my skin. "You like that, don't you?" he asked, his breath warm against my neck. His free hand gripped my hip, keeping me still as he trailed the blade across my breasts, teasing my nipples. A feeling of ecstasy took over my body, as I started to come alive.

"Yes, Lorenzo, I like it," I whimpered as my nipples hardened beneath the blade.

Chad's muffled sobs couldn't escape the tape that covered his mouth. Knowing Lorenzo fucking me would be one of the last things Chad ever saw filled me with an insane amount of contentment.

Lorenzo pressed the blade against my inner thigh, dangerously close to my core. I was too far gone to care. I was at his mercy, and I loved it. I'd never experienced anything like it before. I should have been scared, I should have told him no. But I wasn't, and I didn't. I was more than ready to let my husband play with me. My legs quivered slightly, but I didn't pull away. Instead, I spread them wider, inviting him to fuck me senseless.

"Such a good girl," he growled. "And all mine."

"Yours," I moaned as I watched him effortlessly flip the knife in his hand so the blade was now flat against his palm. My eyes widened the second I realised his intentions. "Lorenzo..." I started, but he silenced me with a sharp kiss, his tongue demanding entrance. I moaned into his mouth, my hands clutching at his shoulders as he positioned the knife's handle at my entrance.

"Just trust me," he said against my lips, a request I couldn't refuse. Slowly, he pushed the handle of his favourite knife inside me, inch by inch as my pussy clenched around the foreign object.

Gasping for breath, I let my head fall back against the table, a torrent of pleasure crashing over me with relentless force. The icy metal pressed against my skin, a stark contrast to the inferno raging within me, each contact igniting electric shocks throughout my body. Never before had I felt such an explosion of life as he thrust into me repeatedly with the unforgiving steel handle, his thumb expertly swirling around my clit in flawless harmony, driving me to the edge of bliss.

"Look at my wife. What a vision," he whispered to me. He pulled the knife out of me slowly, my body quivering as he replaced it with his cock. I must have been too far gone to even notice him removing his pants.

"That's it," he praised as he thrust into me. "Take it." His hips snapped forward, his cock plunging deep into my wet pussy.

"Harder, Lorenzo," I panted, needing him more than I needed my next breath. "Fuck me harder."

He obliged instantly, his hands holding me in place as he obeyed my request. Our breaths came in ragged gasps as our skin slapped together, our bodies colliding time and time again.

Lorenzo's mouth was a torrent of dirty words, his voice low and commanding. "You're my perfect little slut. You love this, don't you? You love being used by me."

My eyes fluttered closed as I revelled in his words, my body teetering on the edge of release. "Yes," I whimpered. "I love it." A tear escaped my eye for no other reason than pure ecstasy.

His thrusts quickened, his muscles tightening as he neared his own climax. "Look at me," he commanded, his voice cutting through the air like a whip. My eyes flew open, instantly meeting his intense gaze as he drove into me with a force that left me breathless. "Come for me, now," he ordered, his words an irresistible force pulling me over the edge.

"Fuck! Lorenzo!" My body erupted around him, unable to restrain my orgasm crashing through me like a violent storm. Blood roared in my ears as I screamed his name, my walls contracting fiercely around his cock as he succumbed to the overwhelming sensation. His hips jerked as he filled me. "That's it, baby," he groaned, his voice dripping with raw satisfaction. "Take every drop."

And I did. He stayed inside of me until every last drop of his arousal remained inside my pussy.

"My good girl." He rested his forehead against mine, sweat beading on his skin. "You surprise me every single day." He smiled as he pulled out of me with a groan.

He wiped the knife on a nearby rag, the blade glinting innocently now, its edge no longer stained with blood. I tried to catch my breath as I came down from the high, my body still buzzing from the aftermath of our encounter.

Chad's muffled sobs filled the silence, his body slumped as he watched us with wild eyes. Lorenzo glanced at him briefly, a smirk playing on his lips. "Don't worry. We didn't forget about you." He laughed as he helped me to my feet. I quickly got dressed and Lorenzo followed suit.

"Do you see now, Chad?" I sighed. "I'm exactly where I want to be."

Lorenzo's arm snaked around my waist from behind, his chin resting on my shoulder. "And where might that be?" he asked.

"With you."

I removed myself from Lorenzo's hold as I stepped closer to Chad. I felt pure satisfaction when I ripped the tape from his mouth, not wanting to wait any longer to hear his screams as I beat the shit out of him.

"You really let him fuck you like that?!" he sneered.

"Yeah, and guess what? I love every single second of it." I smiled, knowing my words hurt him more than a bat or knife ever could. The doors behind me opened as the guys entered the room for support and to enjoy the show.

"Now, where shall I aim first?" I didn't give him time to answer as I placed the bat to his temple. "How about here? I could smash your brain to bits?" I shook my head, lowering the tip of the bat to his eye socket. "Or perhaps your beady little eyes?"

"Just get on with it!" he screamed.

I tormented his body as he continued to thrash against the chains. He could fight all he wanted. He wasn't leaving here, unless it was in unrecognisable pieces.

I lowered the bat to his dick as his eyes squeezed shut. "Open your eyes! Fucking look at me!" I demanded. "How about I smash you right fucking here? This cocktail sausage sized dick? I bet you've jerked off many times thinking of me, haven't you, you sick fuck?" I stood back for a moment, tapping the bat against my palm. "Let me see what my husband thinks." I turned to Lorenzo who looked as though he was ready to devour me whole again.

"You choose. This is your fight, not ours." Lorenzo smiled, giving me the go ahead I needed.

"Rearrange his face!" Red chimed in, looking like a proud brother. *I didn't have one of those anymore. Actually, I never did.*

"Stop playing around and get on with it." Chad's voice broke mid-sentence, as I turned back to face him. I loved the fact he was scared.

I whipped the bat through the air, aiming for his torso. The sound of his ribs cracking beneath it was utter perfection. His yelp of pain only spurred me on. I thrived off every squeak, every cry, and every howl.

"Fuck!" he cried, squeezing those beady eyes shut again.

"Enjoy every single second of it. It's the start of a very long day." I chuckled, swinging my bat to the other side of his ribcage.

I heard the blowtorch come to life behind me as Lorenzo stepped beside me, his eyes dropping to the tattoo that linked Chad to the Bratva.

"Please..." Chad pleaded. "I didn't mean to—"

"Didn't mean, what? Laying a finger on my fucking wife? Betraying her trust? Rallying men her own father banished for your own gain?! Each accusation seemed to fuel his rage further, his words echoing in the room. "The list is endless, you stupid cunt." He lost control, the venom in his voice matched only by the intensity of his glare, and in that moment, I understood the depths of his anger.

"No! Please! I'm sorry!" He begged Lorenzo but there was no point. "Let me die with it, please!"

"You can beg all you want, but your apology means fuck all to any of us." Lorenzo flickered the flame across his skin. The sharp, metallic tang of burning skin filled the air, causing my stomach to churn.

"You don't deserve to die with it. You deserve to die with nothing," I sneered. "These men took the lives of the men who hurt me, and now, they're all going to watch as I take yours."

Lorenzo removed the tattoo along with layers of flesh. The clattering from the chains alongside his screams was so loud it could have woken the dead. His body shook profusely beneath the flame. It was like we were watching an award-winning movie in slow motion. His skin sizzled, his body was a complete mess.

I picked up the knife from the table. It was the perfect choice. I rounded Chad's body slowly then pierced it though his back, just to the side of his spine. His cries echoed in the room. "Ana, please..." Blood trickled down his bruised skin, but I didn't stop there. I plunged my knife straight into his side and looked up at my husband as he watched with pride in his eyes.

"Now, I thought about cutting out your tongue but not hearing you scream would be no fun for me. And to be honest, I feel as though we deserve to hear them." I stabbed him a third time, on the other side of his spine that time. "How does it feel to be stabbed in the back?"

"Ana, you're mine! You've always been mine!" This fucker was getting on my last nerve.

"What would I want with a rotting corpse?!" I ran my blade up his arm to his pinky as I gripped it between my fingers. I sliced through his skin, flesh, and bone before discarding it on the floor.

"You always loved me! You just didn't give us time," he screamed and panted through the pain. Spit trickled down his chin as tears stained his cheeks.

Moving across to his ring finger, I repeated the same process—skin, flesh, bone.

"Tell me, Lorenzo, is fucking her tight pussy as good as I always imagined it would be?" Chad laughed as Lorenzo stepped forward. I moved aside instantly, wanting to see his anger unfold.

"You sick bastard," he snarled as he accepted the knife from my hand.

Without hesitation, Lorenzo leaned forward, his movements deliberate and precise. He pressed the blade against Chad's cheek, just below the eye, and began to carve. The skin parted with sickening ease, the blade slicing through flesh and muscle as if it were butter. Chad's body jerked violently, but Red was there in a split second, keeping Chad's head immobile as Lorenzo worked.

"A Chelsea smile," Lorenzo murmured, his voice almost tender, as if he was admiring a work of art. "Absolutely beautiful."

"I've never seen you look better." I chuckled, enjoying the sight of blood gushing from Chad's face. "There's a special place in hell reserved for you. But then again, hell might be too good for someone like you." I squeezed his wounded cheeks between my fingers and thumb as his lips pursed in pain. "Now, be a good boy, and beg me to kill you."

"I-I'll n-n-never," he stuttered, my grasp cutting off his words, as he fought the urge to slip into unconsciousness.

"That's a shame, it really is. Red, do you want to give him a little incentive?" I asked, stepping aside.

Without another word, Red released Chad's head, grabbing the bat from the ground. "I know it's not original or anything, but fuck, it's going to be fun." Red beamed, excited in a way I had never seen before. The bat flashed through the air with a loud swoosh before knocking out Chad's front teeth. I watched as they scattered to the floor like Tic Tacs.

"Nobody, and I repeat nobody, disrespects our Ana like that!" Red glanced over at me, nodding his head in a *we've got your back* kind of way.

"Before I kill this sorry excuse of a man, is everyone satisfied?" I asked, bringing my blade to Chad's neck.

"We are if you are," they spoke in unison, looking so damn proud.

I *was* satisfied, and I was ready to end him once and for all.

"Any last words?" I slapped his cheek, the sound echoing around us.

"Fu—" he spluttered, clearly in too much pain to continue.

"Fuck you? How original and creative." I scoffed.

I fisted his hair, yanking his head back to expose his neck. I pressed my blade into his skin, watching the blood slowly seep from the wound. I leaned into him, bringing my lips to his ear as I whispered, "Keep your eyes open. I want them to be the last ones you see as you take your final breath."

He obeyed, his gaze locked on the surrounding men, his breath coming in short, shallow gasps. With a swift, fluid motion, I drew the blade across his throat. The sound was sickeningly wet. A sharp hiss as the metal sliced through skin and muscle, exposing the raw, bloody flesh beneath.

Chad's eyes widened in shock, his mouth opening in a silent scream as blood gushed from the wound, hot and thick, spilling over my hand and dripping onto the floor. I didn't flinch, didn't look away. Instead, I watched him, my expression unreadable as his body convulsed, his hands straining against the binds.

As Chad's struggles weakened, my eyes never left his face. His body slumped forward, his life slipping away. I stepped back, my boots leaving faint prints in the pool of red spreading across the floor.

The silence that followed was deafening, broken only by the faint drip of blood and the distant hum of the single light overhead. My chest rose and fell steadily as I surveyed my handiwork. I did what needed to be done. What I had imagined doing while I was locked in that room. There was no regret, no hesitation. Only a quiet satisfaction, and a sense of closure.

"Are you ready to go?" Lorenzo asked, resting his hand on the small of my back. "The guys will dispose of him."

"Yeah, I'm ready."

29

VICTOR

Ten years ago...

Betrayal was something I never thought I'd encounter, especially not at the hands of my ally and best friend, Franco Ricci. But that night changed everything, it changed me.

I stood amidst the wreckage of what was once a thriving warehouse, now reduced to a battleground. The pungent smell of smoke and blood hung heavy, a grim reminder of the betrayal that had brought me here. My eyes scanned the scene, taking in the bodies of my former allies one by one as they laid lifeless, their faces contorted in anguish in their final moments of agony.

I had trusted Franco once, considered him my own fucking brother, but that trust had been shattered just like the broken crates that were scattered around us. We had so many plans. Plans that would have made us stronger and richer than ever, but he had to go and get greedy. He had to side with my own enemy.

I'd always been a man of precision, and tonight was no exception. Every move, every strike, had been calculated to bring me to this moment.

My men fought with ferocity, their loyalty to me unwavering. The clash had been brutal, but my strategic mind had turned the tide, exploiting every weakness, every moment of hesitation among Franco and his men.

In the centre of the warehouse, Franco laid on his back, his once proud figure now broken. I loved it. I felt nothing other than victorious. His breath came in ragged gasps as his eyes widened with shock and pain. A crimson stain was spread across his chest where my blade had pierced him, a stark contrast to his white shirt.

"Ah, Franco, you just couldn't help yourself, could you?" I sighed, standing over him, his hand clutching his wound as blood seeped through his fingers.

"You... You were always the smarter one," Franco rasped, his voice weak and his pride shattered. "But you never understood p-power. It ch-changes things."

My lips curled into a mirthless smile. "Power corrupts, Franco. It blinded you. You thought you could play both sides, but you forgot one thing," I breathed. "I always win."

Franco's eyes flickered with a mixture of hatred and desperation. "You'll never get away with this. Lorenzo, he'll—"

"He's just a boy, Franco." I scoffed. "He's nineteen. He has no idea how we work, what we do, or how to come up against me."

"He'll learn, and one day, you'll regret this." He coughed.

"I have nothing to regret. You were the one who betrayed me," I sneered, crouching down to get closer, slamming my finger into his chest. "You were the one who fucking sold me."

"He w-won't know that." His breathing shallowed as he spoke.

"Papa! Where are you?!"

My head snapped up, clocking Lorenzo as he burst into the warehouse, his young face paling as he spotted his father. His eyes went wild with fear and anger. He was tall for his age, his dark hair a mirror of his father's, but his expression was one of raw emotion.

"Papa?!" he cried out, his voice breaking as he rushed over to us, only to be halted by one of my most loyal men. "Let me go!" he shouted, trying to reach for his own weapon. "You can't do this, Victor! You can't just kill him!" he screamed.

"Your father made his choices, boy. He chose his path and now he has to fucking pay for it." I rose to my feet, watching Franco struggle to look at his son. "You don't know how this life works yet, but you will, and when that time comes, you'll realise that he deserved worse than what he got."

"P-please, Victor. G-give me my b-boy," he pleaded. I had no clue what came over me, but I signalled for Lorenzo to be let go.

"Say your goodbyes, boy." I nodded before heading towards the exit, leaving a teenager to take his father's place.

I didn't know what was said between them before he died, but I knew that, in time, Lorenzo Ricci would come for me. I'd be ready for it. I would never bow down to a Ricci, never let my guard down again.

It should have hurt ending my best friend's life, but it didn't. I felt nothing for him, Carmella, or Lorenzo. This was the life we lived. We could go out one evening never to return home, and that's what happened with Franco. We both left the house tonight, but I was the one who'd walk back through the door. I was the smarter one out of the two of us.

As my men and I exited the warehouse, I heard Lorenzo's piercing scream.

I turned to Artem, pausing for a moment. "Keep an eye on the boy for now. See who he confides in, what he does, where he goes. I want it in fucking detail so I know exactly what we'll be dealing with."

"But he's a boy, Boss," Artem whispered, feeling somewhat sorry for the kid.

"That might be so, but he's Franco's son." I scoffed, thinking about how much I had trusted him. "In the end, the apple doesn't fall too far from the tree."

"Boss." Artem nodded. "And our men inside—what's the plan there?"

"I want their bodies collected before the sun comes up. You will personally contact their families, and I'll foot the bill for their funerals." I entered the car, already forgetting the shit that went down tonight.

I ENTERED MY HOUSE, expecting to see my wife at the staircase. She would sit and wait there if I wasn't home by a certain time, or when she got a gnawing feeling in her gut that something was wrong. Tonight, though, she wasn't there.

"Papa!" Anastacia ran down the stairs, sprinting to where I stood covered in blood. The darkness of what I did never seemed to bother her. She always looked past it as if she was used to it. "I waited up for you."

"You should be in bed," I snapped, forgetting she was only a child.

"But Papa..." Her bottom lip quivered as her huge blue eyes looked up at me.

"What did I say about showing weakness, Anastacia? Straighten the face and go back to bed," I ordered. It had been a shit night, and I didn't need her around. "Deal with her, Artem." I turned my back to them, letting my most trusted right-hand look after her.

I paused at my office door, still in ear shot of them.

"He didn't even say goodnight to me, Arty," she whimpered, letting her fucking guard down yet again. *Did she ever listen?*

"I know, my little fighter, and I know it's not the same, but I'll say goodnight. Will that do?" Artem soothed.

"Yes, please."

I leaned back, just enough to be able to see around the corner.

Artem had crouched down to her level and was wiping away Anastacia's tears. "Goodnight, little one." He smiled. "You have sweet dreams, okay?"

She replied with a nod before her dainty feet carried her up the stairs to her bedroom.

I entered my office, quickly lighting a cigar before Artem joined me.

"Boss..."

"Not fucking now, Artem. I already know what you're going to say."

"She's just a girl. One who needs her father." He continued.

"I don't have time for her, my focus is Miles." I sighed. "You know what daughter's are raised for in our world. She'll be no different."

"Victor."

"That's enough, Artem. She's my daughter, not yours. My say with her will always be the final one." I replied, as Artem kept quiet, unable to say anything else.

Artem had no family. His wife and son had been brutally taken from him, and he never moved on. He couldn't. I knew he disapproved of me acting this way towards Anastacia. Fuck, he treated her more like a daughter than I did. Part of me realised he was a much better father than I ever would be. To her anyway.

I loved her, of course I did, but she was useless to me. Unlike her brother, who could carry on the family name and my legacy. The only use I had for her wouldn't come until later in life when I'd marry her off for an alliance.

30

LORENZO

"You two look well rested after your trip." My mother smiled widely, her eyes crinkling at the corners, as she gently placed our plates on the dining table. The rich scent of tomatoes, garlic, and herbs from the bubbling lasagna filled the air, blending with the warm, yeasty smell of the crusty bread she had just pulled from the oven. My stomach rumbled in response, and a wave of nostalgia washed over me. Memories of sun-drenched afternoons in Sicily with Ana flooded my mind. Making me acutely aware of how much I longed to be there again. "How was it, *la mia bellissima ragazza*?"

Anastacia's face was a picture of confusion as my mother spoke in Italian to her. It was adorable. "She called you her beautiful girl." I smiled, leaning into her as she sipped her red wine, her new favourite since enjoying it at my grandparents' restaurant. She loved it so much I made sure to bring plenty home.

"Thank you for the compliment." Anastacia blushed. "The trip was lovely. It was nice to actually just spend time together with no distractions." As Ana spoke, my mother grinned from ear to ear. All she wanted was for my marriage to work.

"I see my son treated you to the ring you deserve." My mother's face was a picture, as if she knew the second I said *I do* I'd fall in love with Ana.

Fuck... Was I in love with her? Was this intense need to have her and be with her at all hours of the day love? Could a person fall in love that fast? Or were these feelings present from the very beginning and I just never let myself see it? Was I too blinded by revenge to notice and realise what love with Ana could be like?

"Lorenzo? Are you okay? You were a million miles away," Ana asked, placing her hand on mine, bringing me right back to the present, stopping the never-ending questions in my head.

"Yeah, all good." I shrugged everything off, trying to work out what was going on in my heart and mind could wait until later.

"So, my parents seem to be quite taken with you. My mama actually said you were better than she could have imagined. The perfect wife for her little Lorenzo." Mama chuckled as did my wife.

"I'm glad. Besides, he's not so bad, after all." Ana winked at me, and I felt a rush of peace. It was as if her smile alone could take every thought, worry, and stress away.

"People did try to tell you," I teased, draping my arm over her shoulder. The complete turnaround was even giving me whiplash.

"Listen, *figliolo*, I know you're not the easiest to live with and you really did outdo yourself with Anastacia, but I just hope that you two can grow and have a life together." She patted my hand, her eyes falling to the black band around my ring finger. "Plus, I need some grandkids." My mother laughed, throwing her head back in delight.

Anastacia remained silent. I knew she didn't want to talk about children yet. She wanted to enjoy her life a little first, and to be honest, I wanted to enjoy us for a bit. I'd only just got her properly, and I wanted to show her the world before we enjoyed days filled with diapers, lullabies, and baby giggles.

"Oh, I'm just kidding. You two have all the time in the world." My mother looked over at Ana who nodded in agreement.

And we did. We had plenty.

MY MOTHER'S demeanour shifted after dinner, almost as if she was holding onto something but was waiting for the right moment. I knew her all too well to know she was hiding something.

I sipped my coffee as she sat beside me, her eyes flicking between her mug and Ana.

"Mama, what is it?" I asked, turning to face her.

"How did you know there was something on my mind?" She looked nervous and worried, which only made me feel sick to my stomach.

"Mama, come on. I know you," I breathed. "Tell me."

She pinched the bridge of her nose, letting out a deep sigh before apologetically looking up at Ana one more time.

"It's about your father," she whispered, looking down at her knotted fingers. "I know this will be hard to hear." She sighed, composing herself.

I knew it was bad, I had a sickening feeling that I already knew what she wanted to say, what I'd been dreading to believe.

Ana's eyes flicked up to meet mine with a reassuring glance. I'd put that woman through hell, been an absolute bastard, but yet, she still sat there being supportive without needing to say a damn word.

"What's going on?" I asked.

"I found a letter," Mama whispered. "I didn't even know his desk had a hidden drawer but—"

"What was in the letter?"

Please don't say it, Mama.

"The letter was an alliance agreement between your father and Victor's enemy, Quincy Dion." Her voice trembled as she continued. "Your own father betrayed us. He betrayed his best friend, all for money."

The room spun as I processed her words. He fucking lied to me.

When he took his final breaths, he fucking lied. He screwed over everyone who ever trusted him, including his family. He didn't think about the repercussions of his actions when he sold out his best friend.

"Why?" I seethed. "Why the hell did he do it?"

My mother's eyes filled with sorrow. She was betrayed as well. She was kept in the dark just as much as I was. Alright, I was nineteen at the time and probably had no clue what his Don title entailed, but he could have confessed in his final moments. He could have come clean.

"I don't know, Lorenzo, but it was there in black and white. He gave them everything—Victor's secrets, his shipment details, his plans, everything." She gripped my hand tightly. "He arranged for Victor to meet him that night. He pretty much signed his death warrant for him, only it went the opposite way."

My mind raced as I remembered the upcoming days to that night. It all made sense now. He'd been shutting himself away, sneaking around at all hours of the night, and to be honest, I thought that was just part of who he was. I never read too much into it until tonight.

"If you'll excuse me for a second." Ana stood quickly, not wasting any time heading out onto the patio.

"Mama—" I started.

"Go. This is as big for her as it is for you." She patted my hand softly. "I was used to your father's betrayal, you weren't. We don't know how much Anastacia knew, so go after her."

I kissed my mother's cheek. "I love you, Ma."

I headed out onto the patio, my eyes falling on Ana. She had her back to me, and her hair blew softly in the wind. I took a slow, deliberate step forward, my gaze never straying. I was never one to be easily distracted, but she had a way of drawing me in, whether she intended to or not.

"I remember so much about that night..." She sighed, keeping her back to me. "I was so excited to see him that I waited up late. I even put fucking bows at the ends of my braids."

"What happened?" I asked, wrapping my arms around her waist from behind.

"He shouted at me for not being asleep, and then because I showed weakness when he raised his voice, he gave me this look of disgust." She sighed. "No crying in front of him or anyone else. That was one of his rules."

"Ana..."

"Artem, my father's right hand at the time, was the only one who truly ever cared for me in that house. But he disappeared without a trace, and after that day I'd never felt so alone. Sure, I had my grandparents, but they didn't live with me, and even though my *babushka* asked for me to live with her and *dedushka,* my father said no."

"Stop, it's okay, you don't need to talk about it." I cupped her face, as she nuzzled her cheek into my palm.

"I used to want him to love me as much as he loved my brother, but I knew what I was good for. I knew he would eventually use me by handing me off to a man I didn't know." She whispered. "I just thought he'd have the decency to let me meet him first, but I guess that was too much to ask from him."

"I'm so sorry I played a part in that. I'm so fucking sorry, and if I could change it even the slightest bit, I would." I half smiled. "But I wouldn't change marrying you. You are the only person who has kept me on my toes. The only one who isn't afraid to put me in my place, and the one that makes me feel something." I forced her to look up at me.

"Our fathers were as bad as one another, both power and money hungry. I don't blame your father for what he did to mine. I don't even blame you for wanting revenge for what you thought happened." She sounded so sure of herself. "If your father didn't betray mine, mine would have stabbed yours in the back. It was inevitable."

"We won't pay for our father's mistakes anymore, but believe me when I say I'll spend a lifetime paying for mine." I brought my lips to within an inch of hers. "Your father doesn't deserve you, *amore mio*." The Italian endearment rolled off my tongue with a smoothness that made my own heart flutter. Or whatever it did. This shit was all new to me. It was the first time I'd called her that, and I knew it wouldn't be the last.

"And you deserve me, do you?" she whispered.

"Yes, I do. " I smiled, and it was the first time I truly felt as though I was worthy of her.

That I deserved every single part of her.

I pressed my lips against hers, as if needing to seal my words. She responded eagerly, her hands wrapping around my neck as she deepened the kiss. The taste of her, the feel of her body against mine, was a reminder of what we were building together, a bond that transcended the chaos of our fucked up worlds.

BEING HOLED up in my office at the club wasn't my idea of fun today, especially since Rox was the reason I was here. But there was no way in hell, I'd have him come to the house, so here would do. He'd already made his first fuck up, that stupid bastard had been trying to undercut me with shitty weapons, and that was one thing I didn't take kindly to. I wouldn't let some lowlife weasel do me over.

The door clicked open without warning. A female worker slipped inside, her heels clicking softly against the marble floor. She was young, maybe in her mid-twenties, with a pencil skirt that cinched tightly around her waist and a blouse that was unbuttoned in a way that revealed way too much. Her eyes shone with a mixture of ambition and desire. Desire that was unwanted.

Her hips swayed as she approached my desk. "Mr. Ricci," she

purred, her voice dripping with false sweetness. "I just wanted to check and see if you needed anything else. I could...stay late if you'd like."

My eyes flicked down to my phone, my expression hardening. I held up my hand to silence her, but she ignored it, running her fingers along my shoulders. Her touch was anything like my wife's. My grip tightened on my phone, and my knuckles whitened.

"Get your hands off me," I ordered. Of course, she didn't comply. I grabbed her wrist without even looking at her, the force of my hold causing her to gasp. "I said get your fucking hands off me and get out," I hissed. "Before I make you regret it."

Before she could respond, I heard the door slam shut. I half expected it to be Rox turning up early, but instead, it was my wife who strode into the room. She was a vision, dressed head to toe in black. Her eyes narrowed in on me as her lips pressed into a thin line. She wasted no time in moving closer as the waitress's mouth twisted into a smirk.

"He's busy, sweetie, or have you come to join us?" she murmured seductively as Anastacia looked just about ready to kill the bitch with her bare hands. Once upon a time, she would have said go ahead, have him, but not anymore.

"Didn't you hear my husband?" Ana asked, her voice deceptively calm.

"Husband or not, we can still share." This woman didn't have a clue when to shut up, did she?

Without warning, Ana closed the remaining distance and grabbed her by her hair, yanking her head back with a force that made her whimper. "My husband told you to leave, so unless you want to end up in pieces scattered across the city, I suggest you do as you're told and listen."

The girl's face drained of colour, her eyes darting between Ana and me in panic. "I-I'm sorry..." she stammered, trying to pull away from Ana's grip. "I didn't mean to—"

“Shut up,” Anastacia snapped, her voice like a whip. “Get out. Now,” she said with a warning in her tone. “If you breathe a word of this to anyone, I’ll find you, and trust me, it won’t be pleasant when I do.”

She nodded frantically as Ana shoved her head away. She didn’t look back as she fled, the click of the door echoing through the silent office. Ana watched her go with a cold smile before turning her attention back to me.

“It would seem as though my wife has a possessive side when it comes to me, am I right?” I teased, pulling her between my legs by her belt loops.

“I don’t like people thinking they can take what’s mine, that’s all.” She grinned, her eyes softening.

“Nobody stands a chance, *amore mio.* I only want you.” I smiled. “So, what did I do to deserve a visit today?” I asked.

“Nothing.” She smiled, her eyes glinting with mischief. “I just felt like it.”

She grabbed my tie, pulling me up until I was standing toe-to-toe with her. Her hands moved to my belt, her fingers deft as she undid it before making quick work of lowering my pants and letting them fall to the floor. I didn’t resist. My eyes darkened with desire as she stepped back, her gaze bold and unapologetic.

I rested my hands on my desk as she dropped her knees, her skirt riding up around her waist as she knelt on the floor, looking up at me through raven lashes. Her fingers traced invisible lines on my legs. Her touch was light and teasing as she moved her petite fingers up my thighs, her nails grazing my skin.

“Always so hard for your wife,” she whispered, her breath warm against my aching cock. Her fingers brushed against my length, teasing me to no end. All I wanted to do was fuck that pretty little mouth of hers, but I let her take the lead, wanting to see what her plan was for me. She pressed her lips to my hip and kissed across my stomach. Anywhere but where I wanted her mouth. "Let me taste you," she breathed against my skin.

"Do it," I growled, my voice rough with need for her as my grip tightened on the desk.

Her fingers finally slid around my cock, squeezing gently before she leaned in, her tongue flicking the tip. "Fuck," I groaned as my head fell back the second she took me in her mouth, her lips wrapping around me with deliberate slowness. She took me deep as a tear escaped her eye. Her tongue swirled around the head as her hands gripped my thighs to steady herself.

"Fuck, Ana." I moaned breathlessly as she worked me with expert movements that were, unfortunately, short-lived.

What the fuck was she doing?

She pulled back, her eyes meeting mine as she slid her fingers under her skirt and between her legs, letting out a soft moan as she stroked her pussy. I couldn't take my eyes off her as she touched herself, her lips parting to let out the sweetest fucking breathy moans.

"What are you doing?" I asked, my voice hoarse and full of fucking need.

"Showing you what you're missing," she teased, her fingers moving faster as her breaths came in short gasps. She leaned into me, her lips brushing mine as she whispered, "I'm so wet for you. Do you want a taste?"

What kind of question was that? Too right, I wanted a taste.

I fisted her hair, pulling her head back so I could fully see her face. "Stop teasing me," I commanded. "You already know the answer."

"And if I don't stop... What will you do then?" she challenged, her eyes daring me to take control.

I didn't hesitate as I grabbed her by the wrist and pulled her to her feet. I couldn't resist. I ripped open her skirt, letting it fall to the floor around us. "No panties again, Mrs. Ricci?"

"It certainly looks that way." She teased her lower lip between her teeth. I quickly took over, pulling it into my mouth as I pressed her body against the desk with my own.

"You want to play games?" I whispered, lifting her effortlessly onto the desk as she let out a gasp. "Then, let's play."

My hands moved to her thighs, spreading them wide as I dropped to my knees between her legs. Anastacia's breath caught as my fingers slid into her, my touch rough and demanding. "Good girl," I growled, loving how wet she was for me. I sank my fingers deeper and teased her, circling my thumb over her clit.

I pulled my fingers free and licked them clean. The taste of her was the only drug I'd ever need. "You taste so fucking good," I whispered, the warmth of my breath skating across her bare pussy.

"Fuck..." She moaned breathlessly, her head falling back as I leaned in, letting my tongue replace my fingers. I wanted to devour her with a hunger that left her trembling. I ate her pussy like she was my last meal, one I'd die a happy man eating. I gripped her thighs and left my mark on her skin as my tongue teased and worked her relentlessly.

"Lorenzo," she gasped, her nails digging into my shoulders as her body slowly started to quiver, threatening to give in earlier than expected.

But I wouldn't let her give in just yet. Instead, I pulled her back. "Not yet," I whispered between slow, tantalising strokes."I'm not done with you."

Her breath came in ragged gasps as she struggled to fight the ache for release. I loved every single second of making her wait. She opened her mouth to protest, but that was replaced by a moan of pleasure as I spanked her sweet pussy, hitting the spot I knew would drive her wild.

"Fuck!" she moaned, her chest heaving as she struggled to regain her control. Her moans were like a symphony of perfection and listening to them was pure ecstasy. "What are you waiting for?" she challenged, her voice nothing more than a whisper.

My lips curved into a dangerous smile. "For you to beg." I smirked. "For you to *beg* for your release."

"Eat my pussy like a good boy, and I'll beg you," she commanded. I almost combusted, hearing her words.

I slowly traced a deliberate path along her pussy as ragged moans escaped her. I knew exactly where to touch, lick, and nip in order to get her to surrender. Sucking on her clit, she let out a whimper. It only made me suck harder, thrusting my fingers deeper as I curled them inside her.

"Fuck... Please..." she moaned, her body arching into my touch. "Lorenzo... Please..."

"Once more." I needed to hear her plead, needed to hear her whimper as her orgasm was on the brink of exploding through her.

"Please... Let me come, please..." she cried, her voice no longer the whisper it was before.

"Fuck. Come for me," I growled, my voice vibrating against her skin. "Let me taste it. Give me everything," I demanded as my words sent her over the edge.

"Lorenzo, fuck!" She cried out as her orgasm ripped through her. My mouth never faltered as I devoured her, savouring every last drop of her arousal. She was helpless, lost in a storm of pleasure. Her body trembled as I flicked my tongue over her clit one final time.

"Good girl. I knew you could beg for what you wanted," I teased as I rose to my feet, positioning myself between her legs.

"That's the only time I'll ever beg, so don't get used to it."

"Noted." I dipped down, retrieving her skirt before worrying about myself. I helped her back into it, fastening it as best as I could since I'd broken the zipper. "Good as new."

"You know it's not. You did it on purpose." She smirked. "Not that I minded, though. It was hot." She chuckled, stirring something within me. Something so damn good.

"I have a meeting in about..." I glanced at my watch. "Now, actually. You kept me so busy that I lost track of time." I pulled on my pants just as there was a knock on the door. "Looks like he's here now, will you stay?"

"Do you want me to?" She looked shocked, which was cute since she was just as intimidating as my men were, so why not have her stay?

"Of course I do. Stay beside me though," I ordered. "Enter," I called out.

Rox stepped in, his usual smirk faltered as he took in the scene. Ana's presence was undeniable. She was as powerful as I was, and Rox knew it. She had no idea what he'd done, but she knew how to read the room. She knew he fucked up.

Rox's gaze lingered on her, and my jaw tightened. I hadn't forgotten the last warning I'd given Rox about staring at and making remarks about my wife, but he didn't seem to remember those words and threats.

"Lorenzo," Rox began, his tone cautious. "I—"

"Save it," I interrupted, not giving a shit about what his excuses were. "Sit down."

Rox hesitated before taking a seat across from the desk, his eyes flicking between Ana and me. I pulled out my chair, gesturing for my wife to sit down. She raised her brow in confusion, but she complied nonetheless.

She lowered herself gracefully, taking a seat as I stood beside her, my hand resting possessively on the back of the chair as my knuckles brushed her bare shoulder. "This might be my seat, but that also means it's yours," I whispered. Her lips curved into a faint, knowing smile. What's mine was now hers. She was my equal. Just as she should be.

I turned my attention back to Rox who shifted in his seat. Poor bastard knew I was pissed off to say the least. "You dealt us complete and utter shit," I seethed, my voice cutting through the room like the blade that sat in my waistband. "You know that shitty weapons could get my men killed. Did you really think I'd let that slide? Do you think I'm too busy to notice?"

Rox shifted uncomfortably, his hands fidgeting. "It was a mistake, Lorenzo. I—"

I rounded the desk, keeping my eyes locked on the quivering cunt in front of me as Ana seemed to enjoy my calculated movements. "You see, Rox, I don't like mistakes. Can't stand them, actually, and you have made a monumental one. Just as the last one did, and do you know what happened to him?"

My hand shot out the second I was in range, grabbing him by the collar of his expensive shirt that was doused in some cheap, foul smelling cologne. I hauled him to his feet, my temper rapidly rising. "He was hacked apart and buried all over the city. Shame since he was a nice lad, but just like you, he tried to screw me over despite the contract we had in place."

"Listen..." He trembled.

"No, *you* listen. Did you read that contract, Rox?" I asked, surprisingly calm for how angry I was.

"Y-yes..." he struggled.

"Wrong, try again." I laughed.

"Okay! N-no, I d-didn't read i-it!" He clawed at my hand, but it only made me tighten my hold on his collar. I squeezed the fabric and cut off his air supply.

"Top of the class for you for finally telling the truth." I knew he hadn't because the fine print stated he was signing away the rights to his death if he fucked up.

Before Rox could respond, I pulled the knife from my belt, the blade glinting under the office lights. Ana watched on as I forcefully shoved my blade into Rox's side, just missing his lung.

He gasped, his eyes widening in pain as he fisted my shirt.

"Y-you stabbed m-me..." he managed as I let his collar go.

"I know, and you're lucky I'm in a good mood, otherwise it would have been worse. Fatal even," I growled, my voice laced with venom. "One more chance, just one. But one more fuck up, and you're a dead man. You won't even see it coming. It'll be a surprise, and even if you run and hide at the ends of the earth, I'll find you regardless."

"I won't fuck up again. You have my word." He tried to move but realised that the second he did, the knife would bury itself deeper and damage his insides more than it already was.

"Your word means fuck all to me right now." I turned my attention to Ana who had now joined me. "I might have spared you today—because my wife put me in the best mood before you showed up, so you're going to thank her for that."

Rox's eyes darted to Ana, confusion and fear mixing in his expression. His gratitude wasn't fast enough, which didn't sit right with me, so I pushed the knife deeper as he whimpered in pain.

"Fucking thank her. Show her some respect before I let you bleed out," I snapped, my hand tightening around the handle.

Rox groaned, his face contorted in pain. "Thank you," he managed, his voice barely audible.

I smirked, twisting the knife slightly. "Louder."

"Thank you, Mrs. Ricci," Rox choked out, his voice trembling.

"Well done. Now, get out." I shoved him away as my knife practically removed itself. He stumbled back, clutching his side as the blood seeped out and stained his shirt. "And remember, don't let there be a next time."

He scurried out of the office faster than his feet could carry him, leaving me alone with my wife. I glanced down at my watch, perfect timing. "I have some things to finish up here. Red will take you home. Be ready for seven thirty. I'm taking you on a date."

"Let me guess—it's a surprise?" she asked, her lips breaking into a smile.

"Yes, it's a surprise, but I promise it'll be worth it." I winked. "I know you haven't seen the girls much recently, what with me whisking you away after everything, but they'll meet you back at the house to help you get ready and catch up."

"Did you call them?" she questioned.

"I did, and it was worth it to see the smile on your face right now."

She pecked me on the lips, thanking me in the best possible way. "I'll see you later then." She smiled, turning on her heel to leave. "Don't be late, Ricci."

"I wouldn't dream of it, wife."

31

ANASTACIA

"How are you feeling, Ana?" Robin asked, curling up on the edge of the bed.

"Much better. I feel as though I can finally start fresh now that Chad's gone." I sighed, thinking back to the night I took that bastard's life.

"Lorenzo killed him?!" Tay asked, her mouth falling open before she gave me a sinister smile.

"No, I did," I whispered.

"That's our girl!" Robin cheered. "That bastard deserved everything he got, if not more, and I'm glad Lorenzo let you take the lead."

"He did. He offered to do it, but he knew I needed it." I traced my arm where a bruise once was, no longer so emotional from it.

"I knew I liked him!" Tay laughed, sipping her wine.

"No, you didn't!" Robin teased, rolling her eyes before turning her attention back to me. "How's he been now?"

"He's like a different man," I breathed. "He's changed, and I know it's because of what happened to me... But now I think would he have changed if it hadn't have happened, or would he have been the same bastard he was?"

"You can't think that way. It doesn't matter why he changed. All that matters is that he did change and you're happy with him." She took my hand in hers. "You do look happy, Ana, really happy."

"I feel different. I've never felt this way before. I don't know what it is, but he makes my heart—"

"Somersault? Flip? Skip a beat?" Robin's eyes widened with delight, waiting for my answer.

"A bit of everything. Why is that?" I asked.

"Ana, I think you might be falling in love." Tay winked, nudging me softly with her elbow.

"Love?!" I gasped, not knowing if what I felt was love or if I was still in my lust phase. "We've been married for five bloody minutes, I can't fall in love that fast, can I?"

"It doesn't matter how long you've been married for. Love comes when you least expect it, and you, my beautiful friend, are least expecting it." Robin was over the moon, beaming from ear to ear. "Now, time is getting on, let's help you get ready! We don't want you to keep your husband waiting come seven thirty."

"I'm sure he'd wait if she was a little late." Tay laughed.

And I knew he would wait.

That was for certain.

7:25 PM

I GAVE myself a once-over in the mirror before meeting Lorenzo. I barely recognised myself. The girls had well and truly gone to town on my appearance tonight. They straightened my hair to within an inch of its life, and my makeup was completely different, especially for me since I tended to keep my face bare most of the time.

Tay had chosen an emerald green dress for me, a striking

garment that embraced my figure perfectly, until it elegantly halted mid-thigh. The rich, deep hue of the fabric shimmered subtly under the light, adding an air of sophistication and allure. As I admired my reflection, I had to admit that I looked as stunning as I felt, my confidence soaring with each glance. A hint of anticipation fluttered within me as I couldn't help but wonder what Lorenzo would think when he saw me.

I made my way to the top of the stairs, pausing when my eyes landed on the man who waited for me at the bottom of them. He was dressed head to toe in black, his shirt rolled up to the elbows, revealing part of his intricate tattoo. I was nervous, and my stomach somersaulted, thinking back to what the girls said about love.

The second I descended the stairs, the air crackled with electricity. His eyes connected with mine, a smile playing on his lips. "You look breathtaking," he complimented.

"Thank you," I replied with a gentle smile. "You're not so bad yourself," I teased as I stepped closer, his eyes never leaving me with every step I took. Without a word, he pulled me into him and pressed his lips tenderly to mine. He wrapped his arms around my waist, not allowing there to be any distance between us. It was as if he wanted to remind himself that we were real and what we shared was, too.

Just as the moment threatened to deepen, the sound of laughter and loud voices interrupted our intimacy. Of course, it was the guys. They were never too far away. They'd just arrived home, their boisterous presence filling the foyer.

"Oh, would you look at that? Boss man is finally all loved up," Finn joked, earning a chorus of laughter, and to be honest, I couldn't help myself as I joined in.

I watched as Lorenzo's jaw tightened, but I couldn't work out if he was pissed off or amused. "Listen, you lot can all fuck off, alright?" They exchanged glances as their smiles faded before they quickly dispersed, knowing better than to push their luck.

“You know Ana laughed too, right?” Red chuckled as he made his way to the kitchen.

“She’s my wife, so she can,” he replied before returning his attention to me. He took my hand in his, leading me towards the garage. “Let’s go.” He smiled. The carefree and relaxed Lorenzo was back. I followed willingly, my heart racing with excitement and anticipation all rolled into one. “I have to admit, I’m excited to see your face when we arrive where we’re going.”

“Where are we going?” I asked, hoping he wouldn’t keep it a surprise.

“It’s a surprise.” He laughed.

Of course it was. I didn’t know why I expected anything else.

After what felt like forever watching the city disappear from the passenger window, we took a familiar turn, one I knew all too well but many others didn’t.

My breath caught in my throat as tears stung my eyes. He brought me to a place that held a special spot in my heart.

The bowling alley. People might have pulled a face if I told them that’s where Lorenzo took me, but to me, it meant he did his research, finding somewhere that had meaning. It was a place I used to visit with my grandfather, a place filled with so many cherished memories.

“So, is this okay?” Lorenzo asked from the driver’s seat as he took my hand in his.

“Lorenzo, how did you know?” I whispered, my voice trembling with emotion. His smile transformed his rugged features. “I did a little digging,” he admitted, his voice soft. “I wanted tonight to be special for you.” I turned to face him, throwing my arms around him, gratitude washing over me in waves.

"Thank you so much," I murmured against his chest. "This means more to me than you'll ever know."

"Your grandmother was a big help." He beamed as he held me close.

"You went to visit her?!" swallowed hard, my voice trembling despite my efforts to steady it, as I struggled to mask the astonishment that must have been written all over my face. My heart pounded in my chest like a drum as I processed the gravity of the man's actions, my mind racing to comprehend the magnitude of what he had done.

"I did. I know you're close with her. She seemed like the perfect person to ask. Besides, it was nice to get to know her more, too. " He cupped my face, his eyes full of adoration.

Emotion overwhelmed me. Not only did he ask my grandmother, but he also took me to the exact bowling alley my grandfather brought me to regularly. It was our fun spot to hang out away from my family.

"Ana..." He spoke gentler than usual as my eyes met his. "We can leave if this is too much." The care in his voice was more than apparent.

"No, I want to stay." I kissed the back of his hand, "you've outdone yourself, Ricci."

"Well, I do try." He chuckled. "Now, how about we make tonight interesting? If you win, you get to do whatever you want after this, and if I win..." He trailed off, his eyes darkening with a promise that sent a shiver down my spine. "I get to do whatever I want to you when we get home," he finished, his voice laced with challenge.

"Who says we have to wait until we get home?" I teased, exiting the car quicker than he could get out his next sentence. I left my words to replay in his mind until the winner was declared.

"Don't think I'll take it easy on you." He laughed as he caught up to me.

"I don't need you to, but you should prepare to have your ass kicked," I winked as it was clear he was up for the challenge.

The second we stepped inside, I noticed how empty the alley was. The only people around were a couple of employees. As I spun to face him, I almost forgot what I wanted to ask as his smile caused my heart to race and my stomach to flip.

Was it love? Was that what the girls meant?

"Why is it empty?" I asked, although I already knew the answer.

"I booked out the whole place for us," he said as if it was the simplest thing in the world.

I gasped. "It must have cost a fortune!"

"It doesn't matter how much it costs. Your smile is more than enough payback." And just like that, I was stunned into silence. "Now, stop stalling and let's bowl."

And that's what we did. It was everything I could have wished for on a date. We were so relaxed around one another, and I loved this side of Lorenzo. He laughed harder and louder than he usually did, and it warmed my heart. I couldn't believe my eyes either. He was so bloody good at bowling, but not as good as me, which I already expected. He did, however, try his best to distract me here and there with small touches, subtle glances, and unbuttoning his shirt when I continued to score strikes.

"You know this isn't strip bowling, right?" I laughed as I picked up my next ball.

"It could be." He smirked as he stepped closer, but I dodged his advance.

"Not when there are people around." My eyes darted to the teenage boys casually watching us from behind the snack bar.

"You do know that I can make them go away," he teased, tapping his index finger against his lips as if pondering the option.

"I'm sure you could, but leave the poor boys alone." I closed the distance between us, resting my hands on his chest. "Win the game and this pussy is all yours." I grinned. His sharp intake of breath was enough for me to know how I affected him.

"Change your shoes. We're going home." I hadn't worked out if he was joking or being deadly serious.

"Good things come to those who wait, Ricci." I sauntered away from him but didn't get too far because his hands wrapped around my waist in less than a second.

"I think I've waited long enough, don't you?" he asked, his dominance in full force.

"Alright. It all comes down to this final ball. You know the stakes. Give it your best shot." I smiled as he picked up his ball, confidence oozing from him.

He strode past me with a determined look on his face. He hadn't managed a strike all night, so I was feeling confident until the ball knocked down every pin on the lane.

Fuck.

"It looks like I win." He declared with a triumphant grin spreading across his face.

"Hold your horses, pal. I still have my turn." I took my ball and strutted towards the lane.

"Give it your best shot, wife." He laughed.

"Oh, don't you worry, I will." I smiled smugly, releasing my ball as he stared intently at it, waiting for the inevitable. Just like that, I knocked down every single pin. "Looks like we both win," I teased, flicking my hair over my shoulder. "We could go again to declare the real winner?"

Lorenzo glared, his gaze intensifying. "I'm good with sharing the win with you," he agreed, inching closer to me. The air between us crackled with unspoken desire, the promise of what was next to come this evening hanging heavy.

"So, how's this going to work?" I asked, a look of sheer amusement written all over his face.

"Well, I'll allow you to decide what we do after we leave, and then once we get home, you're mine. Mine to do whatever the fuck I want with." He slipped his hand under my dress, cupping my pussy over my lingerie, letting out a groan. "Do we have a deal?" he asked as he moved my panties to the side, sliding his finger inside me.

"Lorenzo," I gasped. He was so forward, not giving a shit if anyone saw.

"I said, do we have a deal, wife?"

"Yes, fuck, yes we have a deal," I whimpered as his thumb brushed my clit.

"Good girl. Now let's get out of here. I'm too impatient to stay any longer." He removed his finger from my pussy and brought it to his mouth, cleaning off my arousal. "Mmm, so fucking sweet."

Rain threatened the sky as we stepped into the cool evening air. My efforts to hurry to the car were in vain as Lorenzo captured me the second the first droplet fell.

"Lorenzo! Stop!" I squealed, trying to make a quick getaway, but the more I struggled, the more his hold tightened.

"It's only a little rain. What's the harm?" As he finished his sentence, the heavens opened and rain poured down.

My dress turned into a second skin as the water soaked through the fabric. Lorenzo's hair flopped down onto his forehead as the rainwater clung to each strand helplessly before running along his sharp, angular features.

"Kiss me," I demanded, my mouth working before my brain processed the words. This man was destroying me in every single way. I went from someone who refused to let him destroy me to someone who craved it with every fibre of my being.

No words were needed. He responded in the way I needed him to as his mouth met mine. I parted my lips as I moaned into his mouth. The rain beat down against us whilst his hand tangled in my sodden hair. "You have no idea what you've done to me, *amore mio*. I don't even recognise myself around you anymore," he whispered against my lips before his tongue delved into my mouth, his body pressing me against the passenger door of the car.

Lorenzo palmed my breast over my dress, igniting a fierce, electric surge within me

"You don't get to claim your prize yet. Not until I've claimed mine." I smiled against his lips as he groaned with disappointment.

"Fair's fair, you're right." He shimmied me to the side, allowing him to open the car door with ease. "In you get, wife." His genuine, heartwarming smile stopped me in my tracks as I continued to gaze up at him like a lovesick fool. *Fuck... Lovesick?!* "You've got me for a lifetime, you know. You don't need to stare," he joked as he brought me back down to earth.

"I wasn't staring, just admiring." I smirked as I slid gracefully into the car. The thought of ruining his seats didn't occur to me as I settled into the leather.

"Same thing." He closed the door and rounded the car, all while not letting the happiness disappear from his face.

Once he joined me inside, he twisted in his seat. His wet clothes crunched against the leather. I slipped off my heels and pulled my legs up beneath me. His eyes darted to my feet to make sure I hadn't dug my heels into the material.

"So, my beautiful wife, where to?" He started the engine, and it roared into action.

"The drive-thru!" I squealed with happiness, but what really made me happy was watching his face twist with confusion.

"Are you high?" He asked, making me wonder if he had ever been to a drive-thru before. He didn't strike me as the type, but I was. I loved it. The greasier the better.

"Only on life! Now, to the drive-thru, Ricci!" I clapped my hands together as he set off. I might have been mistaken, but I was almost sure he was trying to hide his excitement.

He jammed his foot down, driving out of the parking lot and towards the nearest fast food restaurant.

"Put the roof down!" I called out over the soft rock music he turned up full blast.

"I don't think so. It'll mess up my car." He rolled his eyes so hard I feared he'd lose them in the back of his head, which only made me giggle at the thought.

"Not even for your wife? Please..." I pleaded playfully. "I'll pay to have the car repaired, if necessary, just so you can quit being such a damn robot."

"A robot, huh? I'll show you just how much of a robot I am." He cast a glance in my direction.

The roof suddenly retracted. The rain whipped against my skin while we sped along the silent road. I flung my hands up over my head and danced in my seat to whatever song had just come on Lorenzo's sound system. I could tell he was a little uptight about his car, but the fact he went along with my crazy idea made my heart soar and my mouth smile without even realising.

We pulled into my favourite drive-thru not far from the bowling alley. I directed Lorenzo to one my grandfather and I went to plenty of times without telling Papa. After he passed away, I went alone.

We pulled up to the window, and I placed our order. Two of everything on the menu and milkshakes, much to Lorenzo's surprise.

"The guys will be happy you got them some food, too." He smiled as he settled back into his seat.

"Oh, shit! Drive back around!" I said as his finger darted up to his ear in an attempt to block out my shriek.

"Are you trying to damage my ear drums?" he complained. "And what do you mean, drive back around?" He sighed.

"I didn't get food for the guys. Don't drive around. Just wait here." I was about to jump out of the car when his hand wrapped around mine.

"Don't even think about it. We'll drive back around if getting food for them means that much to you." And just as he promised, he went through to order food a second time.

Food secured, we drove out onto the open road.

"Can you put the roof up now?" I asked.

"Wait a minute, why? You wanted it down before. What's with the sudden change?" he questioned, furrowing his brows.

"If you want the truth, I don't want the food to get wet." I laughed as his expression changed from confused to what the hell is wrong with you in a split second.

"So, it's okay for my car to get messed up but not the food, am I right?" He was taken aback, but did what I asked without another word.

"Ding, ding, ding, we have a winner." I kissed his cheek hastily which caused his lips to split into a smile. It was written all over his face that those kinds of small gestures were new to him, and honestly, they were to me, too.

I was changing day by day, and so was he.

32

LORENZO

Anastacia had already gone upstairs while I found the guys to give them the incredible amount of food Ana had ordered for them.

"Evening. Ana got you all some food, enjoy." I placed the food on the coffee table before turning to leave.

"Hold up, Renzo," Red called. "How was the date?"

"It was different, but honestly, I loved every second." I smiled, something that was rare to them over the years.

"Fuck! He's smiling!" Finn teased. "Nah, just kidding, Boss. You do look happy, though."

"Are you?" Gino asked, questions coming from all angles.

"You know what, I think I am." I genuinely was, and the woman upstairs was the reason. "She makes me feel...things. Things I haven't felt before."

Red raised an eyebrow, his voice laced with a mix of banter and sincerity. "Things like love, maybe?"

The four letter word hung in the air like a challenge. "I don't know what love is," I scoffed. "I've never had the luxury of figuring that out, never wanted to, never needed to."

The room fell silent, the weight of my words pressing down on them. I wasn't one to open up, especially about something as vulnerable as emotions. But tonight, there was a crack in the armour I usually wore so effortlessly. Red leaned forward, his tone softening. "You don't have to know what it is, mate. You just have to know how it feels. And if she makes you feel something you've never felt before, maybe that's it. Maybe that's love."

"Maybe, but it's too early to say it even if that is what I'm feeling." I cleared my throat.

Emmet shook his head, a small smile playing on his lips. "You're an idiot, you know that? If you feel it, just fucking say it. You're lucky you've got this second chance with her. Don't waste it. You've already wasted enough time."

My thoughts drifted to the early days with her, something I was doing a lot of lately. I treated her like just another piece in my carefully constructed world, but when I treated her better, she started to let me in and show me who she truly was. And not the woman she had been taught to be, but the woman she longed to be.

"I fucked up in the beginning," I admitted. "You all know it. I just didn't want to listen. I should've been better to her."

Red clapped me on the shoulder, his grip firm and reassuring. "You've got all the time in the world to make it up to her now. Don't fuck it up again."

I nodded, though my mind was already upstairs with Anastacia. I thought about the way her eyes lit up when she saw the bowling alley, the way her cheeks blushed the perfect shade of pink when I kissed her in the rain. If what I felt was love, I didn't want it to end. She was the one in my life I never wanted to lose.

"Right, I'm off to bed, enjoy your food." I held my hand up in a see you later gesture before making my way upstairs.

I never cared much about the future before. I couldn't have cared less if I lived or died, but because of her that wasn't the case anymore. I wanted to find out what my future held, and I wanted to find out with her.

I entered our bedroom as Anastacia was brushing her hair at the vanity, the mirror reflected her image, a woman who had learned to navigate a world she was probably never meant for. She wore nothing more than one of my T-shirts. It drowned her frame.

"There you are. Now we can eat." She clipped her hair up in a damp bun on top of her head before sitting crossed-legged on the bed, our food surrounding her.

"You waited?" I asked, relieving myself of my damp clothes. "You could have started."

"Either we eat together or not at all."

"Is that our new family motto?" I asked, slipping on some sweats.

"I think it might be, yeah." She patted the bed beside her, her eyes shining with happiness.

"I like it." I settled down beside her, leaning back against the headboard. "Now, let's see if this food is as good as you claim."

I unwrapped the burger she handed me, taking a huge bite. All the while, I felt those big blue eyes on me, waiting for me to say she was right. *Dammit.*

"Well?" she questioned, feeding herself a curly fry.

"I hate to admit it, but you're right." I took another bite. She couldn't hide her triumphant smile. "This burger is pretty damn good."

"I knew you'd like it." She seemed so proud of herself as she laid back on the bed, turning her attention back to whatever movie she put on prior to me arriving.

"What are you watching?" It looked like a complete load of shit, to be honest, but she seemed into it.

"Why? Are you planning on watching it with me?" she questioned.

"Perhaps."

But there was no perhaps about it. I was staying with my wife, watching whatever it was she wanted to watch. I draped my arm around her, pulling her close to me. She settled in the crook of my arm, fitting perfectly as if she was made for me, and maybe that was the case.

I watched the nineties movie she was enjoying, and honestly, I had no idea what was going on or who was in love with who, but Ana was smiling, and enjoying every second.

“I have no idea what’s going on.” I complained as she swatted my chest.

“Stop complaining and just enjoy being here in the moment with me instead.” Her fingers brushed one of the scars on my chest as she put me in my place.

Once the movie finished—thankfully, it was only a short one—Anastacia cleared the remains of our food away, leaving it outside of the bedroom door. Once she closed it behind her, she lifted my T-shirt above her head and tossed it aside.

“I think it’s time to claim your prize, Ricci.” Her voice was low and seductive, a raspy whisper that caused my cock to harden.

“Come here,” I demanded, and of course, she obeyed.

She sauntered over to me as if she was the hunter, and I, the prey, but she couldn’t be more wrong. She stopped before me, her eyes dropping to my cock as it fought against the restraints of my sweats.

“Get on your knees,” I ordered. Her eyes darkened the second she dropped between my legs.

Her tongue darted out to dampen her lips, her fingers teasing my waistband before she slid the sweats down my legs, letting them pool at my feet.

She ran her tongue along the tip of my cock as she kept her gaze fixed on mine. Moments later, she took me in her mouth, and fuck me, she was breathtaking.

Seeing this woman on her knees could easily have been the death of me. She fisted her hand around my cock while the other gripped my thigh. The deeper she took me, the more her nails dug into my skin, and I fucking welcomed it as my mind wandered to her raking those nails across my back, leaving her mark in her wake.

I fisted her hair at the nape of her neck, forcing her to take more of me, seeing just how far I was able to push her. “Eyes on me.” She obeyed instantly, her glazed gaze meeting mine. “Good girl.” She fought the urge to gag every time I hit the back of her throat.

Her mouth worked me expertly as a mixture of her own spit and my pre cum trickled down her chin and onto her heaving breasts.

Yanking her head away from my cock by her hair, I watched the tears stream down her face as she struggled to catch her breath. I was torn between fucking her mouth or her pussy. The latter won.

Lifting her effortlessly, I threw her onto the bed as if she weighed nothing. My need to fuck her took over everything else. I wanted to see her face as she moaned for me, wanted to watch her come undone as I made her come all over my cock. I trailed my fingers from her lips to her throat and down the channel between her breasts to her navel until I reached her perfect fucking clit.

“Don’t tease me... Just fuck me.” Her words shattered the silence as well as my thoughts. I ached to hear them again.

“Are you calling the shots on my prize?” I asked, watching as her eyes flared with an intense mix of desire and desperation. Her fingers darted to her clit, stroking and teasing with an urgency that took my breath away.

“Yes... Fuck me, please,” she begged, her voice breaking with desperation as her breaths tore from her chest in ragged gasps.

"Where would you like me to fuck you, wife?" I taunted, a wicked edge to my voice as I moved my finger to her ass, pressing firmly against her entrance. "How about here?" I whispered my words dripping with intent.

“My pussy, please...” she whimpered.

“What my wife wants, my wife gets.” I smirked. “Now, bend over for me.”

She did without hesitation, she locked her gaze onto mine over her shoulder.

"Hold onto the bed. Don't let go," I ordered, watching her do as she was told.

I thrust into her. Her sharp gasp as I filled her confirmed she could handle all of me, every single inch. Her fingers gripped the sheets like a lifeline, as a symphony of sweet moans escaped her. My hand snaked around to her throat, a gentle but firm hold, increasing the intensity of the moment. She shot me a sultry smile over her shoulder as I pounded into her relentlessly. With every forceful thrust, her body tightened around me, enveloping my cock in a vice-like grip, her desire insatiable.

"Fuck! Lorenzo," she moaned. "I want you to come."

"Not yet."

I circled my thumb over her clit as I leaned forward, sinking my teeth into her shoulder as she let out another moan, no longer caring if anyone other than me could hear her. Her body trembled beneath me. Her pussy squeezed my cock as I slipped my thumb, now slick with her arousal, into her mouth, letting her taste herself. Her tongue swirled around my thumb, as she hummed, enjoying the taste of her.

"Good girl." I murmured, my voice thick with admiration and satisfaction. My grip tightened on her throat, as I could feel her pulse race beneath my hand.

"Please, Lorenzo... I can't..." She pleaded, her fingers digging into the sheets. "Please."

I slammed into her once more, pushing her closer and closer to the edge, not allowing her to fall into the abyss just yet. "You're going to come with me, when I say." Her pussy clamps down on my cock as I bury myself inside her. My thrusts became faster, harder and more desperate as my own orgasm built.

"Fuck, Ana." I moan, revelling in how good her pussy feels. "That's my good fucking girl. Taking my cock so well."

Her head fell forward as I felt her body giving in bit by bit, “Lorenzo.” She whimpered, her eyes snapping shut as she tried to hang onto the edge until I gave her the go ahead for her release. “Please.”

"Come for me." I growled into her ear as she finally let go, and gave into the sensation she felt overwhelming her body. My own erupted in pleasure at the same time as hers. “Fuck, Ana!” I roared her name just as loudly as she cried out mine.

My come filled her pussy, and there was no sweeter feeling as I emptied myself into her. My body shivered as I pressed a kiss to the bite mark that decorated her shoulder. “You’re fucking incredible, do you know that?” I said as I pulled out of her with a groan.

She could barely answer, her head hung forward as her fingers remained fisted in the sheets while she tried to catch her breath. Come trickled from her pussy and down her inner thigh. “I’m quite something,” she managed, her breathing slowly returning to normal.

She slowly and gracefully rose from the bed, before making her way towards the ensuite.

“Where are you going?” I called out after her, but she’d already disappeared.

I followed her to see exactly what she had planned for the rest of the night.

“I’m running a bath.” She sat on the bath’s edge as she poured scented oils into the shallow water. She looked breathtaking sitting there. Her cheeks were flush, her lips were swollen, and her skin was marked by me.

“Do you need anything?” I asked, turning towards the shower.

“Yeah, you. Where are you going?” Her voice was as soothing as an angel’s, and it sent goosebumps over my skin.

“I was going to shower and get into bed.” I glanced over my shoulder, her eyes wide with hope, her lips parted in protest.

“Stay with me.” She smiled, looking more exhausted as time went on. “We never got to see if you were a bath man, did we?”

That was true. And who was I to turn down such an offer?

She dipped her feet in first before slowly submerging herself into the water, her breasts bobbing at the surface. She knew I couldn't take my eyes off her as she looked up at me with a come hither gaze.

"Move forward then and let me in." I felt my heart swell in my chest as she scooched forward, wearing the most genuine, happy smile. She allowed me enough room to slip in behind her. Water sloshed around us as she relaxed back into me, her fingers tracking invisible lines on my thighs.

"So, do you think baths will become your thing?" she questioned, craning her head to look up at me.

"It's too early to tell, but honestly, if you're in them with me, then yes." I laughed before imagining coming home to her after a shitty day, relaxing like this while she cheered me up with tales about her day.

Fuck... What was wrong with me?

I used to want to beat the shit out of something, down a few whiskeys, and inhale a few cigarettes after a shitty day. And now, all I could think that would calm me down was her...

Was I in love? Was she in love with me?

"Would you really have killed me that night you stabbed me?" Did you want to?" I asked, genuinely curious.

"Would I have killed you? No, I wouldn't have. Did I want to? Of course I did. You were a bastard." She chuckled as I wrapped my arms around her. Her body relaxed into mine even more than before as her sweet laughter vibrated through me.

"Ana?"

"Yeah?" she responded as she linked her fingers with mine.

What was I doing? Was I about to tell her how I felt? How could I when I didn't know what that was? This whole deal with love was a complete mindfuck.

"Never mind." *Not yet, Lorenzo, not yet.*

Soon, though.

Four weeks later.

Tonight was the night.

I was ready to tell my wife I loved her, tell her I'd fallen *in* love with her, and that I planned to love her for the rest of my life if she'd let me. I didn't need her to say it back. I wasn't saying it for that. It just felt like the right time for me. Something completely new? Yes. But also something I was more than ready for.

I welcomed my mother at the door as she exited the car with a huge smile, unable to hide her excitement, and I adored it. I rushed down the steps to her as she retrieved the first load of white roses from the car. "Here, let me take those for you, Mama. The guys will get the rest. You go on inside."

She walked inside with me, looking around to see if Anastacia was here. "Mama, you know she's not here. The girls took her to the spa and for lunch. I needed her out all day to arrange this."

"You're a good one, it just took you a while to see it." She patted my face, and deep down I knew I was anything but good. "So, have you planned it all?"

"Pretty much. All I can do now is hope she likes it," I breathed.

"She'll love it. What's not to love?" she questioned.

"Yeah, you're right." I looked at my mother's face as she reflected my happiness with a soft smile.

"Right, we've got all day, let's get cracking." She clapped her hands in a, we'd better get a move on motion, before rolling up the sleeves of her cream cashmere jumper. "Lorenzo?"

"Yes, Mama?" I replied, waiting for what was coming next.

"I'm proud of you. Of the man you've become as well as the husband you're learning to be." The corners of her lips twisted in emotion as she stifled a sob.

"Thank you. I'm learning slowly, but surely." I chuckled.

"Yeah, well, remember, Anastacia is learning, too. You can learn from one another." She was right. She always bloody was. "I know tonight is special for you. You wouldn't be doing this if it wasn't, but are you planning to tell your wife you love her?"

"I am." Two words. Two words was all I needed to say for my mother to let the tears escape her. "Because if what I feel is love, I need to tell her. You know I could go out one evening and never come home, and I don't want her never knowing how I feel."

"Don't talk that way. You've got all the time in the world together. I'm sure of it." She squeezed my hand, and I knew she wished my father would have told her he loved her more. "She's too good for me, Ma."

"You need to stop putting yourself down. You're lucky to have one another. What happened between you when you first met is in the past, and it'll stay there." She nodded, always knowing exactly what to say.

Over the next few hours, she helped me prepare the dish Ana enjoyed at my grandparent's restaurant. One I knew she'd love. We made sure all the small details were prepared and ready. She arranged the roses and candles throughout the foyer, bathroom, and dining room, scattering petals along the walkway to Ana's first surprise. I didn't carry a romantic bone in my body, or so I thought. But now, seeing this, changed my opinion completely.

"What do you think, Ma?" I asked, stepping back to admire our handiwork

"It's perfect. You're all set," my mother assured me as she pulled on her trench coat. "Enjoy the evening with your wife."

I planned on it.

33

ANASTACIA

I RELAXED BACK IN THE BOOTH WITH MY ICED TEA AS THE GIRLS SEEMED shifty and a little bit shady.

"Alright, spill. What's going on?" I asked as Robin looked anywhere else but at me.

"Nothing. Lorenzo just thought it would be nice if we all had a girls day," Tay said, but I knew it was a lie. She always had been shit at not telling the truth.

"You two are fooling no one, especially not me." I scoffed with an eye roll.

"Listen, we've been sworn to secrecy, alright! Lorenzo trusts us enough, and I, for one, am not about to ruin it." Robin smiled as if she was completing some secret mission.

"Fine, but we always promised we'd have no secrets." I sighed.

"I know, but it'll just be this one." Tay winked. "It's worth it. I promise."

"We'll see, then." I had no idea what Lorenzo was planning for the evening, but I was excited to find out. I let my mind wander to him, unable to stop myself as I realised just how much we changed together in a short space of time. Though neither of us had uttered the words *I love you*, I felt it in every gesture, every touch. And I knew I was ready to say it, to let him know how deeply I cared.

"Earth to Ana," Robin teased, snapping her fingers in front of my face. "You've been staring at that steak like it's going to confess its secrets. You completely spaced out on us."

I blinked, shaking myself from my reverie. "Sorry," I murmured, forcing a smile. "Just thinking about..."

Tay raised an eyebrow, her fork pausing mid air. "Lorenzo?"

Heat crept into my cheeks, but I nodded. "Maybe. We've been in a good place ever since Sicily. He makes me feel...things. Real, crazy things."

Robin grinned, her dimples deepening. "Girl, you're glowing. Just tell him you love him already, because if we can see it, I'm damn sure he can, too. What's the worst that could happen if you tell him anyway?"

Before I could respond, a commotion near the entrance caught my attention. A man strode into the restaurant, his presence commanding the room's attention. But once I noticed who it was, my heart sank. It was my brother, Miles. His arm was draped around a woman who looked like she stepped straight out of a reality TV show—her hair was long, and poker straight. It was obvious that the relentless bleach treatments had sapped it of anything natural, and left it with a bright, almost artificial yellow tint that glimmered under the light, resembling sunlit straw. Her lips were double the size, if not triple, to what they should have been, and her dress was so far up around her ass it practically screamed, *I'm here to be noticed.* She clung to Miles like a second skin, her laughter shrill and forced.

My grip tightened on my fork. I hadn't seen Miles in months. He hadn't even bothered to check how I was with everything that happened with Chad. *Fucking dick.* I turned back to the girls, hoping to ignore him, but it was too bloody late. His eyes locked onto our table as Tay let out an annoyed groan. And of course, he didn't just wave or smile. Oh no. He made his way over.

"Anastacia." He grinned as he stopped beside our table, his cologne overpowering the three of us as Tay wrinkled her nose. "What a surprise. Lorenzo finally let you out without his protection?" he teased.

"What do you want, Miles?" I scoffed, my eyes drifting over to his date who was practically licking his face.

"Hi," she said, her voice high-pitched and grating on me. "I'm Lozza. It's nice to meet ya." She held out her hand, which I ignored.

"That's nice." I turned back to Miles who currently looked as if he was about to explode. "Oh, I'm sorry. Did you want me to greet your flavour of the week? You've had so many, I stopped bothering. They aren't usually around long." I rolled my eyes before focusing my attention on my plate. "You can go now."

"You can't avoid us all forever. They want to talk to you. Papa's worried about you," he replied, his voice so damn patronising.

"Worried?" I snorted, finally meeting his gaze once more. "Or feeling guilty? They need to leave me alone and worry about their golden boy, since he's the one running around with gold diggers instead of doing what he should be." I laughed.

Lozza's smile faltered, but she recovered quickly, her green eyes narrowing. "I don't think that's any of your business, sweetheart."

"You know what, it's not. It never was and never will be but good luck with him. Just a heads up—he'll be bored of you before the end of your meal," I shot back.

"That's enough. You're just jealous that they favoured me over you. What, didn't Daddy give you enough attention? Didn't Mommy take you shopping enough?" he teased as I shoved my chair back and stood. Miles's voice dropped to a low whisper. "Sit down, Sis. You don't want to cause a scene."

I leaned in towards him, my voice audible to only him. "Or, what? You'll report back to your owners? Do you really think I care what they think of me anymore? I've known for years why Papa didn't mind having a girl. He just about tolerated me, knowing he could use me for an alliance," I seethed. "You always did, and will continue to get away with everything. You'll run his mafia into the ground, and I can't wait to watch it burn when you take the reins."

"You're just a bitter bitch." He scoffed. "Jealous that you were nothing but a spare part."

As if a switch had flipped, I saw red. I grabbed the steak knife from behind me, instantly pressing the tip into his stomach in one swift movement. He swallowed hard as his eyes widened with shock and pure fright. He knew I could gut him with this shitty knife if I wanted to. Despite his size, I was always able to get the better of him, but of course, that didn't matter. It was never enough to please my father.

"I suggest if you don't want your guts to be spread across this restaurant, you take whatever she is and leave," I hissed, shoving him away. He let out a grunt. "The three of you cease to exist to me. You have since my wedding day. I have my friends, my husband, and a mother-in-law that makes my own look worse than the devil."

"Oh, yeah, a husband who wanted you as part of his revenge plot, game, whatever the fuck it was," he spat, anger radiating off him in waves. "He doesn't want you. Nobody will ever fucking want you. You're just there."

"I could stand here and explain my relationship to you, but I won't, because you aren't worth a second more of my time."

"And you can forgive him, just like that?" He laughed, sarcasm dripping from every word.

"As I said, I don't need to explain myself to you. Now, if there's nothing else, run along and play pretend for as long as you can. But once you take over and fuck up—and I know you will—don't you dare come knocking at our door because Lorenzo would rather watch the lot of you burn than help. I mean, he probably wouldn't even piss on you if you were on fire."

"I won't need the pair of you. Mark my words," he snarled, his eyes narrowing as his face reddened with anger.

"We'll see." I smiled as I sat back down, the girls' faces a picture of pride.

He stood there for a moment, unsure of what to say or if he should open that hole he called a mouth. He went with the first option, turning on his heel and stomping towards the exit, leaving Lozza behind.

"What kind of a sister are you?!" she snapped.

"One could paint the walls with your blood if you don't fuck off." I replied, toying the knife between my fingers.

"You're just... You're—"

"Someone you don't want to get on the wrong side of." I grinned. "It looks like your date left already. I told you he gets bored." I didn't bother to look at her. I already knew she wore a sour expression before she scurried off to find Miles.

"I wish I'd have taken a picture of his face! He was a right pissed off bastard!" Tay laughed, unable to contain her happiness. Her and Miles never truly got on, but then again, he barely got along with anyone. He was such a massive bellend who saw himself as superior to everyone and anyone who wasn't my father.

"I wonder what Lorenzo will say about it." Robin said, her eyes filled with joy at the thought of Miles being put in his place by my husband.

"Miles isn't worth it. None of them are, and you know that as well as I do." I shoved a forkful of steak into my mouth, not wanting to give him another moment of my precious time.

"You're right, he's not. Besides, don't let him ruin the evening Lorenzo's planned for you." Robin smiled.

"I won't. They ruined enough of my life. I won't give them any more of it." I had never been more sure of my words.

Hours later, I pushed open the front door, the exact smell from the restaurant in Sicily hitting me in the face. *Wow... He cooked.* But that wasn't what shocked me. What caught my attention was how alive the house felt. Soft jazz music drifted throughout it, the melody wrapping around me like a warm embrace. Bright white rose petals scattered the floor, forming a path that led me deeper into our home. Vases upon vases of roses lined the stairs. To say I was speechless was an understatement. I slipped off my shoes, following the trail of petals as my heart quickened.

"Lorenzo?" I called out, unable to hide the curiosity that tinged my voice.

He emerged from the kitchen, a playful smirk playing on his lips. I couldn't take my eyes off him. He was dressed in black slats and a white shirt rolled up at the sleeves. He was gorgeous.

"You're late," he teased.

"Sounds like somebody missed me." I chuckled, watching as he strode over to where I stood.

Closing the distance between us in less than a few strides, his presence overwhelmed me, but it wasn't enough, I needed more. Before I could wind him up more or offer another smart ass remark, his lips were on mine, kissing me with a hunger that left me reeling.

His hands cupped my face, his touch firm yet tender. I melted into him, letting my fingers tangle in his hair as he let out a soft moan at the sensation. The kiss was a storm, fierce and unrelenting. I tasted the wine on his lips, a hint of garlic, and something else. Something I craved. Something I still had no clue what it was.

He finally pulled away, and a soft smile played on my lips. Lorenzo's gaze lingered on me for a second, his expression unreadable.

"You look beautiful," he whispered, a mere inch away from my lips. I was never good with compliments. They always were few and far between, but recently, Lorenzo seemed to want to shower me with them. I couldn't say I minded. It was different for me, and I had always liked different.

"So, what's all this?" I asked, gesturing to the flowers and music.

A hint of mischief twinkled in his eyes. "A welcome home," he replied, taking my hand in his.

He guided me upstairs, his hand firm on the small of my back. His smile never wavered. It was contagious.

He pushed open the bathroom door, revealing a scene that stole my breath. The room was transformed into a sanctuary of sensuality. Candles flickered along the edges of the tub, their golden light dancing on the water's surface. Petals from white roses and delicate lavender floated in the bath, the colours vivid against the milky liquid. The air was heavy with the scent of essential oils—eucalyptus, lavender, and a hint of something earthy, like patchouli. A tray sat on the counter, holding a glass of champagne and a small plate of dark chocolate truffles. He'd really gone all out.

"For you, wife."

His eyes held mine, intense yet gentle. I had never been treated with such care. It made me wonder if I was never worthy enough until now.

"Lorenzo, it's beautiful," I whispered, pressing my fingers to my lips.

"I wanted to do something for you. We have the house to ourselves, and I plan to dote on my wife for the rest of the evening." He towered over me as he spoke. Then, he knelt before me, his dark strands brushing against my knees. His fingers unknotted the laces of my sneakers before he slipped them off my feet, setting them aside with a quiet thud.

His fingers brushed against the hem of my dress as he stood. "Turn around," he commanded, his voice low and authoritative but laced with a tenderness that made me obey without hesitation. I pivoted slowly, my eyes meeting his in the mirror above the sink. His hands moved to my zipper, sliding it down in a slow, deliberate motion. The dress fell away, pooling at my feet, leaving me in nothing but my pink lace lingerie.

Lorenzo's eyes darkened as he took in the sight of me, his gaze lingering on my body. "So fucking perfect," he whispered against my ear as his fingers traced the edge of my bra strap before he unclipped the clasp, letting it slide down my arms and onto the floor.

"So breathtakingly beautiful." He smiled, hooking his fingers into the waistband of my panties next. "And all mine." He lowered the lace down my legs, and I stepped out of them. "I'll be downstairs finishing dinner. You enjoy your bath and take your time," he breathed, placing a gentle kiss on my shoulder.

I nodded as I watched him leave the room, the door clicking softly behind him. Alone, I felt a mix of vulnerability and excitement. I always hated exposing my vulnerability. I was never allowed to. But the past few weeks with Lorenzo had shown me that being vulnerable didn't have to be a weakness. It took courage.

I lowered myself into the bath, the water enveloping me like an embrace. The petals brushed against my skin, their softness contrasting with the warmth of the water. I leaned back, closing my eyes as I let myself relax after the run-in I had with Miles. I picked up the glass of champagne, taking a sip as every toxic thought about my family slipped away and all that remained was my husband.

After what felt like an eternity, I reluctantly opened my eyes. The water had cooled quite a bit, which told me I spent a while soaking. I stepped out of the bath, my mind calm. I wrapped myself in the new plush robe Lorenzo had hung on the hook beside the tub and headed out into our bedroom.

It still felt strange to call the bedroom ours, especially since I was adamant I never wanted to be married to him in the first place. Life was so different now. Even when I tried to and wanted to resist him, I couldn't. He broke down the walls I built. He chipped away at them slowly when we were at one another's throats and obliterated what was left with his newfound charm and attentiveness.

I crossed the room, making my way towards the vanity, but something laying on the bed caught my eye. The fabric of what looked to be a brand new dress shimmered under the soft light. It was stunning, a soft, pale pink, a colour that I rarely wore, but one I loved. How he knew these things were beyond me.. The cut of the dress was elegant. The neckline dipped just enough to be daring. Beside it was a note, written in Lorenzo's handwriting.

Amore mio, wear this tonight x

My heart fluttered as I picked up the dress, running my fingers over the smooth material. It was a gesture that spoke volumes, a man who not only knew my body but my style. I couldn't help but smile, a warmth instantly spreading through my chest.

I dried my hair in soft waves that cascaded down my back and kept my makeup to a minimum. When I slipped into the dress, I had never felt so beautiful. My bruises had long since healed, along with the memories I once held of that time. Lorenzo, believe it or not, was the only one, besides my babushka, who had helped me through it. Lorenzo had been my friend, my husband, my rock, and most of all, my safe space. I could never thank him enough for that.

I left the bedroom and made my way downstairs, the aroma of dinner wafting through the air as I descended the stairs. Once I reached the bottom step, I took a deep breath, smoothing the dress over my hips. I felt desired, and for once, I allowed myself to simply enjoy it.

I entered the dining room, noticing Lorenzo standing by the window with his back to me, his broad shoulders tense as if he sensed my presence. I paused for a second, breathing him in. As he turned, his eyes met mine, and for a moment, the world stopped. The air between us crackled with unspoken words and desires. I couldn't hide my smile as I took a step towards him and neither could he.

"Lorenzo, this is incredible," I exclaimed. His grin widened, illuminating the room far more than the candles ever could.

"No, you look incredible." He nodded with a gentle smile.

He crossed the room to where I stood, his eyes never leaving mine as his strides quickened.

"I can't believe you did all this." I held my hand up to everything around me.

"I wish I could take all the credit, but I had a little help," he admitted, placing a hand on my lower back to guide me towards my seat.

The dining table was a masterpiece in itself—set with fine china, crystal glasses, and a centrepiece of white roses that matched the others that decorated the rest of the house. Lorenzo pulled out my chair with a flourish, his chivalry on full display.

"Quite the gentleman," I giggled.

"Only for my wife. Nobody else will ever deserve it." He winked, pressing a kiss against my cheek before I lowered myself into the chair

Tonight was the first time we used this dining room. Just the two of us, anyway. It was usually reserved for family gatherings, business meetings, and other formal occasions. But tonight, it was ours.

Lorenzo took his place at the head of the table, a position he was accustomed to as the boss of the Ricci family, while I occupied the chair to his right. A chair that was only ever reserved for Gino until recently. It was a symbolic gesture, one that spoke volumes about my role in his life. He vowed in front of anyone who resided in this house that I would stand by his side as his equal, his confidant, and his wife. That I would be more than what my mother was to my father.

"So, this is why you got the girls to take me out today, isn't it?" I teased, sipping my champagne.

"Of course. I knew they would do exactly what I needed them to do, and I trusted them enough to keep all this a secret." He smirked, looking so proud of himself.

"And who else was in on this?" I asked

"The guys, of course, and my mother." He chuckled, taking my hand in his much larger one.

“You know you didn’t need to go to all this trouble for me.” I felt somewhat guilty that everyone had given up their day to help Lorenzo with his gesture. “It must have taken you all day.”

He leaned forward, his hands gripping the arms of my chair as he forcefully pulled me to face him. “I never want to hear you say that again. Nothing, and I repeat *nothing*, will ever be too much trouble for you,” he replied, his voice firm but tender. “Tonight is about us and what we’re building together—our future.”

My heart raced as I studied his face. The strong jawline, the intensity in his brown eyes, and the way his scar seemed to tell a story I was only beginning to understand. Lorenzo, in turn, was captivated by me in the same way.

His thumb traced the delicate skin of my wrist, his touch sending shivers down my spine. I leaned in slightly, my breath catching as our faces drew closer. The candles flickered around us, casting dancing shadows on the walls. For a moment, the only sound I heard was the soft hum of anticipation.

“I heard about your brother today,” he growled. It was obvious Finn told him since he was the one Lorenzo had ordered to be with me today.

“I handled it. You don’t need to do anything. He’s no longer my brother.” I sighed. “You’re the only family I need.”

“I know you handled it, but just say the word, brother or not, and I’ll kill the bastard,” he seethed. I knew he meant it.

“He’s not worth it. None of them are.” I smiled because they weren’t. “Now, what’s the plan for tonight?” I asked, resting my forehead on his.

“Good change of subject there.” He chuckled, his scowl fading. “So, I thought we’d eat first...” he trailed off, his eyes dropping to my lips before meeting mine once more. “But now, I just want to give you your surprise.”

“A surprise?” I whispered. What else could there possibly be?

"Come and take a walk with me," Lorenzo said, his voice a low rumble that sent shivers all the way down to my toes. It wasn't a request. It was a command. Delivered with the authority of a man accustomed to being obeyed.

"You know it's dark out," I whispered, my voice barely audible above the crackling fire in the hearth.

"Just come with me," he said, holding out his hand. There was a vulnerability in his tone, a plea that surprised me. I hesitated for only a moment before following his lead.

He led me through the double doors of the dining room, the cool night air enveloping us as we stepped out into the garden. The lake stretched out before us, its surface shimmering like liquid silver under the moonlight. But it wasn't the lake that caught my attention. It was the lights, hundreds of tiny, twinkling bulbs that seemed to dance among the trees, casting a magical glow over the entire scene.

"Have these lights always been here?" I asked, my voice laced with wonder as I turned to him, my eyes wide with awe.

"No, I actually had the guys out here this morning sorting it all so we could enjoy some time out here tonight." He gestured to the pathway lined with candles and petals. Again, they were the same petals that adorned the floors inside the house. "Do you like it?"

"Like it? I love it. It's absolutely everything." My heart swelled with a mixture of gratitude and confusion. Why was he doing this? What had I done to deserve such extravagance? Such attention to detail?

I kicked off my heels, the grass cool beneath my bare feet as I wandered along the petal-strewn path. The scent of roses filled the air, their fragrance mingling with the earthy smell of the lake. My attention was drawn to a small, fenced-in area I never noticed before.

"What's this?" I asked, my voice tinged with shock as I approached the fence. What I saw next was the thing that caused my stomach to somersault. There was a bed of roses inside glowing softly, their petals lit up in a way that took my breath away.

"Roses," Lorenzo replied, his deep chuckle echoing in the stillness. He knew full well they weren't just any roses.

I crouched down, leaning forwards as my fingers brushed against the petals. "I know that, but why are they lit up?"

Lorenzo knelt beside me, his presence both comforting and overwhelming. "Because I know that white roses are your favourite, and you used to plant and tend them with your grandfather. I also know they don't bloom all year round, so I had this made for you." He smiled as tears stung my eyes. "Whenever you want to take a stroll through the garden, day or night, you'll see them every single day of the year."

My vision blurred as I looked at him. "Lorenzo, this is..." Words failed me, my emotions threatening to spill over.

He placed a finger under my chin, gently tilting my face up to meet his gaze. "It's a place just for you and only you. Somewhere you can go when you miss him."

My gaze fell to the plaque that was just inside the fence. My fingers traced the engraved letters.

In loving memory of Aleksander Fedorov.

A tear trickled down my cheek.

"Thank you," I whispered. "It's beyond perfect. I never expected anything like this."

"It's because you never expect things that I want to do them for you, *amore mio*. You're the most selfless person I know, and despite me thinking I could never be a better man, you continue to make me one." He spoke so sincerely, meaning every single word, and I believed each one.

Lorenzo stood, offering me his hand. I took it without hesitation, my grip tight as if he would disappear. He pulled me into his arms, his embrace strong and reassuring. For a moment, we stood there, the world around us fading into insignificance. The lake, the roses, the twinkling lights—it was everything and more. I rested my head against his chest, listening to the steady beat of his heart.

"I do have something else for you," he whispered.

Before I could speak, he reached into his pocket, pulling out a small black box.

"Lorenzo," I began, but he cut me off before I could continue.

"Wait, please let me finish before you say anything." He opened the box, revealing a delicate white gold chain with a tiny, intricately designed L pendant. My eyes widened as he gently turned me around, his fingers brushing against my bare skin as he fastened the necklace around my neck. I spun back to face him, my fingers instinctively rising to touch it.

"I know you aren't a massive fan of jewellery. You made that clear on our wedding day," he chuckled, a small smile playing on his lips, "but I wanted to get you my initial. Not because you belong to me, but because I'll always be with you even if I'm not," he breathed.

My throat tightened, my emotions threatening to spill over. I snaked my arms around his waist, my chin resting on his chest as I looked up at him. "I know you are. You're all I need, Lorenzo," I whispered, holding his gaze.

Lorenzo cupped my face in his hands, the coolness of his wedding band branding my warm skin. "Ana, I've never been good with words," he admitted. "I've always been a man of action, not poetry or lovey dovey words, but this is different."

I waited anxiously for what he was trying to say. I knew how ruthless this man could be. He killed without hesitation, negotiated with ruthless precision, and commanded loyalty with a single glance. But this reluctance, this raw vulnerability, was something I never witnessed before.

"Take your time," I murmured, reaching up to touch his chest. My fingers brushed the ink of his tattoos, a reminder of the life he lived before me.

"I've spent my entire life building walls." He sighed, his gaze dropping to my lips. “Walls to protect myself, to protect the few I care about. But with you, those walls don’t exist.”

“They don’t, as in, past tense?” I asked.

“Yes, past tense. You blew those fucking walls to smithereens, and I never realised what I wanted all along.” His thumb brushed my cheek.

I never thought our relationship would be built on more than convenience or duty, but I continued to see glimpses of the man beneath the hardened exterior. The man who would stay up late just to watch me sleep and the man who I knew would protect me to the ends of the earth.

“Lorenzo,” I whispered, my voice trembling. “What are you trying to say?”

He looked into my eyes with an intensity that made my knees weak.

“I used to try and deny it, brushed it off and pushed it down, but I can’t fight the feelings I feel for you anymore,” he breathed. “You’ve become my everything, and that scares the hell out of me, but in the best possible way.”

“Lorenzo…”

“Anastacia, I’m not a religious man, but I thank God for you every single day. Maybe I should wish to turn back time and change the way you came into my life, but I don’t want to, because it got us to where we are now. It gave us a side to one another we might not have ever found. I would die for you, and not just because you’re my wife, but because you’re my everything. You’re my reason for breathing.” My heart raced as he continued. “I love you, Ana.”

Everything seemed to spin for a moment, the weight of his confession settling heavily in my chest. I loved him, too, though I had never voiced it. Not because I feared rejection, but because I knew the burden it could place on him. Love in our world was a liability, a weakness that could easily be exploited. Yet there he was, laying his heart bare, no longer caring about the risk.

Tears welled up in my eyes, unbidden and unexpected. "Lorenzo," I choked out, my voice thick with emotion. "I love you, too," I whispered with a smile.

He froze, his expression a mix of shock and relief. For a moment, he said nothing, just stared at me as if afraid I might disappear. He wrapped his arm around me like a shield as I buried my face in his chest, inhaling the familiar scent of his cologne. His heart pounded against my ear, a rhythm that matched the chaos of my own.

"I never planned to say those words," he murmured, his voice muffled against my hair. "But now I don't want a day passing without you hearing them." He pulled back slightly, his hands cupping my face as he searched my eyes. "You're not just my wife, Ana. You're my strength, my weakness, my everything. And I swear, I'll spend the rest of my life making sure you never regret loving me."

"I could never regret it."

And from that moment on, I never did.

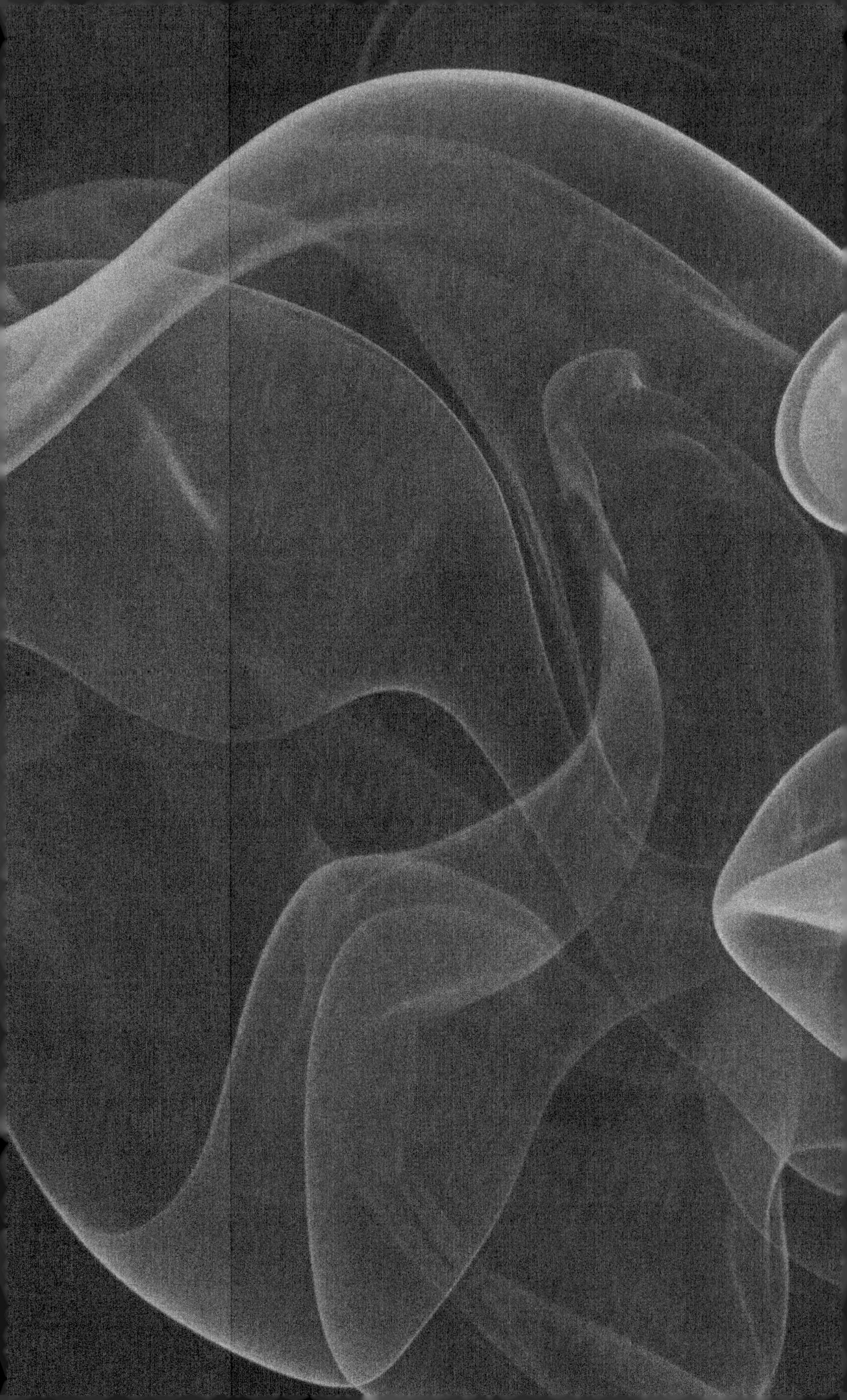

34

LORENZO

Two years later...

The morning light filtered through the small gap in the curtain, casting a soft glow over my wife as she stood by the full-length mirror, taking in every inch of her changing body. Her hands rested gently on the curve of her bump. Her body now bore the proud mark of motherhood, a swollen belly that hinted at the twins growing inside her. She wore a floor-length lounge dress, its soft fabric clinging to her figure and showcasing the bump that I was never able to take my eyes off.

I laid back on the bed, watching her with a mixture of admiration and possessiveness. We had enjoyed a couple of years together, just the two of us, but when she told me she was pregnant, I swore my heart could have exploded. It wasn't because I wanted an heir. It was because I wanted to start a family with her. I wanted everything with her. I closed my eyes, reminiscing for a moment.

"Lorenzo, I'm pregnant." Tears fell from Ana's eyes as she spoke.

"Sorry, what?! Did you just say I'm going to be a papa?" I asked, hoping I heard her correctly.

"I did. You're going to be a father." She pressed her fingers to her lips, unable to control her emotions.

"When did you find out?" I cupped her face, the snow continuing to fall around us and the sounds of laughter coming from the skiers below. It was nothing compared to the joy and happiness I felt in that moment.

"About an hour ago. I was late so I checked my dates, and it all made sense with how I've been feeling," she breathed. "I went to the on-site pharmacy and got a test just to see." She wiped a stray tear that fell from my eye. "I'm sorry I didn't find out with you."

"I don't care whether you found out with me or not. I'm over the fucking moon! We're going to have a baby!" I never thought finding out Anastacia was pregnant would hit me the way it did, but fuck, I had never felt anything like it.

"Yeah, we are," she cried, wrapping her arms around my neck.

"So, no skiing for you tomorrow." My protectiveness was already kicking in. "I'll stay in with you, and you can take it easy."

"Is it going to be like this for the next nine months?" she asked, her face a picture of amusement.

"Oh, abso-fucking-lutely."

"Lorenzo, are you okay?" she asked, bringing me back to the present.

"I was just reminiscing." I smiled, flinging my legs over the side of the bed.

"Wait there. I'm going to change," I said. "I'll take you wherever you need to go."

"There's no need. Tay is picking me up." She rolled her eyes as her plump lips twisted up into a smirk.

"That sounds great, but you can let her know I'll drop you where she and Robin are." I crossed the room, watching as her fingers caressed her bump.

"It's just brunch with the girls, and Tay is perfectly capable of driving carefully," she tutted.

"I don't care if it's a trip to the end of the road. The only one I trust to drive you in this weather is me." I gestured towards the window where the world outside was blanketed in a layer of ice, the sky threatening snow. "It's too dangerous. One wrong move, and—"

"And you'll swoop in like my personal superhero?" she teased, unable to hide the affection in her voice. "You're too protective, you know that?"

I cupped her bump just as one of our babies kicked my palm. "I'm not being protective. I'm just being practical. You're carrying my children, Anastacia. That means you're carrying my whole world. I'm not taking any risks when it comes to the three of you."

She rolled her eyes but couldn't suppress the smile that tugged at her lips. "Fine. But you're going to make me late."

"Better late than never." I headed into the bathroom. "I'll be five minutes. Wait there."

But, of course, she didn't wait. By the time I exited the bathroom, she was nowhere to be found. I pulled on a black turtleneck, followed by a pair of tailored trousers and my winter coat.

I hurried downstairs, already noticing Ana by the front door, her coat draped over her arms.

"You might need to put that on, *amore mio*. It's freezing outside." I took the coat from her and held it open for her to slip her arms inside.

I had to admit, the past eight months I was way overprotective. It was inevitable, though. She was my wife, carrying our children. I couldn't admire her more than I did. Her body was growing our beautiful babies, and she never once let me hear a complaint, despite the pain I knew she often felt. The day we found out it was twins was something else. We were blessed with a boy and a girl, and I vowed to myself and Ana that neither would be forced to marry. They would be equal and never treated differently.

Ana pulled open the door, the cold air seeping in and making me shiver. I placed my hand on the small of her back. "You should've let me get that." I smiled.

“I’m not helpless, Lorenzo,” she replied with annoyance, though she leaned into my touch, feeling comforted by my presence.

Outside, the world was a winter wonderland, the ground slick with ice and the air biting. Red had already pulled the car up to the front door, leaving the engine rumbling softly. Ana started down the steps, her movements careful, but my voice stopped her.

“Hold on,” I called, my tone brooking no argument. Before she could protest, I was there, wrapping my arms around her. I lifted her into them effortlessly. She let out a laugh, surprised but not entirely displeased by my insistence.

“Lorenzo, I’m fine! I can walk!”

“Not on this ice, you can’t,” I said, my voice firm but gentle as I carried her to the car. My arms were a fortress around her, my warmth seeping through her coat. “You three are too precious to me.”

I settled her into the passenger seat, my hand lingering on her leg as I buckled her in. “You’re sure you want to do this? We can stay in. I’ll make you brunch, and we can spend the day together.”

She smiled, her hand covering mine. “I appreciate it, really. But I need this. A few hours with the girls will do me good.”

“Okay, but I’ll pick you up when you’re done.” I tucked her hair behind her ear as she looked at me with soft doe eyes. “Don’t forget, my mother is over for dinner this evening. Apparently, she has a surprise for us.” I smiled, wondering what she could possibly have planned.

I STOOD in the doorway of the dining room, watching as my wife meticulously arranged the crystal glasses on the mahogany table. Despite almost being full term, she moved with practiced grace.

"You've outdone yourself," I praised, stalking over to her. She glanced up, her blue eyes meeting mine.

"It's just dinner, Lorenzo. Nothing special." She shrugged, though her lips curved into a small smile.

"Trust me, it is." I cupped her face as she nuzzled her cheek into my palm. "Dinner smells incredible as well. You made my favourite, didn't you?" I asked.

"I did. You've done so much for me recently, I felt it was only fair I gave you something back."

"I don't need anything back. Just you carrying our babies and keeping them safe is more than enough." I pressed a kiss on her forehead, a gesture I knew she loved. "I love you. All three of you."

"We love you, too," she whispered.

Suddenly, the sound of heels clicking against the marble floor echoed from the hallway. "It sounds like my mother is here." I smiled, but it didn't sound as though she was alone.

I took Ana's hand in mine as my mother entered the dining room, her presence just as commanding as mine. I was right. She wasn't alone. Beside her, stood a man, tall and broad-shouldered. Ana's breath caught in her throat as her gaze locked on his face.

"Artem," she gasped, clutching her stomach.

Artem? As in Victor's former right-hand man?

From what Ana told me, Artem had been more of a father to her than Victor, but one day he just split without a word.

"Artem, is that really you?" she whispered, her voice trembling with disbelief. My mother's lips twitched into a knowing smile as she placed a hand on Artem's arm.

"What's going on? Why are you here? How?" Ana breathed. Artem's gaze flickered to my mother before returning to Ana. There was a weight in his eyes, a mixture of regret and something undecipherable.

"I should've come sooner, I know," he began, his voice rough with emotion. "But your father..." He paused for a second. "Your father made me leave. He knew that when the time came for him to arrange your marriage to someone, I would try to stop it, even though it wasn't my place."

He held out his hand to Ana. She took it without thinking twice. "After losing my own son, you helped fill the void. I saw you like you were my own. The fact that you used to seek me out instead of your father was something he couldn't stand." Artem's own voice trembled as he spoke.

My mother stepped forward, her expression softening. "I've known Artem for years. We reconnected recently, and... Well, the rest is history. I didn't want to say anything because we wanted to see where this went." Mama smiled. "But just know it was incredibly hard for Artem to not come around to see you. He wanted to wait until now, until we knew we were something."

Before Anastacia could respond, I cut in, turning my attention to the man with his arm wrapped around my mother's waist.

"Artem, I've heard great things from my wife about you. Not much but enough to know you're a fucking decent guy." I cleared my throat. "I want my Ma to be happy. God knows she fucking deserves it, but if you hurt her, I swear to—"

Artem held up his hands in a placating gesture. "Lorenzo, I'd never hurt your mother. You have my word."

I studied him for a moment, narrowing my eyes as I tried to work him out a little more. Finally, I nodded, though for now, I'd remain guarded. "Let's sit down and enjoy the dinner my wife has prepared for us."

"Why now?" Ana asked as she lowered herself into the chair.

"Because some things... Some people...are worth fighting for. I should've fought harder against your father back then, but if I had, you wouldn't be happily married now." He smiled, taking his seat.

"No, she would have been. Anastacia and I were put on this earth for one another. It just took us a while to see it." I took her hand in mine, placing a kiss against her knuckles as the smile that brightened my life every single day graced her face.

A FEW DAYS had passed since my mother shared the news of her and Artem. I had to admit, Ana took him returning well. He'd paid more attention to her in the last few days than her father had in years, but then again, Victor always was a cunt.

I stood in the doorway after returning from the basement gym, admiring her for a moment before she clocked me. She always knew when I was near. She wore a pair of my boxers and one of my T-shirts. She never looked so damn beautiful. She caressed her stomach, humming a gentle melody to our twins.

"I can feel you staring, you know." She laughed without moving her gaze an inch.

"I do know, but since when is it a sin to stare at my wife?" I teased, stalking over to her. "Happy Valentine's day, *amore mio*." I smiled before I pressed a soft kiss against her lips.

I breathed her in. The new perfume I'd gotten her for Christmas complimented her perfectly. The sweet smell of Jasmine filled the air around us. It reminded me of our very first date night in Sicily.

"Happy Valentine's Day, husband."

I lowered myself to my knees, flattening my hands on her bump. I could feel our babies kicking and wriggling around. I never thought too much about it before she was pregnant. I never thought how it would be to feel them kicking, to hear their heartbeats, or to see my wife's body changing. Nothing would ever compare to any of it.

"I hope you're not giving your mama too much trouble in there." I chuckled against her stomach.

"Mama cannot wait for them to come out." She half smiled. I knew she was exhausted. She tossed and turned most nights, unable to get comfortable with or without that full body pillow. I never thought I'd ever be jealous of a pillow, but I was.

"Anytime now, wife." I beamed, rising to my feet. "Are you sure you're okay if I head to the club today? I need to meet Rox to go over those new numbers, but just say the word, and Red can deal with it."

"Lorenzo, go. It's fine. Nicolo is staying here with us, anyway," she reassured me, but it didn't make me feel any better.

"And you're sure?" I asked yet again.

"Do I need to push you out the door for you to believe me?" She laughed.

"Alright, alright, less of the threats," I teased. "I'll pick you up some fries and ice cream on the way back." Her favourite craving this whole pregnancy was that combination, and as vile as I thought it sounded, it was actually pretty damn good.

"You better make that two lots. I'm not sharing with you." She relaxed back on the bed as she spoke, taking the weight off.

"Okay, I'll get three lots then, and we can have extra." I smiled.

"I knew there was a reason I loved you." She giggled, unable to hide her amusement.

"You love me for many reasons, *amore mio*." I leaned down to her, brushing my lips against hers. "Call me if you need me, okay?"

"I will. I promise."

I RELAXED BACK in the booth of the dimly lit VIP room as I waited for Rox to arrive. He had never been one to stick to the time, and my patience was wearing thin.

Red, ever the joker, leaned in with a wink. "So, what are your Valentine's Day plans?"

"I'm going to let Ana pick a movie while she eats what she's craving, and hopefully, she'll get a better night's sleep." I smiled, my mind drifting instantly to my wife.

Gino chuckled, clapping a hand on my shoulder. "Ah, guys, they grow up so fast, don't they?" The joke was met with a swift swat on the back of his head from me.

"You're a funny fucker, aren't you?" I scoffed.

The door creaked open, capturing everyone's attention. Rox sauntered in, his cheap aftershave announcing his arrival. His gold canine tooth glinted in the dim light as he flashed a grin. "Lorenzo, how wonderful to see you again! How's the wife? I heard she's pregnant."

"My wife is none of your business, so how about we get on with ours, as I'd rather not be here all day." My tone was firm as I narrowed my eyes at Rox. He took a seat opposite me.

"Wow, don't you trust her home alone?" Rox's smirk widened as my hand twitched. The urge to draw my blade almost overwhelmed me.

"Remember who you're fucking talking to," I snapped. "I won't hesitate to finish what I started last time if you make one more smart ass remark."

Rox's smirk faltered, his posture shifting as he backpedaled. "I apologise. I didn't mean any offence."

"Sounds like you never do, stupid prick," Red chimed in from beside me, clearly unimpressed.

The air in the room grew heavier as Rox poured himself a bourbon from the bottle on the table. "How about I apologise over a drink?"

"I'm not drinking." My jaw clenched, my refusal more than clear.

Rox's eyebrows rose, as if to challenge me. "Too good to drink with me?"

This asshole was on thin ice, and my patience was wearing thin. "It isn't about you, as much as you wish it were. I won't drink while my wife is pregnant."

"Exactly, your *wife* is pregnant. You're not." Rox's grin returned, his tone mocking. "She's not here. She'd never know."

"Maybe not, but that isn't my style. My wife could go into labour any day now which means she'll need me. I can't drive her anywhere if I'm over the limit. I will not risk her life or our babies lives for alcohol, got it?" I hissed. I'd already had enough of this bastard.

"Fine, you win." He held up his hands, giving up completely.

"I did win, yeah." I wasn't talking about the drink, but he didn't seem to know that. I had won in life. The second Ana became my wife, I'd won, and when our babies were born, I'd win again. I'd always win at life with the three of them.

"You know, you're a lucky man, Lorenzo. Not many can balance this life with a family." Rox smiled.

"Many aren't me, though." I strummed my fingers on the table. "Let's begin."

The meeting proceeded with a tense silence, my knife laid flat on the table, its presence a silent warning to the man sitting opposite me with a shit-eating grin. Rox's Adam's apple bobbed as he glanced at it, his earlier bravado replaced by a cautious respect. Gino and Red stood by my side, their presence a reminder of the unity that bound us.

"So, everything is exactly the same, and after that slip up, we've been satisfied with the weapons. We want to extend the contract." I paused. "For now." My smile was faint, but genuine, as Rox snatched the pen from my hand, his eagerness evident.

"And for the future, I've learnt my lesson." Rox cleared his throat, but only time would tell if he had.

The door to the VIP room burst open with a force that made everyone in the dimly lit booth turn their heads, including mine. Finn rushed in, his face flushed and his tie askew as if he sprinted through a storm to get here. "Lorenzo! Boss!" he gasped, unsure of what to call me as he stopped just beside me. I jumped to my feet, my brow furrowed in confusion. "It's Ana!" Finn panted, his words tumbling out in a rush. The room fell silent, the usual hum of conversation and clinking glasses halted as all eyes fell on me.

"What the fuck happened to Ana?!" My voice was sharp, the authority I held cutting through the tension like a knife. I didn't wait for an answer. I started moving towards the door. I clocked Rox from the corner of my eye, relaxing back in the booth with a glass of bourbon in hand, watching the scene unfold with wide eyes.

"Her water just broke," Finn continued, his voice trembling slightly. "She said you didn't answer your phone, and she's panicking." I froze mid step, my hand hovering over the doorknob. I frantically patted my pockets, my heart stopping as I realised it must have slipped out of my pocket in the car. "Fuck! Fuck!" I muttered, my composure cracking for the first time in years.

"Nicolo's getting the car ready with her bag and the babies' stuff," Finn added, trying to keep up with my panicked pace.

"Call Nicolo and tell him to take Ana straight to the hospital. I'll meet them there," I ordered, trying to remain as calm as possible despite the chaos swirling inside me. I paused, turning to Rox, who was still sitting there but had at least set his glass down. "Rox—"

"Lorenzo, I've got it from here. Just go and be with Ana," Gino demanded with a smile. "Me and Red will meet you at the hospital when all is done here."

The amount of time it took me to reach the car was a new record. I couldn't think of anything or anyone else other than my wife. Fuck, she needed me, and I was with that twat upstairs.

I had never driven so fast in my life. The streets of the city blurred past me as I navigated traffic with a recklessness that bordered on madness. I tried to call Ana, but it went straight to voicemail. My heart sank at the thought that she could have the babies before I even fucking arrived. She was closer to the hospital than I was, and the traffic was fucking dire.

I dialled Nicolo's number, the dial tone echoing through the car's speakers. "We're nearly at the hospital. How are you doing?" Nicolo's calm voice came through, a stark contrast to my racing thoughts.

"Don't worry about me. I'll be there. Ana, *amore mio,* are you okay?!" I was almost shouting, my voice cracking with desperation. But I did my best to remain calm for her.

"It hurts," she whimpered in the background, her voice weak but clear. My chest tightened at the sound, my grip on the steering wheel tightening. "I know, *amore mio,* I know, but I'm coming. I'll do my best to make it better, I promise." I had no idea how I could make that happen, but I'd try my fucking hardest for her. Her screams erupted through the line, raw and primal, and my heart shattered.

"Drive safe. Our babies need you in one piece," she managed to say, her voice trembling. Even in her pain, she was still worrying about me.

"I will. Don't worry about me," I replied, my voice hoarse.

"We're pulling into the parking lot now. I'll stay with her until you arrive," Nicolo reassured me.

"Thank you! Ana, I love you,"

"I love you, too," she whispered, her words mingling with her laboured breaths. The line went dead, and I floored the accelerator, my mind racing with thoughts of my wife and the two lives we were about to bring into the world.

I parked haphazardly in front of the hospital entrance and sprinted inside, my Oxford shoes skidding on the polished floor as I followed the signs to the maternity unit. "Anastacia Ricci. Where is she?!" I demanded at the nurse's desk.

The nurse, a kind-faced woman with tortoise shell glasses, typed slowly into her computer. "Let me pull up her records and see what room she's in for you," she responded, taking her sweet fucking time at pulling up that file.

"My wife is in labour. I'd appreciate you hurrying up, please," I snapped, my patience non-fucking-existent. She looked up at me, her expression unflappable. "I said please. What more do you want?!" I added. Another nurse appeared, her eyes widening at the sight of me. "She's in room three-zero-nine. Just down the hall, last door on your right." She smiled, pointing me in the right direction.

"Thank you," I muttered. "You might want to tell your co-worker that urgency matters, especially today!" I didn't wait to hear her reply. I already sprinted off in the direction she sent me.

The moment I reached the door, I paused, taking a deep breath. This was it. The moment I'd both longed for and dreaded. The next time we left this room, we'd be a family. I couldn't pretend I wasn't fucking terrified, but I knew we could do it together.

Time to meet our babies.

I pushed open the door and found Nicolo standing by Ana's bedside, his hand clenched in hers as she rode out another contraction. "Thank God! I can't feel my fingers," he whimpered, his face pale.

"Thanks, Nic. I don't know what we'd have done without you today," I said, crossing the room to Ana. "The guys are on their way. They'll be here in about thirty minutes. Are you going to wait?"

"Of course!" Nicolo replied, his voice a lot calmer now. He headed out of the room, probably to ice his hand, and left me alone with my wife.

"I'm here, *amore mio*," I said softly, taking her hand in mine. She looked up at me, her blue eyes shining with tears while her cheeks flushed a perfect shade of pink. She looked breathtaking, even while she was in pain.

"I thought you wouldn't make it," she sobbed, her voice weak but filled with relief.

"Oh, Ana, I wouldn't have missed this for anything in the world." I smiled. "I don't even care if you break my fingers. Whatever helps with the pain."

She laughed softly, her grip on my hand tightening. "Why would I do that? Then you can't help with the diapers." She chuckled.

"Besides, I only squeezed his hand like that to calm him down. He was freaking out."

I couldn't help but laugh as I ran my thumb over her knuckles. "Whatever will I do with you?"

"I'm sure you can think of plenty," she replied, her voice laced with a hint of mischief. I leaned down, savouring this moment with her as I kissed her forehead gently. "I love you, Ana," I breathed. "And I will love our children unconditionally."

"We're lucky to have you, Lorenzo." She sighed, gritting her teeth through the pain.

I fell silent as Ana rode out another contraction, her grip like a vice around my hand. I held her gaze, my heart swelling with love and awe for the woman before me. Together, we'd face whatever came next. No matter what it was.

As the pain washed over her, I whispered words of encouragement, my voice a steady anchor in the storm. "You're doing amazing. I'm so proud of you."

Her eyes were heavy with fatigue but sparkled with unshed tears. She offered me a weary smile. "*We're* doing amazing," she corrected.

"Trust me, this is all you. I'm doing nothing," I responded.

"You're here, Lorenzo. That's everything to me." Her words, simple yet profound, struck a chord deep within me. A single tear escaped the corner of her eye, tracing a path down her cheek. "We're so lucky to have you."

I leaned in, brushing my lips against hers in a tender kiss, a promise of forever. "It is us who are lucky to have you," I murmured against her lips.

The soft knock on the door interrupted our intimate moment. A doctor entered, her eyes flicking briefly to me before settling on Ana.

"Sorry to interrupt. I just need to check how many centimetres dilated Anastacia is. You can step out if you'd like to, Mr. Ricci," she said, her tone professional but carrying a hint of suggestion as if she wanted me to agree.

"There's no way I'm leaving," I stated flatly.

The doctor, sensing the unspoken tension, directed her question to Ana. "Are you okay with him staying?" she asked, her gaze searching Ana's face for any sign of discomfort.

Ana's grip on my hand tightened as she nodded firmly. "Yes, I want my husband to stay," she said, her voice steady despite the pain etched on her face.

The doctor, seemingly satisfied, proceeded with her examination, her movements efficient and practiced. Ana's face contorted momentarily, a silent testament to the pain radiating through her body. I squeezed her hand gently, reassuring her every step of the way.

"It looks like the two of you are ready to meet your babies." The doctor announced, a smile softening her features..

My head snapped up, unable to hide my surprise as my eyes widened. "What?! That fast? She's only just got here!" The words tumbled out of me in a mixture of awe and panic.

"Mr. Ricci, relax and take a deep breath. Babies don't always wait around, and it's obvious that yours are eager to meet you both." She chuckled, placing a gentle hand on Anastacia's shoulder.

Her words, though intended to soothe, only heightened my anxiety. I was a man who controlled empires. I didn't bat an eyelid when I pulled the trigger to take someone's life, but I felt helpless in the face of this natural force. I took a deep breath, my hand never leaving Ana's, my gaze never wavering from her face.

A midwife entered the room, listening to everything the doctor had to say, before she prepared everything.

I'd lost count of how many minutes followed. All I knew was that it was a blur of pain, determination, and unwavering love. I turned into Ana's anchor, making sure my voice was a constant source of encouragement.

"You're doing amazing, *amore mio*," I whispered.

She nodded her head as the room erupted in a chorus of encouragement, the midwife's voice guiding Ana through each push. Her face was a mask of concentration as my usual composure was completely shattered by the raw emotion of the moment.

Finally, after what felt like an eternity, a deafening cry pierced the air, followed by another, slightly weaker but no less powerful. The midwife, her face radiant with joy, held up two tiny bundles, their cries filling the room with a symphony of life. They were both placed on my wife's chest. Their eyes, though unfocused, held a universe of wonder.

My eyes brimmed with tears as I reached out, my fingers gently brushing the hair of one of our babies. "They're perfect," I whispered, unable to hide the emotion in my voice. "Our family is perfect."

Ana, her face radiant with joy, looked up at me, her eyes mirroring the love and wonder in my own. "We did it, Lorenzo," she said, her voice trembling with happiness. "We created this."

In that moment, amidst the chaos and the joy, the fear and the love, I understood something profound. I had once built an empire on strength and fear, but I finally found my true power. Not in dominance, but in love, in family, in the tiny, perfect beings cradled in my wife's arms.

I BRUSHED a finger over Isabella's button nose, identical to Ana's, as my thumb grazed her pouty lips, a miniature version of her mother's. "Just look at them, Ana. You did that."

Despite the exhaustion etched into her features, there was a glow about her that seemed to illuminate the room. Her gaze met mine before falling to Luca, who was nestled against Ana's chest. He was the spitting image of me, even in his sleep.

"I love you, Mrs Ricci," I confessed for the umpteenth time today.

"Now I have the life I have, I know I'll never be able to live without it. Without the three of you."

"And I love you, too," she whispered. "You're an amazing father already. They're lucky to have you."

My throat tightened, a lump forming that threatened to choke me. I'd always prided myself on my strength, my ability to remain detached, to make the tough decisions. But in this moment, with my family cradled in my arms, I felt a different kind of strength, a strength born from love and vulnerability.

Isabella, sensing the shift in atmosphere, stirred in my arms, her tiny fists balling up as she let out a soft gurgle. I smiled and gently rocked her, my hands surprisingly gentle as I soothed her back to sleep.

"She's stubborn," I observed, my voice laced with amusement. "Just like her mother."

Ana laughed, a soft, melodic sound that filled the room with warmth. "And Luca's got your determination," she countered, her gaze softening as she looked down at her sleeping son. "They're going to be a force to be reckoned with."

My gaze shifted between my children. A surge of protectiveness washed over me, a primal instinct to shield them from the world's harsh realities.

"They'll have the best of both of us," I said firmly. "And they'll have the love and support of a family who will always be there for them."

As I held Isabella closer, the fear of losing this newfound happiness outweighed everything else. I would protect my family with every fibre of my being. Not out of duty, but out of a love that had blossomed in the most unexpected of places.

The future, once shrouded in uncertainty, stretched before us, bright and full of promise. Together, we would face whatever challenges lie ahead, our love a beacon guiding us through the darkness.

We had found not only love in each other, but a home, a sense of belonging, and a future worth fighting for.

EPILOGUE

LORENZO

The past five years flew by in the blink of an eye, but many things remained the same.

Mine and Ana's love for one another was stronger than ever.

Isabella had grown into a sassy five-year-old. She always had something to say just like Ana did. She inherited her eyes, two wide sapphires always sparkling with happiness. She might have looked cute and dainty, but she could throw one hell of a punch. Although, Luca knew about that more than we did.

The older Luca got, the more he looked like me. One thing was for sure, he was a character, always finding ways to make the household laugh. But above all else, he was always there for his sister. He enjoyed spending most of his time with her. Their bond was unlike anything else.

"So, what do you think?" Red asked as he tried to capture my attention. All I heard was the familiar sound of heels coming down the stairs. "Lorenzo, will you fucking listen to me?!" Red waved in my face. He hadn't realised that my five-year-old daughter had heard his beautiful vocabulary.

"Oh, Uncle Red said a swear!" She giggled. "Wait till I tell

Mama," she teased. She wouldn't, but it was funny to see Red sweat a little.

"You don't need to do that, Bells. I'll add a dollar to the swear jar." Red rummaged in his pocket to pull out a dollar.

"How about you just give me the money, and I won't tell Mama at all? If you put it in the swear jar, she'll know someone swore." She smiled sweetly, as if butter wouldn't melt.

Oh, she was good.

"Fine, come and get it." He held out the money to Bella, who wobbled all the way over to him wearing her mama's shoes.

"Like taking candy from a baby." She laughed, and it was the cutest sound I'd ever heard. No wonder everyone was wrapped around her finger.

"You're just like your father," Red huffed.

"Mhm." She turned to me as Red walked towards the kitchen.

"You're lucky I love you, Bells," he called, causing Bella to clap her hands before she shoved the dollar in my pocket for safe keeping.

She was a beautiful little girl. Freckles decorated her nose and cheeks, and her ash blonde hair was like Ana's. She wore a crisp white dress that had layers upon layers of tulle.

"Well, good evening, Princess Bella." I smiled.

"Papa, I need a prince, and Luca doesn't want to be the prince. He said he wants to be the monster," she huffed, folding her arms across her chest.

"Well, how many times have I told you? You don't need a prince." I laughed as I dropped to my knees before her. I took her hand in mine as I kissed her knuckles like a prince would do to a princess. "I'll protect you for the rest of my life."

"But I want a prince to kiss." And there it was, the words every father dreaded.

"Kisses are overrated," I huffed, knowing I shouldn't lie, but for things like this, I didn't have a choice.

"Make sure Mama doesn't hear that," she giggled, wobbling a little.

"Make sure Mama doesn't hear what?" As if on cue, Ana swanned out of the kitchen with a grubby Luca in her arms. His hair was a mess, and his clothes were covered in dirt. That was the day in the life of Luca. He spent most of it outside and then proceeded to track mud throughout the house.

"I think these two need a bath so we can decorate the Christmas tree. What do you think, Lorenzo?" Ana asked.

"Mama, can you bathe me, and Papa can bathe Luca?" Bella smiled sweetly as Ana handed over a mud-ridden Luca, which now meant *I* was covered as well.

"Of course, then we can put your Christmas pyjamas on, decorate the tree, and enjoy a hot chocolate before bed." I tapped Luca's nose with my finger as he wriggled in my arms.

Within seconds, he was chasing his sister up the stairs—obviously to wipe his muddy hands all over her dress. She kicked off Ana's wedding shoes that were, of course, too big and sprinted towards her bathroom.

"Do you think they'll ever get easier?" I sighed.

"No, Lorenzo, I don't." Ana laughed.

She kissed me quickly before darting up the stairs to split the kids up. Halfway up, she called over her shoulder, "Sorry, I forgot, kissing is overrated." She giggled, having no idea I planned on showing her later just how overrated they could be.

WITH THE GUYS at the bar, we had the house to ourselves to decorate the tree with the kids. The twins wore matching pyjamas, I opted for sweats, and Ana pulled on a oversized sweater dress.

"I'll do this side with Papa because he can lift me high, high up!" Bella beamed as she rushed to my side. Luca sat on Ana's lap as they admired the decorations we had acquired over the years. Decorating the tree had become a family tradition since the kids were old enough to help. They loved getting new pyjamas and drinking hot chocolate, too.

I lifted Bella for her to hang decorations as her delicate hand held onto my neck.

"Relax, my little diamond. I won't drop you," I reminded her.

"I know." She smiled as she hung the angel wings on the tree, the decoration Ana had purchased to represent her grandparents. It was the one item the kids took turns hanging. "Those wings are my favourite."

"Mama?" Luca spoke from the other side of the tree.

"Yes, my angel?" Ana responded, turning to look at him.

"I love you lots, like infinity." I could hear the smile in his voice as Bella whispered, "Aww," in my ear.

"And I love you. More than you'll ever know." One thing about Ana, she might have been an incredible wife, but she was something else completely as a mother. These children were her world, just as they were mine, but there was something about watching Ana with them every day that warmed me to the core. She doted on them endlessly."Me and Luca will go and make the hot chocolates. We're trusting you with the tree." Ana narrowed her eyes at me playfully.

"You got it, Mama!" Bella called as they left. Once they were out of earshot, Bella whispered, "Papa?"

"Yes, Bella?" I answered.

"Will I meet a boy who is nice to me like you are to Mama?" she questioned, her fingers twisting in my hair.

"You will when you're old enough." I smiled, but what my daughter didn't know was there'd be no boys until she was at least thirty. *At least.*

"Did you love Mama when you saw her for the first time?" she continued to ask. This girl and her questions would easily send me to an early grave.

"You know, it was different when we met." I paused. "But I wouldn't change a thing. She's the love of my life and always will be." I touched the tip of her nose with my index finger as she did the same to me.

"Papa, you're lucky to have Mama," she giggled.

"And why would that be?" I asked, eager to hear her answer.

"She's pretty and cooks really good food!"

"You're right, I am, but then again, I'm lucky to have all three of you." I smiled, and I really meant every single word. I truly was blessed.

"Papa!" Luca shouted. "I did it!" He bounded into the living room and jumped into my free arm.

"Did what, *figliolo*?" I asked as his sister and I awaited his response.

"I put the cream and marshmallows on the hot chocolate. Mama let me!" He looked so proud as Bella leaned down and high-fived him.

"Did you put extra in ours?" she asked with a devilish grin.

"I put triple!" His eyes twinkled with mischief.

After completing the tree, we all stood back and admired our handiwork.

"I think Santa will love this tree!" Luca clapped as he wore hot chocolate for a moustache.

"Me too. It's the best one we've done," Bella agreed. She had the same messy face as her brother, except she also had dried whipped cream on the tip of her nose.

"Right, you two, let's go and wash these faces and get to bed. Otherwise, we can't go to Pop-Pop's house tomorrow." They squealed with delight and darted out of the living room. Ana wasted no time chasing them up the stairs.

The kids referred to Artem as Pop-Pop, and he deserved that title. He had been great with my mother, Ana, and our children. He helped me, if needed, as well, which he didn't need to do, but it was more than appreciated. Victor never came around. None of Ana's family did. She shrugged it off, but I knew deep down it probably hurt her. We had the support of my mother and Artem, and she claimed that was enough for her.

After a good twenty minutes of alone time, I felt her presence before I saw her. "Are they in bed?" I asked, looking up from the sofa to meet her gaze.

"They're in bed. Not sure how long it'll take for them to get to sleep since they're using those walkie-talkies Red got for them." She relaxed back on the sofa, snuggling into my embrace. "Do you miss it?"

"Miss what?" I questioned, wondering where she was going with that.

"The newborn stage?" She smiled as she wrapped her arms around me.

"You know what, honestly, I do." It was true. I missed when they couldn't sass me and ask about boyfriends and love. But more than that, I genuinely missed the late nights in the nursery with Ana, supporting her through everything.

"Okay..." She breathed. "So, what would you say if I told you we're about to go through it all again?" She blushed, toying with the hem of her sweater dress.

Wait a minute...

"Ana, are you...?"

"Yes, I'm pregnant!" She gushed as if it was our first child all over again. The swelling I felt in my chest was second to none. "Merry Christmas," she whispered, cupping my face.

"I couldn't ask for a better present." I smiled, pulling her into me to claim her lips. This woman continued to surprise me every single day, and today was no different.

She was mine, and I was hers.

We were one.

Now and forever.

Acknowledgments

To my husband, who supported me on this journey from day one, who has been my rock for fifteen years, and who I couldn't be without. Thank you, I love you and appreciate you more than you know.

To my three beautiful children, thank you for keeping me going with those beautiful smiles after many late nights and long days writing this book.

To my editor, Sara, thank you for working with me on this book. You bring out the best in me and my work, and I couldn't be more thankful to work with you.

To my friend/PA, Shaima. Thank you for everything you do for me. I don't know what I'd do without you. Thank you for keeping me on track with everything. I appreciate and love you!

To my Beta readers & friends, Milica, Mary, Sophia, and Ashley, thank you for being there with me on this journey. Thank you for all your input and comments during this process, I don't know what I'd do without you all.

Lastly, thank you to all my readers, I couldn't have written this book without you. I wouldn't be able to live my dream without each and every one of you. I hope you love the rewritten version of Lorenzo and Anastacia just as much as I do.

ABOUT THE AUTHOR

Samantha Jayne is a UK romance novelist and Interactive author for several story apps across the App Store. Her work in the novel app space fuelled her love of immersive narratives, which she now translates into sizzling immediacy of her novels.

She lives in Cheshire, England with her husband, two sons and daughter.

Printed in Dunstable, United Kingdom

66308333R00241